D1601564

PRAISE FOR *SIMULATED*

"*Calculated* was so incredible that I didn't think it was possible for the sequel to one-up it, and yet here we are. *Simulated* has all the mission impossible action you could hope for, paired with a love triangle that rivals the intensity of Twilight's. Be prepared to choose sides and hold on tight. You're in for one wild ride."
— Chelsea Bobulski, author of
THE WOOD and *REMEMBER ME*

"Full of global intrigue and the thrilling adventure of an action movie, Simulated transported me to the lush setting of North Africa as I cheered for an utterly unique heroine fighting for good and finding her place in the world. Action-packed and captivating - I couldn't put it down."
—Becky Dean, forthcoming author of
LOVE AND OTHER GREAT EXPECTATIONS,
2022, Delacorte/Penguin Random House

"Brilliantly crafted, this technological thriller delivers punch after punch of heart-pounding action. The fearless heroine and two equally intriguing love interests had me flying through the pages. I'm in love with this series!"
—Lorie Langdon, author of
the *Disney Villains Happily Never After* Series

"With thrilling adventure and cunning suspense, *Simulated* is the most riveting sequel I've ever read—a masterpiece destined for the stars!"
—Ellen McGinty, author of *THE WATER CHILD*

PRAISE FOR *CALCULATED*

"A high-stakes YA tale of betrayal, revenge, and numbers... An enjoyable thriller with an intriguing, relatable protagonist."
— Kirkus Reviews

"A cunning story of strategy destined to keep readers chasing resolution from Seattle to Shanghai."
– Jennifer Jenkins, author of the *NAMELESS* series

SIMULATED

A CALCULATED NOVEL

SIMULATED

NOVA MCBEE

 WISE WOLF BOOKS LAS VEGAS

WISE WOLF
BOOKS

This is a work of fiction. All of the characters, organizations, publications, and events portrayed in this novel are either products of the author's imagination or are used fictitiously.

For information, address Wolfpack Publishing,
5130 S. Fort Apache Road 215-380 Las Vegas, NV 89148

wisewolfbooks.com

Cover design by Cherie Chapman

Paperback ISBN 978-1-953944-06-1
Hardcover ISBN 978-1-953944-12-2
eBook ISBN 978-1-953944-53-5

DEDICATION

To Olivia for traveling to the farthest lands with me.
&
To the untamed, the rough, and those in chaos—there is
calculated beauty in you.

fractal |'fraktel| *Mathematics*
noun

an infinite pattern or design found in nature, in dynamic systems, in chaos, and in what appears rough or random; broken,
fractured part of the whole

> *"Fractals are just another way of seeing infinity."*
> Benoit Mandelbrot

"A thumbprint in the stars, a pattern in the trees, order in the ocean waves.
There's always a path through the chaos…"

N.J.A.

PROLOGUE

My goal today: don't drown.

It shouldn't be too hard. I'll just be scuba diving on the Great Barrier Reef in the Coral Sea...above ground...fully clothed... in a dry, dark room at Prodigy Stealth Solution's headquarters in Seattle.

When Ms. Taylor, the PSS director, told me she had a way to get my gift back, virtual simulations where 'staying alive' was a main factor wasn't what I had in mind. But the numbers buried in my brain respond to it. Maybe I have a secret death wish lurking deep in my subconscious, or it's simply a survival thing. Either way, I'm here, willing to do anything to jumpstart my numbers again.

"Get comfortable, Josephine," Ms. Taylor says in her stern, calm voice. "We'll have you connected to our neural simulators in just a minute and everything about this exercise will feel real."

I settle into a chair, the only piece of furniture in the middle of the room. Under the smooth material, the odd seat is made of soft gel. As I settle into it, the gel molds to cushion my body. A seatbelt, which is made of the same material, loops across my chest and my waist, gently securing me in place. I barely notice it. Already I feel weightless.

Ms. Taylor's assistants attach small sensors to my fingers and temples as I listen closely to her instructions.

"As with all of your simulations, the room itself will shift depending on the exercise. Last time, the wind pressed against you as you jumped from the plane. Today, you'll feel the pressure of being underwater. You'll be a mile offshore and about 100 feet deep. You'll be given certain challenges to overcome and choices to make. Do you remember the system?"

"I remember." I glance around the room covered in large screens, all loaded with my memories and programs made for me. "You'll give me only 30% of the information and equipment that I'll need for the goal."

"Correct. You must locate the sunken ship, grab the gold coin in the inner cabin and reach the surface on your own. Theoretically, the dormant part of your mind will wake up to the challenge. It'll assemble all the pieces of the puzzle and be reactivated. We are made to survive. This is a private exercise, but do we have your permission to record the results?" Ms. T asks me this every time. The tone in her voice comforts me.

I nod.

"Although this phase is the gentlest of the three simulations we designed for you, it may still trigger areas of your trauma." This is the part where Ms. T demands I look her in the eye. Her unwavering black eyes are steely and full of fire. This woman is a powerhouse. She's worked with countless prodigies, helping them hone their gifts to solve some of the world's most challenging problems, and she just keeps pushing boundaries. I swear Ms. T could have put King in his place with one stare. But underneath her stern features, a motherly heart beats; at least towards me. "Now, if you want to proceed, please say 'I agree' as your verbal signature."

"I agree."

As I sign the agreement with my voice, my heart starts to

pound a bit faster. I never really know what I'm agreeing to. Last month, I nearly froze to death in arctic temperatures trying to find my way back to base camp on Everest. Another time, I came seconds away from plummeting to the ground while skydiving over Abu Dhabi in a sandstorm because I couldn't open my parachute. Most recently, I skidded down a mountainside cliff in Peru on a high-powered motorcycle—just to mention a few close-calls. Although, my gift hasn't "woken up" yet in those dangerous moments, it's flickered. Not for more than a few seconds at a time, but even that small taste fuels my desperate hunger to try again.

Each week I'm thrust into a new series of complex challenges with tech they've designed specifically from the broken pieces of my life.

There are three phases to my sims. Phase one is called: Before Trauma—it's the time before I lost my mom, when life was simple; Phase two is called: Facing Trauma—in these sims I am in China where I lost my gift; Phase three is called: Adventure—these are new challenges to jump-start my gift. All the sims are connected to neural pathways of my brain that shut down after my experiences in China. They also draw on recreated memories and visuals taken from those periods in my life. It's strange experiencing my life in 4-D.

But I'm impatient to get my gift back. Operating without it has made me feel like a small child trying to drive a car—I have to stretch and strain to reach the gas pedal, and I can barely see over the steering wheel, whereas my old life felt like driving a Ferrari on the autobahn.

"This exercise is 30 minutes long. We'll be monitoring your neural activity but the content of what you experience inside the simulation will be private. If you need out, press this red button." She taps the button on the side of the chair.

"I understand."

"Alright," she says, slipping a light helmet over my head,

and gloves on my hands. "Have fun down there. Let your mind do the work. I'll see you at the meeting point."

And just like that, I sink into the clear, blue water.

The sea is warm—somehow I feel it, smell it. The water is a translucent, electric blue. My first emotion is happiness. There is nothing to fear...yet. I stay near the surface. I'm thrilled to be out of my father's house. He's been so protective since I came home that this...feels like freedom. At the same time, unpleasant memories of water during my time in China float endlessly in the back of my mind—Lev attacking me at the pool, Celia's command that I die by drowning, King shoving me underwater for terrifying minutes at a time. But that's all behind me, I tell myself. So after the pressure settles in my ears, I dive deeper.

My diving suit is black and tight. The mask on my face and mouth press against my temples and forehead, connecting securely to my air tanks. My ears echo with the sound of my own breathing. This is the most realistic simulated experience I've had yet. Even the hair on my head feels weightless, floating around me. I marvel for a moment. It's not real, but with each minute, my brain insists otherwise.

The sim doesn't provide a map, but the ship is easy to see. I need to go down further. Thirty more feet? Fifty? I hate that I don't know, hate that I can't estimate more accurately.

When I look up, the surface feels miles away and I shiver even inside my suit.

My neural pathways have come alive now. The sim is making me believe I really am underwater, away from shore, breathing through a tank of air. I don't know how to use the equipment. I'm not supposed to. The pressure against my body is heavy, constricting. I tell myself it's not real, once, twice, three times. But slowly, my brain is absorbed into the false reality.

As I swim along, clear miles of sea stretch out before me. There are no other divers. Just me and the great big ocean. And fish. They swim past me, flashing vibrant colors of red and yellow and cobalt blue. I'm in awe of my surroundings. I want to follow the stony coral reef out farther, forget about the exercise and just enjoy myself. But I know, eventually, something will go wrong. That's when my gift kicks in—the moment I need it.

The sunken ship is now just a dolphin-dive away. I kick my flippers aiming toward it and easily locate the cabin. It's dark inside. I turn on my underwater light. Eerie particles of dust and algae float across my vision as I squeeze through a narrow opening into the cabin. Fish dart to and fro and I want to get out quickly. On a rotting table sits a gold coin. I grab it as instructed and swim out. At the cabin door, my headlamp dies. Everything is gray now. It's still light enough to see, but the sun is setting above me.

A spark of numbers whips past me. It's only a few seconds but an underwater map appears in my head. I know clearly where I am—off the coast of Queensland Australia, not far from where we caught Madame. My mind calculates the distance from where I am to the shore. With it comes a realization. I am alone.

My gift blinks out.

I don't like thinking about Madame. But my mind does anyway. *What if she gets out of prison? What if she knew I was nearby?*

I shake it off. The gold coin is in my hand. Time to swim back to shore before it's totally dark. I'm almost clear of the ship when my equipment gets snagged on a piece of coral. My fin gets stuck too. I can't get free. I'm locked in an awkward position. Shadows of fish around me get larger by the second.

In the gray watery distance, sharks begin to circle. Schools of fish swirl around my mask, blocking my view. I can't see my feet. I try to smack them away. The fish flip back and forth mirroring my panic and continuing to block my line of vision.

Think, Jo.

As I concentrate, a buzzer in my ear alerts me that my oxygen is almost gone. I need to switch to my reserve tank and head to the surface, but I wasn't given any information on how to do that. There are gauges on my arm I don't know how to read.

I tinker with buttons and the dials, but nothing works. My foot is still stuck, and my breathing becomes uneven.

In the back of my mind, something tells me I'm fine. But all I hear is beeping. My heart is beating out of control. My mind darts to King. He shoved me under the water. The capillaries in my face broke. My larynx was damaged for days. I couldn't breathe. I almost drowned.

My breathing comes in ragged gasps now. I'm panicking. Nothing is working! I don't want to be here. I'm stuck in the ocean. Left to die. Again. Another bad set of cards dealt. All my luck is bad.

I yell into the mask, hoping Ms. T hears me. But no one responds. What did she tell me to do? What button was I supposed to push? I can't remember. It's too dark. I'm miles below shore. My oxygen tank is low.

My gift is not kicking in. It's not working! Nothing is working!

"Let me out!" I yell, losing it. Why does everything I do almost get me killed?

The very breath in my lungs will be ripped from me in seconds. Once again, I'm faced with death and no one's here to help me. I'm about to rip the helmet off, let the water rush in.

But a voice stops me.

"Jo. Calm down." It's a robotic voice, distorted but clear.

"I can't calm down! I can't get to the surface. I can't count the fish. I can't measure the distance. I can't make this stupid equipment work. Get me out!"

"Jo. I can help you get your gift back. Breathe."

The voice is calm and confident. It's a male voice, robotic, like a computer program. Thank God. PSS didn't leave me here to die. I breathe as instructed, surprised to find air.

"Look at the coral," the voice instructs softly.

"No. I just need to get out."

"You need to look at the coral. What do you see?" The voice is stern, but so confident that I make one last effort to do what it says.

In the gray water, I bend toward the coral, the edges of each pink branch and arm travel up and down the jagged shore.

"I see nothing. Just bumps, dents and holes. Fish swimming in and out."

"Get closer. Follow the edges, slowly. Take off your glove. Touch it."

I lean in close, take off my glove. It floats away. My fingers rub over the curves and edges of the coral, like braille, they're rough and bumpy. I take another look. Like a snowflake under a microscope, the edges sharpen into view. I squint and see it now. The coral has distinct angles, repetitions, patterns. In every edge it becomes more evident, more beautiful.

Calculations erupt out of me. Instantly I count miles of coral, every divot of their shapes. My numbers reach the coast-lines—dimensions, predictions are everywhere.

I can breathe.

It's clear now why I'm trapped. I turn my foot to a different angle in the crevice where my fin is wedged. It instantly comes free. The equipment is an easy fix too. One switch of a dial and my breathing is calm and regular. I know exactly how long it will take me to swim to the top.

The layout of numbers in and around me are like seeing a loved one come back from the dead. If I could cry under water, I would.

In five seconds, I reach the surface. The distance to shore is 62 feet and it'll take thirteen strokes to get there. I am myself again. My heart beats 480 times victoriously in my chest.

I emerge from the push and pull of the breaking waves and finally stand on my own two feet, fins off. The millions of granules of sand have never felt so soft against my bare feet. Then, ever so slowly, the numbers fade. I'm tempted to despair until I realize that this is the longest my gift has returned since I lost it in China.

Finally, a breakthrough.

My gift has never tasted so sweet. Without a doubt, it's still there inside me. It's trapped, but I have hope now that it can be freed.

My helmet shuts off and the lights in the room come on.

I spring out of the sim-room, celebrating. "It worked. It really worked. You're all geniuses!" I grin. Everyone is smiling and clapping. "The voice, the computer program that helped me with the coral. It brought my gift back. You didn't tell me I'd have help in the sim. I expected to be alone again."

The smiles slip away from their faces.

Ms. Taylor's face goes pale. "What voice?"

"The voice in the sims," I say, startled by their blank expressions. "It told me to look at the coral when I was panicking. My gift came back for five minutes and ten seconds. The longest ever."

They look at each other in a way that makes my stomach sink.

"That program is locked. It's impossible for anyone to enter the sims. We monitor your brain activity from the outside," Ms. T said, glancing again at her team. They are shaking their heads, whispering and frantically scanning the computer screens in front of them.

"What are you saying?" I ask, my skin now cold.

"Jo," she says, "whoever was speaking to you wasn't PSS."

CHAPTER 1

RIVERS RESIDENCE
WEST SEATTLE, WASHINGTON

Four weeks later…

I'm not in China anymore.

It's the first thought in my mind when I wake up. The first thought I've had each day since I returned to Seattle. In the beginning, that comforted me. I was far away from dangerous criminals and collapsing economies and underground prisons that turned my world upside down, but now the same thought feels like lead in my heart.

My right *tranq-earring*, which also serves as my alarm, starts buzzing and whispering at exactly 7:00 am. *Wake up, it's Monday* sings a soft voice that is programmed to sound like my mother's.

At the word Monday a smile spreads across my face. I rub my eyes and jump out of bed. After speaking a command into K2, my smart watch, the espresso machine begins clicking, grinding, spitting, and foaming milk in the kitchen below my bedroom. I have exactly four minutes to hop in and out of the shower before my triple shot cappuccino is ready. I set a timer for only three, because Mondays are not a day to waste time.

Mondays my gift comes back. Mondays are freedom.

Since returning to Seattle, my new life quickly spiraled into what I've always dreaded—a droning bore. I'm getting antsy. I promised my dad I would spend six months resting and recovering from my experiences in China. Those months aren't even half over and already the Phoenix in me feels like a bird with clipped wings. From the outside, everything seems fine, but on the inside, I'm running, trying escape. Except there's nowhere to go.

I keep returning to the same question: How does a math prodigy go from taking down criminal empires and saving world economies to slow walks on the beach and teaching math to high school students once a week? The only answer I've come up with is—they don't.

It doesn't help that each time my gift resurfaces it's like a storm, swirling and brewing over my ocean.

Out of the shower, sipping on my coffee, I thread my wet hair into a haphazard French braid and slip a red beanie over my head. Then I run downstairs to grab my car keys off the driftwood bench. As I pull open the front door, rich, salty air from the Puget Sound buzzes through my senses.

"Dad, I'm leaving now," I yell upstairs. I silently pray that my dad will reply like other fathers: *Ok, have a good day, see you later.* I'm not so lucky.

"Wait, Jo!" my dad shouts from the bedroom, an edge of panic in his voice.

I set my bag down, looking at my watch and tapping my foot. How long until he'll be at my side? His feet don't move as fast as they used to.

Almost three months have passed, and my dad hardly lets me out of his sight. I don't blame him. His daughter was pronounced dead for two years. To him, I'm a living second chance that he won't risk losing again.

Every Monday I do my longer simulations at PSS. Apart from my boyfriend Kai, my *sims* are the only thing keeping me sane. But for the past four weeks, there have only been hiccups of my gift here and there. Nothing like last month when the hacker got into my sim in the Coral Sea.

I'd never seen the PSS team so worried. No one has ever gotten through their impenetrable security before. Ms. T made it very clear that a hacker like that is a threat to PSS, to the program, to me, and to the world. If any hostiles were to get their hands on PSS tech, then no one would be safe.

"Coral Hacker" as we named him, has contacted me three times. After he hacked my sim, I realized it was the same robotic male voice from the strange phone call I'd received soon after I returned to Seattle. The caller had known all about me and my gift. He'd called me *Double-Eight* and claimed to have the same gift as me. He'd said: "You miss it, don't you? The way it defines the universe into beautiful, intricate paths." Then he'd warned me about Kai and said he'd be in touch. After that call, PSS set me up with a new phone with the highest level of security that they could offer—registered in Switzerland and protected like Alcatraz.

But then he entered my sim in the Coral Sea.

The third time was during another sim a couple of weeks ago—a phase three, where I was lost on Denali. As the robotic voice started speaking, I wanted to talk to him, but I pushed the red escape button like Ms. T had instructed me to do if the hacker broke into my sims again. Since then, they've reworked the PSS firewalls and he hasn't gotten through, but still no one has been able to trace him.

The hacker is dangerous, the worst kind of genius, I tell myself. Even so, I can't stop wishing I could ask him how he knew that the coral would unlock my gift.

Dad doesn't know about the hacker. He also doesn't know

that Ms. T chose Mondays for my *sims* because that's when PSS reviews jobs they've been asked to take on around the world and reveals ground-breaking tech and top-secret information. Even if I'm not allowed to participate in PSS jobs right now, Ms. T thinks it's good for me to be a part of these meetings.

Dad finally shows up at the front door dressed in a blue wrinkled Henley shirt and jeans. "I'll drive you over there. I can even wait for your training to be done. Then we can go get dinner together. What do you think?"

My heart crushes inside my chest as the gray-blue eyes of a father longing to protect his daughter peer down at me. "Dad," I say, softly, "we've been over this. I need to drive myself. I missed two years of being a teenager. You have to let me go—alone." I reach over and squeeze his arm reassuringly.

While I have steadily rebuilt my relationships with my sisters, Mara and Lily, Dad's been busy building overprotective protocols around each one of us. Pepper spray. Self-defense classes. Alarm systems. Thank God for Ms. T, who convinced my dad that I'd actually be *safer* if I got my gift back. She also promised him that I'd get to use PSS "perks".

Dad fidgets and takes off his hat. "I'm sorry." He scratches his neck. "You have your phone? Taser watch? Tracker earrings?"

"Yep." I lift my wrist and move my head from side to side to reveal my earrings.

The "perks" are all gadgets that PSS kids have designed. K2 is not only a smart watch but a military computer with holographic features. It also comes with a genius addition—three voice-activated tasers, which I haven't had an opportunity to use yet. K2 can link up to any device in my house, has a tiny cartridge containing 88 seconds of oxygen if I ever find myself under water again, and if anyone other than me triggers it, it sends a message to my emergency contacts. My earrings are typical trackers even if they are pulled out. They have a traceable smart dust that will broadcast my coordinates for at least 48 hours. The earrings can hack anything using Bluetooth technology and also contain a tranquilizer dart if I ever need them as a weapon.

"Backpack?" he says, eyeing the bag at the ground.

I nod. "Emergency snacks, clothes, my extra cell phone, my cuff-bracelet. I know the drill." I'm surprised he hasn't implanted a biotag in my body so he knows where I am at all times.

"Alright," Dad sighs. "See you at dinner?"

"Training might go longer. I've got all three sims today." I don't mention the team meeting. "I'll be back no later than 7 pm." I bite the inside of my lip, hoping he doesn't ask any questions.

He nods, wearily. "Okay, I trust you," he says, obviously stretching his faith. I hug him. He hugs me back tighter. "Seven p.m. I'll be waiting."

I have no doubt he will be. One minute late and my phone will ring. I always answer because I won't risk him getting sick again like he did when I went missing two years ago. "Great, Dad. See you tonight."

With Dad watching at the door, I spring into the salty brisk air towards the electric car I finally learned to drive. Being held hostage and then living in a subway-friendly city, I never had the chance to learn or the need to drive like other teenagers. But I soon realized in America, if you want to be free, you have to drive.

An intense excitement burns inside me as I start the car. I pull out on the road and head toward the university district. "K2, bring up my maps." Holographic screens displaying distance, speedometers, GPS, and a timer are projected around me.

"K2, choose a route with no pedestrians, no police, and

no cameras." A tiny pinch of guilt pricks me. This is not how I should be using PSS tech. If anyone knew they'd probably strip me of my license.

"Calculating route."

K2 projects a 3-D map of the route to PSS headquarters, and I let loose.

All the gauges sync with my mind. I drive attempting to calculate all factors—upcoming turns, other traffic, distance—as K2 delivers instant information audible through my earrings. I want to envision every curve along the route. Somewhere in my subconscious, I know I can match the speed on the speedometer with the speed in my gut.

If my *sims* have proven anything, it's that phase three—when I'm facing danger—is the only time in which my gift sparks, as if it wants to keep me alive.

Now on an empty road, K2 announces, "There is one mile ahead without pedestrians." I press down on the accelerator. Just for a taste. Just for that spark. K2 is only a computer program. An automated helper. He can't calculate everything, but my gift, if it wakes up, can. Finally, my numbers stumble out. A satisfying thrill comes over me. I go even faster, like a fire in the wind, sparks of numbers flying everywhere. I'm so in tune with them I forget the dials and drive, faster and faster. The rush of calculations takes over until K2's robotic voice commands, "Slow down."

I don't listen. Instead, I sink the pedal to the floor.

But just ahead a blind corner appears out of nowhere. Before I can react, my engine dies. My tech goes black. The screen fades.

I slam on the brakes, pulling over to the side. What just happened? K2 has never taken over the car's systems like that before. Then I see it ahead of me—a group of kids chasing each other to cross the street. I gasp, my heart skipping hard.

I didn't see them. If K2 hadn't stopped me...a chill ripples through me. I slam my hands on the dashboard. What was I thinking?

Suddenly, everything reboots. My electric car whirs back to life.

I squeeze my eyes shut. "Thanks, K2."

"K2 rebooting. Suspicious activity. Tech overridden. Unknown user." The system flashes warnings before my eyes.

My heart pounds as I sit staring at my car. It wasn't K2 that killed the motor.

A sudden vibration hits my leg. I startle and slam back against the seat. "Incoming message from an unlisted number, no origin."

Jaw tight, I grab the phone vibrating in my pocket. No one has this number except for my family, PSS, and Kai. It's not my dad. I just left him. It can't be Kai—he's on a job for Private Global Forces and no contact is allowed. And I'm on my way to PSS. No one there would be calling me. It has to be Coral Hacker.

Looking at the screen, my skin shivers as the phone number morphs from New Zealand area code to India to Greece. A text message appears.

Choose Tunisia and tell your idiot boyfriend to back off or he'll be sorry. You have five days.

In less than five seconds, the message has disappeared. There's no trace of any call or text on my phone.

What's in Tunisia?

Without a doubt, the message is from him. Coral Hacker is just as cryptic as usual.

I immediately look over my shoulder scanning the streets. Under my skin, the itch for a fight is simmering.

It's infuriating that he can always find me. It's troublesome that he sends me cryptic messages, like I know what he's talking about. But above all, I despise that he claims to have my gift, then uses it to taunt me.

I'm about to call Agent Bai when the phone rings again. Another international number, just like the text. Great. Now he's *calling* me? Who does he think he is? Suddenly I'm furious. PSS wouldn't want me to answer. But my fear is overridden with a maddening desire to get to the bottom of this.

"Answer!" I shout to the system. I'm ready to give this rogue hacker a piece of my mind—and demand that he tell me how to get my gift back.

CHAPTER 2

Before a robotic voice can utter an obscure warning and hang up, I shout into the phone. "Who are you? What do you want? Why are you calling me?"

A familiar, husky laugh follows. "I might be a bit old fashioned, *Trouble*, but I thought boyfriends call their girlfriends, especially when they haven't talked in a few days." Kai's voice. And he's very amused.

I groan with relief—and surprise. "Ugh. Sorry. Wrong guy." I instantly calm down. His voice still has that soothing effect on me even if his new job isn't exactly safe.

"*Wrong guy?* What's going on? Is someone threatening you?" he asks, instantly serious.

I'm about to answer when it dawns on me. "Wait, why are you calling me? Private Global Forces said no contact with me when you're in the field. It's not safe." A motorcycle growls in the background, and there are horns honking. "Don't tell me you're talking while riding too. Are you crazy, Kai?"

"Not any more than you are, Trouble." The engine revs in the background.

"I told you, you can't call me *Trouble* anymore. I have a very normal, boring life now." Apart from my sims and that ever-growing itch, anyway.

Kai laughs. "Nice try. We both know that will never be true. You'll always be Trouble to me. Trouble that I never want to be rid of—which is why I'm risking this five-minute conversation right now. If Bai found out, he'd kill me."

"Don't lose your job on my account."

"He'll never know. I bought a phone for this five-minute call because I missed you. It's stripped of anything traceable, and I'll destroy it the minute we hang up. Now, can I talk to my girlfriend?"

I imagine the cocky grin on his lips, and I miss him so badly it hurts. I'm also hyper aware of the risks in his new line of work. Ever since Kai helped solve the Madame case in China, he's worked at his dream job with Private Global Forces, or PGF, training to be part of their new field team. But it was after his first field assignment that the hacker warned me about him.

I pull back on to the road headed to PSS and ask, "So how's life where you are?" It's been weeks since we last saw each other in person. To be honest, the separation is killing me. I've already spent so much time away from people I love that it really bothers me we can't live in the same country. Kai and I were just learning how to be a couple, without tension and code names and clandestine operations. Now he's got a job that takes him away for weeks at a time while I'm stuck here kicking rocks at the beach trying to guess their distance and velocity and wondering how long it will be before he can hop on a plane to come see me. After this job is finished, we're supposed to discuss what's next for us.

"Dry. That's pretty much all I can tell you." He sighs deeply. "If you had your"—he stops, correcting himself—"if you were here, we'd have figured out this case by now."

I can't overlook that he almost said "your gift" but I don't blame him. I think the same way. Now that I know my numbers are still there, and just buried inside me, getting my calculating ability back is my main priority.

"Not going well, huh?"

He growls. "We're chasing the wrong thing if you ask me. But I got a lead—I'm on my way to check it out now."

The mischief in his voice is undeniable, which is what makes him such a great asset to their team. He thinks out of the box and he fears nothing. He's the guy who followed me into Madame's claws, into the pit of Golden Alley and King's underground domain. But right now, that doesn't bring me any comfort. For a minute, I understand my father's fear.

"Kai, please be careful."

"Lost your confidence in me so easily, did you?" he asks, chuckling.

"Not one bit. I just want you to be safe, that's all." The first time he returned from a field op, he refused to video chat with me. Later I found out he'd broken his nose, a few ribs, and dislocated his shoulder, not to mention he was covered in new bruises and stitches. When I finally saw him, he'd looked like hell. Black eyes and bandages.

When I fussed over him, he'd laughed. "Now I'm really glad you didn't see me three days ago. Don't worry, Trouble. I loved every minute of it." That was my Kai. Fearless.

"Trust me," he says now as his engine goes quiet. "I'm always safe." His tone turns serious. "I've also got news. PGF offered me my dream job. Not to brag, but I'm the youngest qualified agent to have ever been offered this type of job."

"I'm not surprised at all. What is it?"

He clears his throat. "That's just it...there are some conditions that would make it really hard to accept."

"Like what?" I ask.

Kai inhales a long breath. "Let's talk about it when I get back." The quiver in his voice makes me squirm. "First you need to explain who it was that got you upset. Is someone harassing you?"

"Oh. Right," I say, surprised I'd forgotten. "Um. Pretty sure it was Coral Hacker —the one who sent me that warning about you. He sent me another message. Something about Tunisia."

Kai goes silent. After several beats, he clears his throat again. "Don't let this guy get to you, Jo. After we hang up, call Bai and tell him what you told me."

My breath catches. Tunisia means something to Kai. I hear it in his voice. Somehow that weirdo knows where Kai is. But what's the connection? Why does he care what Kai and I do?

"Jo? Did you hear me?"

"Yeah. I'll do it." Kai's right. I shouldn't let this guy get under my skin—except if I'm honest he already has. The Coral Sea. The way he said my name. His promise to help me get my gift back…it's haunted me for weeks.

And now he wants Kai 'to back off'. So, yes, it bothers me, and no one seems keen to do anything about it.

A loud racket from his side of the line makes me stiffen. It sounds like glass breaking. "Jo?" Kai's voice is masked in static. "Jo, I gotta go…"

"Kai? Is something wrong?" The crackling on the phone gets louder. My throat goes dry.

"Never. Meet you on *the street.*" The call drops. So does my stomach.

I dial Agent Bai right away, but he doesn't answer. I leave a message for him to call me immediately.

For the next few minutes, I drive slowly to PSS telling myself bad phone connections happen all the time. Kai has been in dangerous situations before and survived. The hacker's message has nothing to do with Kai.

I convince myself it's true, because my numbers aren't there to prove me wrong.

CHAPTER 3

PRODIGY STEALTH SOLUTIONS HEADQUARTERS
UNIVERSITY OF WASHINGTON
SEATTLE, WASHINGTON

After scanning my thumbprint, the door swings open to the headquarters of Prodigy Stealth Solutions. A receptionist greets me, I walk through another scan-door, and enter a buzz of brain activity—nerddom—that I love. My shoulders are still tense from my conversation with Kai, my mind still spinning from the hacker's message, but everything about PSS is a breath of fresh air.

Large screens projecting virtual simulations cover the walls. The smartest kids I know are typing away in front of the screens, headphones on, absorbed in great discoveries or trying to solve some of the world's most dire problems. Different labs are in motion, robotic stations are stacked high with wires, and prodigies cluster around whiteboards covered in complex formulas. Others compare data from different news sources for various thinktanks. Everyday math problems and world solutions and new inventions are debated and created. All this activity gives me a sense of purpose. Even without my gift

Prodigy Stealth Solutions believes "once a prodigy, always a prodigy". I want to prove them right.

A few eyes look up as I close the door behind me. Several of the *prods* who have become my good friends wave.

"Hey there, Jo-Bomb. Coffee's fresh." A seventeen-year-old tow-headed boy in a gray hoodie looks up at me. The freckles on his face soften his otherwise brooding appearance.

"Hi, Harrison," I say. "What cup are you on?"

He spouts off a ridiculously complex equation that equates to three.

"Impressive." I smirk. Harrison is not only a tech-genius, he's also our lead analyst and news guy. He's always watching for real-time events that could be of interest to PSS. "What's new in the world this week?"

"Eh. Same old story. Global security in Iran. Crisis Management in Myanmar. Calls from the Global Economic Governance in Spain. The Indian Ambassador Prasad is going to call us for help soon regarding their new energy policy, I'm sure. MIT professors Salzer and Li are officially enemies over the theory of Quantum reality. G7 wants us to come to Camp David to discuss the new energy policies."

"*Aiya.* Any lighter news?"

"NASA finally got their long-life, long-range satellite to work thanks to another anonymous tip. We may find aliens soon." Harrison winks. He's obsessed with space tech and anything extraterrestrial. "I just don't understand why we can't set up a PSS outpost near Area 51. We'd have better Wi-Fi, more solar power, and aliens..."

I laugh and turn my attention to the redhead to my left pulling out her ear buds.

"Hey, JoJo."

"Hi, Pens," I reply. "How many cyber-attacks this week?"

Her real name is Penny, but everyone calls her *Pens* because she can simultaneously write with two hands, two different reports. Her brain literally divides into two and can work on two things at once. I've never seen anything like it. She's one of the three main hackers in PSS and a brilliant cryptologist too.

"Hundreds. It's been really bad this week. But don't worry, I've got it covered. No one has gotten through our firewalls, and I've shut down a mob of hackers. The US government can thank me later. How's your father, any breakthrough?" she says, pulling her long red hair into a messy bun on top of her head.

I groan. "If my dad has his way, I'll stay in Washington State forever, teach full time at the University, and never journey farther than a 10-mile radius from him." I sigh. It's getting tiring. This quiet life just isn't me. It never will be. The other day I had to read the Chinese dictionary for fun.

"Don't worry. Once your six months are up, you can take a PSS assignment again. Maybe even go abroad. Speaking of... how's Kai?" Pens asks, waggling her eyebrows.

Harrison perks up. "Yeah, when's my bro-crush coming back?" Harrison gives me a mock air-punch. "I've been working on my Kung Fu. Kai said next time he comes around he may even teach me the 'death kick' move he's been practicing."

My call with Kai rushes back to me. I consider telling them about it but decide against it. Technically, I'm not supposed to be in contact with him. They don't even know what he does.

I shake my head at Harrison. "It's not a *death kick*. And he's fine, I think. He's traveling now. Not sure when he'll be back." I put my bag down and lean over an Asian boy bent over his keyboard.

I poke his shoulder and smile. "Hey, Eddie, invent any new tech this week that won't get us in trouble?" Eddie's a wizard. Not only does he speak five languages, but he's an inventor, an electrical engineer, and a music whiz. Some of the prods truly think he comprehends information twice as fast as a normal human, that's why they call him "Sp-eddie."

"Very funny," he growls and leaves the room.

"What's up with him?" I ask.

"Gov-Ops called about one of his inventions. It got vetoed, and apparently, we are on some kind of probation because of it. We have a meeting about it after acquisitions." Pens shrugs.

Oh no. Poor Eddie. He's new to the team. A pure genius but he's 0-4 for approved ideas. Back in his home country, his gift was manipulated by a terrorist group for so long they kind of skewed his view on things. But Ms. T found him, freed him and gave him a chance to use his genius for good. His creations, though built with good intentions, always end up getting tossed into the PSS Blacklist—a virtual file containing hundreds of dangerous inventions that should never see the light of day. But here, there's no shame in dangerous ideas. Without limits, kids and their ideas can grow.

That's what makes PSS so successful—everyone here thinks outside of the box. They've been trained not to accept what others believe is impossible. They think beyond limits of impossibilities and probabilities. They experiment with everything in their genius brains, and no one tells them it can't be done. Which is why PSS prods sometimes come up with unintentionally bad ideas. We've learned the question *"What if?"* can be dangerous.

What if the narrative of a nation could be changed with one AI computer program? What if we could carry undetected bombs in our fingertips? What if drones could manipulate the weather? What if one software program allowed a government unlimited power to any system they chose? What if we could have a truth serum activated by a kiss? Well. Those ideas, to mention a few, were blacklisted by the government. Mostly because their safer counterparts weren't fully developed yet. Like *FingerTips*—there was no effective way to dismantle the bombs if they weren't going to be used.

I take out my phone, eager for a text from Bai. Nothing. I

text him another *911* then plunk it down in front of Harrison. "It's been compromised again."

Harrison brushes a blond mess of hair from his eyes. "Coral Hacker? Seriously? How did he get in this time? We've been sweeping for his malware signatures across all systems 24/7!" He squeezes his fist in the air.

I shake my head. "I'd really like to know."

Harrison inserts my phone into the dock that allows him to access it with his computer. "I'll run diagnostics again. We're going to find him, lock him out of our systems forever, and bring him to justice. But dang it, if he wasn't threatening our very existence, I'd give him props, and maybe even offer him a job. I admire his work."

Everyone groans. "Harrison."

"Fine. He's public enemy number one. I'll find out how he's getting in and close the door."

"Thanks," I say, feeling a bit conflicted. It's the right thing to do but it's not what I want to do. Ms. T is convinced Coral Hacker has probed our other files, and if he can break in here, he can break in anywhere.

A part of me wishes I hadn't given my phone to Harrison, who will surely lock him out for another few weeks. That means a few more weeks without my gift. I should be afraid of this hacker. But I'm not. I can't decide if he's trying to help me or trick me.

I turn my focus to why I love Mondays. Today could be the day I have another breakthrough on my sims. "All right everyone. I'll see you at the meeting after my sims."

Pens follows me to the door. "Don't hurt yourself in there, JoJo. You've been working like a beast lately on those sims. These simulations aren't designed for someone to engage with them for hours at a time. And I've monitored your heart rate. It always skyrockets during phase three."

I grimace. It's true. I have been going a little overboard, but they don't understand. At first, when the numbers all vanished, I made my peace with it. I thought it was a new start. But then, when they started resurfacing, and I remembered what it was like to have them. It made me miss them even more.

"Pens, if you lost your gift, you'd do the same to get it back. And I'm fine, really. Every time I go in, I get stronger. That part of me wants to return. I can feel it. I just have to work harder."

Ms. T walks in. "Pens is right." Her black curly hair is pulled back into a ponytail, and she somehow looks younger than when I first met her. "You need to take it easy on your sims. I've made you and your father a promise—and it doesn't involve you burning out or going crazy. Now log in, then come to the sim-box."

"Be right there, Ms. T," I say, opening the computer to log in.

Harrison taps my desk. "Hey. That guy is good. Clean logs, no history. But you're good to go. I double checked everything. No weird robotic voice will hijack your phone or your sims today." He gives me a thumbs-up and I clamp down hard on a rush of disappointment.

Coral Hacker broke laws and the most complex electronic barriers imaginable to get inside PSS, and God knows where else. He's dangerous, a potential threat, possibly malicious. Logically I know he shouldn't be in my sims...it's just that the robotic voice helped me when no one else could. I try to smile a "*thanks*" to Harrison but there's an idea swirling in my head that I can't let go of. PSS is determined to catch him, while I'm desperate to figure out who he is and what he knows, and why. The *Phoenix* in me wouldn't sit around waiting for him. I know exactly what that girl would do. Which gives me an idea. PSS and I are both intent on finding him—what if we could both get what we want?

"Hey, Harrison," I whisper before he walks away.

"Yeah?" He leans in closer.

"What if we could catch this guy?" My voice is low.

"What do you mean?"

"Instead of blocking him, let's throw out some bait. Find his vulnerability. Then decloak him. He contacted me today. What if he's still watching?" I glance over my shoulder at the room. No one else is paying attention but Pens.

"Ms. T would kill us. Any time there's a breach at PSS, our information could be stolen."

"Not if we get to him first."

Pens creeps over. "I can hear you, you know," she whispers, "it's a totally stupid plan."

I bite my lip. "Fine—"

"But I agree. I want to catch this guy too. No one breaks my code and gets away with it," she says vindictively. Pens brags all the time that she's written code since she was five. "Besides, I've never seen Ms. T want a guy taken down as badly as Coral Hacker."

Felicia pops over, bumping me with her hip. "What's going on? If World War Three is happening I need to know how to stop it too." Behind thick glasses, a pretty girl with dark brown curly locks gives us a perfectly white smile. She's a tech nerd with a hacking ability so great she had to sign agreements with the US government controlling what she can do.

Harrison fidgets when she joins us. He has it bad for her. She debates all his theories and messes with all his algorithms, but it's obvious she likes him too.

"Coral Hacker," I say. "We're setting a trap for him in my sims."

"Seriously? He's a criminal," she says, looking straight at me. "With today's meeting, it's not a good idea. What if he gets into our system?" Harrison nods at her voice of reason.

"He won't," Pens says, "Harrison and I will guard the walls like Godzilla. We'll give him one hour to find his way in. When he does, we'll trace the origin of his DNS back to his IP address. Then we find his identity and expose him for good."

"You'd better know what you're doing," Felicia whispers. "Use our Rogue server. I didn't tell you that." With a wink, she slips away.

We all stare at each other as if we're about to go cliff diving without knowing if there are rocks below. Then everyone nods silently and quietly steps back to their desks like we didn't just plan an ambush against ourselves. But my blood is finally flowing again.

I sit down at my desk and log in. Harrison pulls up his hood, like he's already hiding, then sends me a skull emoji and a thumbs up. Pens sends me a countdown of t-minus ten minutes. Time ticks by agonizingly slow until the final punch of a few buttons. They've unlocked a door and set a cyber trap, which means there's no time to waste.

My heart surges as I stride into the sim room. My gift flickers, calculating the odds of Coral Hacker taking the bait. Even if it's just for one hour, he knows things and I need to find out what.

Ms. T greets me at the door. "Ready?" she asks.

"Yeah. I've got a feeling about today," I say, ducking my head for fear she'll see through me.

"Hmm," Ms. T grunts. She goes to the door and turns. "Try not to do anything reckless, okay?"

"Sure," I say, but I know I already have.

CHAPTER 4

The sim-box's walls are covered with screens, small speakers, and heat sensors. As usual I settle into the gel-body-forming chair.

"How are you today, Ms. Rivers?" Mr. Barrios, a senior analyst, says attaching the neural connectors to my body.

"Fine, thanks. Can you please put me into phase three first, Mr. Barrios?" I ask. I'm eager to have the rush from my gift. I need to remember who I am. It's there, and it wants to resurface. But Mr. Barrios frowns.

"Sorry, Jo," he says, "Mrs. T says you've done a lot of phase three, but you've skipped too many phase one and twos. According to our calculations, you need all three to get your gift back. She's ordered that you do all of them for the next week. Even at home."

I sigh. I don't do it on purpose. It's just that phase one—the time before my mom died—is hard. I like being there. I even like the recreations of my mom. It doesn't sting as much as it used to coming out of them, but they're slow, and there's never anything that sparks my gift at all.

Phase two, on the other hand—my time in China—is an emotional left hook to the head. It's where I became who I am today. Where I met Kai and Red. The place of fire and pure gold and strength. It also triggers Phoenix and my greatest fears.

When Madame is in them, they're too real. Too skin crawling. But I buckle down and take it all in. I need to be reminded that fear can always be overcome.

And yet, my gift doesn't spark in phase two either.

Ms. T claims my subconscious will see things I didn't notice in the moment during my time of fear. By reliving a point in time, my perspective will change and hopefully trigger my gift. It might resurface in new ways, she'd said. It's all theoretical, of course.

Phase three is the only simulation where I gain new ground. I'm still not sure why they always turn into near death experiences but if anything can kick start your life, it's nearly dying.

Mr. Barrios clears his throat.

"Alright," I agree. It's their design. "Send me to phase one. But can we automatically transition this time? I don't want a break in between." Besides, I don't have time. We only have one hour.

"You know zero process time causes unnecessary anxiety in the brain," he says. "It could disrupt your neural patterns and complicate the sims. I recommend a break, even if it's 1-2 minutes."

"I'll be fine. I just want to jump in today," I say. "Who knows, it might spark my gift."

"Fine," Mr. Barrios says, his lips puckered in thought. "We can do that. I'll set them at 20 minutes each for the first round. They'll transition automatically."

Perfect. One hour. And I'll be in there the whole time. If the hacker is watching, he should be able to find me.

"You know the drill," he says, prompting my verbal permission before he leaves the room.

I nod, eyes closing. "I agree."

The lights go out.

A familiar lavender aroma grabs my senses as the lights slowly transition from semi-darkness to bright. My bare feet sink into soft, fuzzy carpet. "Mmm," I hum. My old room. My eyes adjust. I stand, looking at a fully stocked bookshelf. My old bed is covered with the patchwork quilt my mom made. My desk is piled with math books, journals, and trophies. It's exactly as it was before mom died.

My mind sinks deeper into the sim connected to my neural memories of being thirteen. I'm happy, content. Nothing is wrong. There is everything to look forward to. A part of me knows it isn't true, but I give in for a moment.

I go to the bedroom door, eager to see who is home. Will I eat lunch with my mom? Play games with my family after dinner? Outsmart my old math tutors? Give Tails, my cat, a scratch session by the fireplace?

"Mom?" I call out, listening. No answer. "Dad? Mara? Lily?" No sound comes from downstairs. Not even a meow.

My smile fades and a pinch between comfort and loss sweeps over me. The thirteen-year-old girl in me shivers. I was rarely left alone in the house. A moment of reality hits me—I've never been alone in phase one before. I retreat to my room. Whatever I'm here for must be in there.

I wander around my room looking at memorabilia. A shelf covered in small sticky notes with codes and equations. A calendar on my wall with different symbols crossing out each day. I check through the notes and dates like usual, but nothing stands out or sparks my gift. No sign of Coral Hacker either.

Slowly slipping back into my thirteen-year-old self, I plop myself down into the swivel chair at my desk. I'd spend hours each day at this desk. My old laptop is glowing blue, a string of old tabs open. I take a closer look. School assignments, math forums, book chats, and my old blog, www.you-get-my-digits.com. I laugh out loud. How had I forgotten about that blog?

My APP-Site was the highlight of my thirteen-year-old life. Mom had inspired me to start a forum for gifted kids, creating a space to meet others like me. Those friends kept me sane. They were there for me when others couldn't be. A youthful buzz of energy shoots through me.

I click open my chat room, excited to connect with my old math pals when it dawns on me. These friends might not be excited to chat with me after what I did to them.

My chat room message board pops open. Hundreds of unread messages and old unanswered chats stare back at me. My stomach sinks. Worried friends. Broken promises. Kids who confided in me, needed me. Friends I failed. My stomach tightens as I scroll down.

FROM <read.write.math> SAL: Jo, where are you? You missed EQUATE. You were the main speaker... Ten unread messages. A rock settles in my stomach. Sal and I used to be close. EQUATE was her first teen conference. I left her hanging in her biggest moment.

FROM <math.wizard.girl> AYAKA: Jo, you're not responding to anyone so I'm hacking your computer to see if you're ok... Five more unread messages. I shake my head, reading faster.

FROM <*mathfreakgeek*> Daanesh: Jo, check in, or I'll refuse to do your math homework anymore, lol... Three unread messages. He used to challenge me and keep me sharp.

I remember the day I logged out. Never went back. I left them all hanging like they didn't exist. And I never explained why. What a horrible friend.

A surge of grief and regret rises in me. I want to hit reply right now. Answer them all. Ask them to forgive me for abandoning them. Tell them why. That after my mom died, I didn't have the emotional energy to be around people, that running a math forum seemed pointless without the one who inspired me to do it in the first place. I'd tell them I couldn't think straight. That I cried myself to sleep. That Mara was angry at me. That I focused on school. Worked with my dad. That it was a dark time...then Madame came... No. I wouldn't tell them that part.

I scroll down through the hundreds of messages, faster, searching for one name. When it pops up, all my courage is lost.

FROM *<son.of.a.mandelbrot>* Twenty-five unread messages.

My face flushes with heat and my stomach ties itself into a hundred knots. I'm a thirteen-year-old girl staring at the screen, my fingers trembling. The one person who deserved an explanation the most never got one. What do those twenty-five messages say? Do I even want to know? My eyes squeeze shut, and I breathe. *This is a sim*—the thought comes sharp and fast. *It's all in the past now.* Instead of opening his messages, I close the computer. I'd rather remember him without messages telling me how I hurt him.

I push the chair back, and open a drawer, searching for an old journal. I find it under a few papers and knick-knacks. Tucked in the middle of it is a postcard of the Mandelbrot Set Fractal, a famous mathematical phenomenon, the origin of his virtual name. The only time he sent me something physical. I remember thinking he'd sign his real name on the back, but he didn't. I was disappointed.

My finger runs over the smooth card. I'm about to turn it over, to re-read what is written on the back when a flicker of numbers rolls over the complex lines of the Mandelbrot.

I freeze, not willing to lose the moment. This has never happened in phase one.

My eyes hone in on the picture and a sharpness comes over me. I look deeper, my eyes running over the lines of the symbol. Slowly, a spark, a drip, a taste of my gift. I blink, and the measurements of my old room become a blueprint, like a light turning on. The numbers are so familiar I nearly cry. Equations connect everything from my bed to bookshelf to all the memories of my childhood. Laughter bubbles out of me until the lights snap black, and my head starts spinning.

My back is against a brick building. My hair whips across my face in the sharp wind. I'm dizzy as I gain my bearings on where I am. No process time, like Mr. Barrios said. The transition is heavy this time.

I focus on what is in front of me. The Shanghai skyline. Downtown. The Bund, *Waitan*. I'm near Chan's old office. I'm not 13 anymore. I'm 17 and in the city that both destroyed and forged me into who I am. Strong. Brave. Fierce.

I'm breathless, as my mind catches up with my location. I need to be fully here for my assignment, for Harrison and Pens as we wait for Coral Hacker, but I can't seem to shake my feelings from the last sim.

My gift was at my fingertips.

My head buzzes. I can't think about that. There's no time.

It's night. I'm outside in a square. There are thousands of people around me. Scents fill the air. Oil frying, car exhaust, and dust. I feel like I'm home, but I know it won't last long. I check my pocket. Sure enough there is a note like always in phase two.

Your assignment: Get to the factory. You have twenty minutes.

Easy enough. There's a bus stop across the street. I go to cross the street, ten feet ahead, when all of a sudden, my back is thrust against the same brick wall again. I shake my head. That was weird. Somehow, I've missed the bus.

Several new choices are before me. The subway station is several hundred feet ahead of me. But it'd be busy now. Hailing a taxi would take too long. I decide to run.

My feet charge ahead, my head darting left and right. Excited to be out in the night air, I dodge pedestrians, crossing in and out of my path. I pass an old favorite restaurant that Kai and I frequented. People are gathered at round tables, laughing and eating. I try to count them.

Running faster, things like cars, bikes and old faces become obstacles.

I run past boutiques as their doors close for the night. I dodge shop owners trying to sell to me, and gate guards wanting to question me.

Finally, I make it out of the brightly lit downtown area and onto the shadowy street where the factory is. It's dark, but I know the way. I run faster, knowing I'll beat the allotted time. I'm almost there when there's a bright flash that blinds me and I'm back against the brick wall where I started. The note is once again limply hanging in my hand. I look at it.

Your assignment: Get to PSS. You have twenty minutes.

I straighten. *PSS? What is happening?*

I look around confused. I'm still in Shanghai. Is this a malfunction in the program? Then I remember what Mr. Barrios said. Having no process time could disrupt or complicate the sims or my neural patterns. Apparently, he was right. The red button on my chair is tempting. I could easily push it and get out. Restart the system. But I can't. Harrison and Pens are depending on me for one hour.

I'll complete my first assignment. Get to the factory.

I run, this time avoiding a group of rowdy boys and bustling carts. I cut corners to avoid red lights. I'm almost to the factory, nearly touching its gate when—*flash*—

My back is against the brick wall again; the note still hanging in my hand. I pull it up in front of me.

Your assignment: Get to Kai. You have five days.

My whole body shivers. I'm still panting from running. I look up, searching for threats. For Coral Hacker. But Shanghai is calm. Nothing to fear that I can detect. It has to be a mental disruption. I've been thinking about Kai since our phone call.

I'm determined to make it to the factory when up ahead a woman who looks like Ms. T catches my eye. She speeds over to a circle of people who are yelling in the square.

Ms. T has never been in a sim. It couldn't be her. But I run after the lady anyway. "Ms. T!"

As I pursue her, a little Chinese boy on a bike rides urgently toward me. I go to dodge him but stop. My eyes must be playing tricks on me because I swear his face is changing. Like a digital program morphing into another. He is not Chinese anymore, but darker, with new distinct features, no longer Asian. The square is also changing. I don't know where I am. Is this the hacker? Or a disruption? If it's him, I need to find out where he is.

I shake my head. *Focus. Just make it to the end, Jo.*

Voices yell, pulling my attention to the right. They are gathered in a circle, watching something. A fight. I search for the Ms. T look-alike in the crowd. I spot her and gasp. Madame is beside her. Too close. I have to warn Ms. T.

My gift starts sparking like flint against stone. Madame is talking to an X girl with a short skirt standing beside her. *Oh no.* I have to warn the girl too. I run faster trying to reach them, but the circle keeps moving farther away as the fight gets more violent. The woman who looks like Ms. T is swept into the crowd. Madame walks away, the X girl at her side, walking in perfect sync. I harden, an instinct inside me takes over. I run toward her until a man emerges from the fight, bloody, and follows Madame and the girl. My mouth drops open. I'd know his gait, his frame anywhere.

"Kai?"

Before he turns, a wall of black engulfs me.

∞

A loud noise beats above me. My eyes snap open to a blue and white haze. Sky. Blades.

Voom. Voom. Voom. Voom. My hands are gloved. I'm gripping controls on an aircraft I don't know how to fully operate. I'm high in the sky. The West Coast of Washington State is below me. I'm in a helicopter. This time, I reorient myself quickly. I've done the helicopter sim many times.

I close my eyes until I feel the high winds on my face. For a moment, I forget phase two and the hacker-prod who could be in the system, and just breathe in and out. Ever since I was young, I've always wanted one thing: The impossibility of soaring and falling through the clouds, flying just like the birds above our beach house. After all these years, I get my wish. *Sort of.*

I'm extremely happy. It's summer and I'm flying above a beautiful coastline. I'm five thousand feet above the ground, according to one of the many gauges.

After many times attempting to fly this thing with only 30% information, I still can't get it right. But I'm determined to learn.

Each time I get close, a problem starts. Right now, the sound of the blades pumps loudly in my ear while I notice rapidly blinking lights—40 dials, 200 buttons, 30 switches, not sure how many gauges.

The helicopter simulation is supposed to reboot my brain, but it makes it spin instead.

Now the smell of smoke is pungent. Fire below me? Fire in the engine? The helicopter is broken. I need to land fast.

My gift flickers to life. I've got a 50/50 chance. In a split second, a possibility, an option, a route is revealed in my mind's eyes. But it flashes out before I see if it's safe. But one thing is clear. I've dropped in altitude. I'm flying too low now and must pull up.

Mountains, jagged cliffs and water. Last time it was desert. I've even flown in the jungle. I've learned all the routes and still I don't have what I came in here for. What if I try to crash? My mind would be forced to save me—like a shot of adrenaline to the brain. I dive low, ignoring all the warning signs.

My gift is sparking like crazy. I will taste it today. The blades chop and the wind presses against me. I am flying. I am falling. The red warning light glows hot in my peripheral. I ignore it, and go faster, lower. A peak is approaching when a robotic voice like the one in my car this morning shatters the sound of the blades.

"Slow down."

My breath catches. Coral Hacker. He came. He speaks again and my skin goes cold.

"You shouldn't have opened this door. You're going to regret that."

It's not what I expect him to say. It's a *threat*. Regardless, a confused hope soars alongside me. I won't waste this opportunity to speak with him. "Tell me how to get my gift back."

Silence.

The helicopter is still fighting to stay in the air. I know how to make him speak. I let go. The helicopter spins out of my control. Spiraling. Just like me. I'm getting dizzy. Sick. The numbers in my brain jumble into one large mess.

The voice, low and robotic, crackles in the speakers. "I already told you what you needed to know to help them. Now slow down..."

What? Help who?

"Tell me who are you and I'll slow down."

I'm panicking. Losing elevation. I need my brain to jump-start. I don't care if I have to crash to do it.

Silence. No response.

My anger skyrockets.

The helicopter is plummeting. I'm tipping it on purpose. My gift responds, numbers are appearing like a forest instead of just a few trees. I won't slow down now.

Whoever the hacker is, he won't tell me. So I don't care.

I go after the sparks of my gift, chasing the fire. My gift will save my life.

I'm falling, plummeting. I'm choking on the wind.

"Focus on the coastline."

At his command, my eyes shoot everywhere until I find a small snapshot of the ground. It's shaky, but I lock onto the coastline, and something brilliant happens. A shot of numbers splits up and down the coast. A pattern emerges. Everything comes into focus. Not sparks or scattered erratic numbers. My gift is fully turned on. But it's too late. The helicopter is out of control. The ground is too close. Alarms are going off, too loud to count.

The screens go black.

Two large hands grab my shoulders. I push them back. "No! Not yet!"

A white light blinds me. My eyes close tight as the room lights up.

Harrison pulls me back. "That's enough."

"I almost had it. My gift was right there! The hacker was inside too."

Harrison doesn't argue with me. He shuts the sims down. The belt pops open.

I let out a breath, touching my forehead. It's covered in sweat. My body pumps with adrenaline. Bouncing from sim to sim. The Mandelbrot. Kai and PSS in sim two. My gift switching on as I crashed. *It's still on.* I know this because it's calculating my heart rate. For a second, I note it's 194 beats a minute. Then like dusk to dark, the numbers fade.

Harrison is shaking his head. "Get your stuff and come into Com-Hall. It's an emergency."

The hacker's voice rings in my ear. *You shouldn't have opened this door. You're going to regret this.*

He's right. What have I done? Whatever is wrong, I just made it worse.

CHAPTER 5

Com-Hall is a secure conference room with no windows and a long oval table. Ten prods sit around the table with buds in their ears, tech on their wrists, and tablets sprawled out in front of them. Everyone is glancing at each other nervously. I don't meet their eyes. It's not every Monday Ms. T calls for an urgent meeting, on top of job acquisitions. And it's certainly not every Monday I decide to be stupid enough to break one of the most fundamental rules and let a dangerous hacker have his way in our system. *What have I done?*

I take my seat, mouth dry. We're surrounded by PSS tech so micro you wouldn't be able to detect it, reminding me of how easily they track everything. A mole on someone's skin, for example, could be a mini-camera or a bio-detector. I sigh.

Ms. T is not in the room yet, so I take a moment to process what just happened in my sims.

Harrison and Pens rush in and sneak to my side. The look on their faces makes me wish I had actually gone down in the helicopter.

"How bad is it?" I ask, clenching my jaw.

"Well, as you said, Coral Hacker got in," Harrison whispers.

I nod, wondering how much I should say. "And?"

"He was sneakier than we thought. He had help. While Coral Hacker was in your sims, his accomplice slid in and cracked our secure database and stole a file."

My eyes close, a dread sinking into my gut. "Which file?"

"We don't know which one yet. It was a virtual, holographic file. He's that good." Harrison exhales, his eyes narrowing.

"Or that bad," Pens adds.

Pens leans in. "Whatever file it was, we'd better find out before Ms. T or Mr. Barrios does." We look at each other grimly.

I push up my sleeves and start tapping the table. *Stupid. They told me he was dangerous.* I didn't listen. Without my gift I keep making really bad decisions.

"We'll get it back," I say. "*I'll* get it back. No matter how long it takes. We can start after the acquisitions meeting. Where is Ms. T, by the way?"

Pens shrugs as she and Harrison exchange a look. "She told Felicia to start without her, which is a first." My body stiffens. It isn't like her to be late. A different Monday indeed.

My head hurts. "I'd better get coffee." I make my way to the counter where a voice activated espresso machine named Ledger greets me as it picks up my voice waves.

"Hello, Jo," the robotic voice says. "What can I get you today?"

"Hi, Ledger, a triple shot macchiato, extra strong please." Ledger gets to work while humming a Chinese folk tune I taught him. It doesn't bring me joy this time.

Felicia enters the room with her clipboard and sits at the head of the table. "Alright, prods, Ms. T will be in soon. We've got some fantastic new opportunities this week..." Her tone is optimistic but the awkward smile on her face says otherwise.

"Felicia, tell the truth," sighs Eddie. "This week's PSS jobs are mind-numbing." Of course Eddie would say that.

"Boring is still important," Felicia retorts.

"*Boring* is what I need to tell my dad," I whisper to Pens.

But it won't get my gift back. My mind jumps to the helicopter sim where my gift surfaced with the rush of an adrenaline high. I shake my head. *What are we going to regret? What was he telling me? What do Kai and PSS have to do with this? What did he take?*

Felicia reads the assignments one by one. Torturously slow. The assignments are located all over the world: Seoul. Abu Dhabi. London. They all involve an economic, agricultural or technological problem, all of which involve a ton of reports and accounting. Apart from a few enthusiastic yesses from kids who actually like reports, moans and groans fill the room. Definitely not as fun as the jobs that require inventing, testing new products, or hacking into things.

Felicia continues reading the brief job descriptions as the team logs possible solution starters into the thinktank app. But I can't focus. PSS jobs usually get me excited, but not today. I can't stop thinking about the missing file. And I need to talk to Agent Bai or Detective Hansen about Kai, tell them about Coral Hacker. Besides PSS doesn't need me for these jobs. Everyone on the team is more than capable of solving these problems.

We're not finished with the job list when Ms. T marches to the front of the room. Her short but commanding presence steals our attention. Her straight back coupled with the stark expression on her face reminds me of a military leader coming back from combat. Each step on the tile floor is tapped out for us to count. The way she holds a file in her hand, like it's evidence of a murder, silences us all.

"Team, can I have your attention? I have grave news."

CHAPTER 6

Lights in the room snap off and a glowing red bulb turns on. A zing from an overhead buzzer vibrates the table and every piece of tech, tablet or smart watch in the room zaps to black. *Dark-Eye*. It's a protocol I've only heard about. PSS is now completely locked down, highly secure and soundproof.

"Don't worry, everyone. We'll be up and running again soon. None of your information will be lost," Ms. T explains.

Five other PSS mental calculators who I don't know well squirm in their seats at the tension. They don't take field jobs and only provide internal assistance to the teams. Right now, they're fish out of water. The field team sits still as ice, hyper-aware, but not afraid. For me, this tense atmosphere almost feels normal, like I'm back in China.

"Earlier today we received a warning from the Government-Ops sector that unless we sterilize our Blacklist by the end of this week, they'll have to shut down PSS. Which means, Harrison, we need to lock up that virtual file in Cyber Island."

I raise my hand. "Cyber what?"

Ms. T glances my way. "All of the programs created by PSS are fully encrypted. Every time the program runs, a public-key and a private-key is fetched from the Cyber Island command server. If there's a potentially sensitive file, we'll lock it up in our *Cyber Island*. If there's tampering, then the command server will not respond with the appropriate key to decrypt, instead, it will respond with an order to delete the file and everything related to it. That way, even if the attacker has backups of the program, it would be nothing more than jumbled text without the encryption key. Basically, it's a kill-switch for our Blacklist files."

"You know, so the world can be a safer place," Eddie says, shaking his head.

All of PSS's inventions, including everything on the Blacklist, contain cutting-edge technology or scientific breakthroughs that only certain government experts are allowed to review. Some of these technologies are sanctioned for public use, conforming to safety and privacy laws, while others are for government and scientific use only. All PSS breakthroughs are highly sensitive, but Blacklist tech in the wrong hands could be truly dangerous.

Ms. T's lips flatten to an angry slash. "Which brings me to the grave news. We've been hacked. The perpetrator penetrated our system and knew exactly what he was looking for. A virtual holographic file containing Blacklist tech."

The room gasps. No one can steal a virtual holographic file without stealing a PSS invention called the Holothumb, a holographic thumb drive to carry the designs in. It's new PSS tech, and it's a big deal. Whatever the thief stole will now be encrypted with his thumbprint.

"That's right," Ms. T says. "After looking into it, we discovered a trail. There's evidence the hacker has been in this secure database before." She stares at all of us, her eyes dark like a storm is brewing. "What I'm saying is, our entire Blacklist is in the wind."

The gravity of guilt is crushing.

I nearly fall from my chair. *Idiot.* How could I let this happen?

I tuck my hair behind my ears and jam my fingers into my temples. Have I lost my mind? Newton's third law runs through my head, shaking its finger at me. *For every action there is an equal and opposite reaction.*

My mind darts to my sims—my assignment—Kai, PSS, Ms. T, they were distractions so he could take the Blacklist file. The desire to get my gift back has now made the world an infinitely more dangerous place. Anything else I do might make it even worse.

Ms. T passes a paper to her left. "Eddie, I want you on this immediately before it leaks to the government. Harrison, you wrote the Cyber Island program so get on it. We have to do anything it takes to strip the Blacklist from every server it's ever touched."

"Yes, Ma'am." Harrison rubs his forehead, which now gleams with sweat.

This is my fault. I did exactly what Kai told me not to. I let the hacker get under my skin. Ms. T told me he was a threat. He wasn't trying to help me. He was using me to get the Blacklist—which means he *is* more dangerous than I let myself believe.

Under the red light, Pens and Eddie shift in their chairs exchanging anxious expressions and twitching with nervous energy. Harrison and Felicia are already buzzing with strategies on how to trace the list. A fire roars inside me so hot I feel like I'll combust if I don't do something right now. I will get my gift back. I will find the Blacklist. When I track Coral Hacker down, I'll stop him, expose him once and for all and bring him to justice.

Ms. T can feel the energy in the room. She claps her hands for attention.

"PSS rule number one. We never give in to panic or defeat. We work hard and in innovative ways. We got here by believing we could accomplish anything. I don't need to remind you of the past solutions we have come up with." She takes a deep breath, before the lights blink back on. "We will find the list and the hacker. That said, we also can't forget our other responsibilities and those who need us." She turns to Felicia. "Update me on acquisitions. Which job did we choose?"

Felicia snaps up the list. "We haven't selected a job yet." Felicia says, distracted. "There's actually one last proposal to consider. It's labeled *crisis management* but in the details it looks like an Internet security reboot. The notes say their system is on the brink of breaking down; software's causing crashes, and there are lots of hacker-vulnerabilities."

Everyone groans under their breath as she continues reading the proposal. It's a boring job.

"They could hire anyone to do this work," Pens whispers to me. "Why call us?"

Felicia clears her throat. Clearly no one is interested. "Alright then, Eddie and Harrison are evidently more interested in the new diamond drill tech for oil discovery in Namibia. Pens chose deep-dive fishing sub tech to tap into the world's untouched fish population, so since the job in Tunisia is a no-go, let's vote between one of these."

My head snaps up so quickly it hurts. "Wait," I gasp. "Did you say Tunisia?"

Felicia nods.

My chair flies back hitting the wall as I stand abruptly, surprising myself as I blurt out, "You have to take that job."

CHAPTER 7

To say it's out of character for me to raise my voice for any job during acquisitions is an understatement, which is why the room falls silent and all eyes are on me. If only they heard what was in my head, maybe they'd understand.

Choose Tunisia. You have five days...

I straighten my shirt, wiping my sweaty palms on my pants. I must look like I've seen a ghost. In a way, I have. This can't be a coincidence. Harrison and Pens are questioning me with their eyes, wondering what I'm up to.

"Interesting." Ms. T folds her arms across her chest. "Want to explain why you think we should take this job?"

For two months I've listened in the back corner, taken notes, daydreamed that my gift comes back in full force and I'm the one who has the brilliant answer to solve all the problems of the world. But in reality, I haven't been able to offer much more than an equation or mathematical perspective.

I grin awkwardly, my shoulders shrugging. I'm not sure if admitting to the team that Coral Hacker is pointing us toward Tunisia is a smart idea. It could frighten them—or him.

I slowly take my seat. "I'm with Felicia on this one. Boring jobs are also important," I say, looking around the table.

Felicia is staring at me like I've lost my mind.

Ms. T cocks her eyebrows at me. She doesn't buy it.

"And Harrison, our news guy," I say, thinking on my toes. "Weren't you talking about Tunisia earlier?"

Harrison gives me a blank look, clearly not excited I put him on the spot. But he catches on quickly. "Um, right." He nods. "Actually, I did read about it this morning. The second biggest election in Tunisia's history is happening this week and there is a group of radicals have been causing some tension in the capital."

Ooh. I shudder and my hands go cold. That's not good.

"Hmm. Any more information on the job?" Ms. T asks Felicia, her curiosity piqued.

Thankfully, Felicia takes over. "Sure. First off, this job has to be done in person. Their main concern is an information breach in the Ministry of Education."

Pens darts me a sideways glare. Her lips are pursed, and eyebrows gathered in a tight knot. She's angry and wondering what I'm not telling her.

My head cocks to the side as I mouth, *The Blacklist.* But she still doesn't get it. I just shake my head.

My mind is sparking, and my stomach is churning. Coral Hacker's message. Ms. T in my sims. The stolen Blacklist. This job in Tunisia is connected.

And so is Kai...but I can't tell them that. Coral Hacker told me *I had all I needed to help them.* I'm confused. Is this hacker helping us? Or is he baiting me to go to Tunisia? If he's a threat, then why would he tip us off? And if he already has the Blacklist, why would he need anything else from PSS?

Numbers trail in and out of my vision. Like static, they only half appear, then sink under the surface. It's like looking into a shattered mirror. Even so, I'm sure Kai and the Blacklist are there.

Harrison locks eyes with me, rubbing his chin. "Ma'am,

we've done this job long enough to know that aiding countries during a transition is important." Harrison has no idea why he's helping me, but he knows it has something to do with the list.

Ms. T pipes in. "What's important right now is tracing the Blacklist. An internet security job is too easy for PSS. I suggest we pass on a recommendation, then accept the job in Namibia."

That feeling, deep in the pit of my stomach tells me she's making a mistake. This job is connected to the Blacklist and PSS has the right to know.

I'm staring at Pens and Felicia, shaking my head *no*. Felicia shoots me a '*what is going on*' look then says to the team. "Ok, let's put it to a vote. Namibia or Tunisia?"

"Prods!" Harrison snaps his fingers, and everyone huddles into a group, excluding me from their decision. It has never bothered me before because I can't take field jobs, but today it makes me nervous. They talk for a moment, maybe several minutes, before moving back into their original seating order.

The team turns to me. All of them have odd expressions plastered on their faces. Maybe they decided I couldn't be trusted after my stupid plan to catch the hacker. Maybe they're right.

Felicia clears her throat, then stands to make her announcement. "We'll take the job in Tunisia on one condition."

"Which is?" I ask, my feet go cold in my shoes.

Pens smirks, a mix of mischief and determination in her eye. "You're coming with us."

CHAPTER 8

You have five days.

A sharp hiccup in my gift kicks into gear. The numbers inject such a rush of adrenaline that it's like a roller coaster ride of a hundred miles per hour and I don't want to get off. For a glorious moment, I imagine myself stepping out of an airport; my father is supportive, and my gift is in full force.

Within five seconds, three graphs and nine maps of Tunisia I didn't know I had stored away are pulled up and I'm mentally tracing highways all over the region. The equations then stretch into coral and coastlines and the imperfect symmetry of Kai's face. Finally, they all land on one thing—the hacker's robotic voice.

If I go to Tunisia, I will find him. He will help me get my gift back. I don't know how I know it, but I do.

Ms. T patiently studies me. By the look on her face, she suspects my gift to be at work. I'm smiling from ear to ear until the numbers snap out like whiplash and the ride is done. I want to hop back on again, but it's closed.

Reality rushes in like a headache after a sugar rush.

Tunisia is out of the equation. I've done enough damage today. My dad would never allow it. And I won't make the same mistake twice by trusting a lunatic I don't know. Kai, no matter how much I worry about him, can take care of himself.

"Sorry. I can't go. You know I'm not very useful without my gift and my father won't allow it." The words come out like weak traitors. They know—like I do—it's the opposite of what I really want, the opposite of what I should do. Especially if I'm the one urging them to take this job.

PSS is already in serious trouble. The Blacklist is gone. What if I am leading them into more danger? This could all be a trick if Coral Hacker is luring us there. And what does it have to do with Kai?

Breathe. I force myself to think positively. Kai knows what he's doing. He's due back in Shanghai in a week. Job done. I refuse to get worked up by the groundless ideas in my head.

"Jo, you think outside of the box more than any of us..." Felicia says. "Can't you find a way to convince your dad?"

My gut is screaming in agreement with Felicia, and I've learned not to ignore that feeling but I can't traumatize my father again. "He'd flip if I asked to travel to a country with heated elections coming up. His health is finally recovering."

"It's the shortest job we've done in months and it's an office job," Pens says. "Since China, all of our protocols have changed. We operate under full security with privately hired bodyguards now."

By the looks on Harrison, Eddie, Pens, and Felicia's faces, they're not going to give up. Most likely their gifts are even showing them ways to convince me. They've seen my sim records. They know about the rush in my blood compelling me to take risks in my sims. I'm a liability. Simulations are one thing, reality is another.

"I'm sorry. If my gift was back, I'd consider it, but..."

Ms. T stands. "Jo, can we talk privately?" By the look in her eye, I have no choice but to follow her.

∞

The woman stepping out of Com-Hall is not afraid of mistakes or failure. The truth doesn't scare her either. When she found me, she promised she wouldn't let me lose who I was. She swore she'd be my advocate even if no one else would. I believed her. There's no reason not to come clean. Still, it doesn't mean it'll be easy.

As soon as the door closes behind us, Ms. T cocks her head to the side. "Josephine, what aren't you telling me?"

I shove my hands into my jean pockets and bite my lip. Even though she's shorter than me, she stands as confident as the President of the United States. But more than that, she stands there as a woman I admire. A safe and caring woman who actually believes in me.

She has poured her trust and support into me these last few months. I haven't had that since my mother died. I don't want to lose that.

I shake my head. After what PSS has done for me, I have no other choice but to tell her it's my fault we're in this predicament.

"Turns out this job might not be so boring after all," I say picking at a frayed thread from my jacket string. "I have reason to believe whoever stole the Blacklist is there."

Ms. T's face tightens. "Hmm. What else?"

"And Coral Hacker..." I pause, breathing in, "texted me today about Tunisia. I thought we could trap him in my simulations...he showed up. Now the Blacklist is gone because of me."

She clears her throat. "Then he is trickier than we thought."

"Why?"

"He used a program called Still-Night. We blacklisted that program four years ago."

My face pales and my heart skips a beat at the revelation. "That would imply—"

"Yes, he has been breaching our security for much longer than we could have imagined, which means he's more dangerous than we first thought. And if he told you about Tunisia, we have to assume this is a trap."

It's logical. I want to agree, but something doesn't add up. Ms. T implied years of theft, but Coral Hacker first contacted me six weeks ago. It's true he knew all of my former names, but the way he helped me in the sims wasn't malicious. My fingers tap K2 with a sharp pinch in my stomach. The Coral Hacker stopped my car this morning so I wouldn't hit those kids. How can someone like that be bad?

"What if Coral Hacker didn't steal the list?" I ask. "What if he's trying to help?"

"What if he's trying to steal more from us, Jo? He's beaten us a few times. And let's not be blind in all of this—his goal is you. You're the only one he contacts." Her tone is serious.

"Which is why I shouldn't go. Even if my dad would allow it," I say. "I want to help, but without my gift, I'm clearly a liability. I shouldn't have even suggested the team go there. It was stupid and dangerous…"

I swallow hard, thinking back to the helicopter and the robotic voice. *I can help you get your gift back…that's not the way…I've given you all you need to help them.* With my history, it's ludicrous I would believe this hacker will make good on his promise.

"I'm not saying we back down," Ms. T says. "I believe in my kids. This hacker might be smart, but we're smarter. Right now, he's our only lead, and just like you set a trap, I think we can too. We don't give in to fear around here—ours or anyone else's."

Her eyes fix on me. It's not the first time I've heard her match the edge in my voice or the resolve in my stare. I bite my lip. "So you aren't mad that we…?"

"Oh, no. I'm livid. You broke the rules, and it was incredibly foolish. But I believe in the prods I choose. There's never been a job without some risk. We need our Blacklist tech file back. And this is a chance for you to make up for your mistake to your team." She doesn't flinch.

It's been a while now that I've wondered about her past, if she's faced more than she's told me. Even without the ability to count cards, I'd bet she's been in my shoes somehow.

"You know my father won't allow it," I say, bringing up the other issue.

"Your father used to be a very confident CEO who made risky decisions every day," she says, her lips tight. Suddenly she smiles at me, a whimsical look in her eye. "Besides, everyone agrees it's a boring job, right? Maybe he'll make an exception." She taps the side of her nose with a long slender finger. "I just may have a way to convince your father if you want to come along."

"I don't know."

"Think about it. Go meet with the team. I have to make some calls."

"Yes, ma'am."

I leave Ms. T's office, heading back to Com-Hall. The moment I enter, everyone's eyes focus on me. Their social intelligence training is hard at work, surely seeing my conflict. If I were in China, I wouldn't be hesitating right now.

Pens is taking notes with both hands and it dawns on me. All the students here are operating within their gift, except me.

Red taught me to follow my gut and trust my gift. My gut says I need to join them in Tunisia but without my numbers I'm likely to make the wrong call. Like in the car and helicopter, like with Coral Hacker. In China, I operated as a rogue individual. But PSS is a respected company. After today, I can't mess up anymore.

Pens and Harrison look at me for an answer.

"Sorry, guys," I say.

They're about to argue when my phone buzzes. I glance at the name. It's Bai. Finally.

"Excuse me." I bolt out of the room, hitting accept. "Bai?"

"*Jo, ni zai PSS ma?*" he asks in Chinese.

"Of course I'm at PSS. It's Monday. I need to tell you something."

"*Kuai yi dian,* step into that private room of yours," he says, sharply.

I rush into my sim box, which is soundproof. "I'm in," I say. "Have you heard from Kai?"

"That's why I'm calling," he says, his voice even more serious than usual. "Kai's gone dark."

"You mean offline?" I ask, hopeful.

"No." He clears his throat. "His biotag isn't registering."

A lump sticks in my throat. "What does that mean?"

"In our line of work," he says, a deep chill in his voice, "he's either gone rogue...or he's dead."

CHAPTER 9

Tell your boyfriend to back off.

Coral Hacker warned me. And I did nothing. Said nothing to Kai.

"No," I say pacing the small room so fast it feels like it's spinning. "Kai's alive."

"Jo, it's been three days since he checked in," Bai says, devoid of emotion like he's just spouting off the facts. He's upset, but he's tough and I can feel him preparing for the worst. "Today the tag went cold. Two hours ago."

Bai doesn't know I spoke with Kai. He called and told me about a lead. "Look," I say, "He was alive three hours ago."

"How do you know?" Bai snaps into the phone.

My face twists up with regret that's already stinging me in the gut. I really shouldn't admit this to his boss, but desperate times call for desperate confessions. "Don't be mad but Kai called me this afternoon."

"That boy...!" Bai curses in the background. "He knows our protocols. There's a reason we stay offline. That call could be the very reason he's dead!"

My jaw tightens. "No, he was fine. And he's not dead." My numbers knot up in my head, and I have to squeeze my eyes shut to make them go away so I can focus. "I admit there was some kind of trouble, but I'd know if he was dead. I'd feel it." It's strange to think, but I think the hacker would also tell me if he was. I think my gift would know too. "Just because his biotag isn't working doesn't mean he's dead. He could've disabled it. He could've gotten into an accident or there was a malfunction. Or…"

"Biotags are extremely hard to dismantle and unless you're beaten half to death they don't malfunction." His voice cracks. "Jo, he's my cousin. I don't want it to be true either. But you knew you had to prepare for this possibility. And it's better than him going rogue."

My eyes close, picturing his face. "He'd never go rogue."

"You don't think so? He's good at what he does, Jo. Better than most guys I've seen, but *jiche*, he's arrogant. This wasn't his mission. He doesn't know when to back off."

Tell him to back off. My throat tightens. The hacker also said I could *help them.* "What other info can you give me? Maybe PSS can help. You know we have access to all the right tech."

Silence. I can picture Bai weighing the pros and cons of gaining our Intel and getting roasted by Director Kane for telling me anything. "Jo, you know the rules. Our partnership in the past was different. You were different."

I want to scream at him, remind him who saved the entire economy from crashing. That I am still the same person who lived and breathed the Pratt and figured out how to take down King and Madame. But he's right. I don't have a mathematical advantage anymore. But I do have one thing he doesn't. A connection to Kai. He called *me.*

"I can still help. Just give me anything you can."

There's more silence, then Bai lets out a long sigh. "Kai was on a solo trip watching a pretty tame contact that was going to get him a meeting with an important person somewhere in the Middle East."

Somewhere. "You don't know where he is?"

Bai grunts. "That's classified."

They have no idea where he is. Whatever tech he had is now destroyed or worse, being used against him.

"What are you doing to get him back?" I say, focusing at the screens on the walls and willing my gift to resurface.

"Everything. Look, if he's alive, he knows what to do in this situation, and our guys are there on the ground as we speak." He draws in a deep breath. "Kai's a natural. He's well trained. Better than anyone I've taught in years. He'll make the right call."

That's what worries me the most. He'll do what's best for everyone, not necessarily for himself. "What can you tell me about this *pretty tame contact?*"

"Kai was tailing a crooked professor name Montego, that's all I know." Bai swears in Chinese. "I shouldn't be telling you this."

"It's not much, but I'll do everything I can," I say.

"It's not your fight, Jo. Just wait it out. Keep your eyes and ears open, let me know if you hear anything. But stay back. Don't get involved." Bai's voice is harsh, full of warning. He's on edge. He doesn't want anything to be wrong either. "Kai wasn't supposed to call you—I won't mention it to Director Kane this time because of your unique relationship with him, but Jo, if you want to help, stay safe and let us do our job."

"Kai is more than just my boyfriend, *Da-ge.* He saved my life. His family is the only reason I'm free. I can help. I know it."

"It's not safe. I've probably already told you too much," Bai says, a tone in his voice that says we're done. "I'll let you know when we have news."

Not safe. A buzz of adrenaline under my skin causes my hand to start tapping, an old habit I had when my gift was at work. Whatever is out there is calling my name. The hacker could have called anyone, but he called me.

I laugh, a bitter edge to it. "You don't even know where Kai is."

Agent Bai is silent. I can even picture the way he narrows his eyes when he gets smug. "And you do?" he snorts.

My gift sparks strings of longitudes and latitudes forming a map in my head and igniting a flood of adrenaline. Two seconds later it's gone but the feeling isn't.

"Not exactly," I say. "But I'm going to find out."

CHAPTER 10

The door to the Com-Hall swings open as I rush in and set my hands down on the table in front of the team. "I changed my mind about Tunisia. Count me in."

"All right," Pens says. Her keen eyes narrow on me as she crosses her arms. "Any particular reason why?"

All four of them are giving me weird looks. They know something's off with me. Over the last few months, these prods haven't just been colleagues to me, they've become friends. Even now, they're willing to go along with Tunisia even if they don't have all the facts. But before I can answer Pens, K2 informs me that I have an incoming message from my dad.

He's checking in already? I groan. Today is one long string of fire drills.

"I've gotta get home early today," I say, grabbing my stuff. "Tell Ms. T she'd better work her magic on my dad. I'll do everything I can to come but no matter what I do, you have to choose Tunisia. Trust me."

I head for the door, without even a glance behind me. Thanks to my missing gift, I trip into a table.

Harrison catches me by the jacket. Pens and Eddie come up, too.

"Seriously, what made you change your mind?" he asks. "Who was on the phone? Looked like more bad news."

"Sorry." I feel bad keeping quiet because PSS has a code of conduct—full disclosure. But technically, I've only signed on to do my simulations and operate as a provisional member of the team. Besides, I don't have liberty to talk about Kai. I straighten my jacket.

"You know we can hack that call, if you don't tell us," Felicia says, sneaking into the conversation.

My eyebrows tighten and I shoot her a dirty look.

"Fine, we won't hack it. PSS never uses our gifts against the team." She shrugs.

"Not to mention privacy laws and all, Felicia," Harrison adds, bumping her. "What she means is, we're on your side. We want to help." Pens and Eddie are nodding beside him.

"Me too." Felicia tightens her lips. "I should have helped you guys with the cyber trap. If I had, we might not be in this predicament..."

"We can't second guess that now...because you're right. It may be worse than we think. But Tunisia is the key."

Felicia studies me for a moment, kind of like Mara used to do when we were younger. "Are you sure this isn't a trap?"

I shake my head. "I'm not sure about anything. But losing the Blacklist is my fault," I say. I could leave it up to the team to get the list back. But I can't abandon Kai. I won't let anything happen to him. "To get the list back, I need my gift, and the only way I'm going to get both is to find Coral Hacker."

"What are you going to do?" Pens asks.

I shake my head, a crooked grin pulling at my mouth. "What any nerd would do—invite him to chat, prodigy style."

CHAPTER 11

RIVERS RESIDENCE
WEST SEATTLE, WASHINGTON

There are few things worse than a daughter overhearing the man who raised her weep in his room in the dead of night, whispering prayers into the dark, *Dear God, why wasn't it me instead of her?*

This is what runs through my mind as I watch him digest my proposal.

Before I was taken, I never understood the stories where the victims didn't want to tell their loved ones what happened to them. I do now. They were sparing them from nightmares and guilt. After we returned to Seattle, I told Dad only a fraction of what I'd gone through. I wish I hadn't. Those dark nights of his have only recently stopped.

But my dad still thinks his little daughter returned yesterday. He doesn't really know the fire-forged girl I've become, and honestly, I'm not sure he's ready to see me—the real me—just yet.

I keep the thoughts that remind me of King or Madame to myself because most of them wouldn't be appropriate to share at dinner. Nor would the things that were funny in the Pratt be funny here. And my family doesn't speak Chinese, either. So often, I stay quiet. They interpret my quietness as a wounded spirit still needing restoration. Which is why asking to leave now feels like asking my dad to throw me back into cell 88.

I shove a heap of mashed potatoes in my mouth as I calmly answer questions about the job in Tunisia.

"It's only seven days," I explain. "We'll be lodged in a secure government-protected building...and a swat team of bodyguards are assigned to us when we go out..." I trail off as Dad goes still and closes his eyes.

The dinner table is as silent as a mausoleum. Mara, Lily, and I are all watching Dad. He's not eating. His eyes are closed and he's massaging a crease down the center of his brow as he listens, methodically breathing in and out.

Mara silently pushes broccoli across her plate with the side of her fork. Lily slowly slices pieces of filet, watching Dad. I swallow and continue.

"It's the most boring job in the world. Installing new security software, boosting performance, basic maintenance..."

"But it's in *Tunisia*," he reminds me. "Far away. On another continent."

"I've always wanted to go to Tunisia," I add, as if that makes it any better.

Mara shoots me a look. Immediately I regret my comment—she's right. It's overkill.

Dad tears his eyes away from the mashed potatoes and looks straight at me. "You've mentioned Sicily, The Maldives, Chile. Not once have you talked about North Africa."

I shrug, laughing it off. "What I meant was since I lived in Asia, traveling anywhere is exciting to me."

"Jo, I'm your dad." He narrows his eyes on mine. "Tell the truth."

I sigh, considering his request. He deserves some honesty.

"Fine, I know our six months aren't up yet but I'm having cabin fever. I feel like my gift is getting worse because I'm feeling claustrophobic. Then I did something really stupid in my sims at PSS and lost a file that was important to them. So when this opportunity came up, I thought it might be a good way for me to pay back all the time and money they've invested in me. Ms. T won't lie. Every job has a level of danger. So does going out your front door. This isn't any different. But this time, I need to help."

He studies me, weary lines showing around his mouth. Everything I said is true so I can stare back and not feel too guilty. I can't tell him about Kai or the Hacker—that would make his heart stop. And technically, I can't mention either—they're classified.

"You know Ms. T's new protocols for travel mean we'll have a team of security guards," I add.

"Yeah, she called me about that already. Goliath Guard Services. *Goliath*?" He shudders. "Doesn't instill much confidence. I mean, come on. Everyone knows that story."

I smirk. "Apparently they're the best security service in North Africa," I say, wondering what else Ms. T told him. "The bodyguards will be with us 24/7. From the minute I leave this house until I return, I'll be fully protected and back before you know it."

He shifts his feet under the table. "I've heard that before. How did that work out?" Dad is not convinced.

"I understand you're worried," I say gently. And I do. A part of me truly wants to comfort him but then there is another part where I want to scream. *You're my dad! You used to own a Fortune 500 company! You're brave and strong—you risked everything to find me. And I'm just like you. I can't sit still when someone I care about might be hurting!*

I want him to wake up and face his fear. I want to show him the scar on my neck and tell him it's not going away, but we got through it.

But I can't. The look in his eyes is too fragile. I back off.

He sets his steak knife down. No one is eating.

"The capital is a mess right now," he says. "Tunisia has a heated election coming up. Not exactly a great time."

My eyebrows shoot up with surprise.

"What? You don't think I read the news?" he says, shrugging.

"If you did, you'd know Tunisia is a democracy, an open free country and has been for years. It's also tourist season."

"Hmm." He smashes potatoes with his fork. Surprisingly, he hasn't said no but my arguments haven't won him over yet.

"Dad," Mara says, breaking her own silence. "I know you hate to hear this, but you have to stop trying to control everything. It's been months. We've all felt like we're on lockdown. It's not healthy."

He sits up, his face remorseful, peering up at his daughters. "Have I really been that bad?" All of sudden he's listening to reason...from Mara?

"Dad, come on. You gave us seven p.m. curfews like we were ten years old. We all wear tracker earrings, and you call us every few hours. Jo and I are technically adults. Lily is 16 and can hardly have a life because you screen all the boys and then scare her into thinking they're all potential kidnappers."

Lily nods her head vigorously. "Dad, the last time Cullen came over you took his fingerprints. Now everyone at school thinks we're freaks."

"Good." He beams. "Only the ones with nothing to hide will come over."

"Dad," Mara says in a stern voice. "You taught us to be resilient. Sure, we lost mom, and Jo for a while, but look what she accomplished in our absence. You can't forget about who she became. She's a hero who saved the world. Don't you believe in her?"

Mara speaking about me like that fills me with courage because someone sees who I am. She's spoken the words I've wanted to communicate for weeks but didn't for fear of breaking Dad. He's never had a chance to know the girl I became in China. Phoenix. The fire I lived through didn't destroy me—it made me strong. At first, he was proud and applauded me. Then after we got home, fear took over. I was fourteen all over again. In his mind, he had failed to protect me, and he resolved never to let me be hurt again. He didn't see that his loving protection was keeping me caged.

Mara places a hand tenderly on Dad's shoulder. She's matured so much during my absence. "I realize we still need to rebuild and repair our family, and there's more to do. We'll have time, but control and fear won't lead us to a healthy place."

I put my hand on Dad's. "I'm not just a survivor, I'm a fighter. There's a difference. You have to trust who I am."

Dad inhales deeply and nods his head like he's listening for the first time in three months.

In moments like this, I miss Red and what he taught. I imagine what he'd say to my father. When life doesn't work out the way we think, and we end up in the dark, we have a choice—either stand up and keep going or cower in the darkness—but only one choice leads to the light. But Red's gone, and my father has to make his own choices.

"Girls," he finally says. "I'm sorry I treated you this way. I do believe in you. All of you." He stands and walks toward the hallway leading to the den. "Just give me some time to think it over, OK? I'll be out in a bit."

Mara, Lily, and I wait until he's gone before we say a word. As soon as his door clicks shut, I put my hands on the table and groan.

"Tell me the truth," I say, "Am I killing Dad by springing this on him?"

Lily folds her napkin on the table. "To be honest, I'm surprised you didn't do it earlier." Her phone rings. "It's Cullen. If things go well tonight, maybe he'll get to come over without surveillance." She excuses herself and leaves the room. Mara and I are left with our cold potatoes.

I take another bite because I've learned to eat even when I don't feel like it. It's a survival habit. Those movies where the victim doesn't eat don't make sense to me anymore. I tried that once in the Pratt, and Red told me, *Truth should dictate your actions, not emotion. One is a master, the other a servant.* Then he added, *And don't let food slip past you ever again. The last thing you need is a weak body.*

Besides, I'm still enjoying all these home cooked meals.

"He's going to let you go," Mara says breaking the silence. "I've watched Dad the last two years when you were gone. He's just working up the courage to do what he knows he should do. It won't be easy on him. Or us for that matter." She sets her napkin down. "Jo, I see the fire burning in your eyes. Teaching math at the university won't satisfy you. The person you've become is fierce, but still compassionate. Like mom. But you have to promise me, you'll come back in seven days no matter what happens. Or I may become just like Dad." Mara searches my eyes, seriousness creased in her brows.

Promises, no matter how many good intentions are packed into them, aren't always up to the person making them. I think of Kai. He promises me all the time he'll be ok. He promised PGF he'd stick to the mission, and well, he didn't do that either. A sad smile pulls up on my face. "I'll do everything I can to get back here safely."

"You're thinking about Kai now, aren't you? It's always the same look on your face when you talk about him," Mara says, surprising the heck out of me. She's more perceptive than I thought.

"Yeah." Mara squeezes my elbow. It feels good to have a

big sister again, always watching out for me.

"We've all noticed how unsettled you are every time Kai goes on a trip," she says. "You miss him, don't you?"

I nod. "A lot."

"Do you love him?" she asks.

"I..." I'm not sure what to say. Kai has told me he loved me since China. But I've never said it back to him. I've always hesitated. I don't know why. I've been trying to figure that out. He saved me, he knows me, he understands me. I admire and respect him, and can't think of a better guy, and yet the words won't come out of my mouth, like there's something blocking them. But now, I couldn't bear it if anything happened to him and he didn't know how I felt. Mara sees my discomfort and changes the subject.

"It's ok not to know." Mara smiles. "What will Kai think about you going to Tunisia?" Mara is too smart for her own good, or she's my sister for a reason, as Red would say. She's been watching me. She's noticed I've needed Kai and he hasn't been here. I turn my head to the side and look out the window, knowing that someone I trust needs to know about Kai.

"Mara?" I say, my voice low. "I have to tell you something. But you can't tell Dad or Lily until it's over."

Mara stares back at me, full of fire. Her eyes are not like Dad's. They believe in me in a way only a sister can. We've come a long way. Dad couldn't handle all the stories, so I never told him details. But Mara was different. She wanted to hear it. It wasn't much, but I told her about the abuse, the underwater torture, punching Chan in the nose. The fights I saw. The cold nights. She hated hearing my hard stories, clung to me, and held me with tears. I let her. It restored our relationship, but for her it was something different. It made her brave. It taught her she could overcome. It made her want to be stronger, better. My stories built her up. Mara has already proven she can handle whatever I tell her. She deserves to know what her sister is really doing. And the truth, in case something goes wrong.

"If you promise it doesn't involve smugglers, I won't talk."

"Kai has gone dark. He left his mission. No one knows where he is or if he's alive. But there's a lead in Tunisia. PSS is going to retrieve a file that has been stolen by a hacker." I shake my head. "But I'm going to find Kai. And to figure out how all of this is connected."

Mara gasps. "So this isn't some boring trip after all."

"I have to go," I say. "I believe he's alive and that I can help him."

"Jo..." She tightens her fist around her napkin, face as stern as Dad's.

"I know. But, Mara, if anything happens to Kai, I'll never forgive myself for not trying."

Mara snags my hands and squeezes. "I understand. When Dad wanted to move to Asia because he thought you were alive, we thought it was slightly extreme, but we agreed. And you were there. Then I met Chan for the first time and had no idea how you could go head-to-head with that guy. The world wouldn't be the same without you. Literally. And if Kai needs you, you should go."

"You won't say anything to Dad?" I ask.

"I swear." Mara draws me into a hug. "This is who you are, Jo. Don't run from it."

"Thanks." I hug her and K2 beeps. Harrison is waiting.

"Excuse me," I say. "I have a hacker to find."

CHAPTER 12

In my bedroom, I sit at my desk and connect my PSS earrings to K2. Instantly Harrison is in my ear. "I'm here. What do you need?"

"Send out a signal for me with an IRC," I say, opening my computer. "I just want to ask him a question."

"Are you sure?" Harrison asks. "I can't track him if he enters your sims."

"Don't do it through my sims. Do it through a public line."

"Fine," Harrison says. "I'll send out an invitation for the hour. If he doesn't reach out, I'm pulling the channel." I'm about to object when he adds. "Don't forget what he did to us earlier, Jo. I'm making sure he won't steal your identity and fry the remaining bones of PSS. If we want to do things right, we do it my way. I'm putting trackers on every signal I set up. I want to capture any trace of his IP or DNS I can. These kinds of hackers have a base somewhere. That's what we need to locate."

"Fine. You do your thing. I need to check on something else."

Harrison signs off and I hop on to '*the street*' or *Wall Street* where a month ago Kai and I set up a hidden portal behind our accounts within the website. Basically, it's a way to chat that no one else can access, where he and I can secretly and safely send messages to each other while he's on a job. We also created ciphers to communicate in case of emergency; if something's wrong, we invest in a certain stock from his father's company.

My fingers glide over keys and passwords but I find nothing in either of our accounts. I scroll the different pages looking for hidden messages behind each page. An anomaly catches my eye. There's been activity here that's not in our usual code. I go to invest in the 'emergency stock' when to my surprise, I've already made four miniscule investments today. Except I haven't.

Naturally, I look for a connection between them, and there is none. Even my messages have stock reports I didn't request. Someone is *hacking* my account. I can only guess who.

I go ahead and invest anyway, then use our portal to ask Kai how he is. Then I push my computer away and lie on my bed. All I can do is wait and make sure I don't grind my teeth into nubs.

Very slowly, my mind drifts to sim one, and that old journal. My father sold our old house, but he kept all my stuff. I wonder if that journal is packed away somewhere. I go to my closet and pull out a box labeled "Jo's Journals". Under a heap of notebooks full of equations and diaries full of grief, I find it. The bubbly, hopeful journal I kept on my desk as a 13-year-old. I open it up to the middle. The postcard of the famous Mandelbrot Fractal falls out and into my lap. The chaotic, infinite design on the front stares back at me. I wait for my gift to flicker like it did in the sim, but the card is lifeless. I wonder why this image sparked it earlier. Thumbing over the colors, still vibrant even though it's been in a box for four years, I decide to turn it over. I'm instantly hit with emotion.

Digits,

This is the Mandelbrot Set, also nicknamed the Thumb-print of God. This tiny fractal changed the world, you know. It showed us all that even in chaos, there is calculation. It's become somewhat of an anchor for me. No matter how rough, chaotic, infinitesimal or untamed life appears, this simple trace of order always leads me back to hope.

In a world of chaos, you're my fractal.

Yours,
Mandel (Son of a Mandelbrot)

A wave of goosebumps tingle over me, followed by nostalgia poured out like warm sun. His small note crushes me. We understood each other in a way no one else did. And that week he needed me. His parents, who were already cruel, were harder on him than usual. Far from my parents who allowed me to learn in my own way, they controlled his every move and never allowed mistakes. They required too much, used him for their own recognition, forced him into situations that made him uncomfortable. The pressure was too much, and no one understood him. But I did. He had a heart of gold. I remember when he reached out, how broken he was that week. "Sorry," he apologized. "You're the only safe person I can think of to talk to."

"I'll always be here for you," I told him. Too bad that wasn't true.

Sharp and numerical memories of him crawl under my skin as a smile climbs to my face. "My master classes are scary," my thirteen-year-old self confided in Mandel. "The older students are intimidating."

"No way, I'm sure it's the other way around," he'd comforted me. "Tell them that you completed a course in mechanical engineering in 4th grade. That'll work." His words made me laugh.

Once, we made a plan to act like we'd "lost" our gifts so we'd be free. We'd be nobodies who traveled the world. He'd voyage by sand and I'd go by water. We'd find each other in the middle, navigating by the stars like they did in the old days. New maps and books would be written under old grumpy names, like Edna and Orwell. No one would be the wiser.

The thought of him makes me sad. I wonder what he'd think of me actually losing my gift. Would he be happy for me? I'd have to be brutally honest and tell him it's not like what we'd imagined, but more like getting your right arm cut off.

Thankfully, the *me* today, can still be *me* without it. But if it had happened at thirteen, I would have run to him. I trusted him. Even crushed on him without ever seeing his face or knowing his real name. One night, Mara snuck in and found an open chat box, and blabbed to him about my crush. I was so embarrassed that I didn't chat with him for weeks. But he never stopped sending me notes. He was such a nerd. Always talking about fractals.

I wander over to my desk and pull up my old blog. A slight prick of guilt wakes me. What would Kai think about me reading old messages from a thirteen-year-old crush? He'd laugh. It is pretty ridiculous. But as I click on the chat board it feels different than in my sims. My emotions are heightened, on the edge of my skin. There are no flashbacks. Just my memories and me, and this silly postcard in my hand. I find my chat board and scroll down to his messages. This time I find the courage to open them.

<From sonofaMandelbrot: Digits, where are you? You haven't responded in days. I'm worried. Is everything ok?>

<From sonofaMandelbrot: Digits. Heard about your mom. I'm so so sorry. I want to help. I'm here if you need me. Please respond...>

<From sonofaMandelbrot: Jo. I miss you. Please let know if you're ok. I need you too...>

My chest tightens. I can't bear to read any more. I never explained. Never said goodbye. Never told him I was ok. Of course, I wasn't ok. Not after my mom's death. Not after Madame. Guilt curls inside me but I shrug it off. Why do I care about this right now? I don't need to carry this weight. It was years ago. I'm sure he's fine now. Probably doesn't even remember me. He's what, 18, 19 now? We were kids.

After my mom died, I grew up fast. I focused on school. Pursued my PhD. At college, I discovered real boys. I let go of Son of a Mandelbrot, the boy behind an avatar, who I'd never actually seen. My slight obsession with Samuel Davis—the beautiful econ student. Then Rafael, the Italian crime boss's son in the Pratt, and finally Kai. Looking back, Mandelbrot boy was hardly real. I never even knew his name.

I set the postcard down and check K2. It's been over an hour. I guess Coral Hacker doesn't play by Harrison's encrypted rules. Probably knows he's being set up.

Harrison confirms he's signing off, and I should too. But I don't. Back in the day, the kids on my blog would use an old cyber SOS to send messages to hackers. It's old school. But if this hacker is watching me, he'll pick up on it. It won't be laced with Harrison's traps, but it's worth a try.

I send out a simple encrypted beat. *Reach me*—it says under layers of code at three locations—my phone, a website for a restaurant I usually order from, and my university math department. This guy has tabs on me, and I need to know how he is doing it, where he is looking.

The minute I press send, an alert goes off and sends me flying into the back of my chair. That was fast.

A chat box from my old blog pops up. An anonymous messenger. My heart pumps straight into my throat, my words already laced with fire.

Before I click on the message, I begin an old school tracing method, but I'm caught like a little kid trying to sneak cookies. The message scrambles, too encrypted to trace. The signal bounces, as if he's using tor nodes all over the world, and even passing through satellites, and is gone before I know it. *Who is this dude?* I shake my head, eyes wide with wonder.

I don't know who I'm dealing with here, but it's high time I found out. My finger hovers over the button about to click when a knock on the door sends me spinning around to face whoever is entering.

Dad opens the door finding me breathless. "Mind if I come in?"

I bite my lip, staring at the screen. I gently close the computer. I guess my chat will have to wait.

"Of course, Dad."

CHAPTER 13

Dad adjusts his cardigan and wanders in, taking a seat on my bed.

The worried wrinkles by his eyes and mouth have eased now and when he straightens his back and lifts his chin, a glimpse of my old dad returns.

He picks up the postcard and gives it a once over, then looks at me.

"I know the chances of a second kidnapping are extremely low," he starts out. "But Tunisia is still very far away, and in a region with conflict. But I've talked with Ms. T and she assured me that you'll be hosted in the most secure government lodging in Tunis. No hotels, no public transport at all. Ms. T and I made an agreement and she promised you will be guarded at all times." He stops to swallow and breathe. I almost can't believe my ears. He's conceding. Thank God.

He draws in another large breath. "She's hired bodyguards to watch the team and then there will be a separate one to guard you personally at all times—there are no exceptions, Jo. He'll be with you night and day. Your only privacy will be in the bathroom." He gives me a sympathetic glance. I smile back like it's tough, thankful he doesn't know I hardly had that in the Pratt. His idea of privacy and mine are completely different now. But I pretend, for his sake.

He continues, "I'll expect morning and nightly check-ins by phone so I can hear your voice. If you agree to this, then you can go."

"Morning and night check-ins by phone? Dad, are you serious?" I bite my tongue. It's another one of those moments where I want to tell him I am not a normal teenager. To spell out everything I lived through, yet I can't. I never want him to know. It's better this way. And getting my family back was the greatest gift in my life.

"Help me through this, Jo." His face tells me he can still pull that card. And I let him. I mouth the exact words as they come off his lips. "You realize that I lost my daughter once, right?"

I let out a long sigh.

"Just this once, until I see you can return without injury or abduction."

Two daily calls and a 24/7 bodyguard. Who knows what the hacker has planned for me, but I doubt it can all be done in the bathroom. How will I ever be able to help Kai without my dad finding out?

Maybe I'm going about this all wrong. If my dad was Chan, I'd be bargaining with my best game face on. I look up at my dad. He's peering at me full of hope and worry, and all I see is the man who could barely walk into the Chinese conference room, run over to me and not let go of me for three days. My gut sinks into my shoes.

"Dad," I say as gentle and serious as I can, "I'll do phone check-ins but only once a day. The time difference is hard enough as it is. And I need to work when I'm there. I'll help you if you help me."

"All right," he agrees too quickly, as if he bargained high on purpose—and I lost. I forget he was once a brilliant CEO too. I inwardly groan that he got the best of me. "Now promise me you won't do anything risky, and you'll come back."

A buzz ripples under my skin. I sneak over and wrap my arms around him. "I promise to do everything as safely as I can. I work for a very stable company now. With rules and regulations, remember?"

He hugs me back, releasing a breathy half-laugh. "What would your Mom say right now?" He sniffles a bit. "I'm glad she never had to live through your disappearance and at the same time I don't think she'd want me to have such tight restrictions around you girls. She believed in each one of you. She'd help me let go and trust. Truth is, I know how capable you are and I'm really proud of you. Whatever it is you have to do, I'm sure you can do it."

"Thanks, Dad." I stay in his arms, resting on his chest. The same pine scent of his cologne stirs up childhood memories of safety and belonging. We talk for a few minutes and then finally he tells me he's off to bed.

After he leaves, I rub my tired eyes but still open my computer and click on the message. There's a number written out with the country code for Iceland. Frenzied equations pop inside me like little fireworks. But I pick up my phone and push each number.

Not even a full ring before the line opens. "You reached out?" Coral Hacker's robotic voice just like in the sims, steady and even. My whole body quivers.

"So, you are watching," I say. "Who are you?"

"We have more important things to discuss."

"Like how you stole the Blacklist?"

A scoff. "That wasn't me. That was a double hack."

"You expect me to believe that?" I'm angry and I want answers. "Where is it?"

"I warned you about PSS, like I did about your idiot boyfriend. You didn't listen." The robotic voice glitches.

My heart stings when he mentions Kai. "Is he alive?"

"For now. But the odds don't look good."

"How do you know about Kai? What else do you know about PSS?" I demand, the rough part of Phoenix resurfacing. I wish I had my numbers to back up my game.

"Listen, Josephine Rivers, I wouldn't have called you at all if I thought there was another way. Unfortunately, you're a little indispensable at the moment. You may not like it, but you need my help too. And despite what you just told your dad, you're walking into a lion's den. Are you sure you want to do that?"

My heart races as my gift starts firing in random directions. Amidst the chaos of jumbled numbers, I try to calculate what I've missed, even during this phone call and how he's listening in on my conversations. My dad was right. This *is* dangerous.

"For Kai, absolutely," I snap at him. Not to mention for PSS. We're in this predicament because of me.

"That's noble of you but your boyfriend's not worth it."

"What are you talking about?"

The robotic voice lowers an octave. "Do you even know why your boyfriend likes you?" He doesn't ask like it's a question.

"I can think of a few reasons," I say. "Sounds like you have another one. So what is it?"

"He's only attracted to one thing."

"Ugh. He's not that type of guy. You couldn't be more wrong."

"I don't mean *that*. He's attracted to danger. And you're dangerous."

I laugh out loud. "I'm a math nerd with a PhD in economics. And if you're referring to China that was not my choice. I played the cards I was dealt."

"No. You took risks you didn't have to. Ran forward instead of away. That's why he likes you. That's why he calls you *Trouble*. And that's also why he left after a month of you turning into a boring math nerd sitting in Seattle."

The hacker's words mess with my mind because I've asked myself why Kai left. But Kai has called me Trouble since I met him. And he does love trouble. But that's not his reason for liking me. I'm letting this stranger—*this hacker*—get under my skin. He's doing this on purpose. Driving a wedge between Kai and me. One I won't allow.

"You don't know me or him and that's none of your business. Right now, all I want is the Blacklist file returned to PSS and information on how to help Kai. You either help me or not."

He clears his throat. "Fine. Don't use your PSS buddy's trap again. Find me with your cyber SOS or on K2. Pack your sim glasses. I'll be in touch when you arrive in Tunis."

"Why should I trust you?" I ask.

"You shouldn't. But if you do, I'll help you get your gift back while you're here."

My breath catches and my heart pounds in my chest. He's lured me with my gift before...he knows it's irresistible bait. "Tell me who you are."

"It's all written in the stars, Jo."

The audio goes dead—then it dawns on me. He messaged me through my old blog—the one place I didn't put a signal.

CHAPTER 14

SEA-TAC INTERNATIONAL AIRPORT
SEATTLE, WASHINGTON

It's almost midnight and I'm not done packing when Ms. T sends a message on K2. It's a screen shot of plane reservations at 02:00 a.m. leaving from the private airport. A voice message from K2 follows, "Goliath Guard Services is outside waiting for you."

I hold my watch to get a visual of a vehicle and a tall man standing outside it. I message back. "Be right out."

My heart skips a beat when I think about leaving home. I've never forgotten the reason I'm alive—to live with purpose wherever I am, whatever I'm doing—but it doesn't mean fear doesn't show up and try to bully me. Thankfully, Red trained me to bully that liar back into its hole. Victory is often just across the threshold of fear, he used to say. And that is what I need to focus on right now. But Tunisia is more than just getting the list or stopping the hacker. It's about Kai and my gift—the two things I need to move forward.

I throw a bunch of clothes, mostly long pants and loose shirts, into a bag. It's a conservative country, and I need to dress accordingly. The Mandelbrot postcard is beside my bed.

I pick it up and stuff it inside my bag as a reminder that my gift is still hanging on.

The house is quiet, and I already said goodbye to my sisters, but I promised to wake Dad before I leave. I tiptoe in and gently rock his shoulder. "Dad, they're here."

He squints at me groggily. "I'll walk you out," he croaks. He climbs out of bed yawning, throws on a sweatshirt and helps carry my bags outside where we find a giant dark-haired man who is at least 6'5, standing next to a black van. Goliath services indeed.

He tips his head to my dad. "Mr. Rivers."

My dad and I both pause. An internal warning buzzes as memories of me walking to Madame's boat come unbidden to my mind. But this time Ms. Taylor pops out of the passenger side of the van and I can breathe again.

"Jason," she greets my dad kindly. "Jo is in good hands, I promise."

"Thanks, Marigold." My dad shakes her hand three times to make sure it is her. When did they get on a first name basis? It's weird. Then he turns to my bodyguard. With a nervous smile, he shakes his hand, scrutinizing him. "Do you have children?"

"No, sir. None of my own."

"Hmm. Well, I'm putting my daughter's life into your hands. I trust you can handle that?"

"Yes, sir."

As they stow my luggage in the van, Dad's hands curl into nervous fists and he holds his breath. My heart melts. *Oh, Dad... what am I doing to you?* I promised him I'd start a new life.

He draws me into a tight hug. "Don't ever take your tracker-earrings out." He whispers as he bends down. "If you miss a call, I'll know something is wrong."

"I won't miss a call, Dad. Everything will be fine." I point to my watch. "I've already programmed K2 to remind me. Thanks for letting me go. Love you."

My dad is visibly shaking, but he straightens his face. "I love you too, Jo." He lets go of me. "All right then, don't get into trouble."

I flinch at his choice of words and give him a weak thumbs-up, then hop into the van.

The car whirs to life and Ms. T picks up her phone to alert the pilot we're on our way. Goliath leans over to speak with me.

"No harm will come to you under my watch," he promises. "You will never leave my sight. Your goals will be my goals, and my life will be at your disposal."

Wow. Hardcore. "Thanks," I say. "So, what's your name?"

"Goliath is fine," he says with a straight face.

"Is that a company policy?" I ask. "Or personal choice?"

"Sorry, Miss Rivers. I don't answer personal questions."

"O-kay." I nod, not sure what to make of my new bodyguard. My numbers could have figured out this guy in ten seconds. Without them, I want to judge his coldness and his refusal to open up but then I smirk. *You used to be fun like this, remember?* Phoenix—the girl fresh out of the Pratt—said a similar thing to Chan not so long ago after she punched him. My past has come back to bite me in the rear.

CHAPTER 15

INTERNATIONAL AIRSPACE
ATLANTIC OCEAN, NORTH AFRICA

Dawn spreads out like a lavender field across a sky spotted with pink clouds. Even though it's gorgeous, my adrenaline has worn off and I can't stop yawning. The private jet will land in Tunis in a few hours. Everyone else is asleep except for our three bodyguards, Pens and me. The bags under my eyes feel deep enough to fit my old calculus textbooks inside.

As I stare into the sky, thoughts of Kai and the Coral Hacker dominate my thoughts. I try to focus on the coastline, but there are too many clouds and I keep drifting to Kai's face after his last mission. The bruises and black eyes. I can't imagine how much worse he might look now, given that his biotag is dead. What did they do to him to make that happen? I don't even want to think about it. I hope he's ok.

Pens planned on sleeping during the flight and took some Dramamine, but it had an opposite effect on her. She's talked my ear off for hours now.

Flipping another page in the Tunisia Tourist magazine Pens hums, "After we catch the creepy old hacker, and get the Blacklist—which we will—I'm hitting the streets of North Africa, baby. I want to inhale spices of all colors, eavesdrop on Arabic conversation, shop in the *souks*—that means 'markets'—and eat all the things…Ooh, yum…Couscous. Lamb kebab. Have you ever eaten Chicken Tagine?"

"Um, nope." I frown at her. "Pens. We've got a job to do. Most of our time is going to be spent locked in government buildings. And there's no telling what will happen if we can't get the Blacklist file." But I've never actually been on a PSS field job before. "Am I wrong?"

"Jo, we always do our job. But we're not undercover agents or slaves. We're hired professionals, working quietly. When we go abroad, we always leave room for sight-seeing. Chances are, nothing will happen with *them* around." She rocks her head to the left.

My bodyguard seated on the other side of me, ever vigilant, moves ever so slightly at Pens' comment. He's listened to everything we've said during the flight. I couldn't even use the jet bathroom without him standing outside the door the whole time. His subtle glances at me every few minutes are getting really annoying.

He's facing straight ahead but his ear is clearly attuned to every word I utter. I turn, obvious now, openly examining him. His dark brown hair and well-aged tan skin put him around 35-40 years old. He's inconspicuously dressed. He's very tall but he'll totally blend in where we're headed—that's the point. If I glanced at him on the street, I wouldn't have pinned him as a bodyguard. But when you take a closer look, you can tell he is, in his own way, calculating everything. Even without numbers, I know he's ready to strike at any moment. It makes me shiver.

I remind myself the only fights we engage in at PSS are on a keyboard.

I lean over to him now, definitely in his bubble, and whisper in a deadpan voice. "How many ways do you know how to kill a man?" I want to see how much he'll take from me. So far, he won't have any of it.

"That's classified," he says, not even the slightest break in his expression.

Hmm. "Any tattoos?" I lean in, scrutinizing his arms.

"No."

"Are you going to put a tracker in me as soon as I doze off?" I squint at him.

"No."

"Do you have a weakness?" I ask, eyeing his bicep.

"No."

"Are you ever going to sleep?" My lips scrunch up to one side, an eyebrow cocked.

"Not while you're awake." The straight lines of his lips don't budge.

I roll my eyes. "Fun, great for you. Wake me up when we get there."

Doing anything with this giant ball of sunshine next to me is not going to be easy.

I lean on the cold plane window wondering if I should try to sleep. The clouds part, and few morning stars still twinkle. The hacker's words swirl in my mind. *It's all written in the stars, Jo.* Maybe it's a cypher or an equation he thinks I should know. PSS will figure it out—if I tell them.

I look over at the rest of the team. Everyone is asleep now. Even Pens finally dozed off. I grab my backpack and pull out the Mandelbrot Fractal postcard once again.

I remember the day I asked Mandel about his alias. "Why '*Son of a Mandelbrot*'?" I'd said, hoping he'd turn on his video.

"At first, it was because Benoit Mandelbrot studied Roughness and Chaos Theory and how he found order in them. My life felt rough and chaotic at the time, so that resonated... you know about my parents..." He breathed in. "Mandelbrot was also educated by his uncle. His uncle hated traditional education and made him play chess and study maps and explore things outside to learn. I'm convinced that's why he was a genius. He saw math in ferns and Romanesque broccoli and coastlines and galaxies, and he taught us that fractals are just another way to see infinity..." He'd stopped. "Am I talking too much?"

"No," I'd said, completely enamored. "Keep going..."

He'd let out a shy laugh. "Ok...well, that's how he discovered the Mandelbrot Set. Infinitely complex designs in the messy things of our world. Mandelbrot called them *fractals*—broken pieces—he made me feel like even if I was broken, I still had purpose, was still a part of the whole. His life work is my greatest inspiration. It's what keeps me going...well, I mean, besides you..."

The airplane skips under a bit of turbulence and the memory fades. He and the kids from my old blog were so brilliant they all could've joined PSS. I sigh at the sense of loss. Even if I was never kidnapped, people move on, grow apart. It happens even in normal life.

I'm glad to have found my place at PSS. Right now, they're risking themselves for the Blacklist because of a hunch. They're confident they can get it back. They don't understand the risk involved. But I do. And I'm leading them into it anyway. And for what?

Focus, Jo...On the coral...I can help you get your gift back.

The low robotic voice, once a whisper, now crashes in my head. His offer churns in me like a hungry sea hunting for boats. Apparently, I do have some lurking death wish inside of me. Because despite all the warnings, I want to meet this hacker face to face.

CHAPTER 16

TUNIS-CARTHAGE INTERNATIONAL AIRPORT
TUNISIA

Tunis glows in the late morning sun as we touch down. Thankfully, I drifted off for a couple hours of sleep and now I'm surprisingly awake.

A private van pulls up and a driver in a red hat hops out to greet us. "Welcome to Tunis, our beautiful capital," he says in a thick accent. He collects our bags, and we are off, pushing our way through thick traffic in a 15-passenger van.

Each of us is wide-eyed, gawking out the window as the driver points out different sights. "That is Boukornine, the mountains of two horns," he says, pointing to the green hills in the southeast. "There is the Lac de Tunis. And Carthage is that way, very old. You must go."

Exiting the highway on to a lengthy palm lined street, the driver tells us we're on Avenue Mohammed, named after the Sultan of Morocco, who helped Tunisia gain independence from colonial powers. Then he points out the 'Mongela' an intricate clock tower, announcing our arrival to the center of the new city and a street called Avenue Habib Bourguiba.

Wide sidewalks line the boulevard, and seemingly end-less rows of outdoor cafés are full of people. French style fountains, statues, and shutters on the windows fuse with minarets and huge elaborately decorated doors popping out like perfect photographs.

My head twists, trying to take in everything—palm lined streets with vendors selling bunches of jasmine and brightly colored wool rugs. Women with veils carrying baguettes under their arms. Cascades of magenta flowers hang over walls.

French and Arabic are written on doors, signs, and bill-boards. The Arabic script snags me like a moth to a flame. Even though I can't read it, my mind hiccups and hums like it's music. I wish my mind would give everything numerical definition. But it doesn't.

As we reach an older part of town, covered walkways made of cobblestone catch my eye and make me curious about what's around each corner. The van windows are open, inviting new smells of freshly baked bread and spices I don't recognize, mixing with salty air from a different ocean. My mind's a hive of activity.

My gift used to keep track and log every detail. But not now. Without it, I need time to register it all. How does a normal person remember everything? But I know the answer. Red would tell me to *man zou,* or 'walk slowly' as they say in Chinese and take your time. Even then, you'd miss some things, but the joy would be discovering it on your next walk.

Sadly, there's no time to *man zou* on this trip. We're here for only five days—and it's not to see the sights.

"We're nearing Medina now," the driver says, after passing an old city gate he called *Bab Saadoun.* "This is the Kasbah. You'll have to walk the rest of the way." We pull over on a narrow street bursting with bougainvillea against a dusty white villa. "You will be staying in *Dar Alzaytun,* the House of Olives, behind Saint Croix, a French church built in 1837.

It now houses the government offices of the city of Tunis." He motions to an old building with a bell tower on it.

There are motorbikes parked along the roads, and the cement is cracked but clean. The area looks old but well-kept, with an occasional spot of graffiti.

As we exit the car, a number of helpers arrive to carry in our numerous bags, ignorant of the expensive technology within.

We enter the *Dar Arabi,* a traditional Arab styled house, under a domed archway and come into an open-air central courtyard with small tables. Around the courtyard, there are rooms tiled with beautiful patterns and beds with wooden headboards carved with meticulous tiny designs. Each rug is woven with intricate, bright patterns featuring fish and camels. My mind is stimulated for the first time in weeks.

Ms. T reminds us, "Our official cover is that we are students on a visiting scholar exchange. We'll do official tours and pretend to be tourists in old town Medina."

"Not the most terrible job." Harrison fist bumps Eddie.

"After we solve the problem." Ms. T says. Her hair is pulled back now, and even though we had a long flight she's in an old-style dress suit and looks younger and more herself.

In the courtyard, Ms. T barks orders. "Everyone has one hour to freshen up. Then we have an official meeting with the head of security for Tunisia's Ministry of Education." Ms. T looks sympathetically at me. "Jo, Mr. Abdelqadar will be in the adjacent room to yours. You will leave and enter through his room always. Your door will have permanent security out front."

I look up at him. "So, Goliath does have another name."

"You can call me Qadar," he says, then extends a hand down the hallway in the direction of my room. "Ms. Rivers."

I walk forward, rolling my eyes. We enter through his door. Before I can go into my room through the door on the far wall, he bars my way and instructs me to wait for him to inspect it.

Once he deems it safe, I head inside.

"I'll be out in an hour," I say, and close the door.

If I hadn't spent a year in underground tunnels with all kinds of strange men sleeping just a jump away, this might be awkward, but as life goes, it feels oddly normal having someone hovering nearby watching my every move. I remind myself that I've gotten very good at escaping and planning around annoying obstacles.

My room is spacious, with a nice sized bed covered in a white spread with a streak of blue. On top, there's a small Arabic phrase book I assume they give to all their guests. I pick it up. Inside there is a note. *Reverse. Learn to read the world differently.* Since Arabic is read from right to left, it's a clever invitation.

The rest of the room is simple. There's a door on the far wall leading to a private bathroom, a wide countertop holding an espresso maker and a mini fridge, and a large window. I try to open the window and grit my teeth. Tighter than a rock. It's permanently sealed. There's no getting in or out of this room without Goliath.

I shower quickly, make myself a coffee, and unpack. K2 is programmed for Tunisia with maps, popular restaurants, shops, and more. "K2, tell me about the neighborhood."

His soothing voice obediently starts spouting off facts. "The Medina is the old town of Tunis and has been a UNESCO world heritage site since 1979, containing over 700 monuments, palaces, mosques, mausoleums and—" K2 cuts out just as my gift starts flickering. K2 sputters. "System overridden. Standby."

I grab my bag and rush into the bathroom, closing the door behind me. I dig out my sim glasses and put them on.

The screen over my eyes fills with numbers and coordinates in Tunisia, appearing and disappearing, then scrambling before everything goes black.

Coral Hacker. He's checking in. Letting me know he's aware that I'm here. My stomach flips. I'm both troubled and relieved that he's keeping in touch. If nothing else, he's reliable. *No.* I toss that thought away. *He's dangerous.* He knows too much, and the way he's invaded my sims and connected to my gift, alarms me. Harrison thinks he's a creepy old man, but maybe he's like Red. Whoever he is, I can't identify his effect on me. It's nothing I can explain, just a feeling under my skin.

After the coordinates disappear, a pre-recorded robotic voice starts playing.

"Welcome to Tunis. Step one—shut down the Ministry of Education for three days. Step two—help your *boyfriend* and get the Blacklist. There isn't much time, so make plans to meet me tonight. Alone. I'll send a location later.

"Step three—do your sims. PSS is right—they're important. Your subconscious is recalling details no one else will know. You need them.

"Finally—time to reverse. One new direction can alter your brain in great ways."

So the phrase book is not standard-issue for all guests. Which means Coral Hacker was somehow in my room. I shiver as the connection ends and the smartglasses turn off, but the robotic voice echoes in my mind.

Your boyfriend. I didn't miss his patronizing tone. It's obvious he has something against Kai, and I can't rule out the possibility that he's using Kai as bait. I just hope he doesn't want to hurt him. I fight away the image of Kai with black eyes and stitches on his lip.

Shut down the Ministry of Education. He brought us here for a reason. Shutting anything down in a foreign country won't be easy. He either doesn't know what he is asking or worse, he does know, and we have to carefully assess each move.

Meet me tonight. Alone. My stomach fizzes and sloshes like I just drank a can of soda. It's nerves. Or jet lag. Or just a terrible idea. But I've been here before. The crossroads where risk is the only way forward, and the reward of what you seek drives you on. Before you know it, one small risk becomes another. Less than twenty-four hours ago, I was in Seattle, now I'm in Tunis, sitting on a bathroom floor.

Sneaking out won't be easy. Not with Ms. T or Goliath nearby. I swore to my dad, my sisters and myself that I wouldn't put myself in harm's way. But to help Kai and PSS, I'll do all of these things and more.

K2 blinks a warning. A sensor I've never used before called, *Reminder*. "Ms. T said you had one hour until the meeting. Time's up. Don't be late and remember, punctuality is appreciated."

"Thanks, K2," I say looking at my watch. K2 starts spouting off facts about Tunisia right where he left off. An idea knits in my head and before I walk out the door, I have a plan.

But that doesn't mean it's a good one.

CHAPTER 17

THE KASBAH, TUNIS
DEPARTMENT OF INTERNAL SECURITY

At a round table, supplied with unmarked, fancy water bottles, pens and paper, Mr. Ayadi, a state representative welcomes us. "Thank you all for coming to Tunisia. As you know, very important elections are happening this Friday. As we get closer to election day, we've experienced occasional shutdowns and malfunctions of our computer systems, and simultaneously, false information being spread throughout the media and on-line platforms. We think it's some kind of virus. Over the past six weeks, we've talked to scores of private internet security companies. We've tried everything to discover what or who is behind this—without result. Which is why we contacted you."

I sit with the team, gauging the adults as they brief us on details. There are people from the police department, government security, tech analysts, and even some leaders from Parliament. As they continue to describe the situation, I glance around. It's a high-security official meeting room but the amount of tech is very limited compared to the PSS team, who are decked out. Every earring or pen or watch contains some kind of sniffing or spoofing device or tracing system gathering intel on everything in this room. Except they all look like good students, taking notes and smiling, nodding politely, not security analysts.

But I can see their minds at work. Pens, with one hand, takes notes on everyone in the room—their names, their mannerisms—and with the other hand, types notes into her smart watch. Ms. T is a master of social intelligence. By the end of this meeting, she will know who the real boss is here. So, this is what it's like to be on an official PSS mission team.

Mrs. Youssef, a woman in the security department, with long dark hair and a nice dress suit speaks up, "Our security analyst, Mr. Abdellatif," she says, pointing to a young man in glasses across the room, "discovered the Ministry of Education has had an uptick in data usage. He believes that's where the virus is located, but he can't find any proof."

I scan the data they've provided for us, willing my gift to appear. My numbers come into focus for seven seconds before fizzling out.

"Eddie. Pens," I whisper. "Hop on one of the computers they've made available and check any activity embedded in the Ministry of Education's website."

Ms. T sees me concentrating and comes over to me, whispering. "What is it?"

"Coral Hacker thinks we have to shut down the Ministry of Education's main server to stop the problem."

She rubs her forehead. "Shut down an entire ministry. Right before an election?" she says with a look of distrust.

"I agree we have to be careful, but I don't think he's trying to sabotage anything," I say. "I think he's showing us how the Blacklist and the election are connected." But how does Kai fit into this? Bai said he was eliciting information from a professor.

"Jo, we can't just trust this guy," she says. "He stole our Blacklist-tech. If he knows about the Ministry of Education, he's hacked into the government mainframe. He's a criminal."

It was a double hack. The doubt in my mind is heavy and clouded. I should believe Ms. T. Coral Hacker is a criminal and I've vowed to catch him. But before we do, we need him. Need him to believe we are working together. He has what we need, *what I need.* He's the key to Kai and my gift...

"Just consider it," I ask, a shiver shooting down my arms. "To get the list back, we just might have to do things we don't usually do."

Pens, who is still writing everything our hosts say with one hand, motions for us to come over. "I found something."

"Already?" Mr. Ayadi says. He glances at his staff and then Ms. T. "*Wah,* these kids are fast." He nods to Pens to speak.

"Major tampering, sir. There are signs of a very sneaky virus. It's an advanced program with ransomware aiming to take control of your system. It has AI bots that can carry encrypted messages, corrupt and steal files. Basically, someone is using the Ministry of Education's server as a base for a major cyber-attack against the government's infrastructure. It's malicious at its core. And they're *veiling* everything they do so no one can identify them."

"How is that possible? What are they planning?" Chief Administrator Trabelsi asks. But as soon as Pens says *veiling,* the team pales. Veil is PSS tech. This may be worse than we thought. "Can you find them?"

"We're working on it, sir," Pens says, her eyes glued on the screen, concealing her horror of even hinting at PSS involvement. If word of Blacklist technology being used in Tunisia gets out, PSS will be fried by US Gov-Ops. "The program they're using is heavily encrypted. It's like tracking someone in the dark. We need some time. Team, can we please assemble?"

Ms. T cocks her head at me. Coral Hacker was right. Blacklist tech is at work. My heart skips a beat. Maybe he can be trusted—unless he's the one behind these attacks.

The team gathers around a separate table in the back of the room. Pens leans in, her voice low. "This is bad. PSS tech is all over this. They're messing with the infrastructure of the government. They're planning to seize control of the whole system. And whoever is doing this won't be happy we're interrupting."

I frown. "And they're using Veil?"

Veil is a cover-up software that takes code and obfuscates it so no antivirus can identify it. Veil can do three things—allow hidden operations, send AI bots to accomplish whatever goal is specified, even producing fake news articles and videos according to one headline. Basically, it can change an entire internal data system.

Felicia pulls up more information. "Using what we know of Veil, I traced one of the AI commands back to a third party in the elections. They are a very extreme group of radicals. The party leader's name is Amir Ben Slimane."

Pens huffs loudly. "This is how they plan to win the election."

Harrison hands me another file. "If we don't stop these attacks, this radical party will use our tech to rig the election in their favor, and they'll gain total control of the country and its government by the end of the week."

I look up at Ms. T. "Which is why PSS needed to take this job. There's no telling what other tech they have. Our team is the only one who can trace Veil's code and stop it."

"Then we get to work right now, tracing our code and locking it up in Cyber Island," Ms. T says.

Felicia looks at us. "We've got another problem. I've traced it as far as it can go. But whoever stole it, created a back-up on a holothumb. Which means, until we have that specific device and the thief's biometrics, our hands are tied."

Ms. T sucks in a deep breath. "This is serious. Our tech cannot keep circulating. We can't trace the Blacklist unless we find that holothumb. Until then, we need to shut down these attacks and clear the Ministry of Education of Veil bugs. Harrison. Eddie. You know what to do." They get to work immediately.

I'm left with Ms. T. We're staring at each other. I could be wrong, but I think we have the same idea. The hacker.

"I think I can get him to tell me what he knows," I say. "Maybe he knows where to find the holothumb."

Ms. T leans over, her voice low. "Are you afraid of him?"

At first, I don't know how to answer. Yes, he scares me, but not in the way she's thinking. I can't prove it, but I don't think he'll hurt me. It's more like falling down a rabbit hole, not knowing what I'll find.

"No," I say, finally.

Ms. T nods. "Good." She stands and approaches Mrs. Youssef and Mr. Ayadi. "In order to do our job, we need to shut down the Ministry of Education for three days. Websites. Domains. Servers. Everything."

Gasps and appalled objections mix with paper shuffling in the room. The head of security shoots the State representative a worried glance.

"Don't worry," Ms. T explains, "our team will find an alternative solution for the work of the Ministry to go on without interruption."

They look shocked and skeptical. A rush of whispers in Arabic flutters across the room.

"Let me make this clear," Ms. T says in her stern voice. "Your country is in danger. Either we shut down your system or these radicals will."

They reluctantly agree, discussing strategies to engineer work-arounds for the Ministry employees. Pens and Felicia answer a few questions before joining Eddie and Harrison. The team gathers in a small circle.

Ms. T leans over to me. "Leave the Ministry of Education and the leaks to us. You go back to your room and connect with the hacker. Find out everything he knows. For some reason he only wants to talk to you. Do anything you need to help us get the Blacklist tech out of the hands of these radicals."

My eyebrows shoot up. Huh. I just got direct verbal permission to meet Coral Hacker tonight. Looks like I was worried for nothing. I'm stalking toward the door, making plans in my head until she stops me.

"Just remember," she adds, "No one leaves this building."

CHAPTER 18

The sun is an hour from setting with no reply to my cyber SOS or a location from the hacker. Apparently, Coral Hacker does not play well with others. Goliath is in the room next to me, always guarding the door. And I've checked *the street* for messages from Kai six times but it's still blank. The very least I can do is work on getting my gift back.

Coral Hacker basically instructed me to do my sims, agreeing with Ms. T that it was important. He said I'd pick up on clues others won't. Right now, we need that. But I'm hesitating. During my last sims, I almost crashed in a helicopter. Kai was bloody in the square. And the Mandelbrot Set postcard breached my defenses in a way I haven't felt in a long time. The sims feel foreboding, yet, with my gift back I can help Kai.

My sim glasses are on the bed. For simulations to be done outside the sim box, PSS invented the most advanced smartglasses on earth in terms of virtual, mixed and augmented reality. They secure around your eyes and ears, and stimulate nerves in the temporal lobe, inducing a dreamlike state to make the experience more real. I reach over, pull on the glasses and lie down on the bed, taking a deep breath. "K2, please load sims 1-3. Decrease the session by half please. Minimum process time."

I close my eyes as the screen goes black.

There's no scent of lavender to greet me this time, but a pine and cedar candle burning in the window. I'm thirteen and my face is snuggled into my pillow. I'm just waking up. My phone is alerting me of unread messages. I grab it and notice the date: December 25th.

I sit up in my bed. Outside my window is our old backyard. The green grass is frosted over, and the sky gray. My body and mind shiver, confused. Obviously, I know I'm in Tunisia where it's not cold, but everything is so real that I'm sinking in. Even my bare arms feel like they need a sweater. Since my bed felt warm, I sneak back under the covers, and silence my buzzing phone. There are Christmas messages from my friends. My face is beaming, no worry about anything. I can even smell pancakes and coffee wafting up from downstairs. I'll check my messages then run down to see everyone. An excitement to open presents bubbles inside me.

Scrolling through my messages, I notice that one is from Son of a Mandelbrot. My heart skips a beat. I always read his messages first. But right now, I feel funny about it. A glimmer of reality slides in. Kai is missing and here I am reading old messages between two kids. But it's a distant past. Besides, this simulation is designed to help me. I click on it.

Inside his message is a link to a hidden page on his website called "gift for jo". I click on the link and a snowflake pops up. Lots of them. Each one is unique and beautiful, and completely covered in mathematical equations. I shake my head. $fc(z) = z2 + c$ the equation for the Mandelbrot Set, is embedded into his design. As I keep watching, each snowflake-fractal begins to grow larger, and a new one reforms from the center, a typical fractal display. Eventually, the image changes to a picture of me covered in snowflakes. Me—or the thirteen-year-old girl—laughs out loud. I thought it was the coolest gift.

Below the snowflakes, I re-read our back-and-forth messages, a tingle of warmth coming over me.

<From Yougetmydigits: *Merry Christmas, Mandel. You there? I got your gift! Did you make this from your research? Thank you*>

<From sonofaMandelbrot: *Digits, Yes, I did. Can't believe you remember that project. Like it? I know you wanted snow this year for Christmas, but it doesn't look like it will happen in Seattle until February. I wanted to gift you a billion snowflakes but as it is, I can't control the weather yet—don't worry, I'm working on it. One day you will eat fractals falling from the sky! In the meantime, this display will have to do.*"

<*Haha. Can't wait. Anyway, I love it. It's beautiful.*>

<*Right? Snowflakes are one of the most beautiful fractals the world has to offer, (apart from our galaxy, of course.)*>

<*You and fractals, lol. You and Benoit Mandelbrot are always so deep. Didn't that guy ever look for patterns in anything less meaningful? Lol.*>

<*Actually, yes. The financial world. Stock markets. He discovered a bunch of patterns and even found a way to crack the code so to speak to make predictions of what was to come. Meaningless to me, I guess, because I don't care about money, but others went crazy over it.*>

<*Huh. That's interesting. I'll have to check that out. My dad loves the stock market. He invests to make money for his company. Who knows, maybe I'll crack a new code and help my dad?*>

<*No doubt you'd be amazing. If Mandelbrot taught us anything, it's that secret messages are hidden everywhere in our world just waiting to be found by those who look closer.*>

<Eesh. Prob have to go soon. My parents are summoning me for breakfast.>

<Must be nice...I'm avoiding my parents...>

<Even on Christmas???>

<Especially on Christmas. But don't worry about me. My mom's brother will come over and he's cool. Talk later?>

<Yeah. Merry Christmas, Mandel.>

<Merry Christmas, Josephine.>

My head spins with memories I'd forgotten. That was when I actually started watching the financial world. I guess Mandel was to blame. Before my time in the sim is done, I pull up the snowflake gift once more and marvel at its beauty. Knowing each snowflake is different, I wish a pattern would emerge. None do. But as I watch, a strong desire to play in the snow itches in my chest. I haven't seen snow in years. I remember Mandel claimed that eating snow was a pleasant way to consume fractals, and I laugh. Then, slowly, the infinite equations on the snowflakes become time zones and plane routes and birthdays. My system is flooded with graphs until K2 suddenly glitches and my sims are terminated.

It's him. A robotic voice fills my ears. "You didn't make arrangements to come tonight."

"We shut the Ministry down. But you knew about the holothumb, didn't you? Now how do we get it?" I demand.

"We'll talk about it when we meet tonight. I don't trust anyone else."

"Yeah well, no one here trusts you." My mouth dries up because I'm stalling. I've made up my mind to meet him even though it's very possible this hacker could be King all over again. A swarm of numbers simmer below the surface of my skin and the dimensions of the room vaguely appear but in a tangled mess that makes my head ache. In the past, my numbers would have helped me predict danger. But they're useless now, especially regarding the hacker.

The low robotic voice softens. "I get it. The odds of me being safe are low. If I were you, I wouldn't trust me either. But I keep my promises." He's silent like he knows I'm weighing his words.

"Go to the window on your right," he says, surprising me. "Why?" I ask.

"An exchange of trust. What do you see?" the voice directs.

Hesitantly, I move toward the only window in the room, I peer through its thin glass. "Lots of buildings, brown dirt, cement walkways, people, cars, a tree."

"Focus on the tree. Imagine its roots, then move your eyes up its trunk. With your mind, trace each branch like you were drawing it with your finger. Think of every vein, every angle of the leaf to its very edge."

I feel silly doing it, but I really have nothing to lose.

The trunk is thick. I follow the bark up and choose one branch to follow. That branch shoots off to another one, and then to a thin twig, which leads to a leaf. The next branch is the same. Each branch is its own tree. I close my eyes, and imagine a small pattern emerging, like brushstrokes. When I open my eyes, the tree is dripping with numbers. Unprompted by danger, without struggle, my gift pours out a bit more, like a faucet turning on. One branch here is numbered another one there is measured. It's flooding over onto the distance around it—measuring the landscape and the distance between me and the tree and—

"Your gift's back, isn't it?" His robotic voice snaps me from the illusion and my gift fades, leaving me wondrous and lost.

"How did you know that would happen?" I ask.

"A calculated guess." The robotic voice softens. "There's always a design. Designs make patterns, patterns produce equations. I promised if you came to Tunis, I'd help you get your gift back. But time's running out."

"Fine. Where do I meet you?" I agree, perhaps too easily. He is baiting me. And I'm taking it. I'm a kid and he's offering me candy.

"National Bardo Museum." A map shows up on K2 as he speaks. "I'll be inside."

"How will I know who you are?" I ask, my heart beating at the thought of meeting the hacker alone. K2's seconds tick by.

"Don't worry. I know who you are."

CHAPTER 19

Ms. T stares at me wide-eyed. "You want to do what?"

"Retrieve a *clue* from the Bardo Museum." I do not tell her Coral Hacker will be there. She'd never let me go. "You told me to establish a connection with the hacker and find the list, and he sent a clue," I say, calmly. My plan to meet Coral Hacker alone hinges on if Ms. T allows me to go with only Goliath accompanying me. "All I need is one hour to scope it out. Goliath can stay with me the whole time."

"I don't like the way this sounds. What if he shows up?" She paces the room, eyeing me. I hold her gaze. I don't want to lose her trust. She's been good to me. But the last thing I want to do is endanger the team. I have to find out what's really going on first. Which means, I have to go with or without her permission. But Ms. T is not the biggest problem here. It's Goliath.

"The clue is in a public location, which I will be visiting during regular business hours."

"You know there was a major terrorist attack there some years back?" Harrison pipes in.

Pens elbows him.

"Never mind," he mutters under his breath.

"His goal is you, Jo." She shakes her head like she means business. "There's a reason he's breaking into *your* sims."

"I'm not afraid of him. He has what we need." My teeth clench, hurting my jaw. "Isn't this the reason you brought me?"

"Our goal is the Blacklist and the safety of this country and our team. After what we found out today, this situation is more dangerous than we thought."

Pens raises her hand. "With all due respect, Ma'am, with the Blacklist in the wind no one is safe. We are the only ones who can trace it. And I don't need to remind you of this, but PSS will be shut down if we don't destroy that information."

Kai's face is in my mind, haunting me. My hand is tapping. Time is running out.

There's a knock on the door.

"Come in," Ms. T sighs.

Goliath steps in. "Ms. Taylor, I'm a personal friend of the curator of the National Bardo Museum. I've just made a few calls. They're willing to offer heightened security, which they've already engaged. Jo will be safe the whole time. I won't let her out of my sight."

A strange gratefulness comes over me along with thick suspicion. Goliath is an obstacle I don't need but apparently when he said *my goals would be his goals*—he meant it. But what's in it for him?

"Our objective is to best him—not the other way around." She paces a bit more, and I know I've won. "I can't believe I'm saying this. But if it's just a clue, and he won't be there, you can go. On one condition." Ms. T calls over Harrison and Pens. "Set her up."

Pens and Harrison rub their hands together.

After ten minutes I am so decked out with micro-tech it's ridiculous. Despite the risk, the team is excited and they're swarming over me like I'm the coolest thing since Tesla.

"We're still nerds, ok? We've never had the chance to use this tech before." Harrison's smile is devious.

Pens holds my chin. "Open." She squirts something in my mouth. It tastes minty and sour and makes my tongue stick to the roof of my mouth.

"What's that?" I ask, swallowing it down.

"Hold still." She smears some lipstick over my lips.

"Oh no. You can't be serious. Sway?" I ask, incredulous. "Sorry. I refuse to kiss anyone for information."

"Especially when he's probably a creepy old hacker who hasn't changed his underwear in God knows how long," Harrison gags. "Ew."

"The lipstick serum—if ingested by another party, makes them dizzy-drunk and open to suggestions without remembering a thing. I squirted the antidote in your mouth. I know you're going to check out a clue, but if our creepy hacker debuts, you could get all we need from him." She obviously thinks it's cool, but there are certain lines I won't cross.

K2 beeps. Time to go. "You're ready." Wow. In less than ten minutes my body is covered in tiny pieces of equipment that have facial, voice, and biometrics recognition scanners to catch this hacker.

"Look," Pens whispers, hiding the worry in her voice. "This is actually dangerous for you. Are you really doing this for the list? I mean, are you sure Coral Hacker can be trusted? Do you think he really has what we need?"

I nod, thinking of the tree and the design. "He has what I need. You're a polymath. You know as well as I do that the answer isn't always where we think it is."

"I'll be online with you the whole time. If there's any doubt about your safety, use the tech," Harrison says.

Standing at the door, my dad's voice rings through my ears. *You have your bag? Your watch? Your earrings?* I touch my earrings one last time to make sure they're on. I'd better be right about this.

"I'll have answers soon." I wink and saunter out the door. I managed to get out mostly alone.

Now, all I have to do is take down a giant.

CHAPTER 20

Sometimes, there are no options other than a bad plan.

Riding to the Bardo Museum, Goliath stares straight ahead. Coral Hacker won't like that I have a two-ton brick wall accompanying me. There are only two ways I get to go in alone. I sort of like Goliath, so I'll try diplomacy first.

"I know Ms. T said you can't leave my side, but I don't want you to go in with me," I say, politely and firmly. "I'll be fine. I'm just touring the museum for clues. It's not like there's anywhere to go. I already did a perimeter study." I wave a map of the area and building blueprints displayed on K2 in his direction. "There's only one entry and one exit. And you said they'll have extra security. On top of that, I'm loaded with tech."

He doesn't say anything for a moment. "Look. You're important. I'm here to protect you with my life because the person that hired me cares for you."

I sigh, remembering how my dad donated most of the funding to cover the bodyguard costs.

"I won't do anything stupid." I bite my lip. "I know you read my file—Ms. T told me she briefed you on my past. So, you know I'm not fragile."

We stop at a red light. He whips his gaze to me. "I didn't say fragile. I said *important.*" He sighs. "Lucky for you I know the museum is safe. I didn't just ask for extra security. I booked a private tour. No tourists and no staff. I also prepared a lockdown of the entire museum except one door. No one's getting in or out. You will be alone. Except for me, of course."

Oh snap. Goliath isn't messing around. "Look, I'm giving you one last chance to let me go in alone."

"Sorry, Josephine. You're not the one I take orders from."

Oh well. I tap my leg, considering my other option. He won't like it, but he had his chance.

We pull over, parking near the museum. I wait for him to put the car into park and shut off the engine.

As soon as he does, my wrist points in his direction. I've wanted to try this for a long time. "Everything should get its chance for a maiden voyage."

"Wha—?" But the giant can't even finish his sentence. He has been struck down. Not by a tiny rock, but the lowest setting of a Taser-Watch created by a bunch of nerd kids.

Goliath shakes and trembles. I slam my arm against his chest to prevent his head knocking on the steering wheel. His eyes roll back into his head and close. I guess it works.

I buckle him back in and put a hat over his face. Anyone will think he's asleep. I've got to move. He'll be out for just over an hour.

I take the keys and lock the doors. "Sorry," I say, before shutting him inside. "I warned you."

CHAPTER 21

NATIONAL BARDO MUSEUM
LE BARDO, TUNIS, TUNISIA

The Bardo security guards confirm the museum is empty.

I pass through the glass doors and into halls of beautiful archways. The silent hosts of history greet me. This museum contains mosaics, relics and art from the Hellenistic, Phoenician, and Roman times, some nearly 3000 years old. The only sound is my feet on the stone floor as I meander slowly through the museum halls, allowing the mystery of ancient eras to entice me.

I wander for ten minutes and there's no sign of the hacker.

I wonder how Goliath was able to swing shutting down the whole museum for a private tour. It can't be a personal favor. This is a national museum housing some of the most important ancient artifacts in the world. My dad must have given him extra cash to do anything to keep me safe. Or did Ms. T? She has every reason to—PSS's future is on the line if we can't find the Blacklist, not to mention the safety of Tunisia, Kai's life and my gift...twenty minutes now.

The last of the sunset seeps into the room from high windows lighting up the dim halls like small torches. For a moment, I forget about the hacker and am completely absorbed by the echoes of ancient stories on the walls and floors.

All the mosaics, made of broken pieces of marble, ivory, and stone, are meticulously put together to create a whole picture, and there are...repeated patterns everywhere. In mathematics, tessellation—like the art of tiling mosaics, is well known. I see now why Coral Hacker wanted me to come here. It's a playground for people like us. Mosaics are like puzzles and equations. My gift thrums in the back of my mind, dying to come out and play.

Homer and the Odyssey; Diana the Huntress; Byzantine kings. Small tiles of earthen tones depict scenes of history and myth, victory and defeat. I read the displays about four relics and study two more mosaics on the floor. I'm gleeful to learn that some mosaics used to hide secret messages that only insiders could interpret. It's genius to embed codes into art, especially art so intricately crafted. I wonder if a prodigy first thought of that.

I'm tempted to focus on finding hidden code, to pull my gift out from wherever it is hiding. I want to decipher every mosaic in this museum, assign numbers to every tile and find their secrets. But I'm reminded of the helicopter and how forcing it has made me spin out of control. I need to be alert to meet Coral Hacker. If he ever shows up.

I check K2. Nothing. I'll give him five more minutes.

I come to a smaller piece of art made of ceramic tiles at an intersection of the museum. A man is depicted surrounded by lions. Tiny fractures of light hit the stones all around him. The man doesn't look scared even though he should be.

"It's Daniel."

A male voice shatters the silence and sends my heart thudding. There's no digital alteration, and the boy's voice is low and gentle. My gift wakes up. Numbers come at me, but in a way I've never experienced before. I'm measuring nothing but decibels and sound waves—a frequency in the air. My breath catches as I realize the numerical oscillation is from his voice, and the sound waves are moving between us. *What is that?*

"Daniel who?" I say, watching for it again.

"Daniel in the lion's den." The frequency skips, the energy rippling like a graph in my direction. My mind calculates a stream of hertz, periods, oscillations, and wavelengths. Coral Hacker. He's on my right, in the shadows. I don't have to move to know this.

Ms. T said if my gift returned it might emerge in new ways. Is this part of it? This is totally new. My heart shifts remembering that I used to love calculating the ocean's waves. It was music to my soul...but voices? Not once did numbers ever attempt it. It's unprecedented. I never thought it was possible.

The shifting of his feet snaps me back, and a different kind of warning washes over me—the talk of lions.

I turn toward the voice. A tall figure moves in the corner, his face hidden in shadow. An outline of dark hair falls to his cheekbone, only a hint of light on his lips.

"Daniel was a good man," I say, breathlessly, "but it didn't matter. He was still set up by people who tried to kill him. Only they couldn't. I've been there before. I know how that feels."

Coral Hacker lets out a harsh breath, like a laugh, only it's not funny. "What this picture doesn't show are Daniel's friends who had to wait all night to see if he would live. What a long, hard night it was. I know how *that* feels. I've been there before."

My heartbeat zips through my chest, twice as fast as usual. His words are one thing—what the heck is he talking about? —but his voice and that frequency run side by side with my own voice. The synergy between us won't let me go. It freezes me to the ground, taking note of every unique pitch in the air.

How am I measuring the sound waves of another human's voice? Is this happening to him too? Is it because we have the same gift? Are my numbers protecting me, finding a way to identify him? Whatever it is, it's amazing, but it also sets me on edge.

K2's taser buzzes lightly on my wrist. I look down. My smart watch is scrambling. My eyes snap up to the dark corner where his face is still hidden. "What did you do?"

He clears his throat. "Your tech has been inaccessible since the minute you entered the building. Sorry. I had to be safe. Especially after what you did to your bodyguard. Poor guy."

My eyebrows knit together. "How did you disable it?" Ms. T loaded me up with every kind of tech she could to snag this hacker and now it's not going to happen. At least they'll still be able to trace me. I reach up and touch my earrings. Thankfully the smart dust in these cannot be overridden. They are completely dependent on my body temp to keep running.

"Practice."

I step forward into the light. I want to get this meeting started. The museum is silent, the air still and dusty. Any minute I'll know if this was a good idea or a bad one.

"This way," he says, the frequency faster now. "We don't have much time." He turns and I follow his lead through the empty, poorly lit hallways.

As we snake through the museum, he points up at the walls. "These mosaics were made to communicate stories, codes, secret messages. Most of which were illegal at the time. It was a creative way to get the job done and not get caught. We're like these mosaics. We find new ways to talk to avoid danger."

"I'm not interested in analogies," I say, Phoenix surfacing again. "What's dangerous is if PSS doesn't get the Blacklist back."

"That's why we're here." He beckons me down a dark hallway. "On the roof. It's safer."

He leads me up a staircase. I still haven't seen his face, only the dark, silky strands of the back of his head. His frame is similar to Kai's. Not super tall, not short. Not particularly muscular, but definitely strong. His shoulders are wide, his gait confident. His clothes are simple—jeans, t-shirt and gray button up. Is he American? A local? One moment, his accent is there, the next it's gone. Which means, he may have grown up in multiple countries. The robotic alteration made him sound older, but his voice is clearly younger, possibly closer to my age.

There's a small door and we slip into another staircase, with a metal ladder, definitely made for workmen. I follow him up.

"Thank you," he says as we climb the final steps.

"For what?" I ask, my gift spinning in a knot as our voices continue to intertwine. What is this connection to him?

"For trusting me," he says, his sound waves spike in amplitude.

"I don't trust you, not with how much you know," I say, my throat dry. It's not exactly true.

The roof door is open, despite Goliath insisting that everything was on lockdown. It leads outside.

"Then why did you come?" He walks out slowly, unrushed. His back is still turned to me.

I hesitate. Going outside unwatched could be a really bad idea. Without equations, I can't discern his movements, like I did with Kai long ago. But then I remember he stopped the car so I wouldn't hit those kids. Showed me the coral so I wouldn't drown. And he promised to help me with my gift. But there's an even more important reason for me to follow him out on to the roof. "For Kai," I say.

A long pause follows. "Then I hope you won't be disappointed." His voice wavers slightly, like he's nervous. It's the first time I've heard a chink in his armor. Even as a robotic voice, it was always calm, steady.

Finally, I step outside. The clouds shift and the rays of a

pink setting sun shines on both of us. We are now exposed, face to face.

My numbers escalate like a tsunami sweeping up water and holding the wave at point break. Calculations faster than lightning shoot through me, evaluating everything about him. It's beautiful and heartbreaking the familiar way numbers tell me the story of his face, showing me every shape and angle and curve and scar. His features are as striking as his gaze is deep, and I shiver as the numbers clearly paint him in an even more beautiful way. I took for granted this feature of my gift. It feels so good to see someone like this again...but it's short lived. The numbers snap out and I'm left breathless, with no equations.

Not so with the hacker. His numbers keep going. I can tell. His eyes dart all over my face, calculating me. Evaluating me through formulae and design, the beauty of a mathematical language that I lost. Jealousy churns inside. I have nothing but my five, maybe six senses to evaluate him; it feels insufficient. Naturally, I do it anyway. We silently stare at each other, intensity building.

His jaw is strong and dark, curved in all the right places. His full lips are slightly sunburnt. His eyes are deep and brown, like mahogany. His brown hair, dark as his eyes match a shade of stubble on his jaw. I have never seen him before. I'd have remembered this face.

He examines my face too, making me more self-conscious than anyone I've ever been around. My gift turned against me. He sees me the way I used to see people; the way I saw Kai in all his imperfection, the numbers revealing countless hidden things. I'm exposed in a way I've never been before with another human. It's vulnerable. I'm glad no one ever knew how it felt when I looked at them.

"Hi, Jo," he says breaking our silence.

When our eyes meet, that frequency oscillates like thunder

between us. It startles me so much my foot shifts and I'm thrown off balance. He reaches for me even before I stumble.

His hand is on my arm. By the look in his eyes, he knew I'd misstep before I did. I growl under my breath at the numerical advantage he has.

He drops my arm.

"Please stop looking at me," I say. "You're making me nervous. I know what you see."

"Sorry." He backs away, his eyebrows knit tight. "Looking at you in person knowing you are...I mean, knowing you have the same gift is different than I thought it'd be."

"*Had* the same gift. Unless you help me get it back," I say, sharply as I back away.

"It's not gone, just hiding. You'll get it back. I promise." He sucks in a deep breath.

A lot of people have said that to me at PSS, but when he says it, it carries weight. No one else has my gift. No one else spoke into my sims the way he did. He moves to the wall running along the length of the roof. He rests his arms on the concrete and looks out over the old city. He's standing several feet away now, as if to make me more comfortable.

I walk up beside him, leaning over the wall to peer down at the dusty streets.

"You already know so much about me. Do I get to know your real name?" I sneak a quick glance at him.

"We're not here for me, remember?" he says, suddenly moody. "I'm not important." He brushes a dry leaf off the ledge and watches it float to the ground.

His words coil in my stomach because they couldn't be farther from the truth. Dangerous as he is, he *is* important, at least to me. He holds the key to my gift and to Kai. Since the first time he spoke to me in the sims, I've wanted to know the person behind the voice.

"No," I say. "You know my name. I get to know yours." We

lock eyes in a stare-down as he considers my request. My lips tighten and the serum is sticky on my bottom lip...my cheeks flush at the ridiculous idea. I could never do it. Don't want to. My eyes flick away, hoping he can't read my thoughts the way I would have done to him. But I'm not so lucky.

His eyebrows rise. "A bit forward, don't you think?" he says, his eyes darting to my lips too. *Dear God*, I inwardly groan, *he knows about the serum.*

"Noble." His large eyes pierce mine.

"What?" I ask, assuming he's still teasing me.

"That's my name," he says. "You need my last name too?"

Noble. Coral Hacker's name. I almost laugh at the irony until the frequency sends ripples along the graph in my head, light and soft like falling snowflakes at the sound coming off his lips. I shiver. Names so easily shift our perspective. We're attached to our names and they're attached to us, personal and deep. Like the ground breaking open, names can reveal things we never knew were there.

He's more real now than when he spoke in my sims, more real than even five minutes ago, all because he has a name. However. *Noble*—the name almost feels too personal to say— owes me much more than that.

His invasion of numbers starts again. I cock my head, breaking off his gaze. "Let's get started."

CHAPTER 22

A week ago, if someone had told me I'd be standing on the roof of the National Bardo Museum in Tunisia at sunset meeting a prodigy hacker to stop a coup and save Kai, even with equations to prove it, I would have called him crazy. But I've learned—more than most—that life can change with one boat ride, and unless you learn how to bend, you will break.

"Time's short," I say, sounding a bit like Ms. T. "You have a lot to explain. Start with Kai. Is he..." A lump rises in my throat. I can't even bear to say it out loud.

"He's alive. For now," he says, the frequency spiking again. He flinches in sync with the spike.

"Thank God." I exhale, and release fists I didn't know were clenched.

Noble scratches his eyebrow. "Your boyfriend's stupid, but at least he's brave."

I bristle at his words. "Kai is anything but stupid. And yes, he is one the bravest people I know."

He rolls his eyes. "Fine. He's not stupid in *that* regard. He knows how to do his job." I don't miss the annoyance in his voice. "He's a quick thinker. And an even better liar. On Monday, he successfully infiltrated a global crime syndicate called The Loyalists. Surprisingly, he's holding his own."

I bite my lip, suppressing the pride threatening to show on my face as well as the fear in my heart until I remember. "Wait, that's not why he came to Tunis."

"No. His agency sent him to elicit information from a professor who's involved with the radicals who are messing with the elections. Kai got the professor to talk, who leaked information about the Loyalists and a transaction that will happen on Friday. After Montego agreed to vouch for him, Kai left Tunis to find the Loyalists. Without his director's approval."

On the phone, Kai told me their team had been *missing something* and that he had a new lead. "What are you saying? The radicals aren't important?"

"The radicals are child's play compared to the Loyalists. A red herring. The Loyalists are taking advantage of the chaotic elections to set their own plans in motion. But Kai went seeking the Loyalists with an active biotag, which means the idiot has no idea how dangerous this syndicate really is or the kind of tech he's dealing with. Your boyfriend probably thinks his agency still has eyes on him and he's safe." Noble shakes his head.

"Then how is he ok?" I ask.

"Thankfully, I located the tracker on his biotag and disabled the signal before they traced it," he says.

"Ah, so that was you."

"If I hadn't turned that signal off, he would be dead." His voice is low, hard to read. "They would have identified his bio-tracker within seconds and knew he was a spy."

"So I'm supposed to thank you?" I say.

"Forget it." He looks at me like I'm going to believe him. But he hasn't given me any proof yet.

"So how is this connected to the radicals in Tunis who have PSS tech?" I ask, trying to piece this together.

He opens his bag and pulls out an old school folder. He sets a photograph on the ground, his eyebrows raised in question. "Does this face ring a bell? He was your boy's mission."

A meek looking man with glasses, tall and skinny, sits in the picture. I shake my head. "Never seen him before."

"Good." Noble taps his face. "His name is Professor Fuller Montego. He was behind the double hack at PSS. He has the Blacklist file on a holothumb. He's been selling PSS tech to the radicals, so they can wreak havoc on the elections as a diversion for the Loyalists to get their people into power. And yes, the radicals are staging a coup d'état that your team came here to stop. I warned you to get PSS under control." He avoids my eyes but continues. "But the coup is the least of our worries. As Kai learned, the Loyalists recently declared a new empire, led by what they call the "Successor". In exchange for loyalty, the Successor will provide a master-file that belonged to their former leader. It contains contact names and information for a global crime network and detailed, worldwide plans to be set in motion. And for a fee, the Successor is also offering the Loyalists cutting-edge technology, which Montego is providing." He gives me a look of understanding. "If the Loyalist deal happens on Friday and they get their hands on the master-file and the Blacklist—the whole region will erupt in chaos. And it will domino everywhere else in the world once that tech spills."

No. My head is spinning. It is much worse than we thought. But all of this could be a lie too. He's a hacker, for crying out loud! I don't know him. He could be manipulating me into helping him. For all I know he's the "Successor" leading this Loyalist group.

"If the Loyalists don't have the Blacklist yet, why don't you just stop Montego?" I ask, playing along, studying him.

"Two reasons. Kai's life depends on Montego showing up with the Blacklist and vouching for him. I assume you care about that. Second, there's no other way to stop the

Successor and get the master-file, which includes older PSS tech, like Still-Night. With Kai on the inside, we can help him get both the Blacklist and the master-file. But first we have to communicate with Kai and there's only one place he checks in regularly."

The expression on his face explains it all.

"The tampering with my stocks. That was you." So. Nothing is private in my life with this hacker around.

"If there was any other way, I would've done that. And yes. I unsuccessfully tried to tip off Kai so he wouldn't get killed. But even a genius can't crack a code between two people in love." Noble sarcastically narrows his eyes.

My head whips left like I've been hit with cold water in the face. *Two people in love.* The subject of love still makes me uncomfortable. Kai's always been patient. But saying those words is like tearing out a piece of my soul that can never be put back in. I don't say them lightly, which is why I haven't said them to Kai yet.

I look at Noble. He's making things sound simple but there's some information that doesn't match up. "Look, I'm not just going to believe you. If you want to help Kai, call his agency."

"I can't. I've calculated that possibility and it doesn't work out. The only equation where the Loyalists are stopped, the Blacklist is retrieved, and Kai stays alive is the one where you're involved."

Our eyes meet with the frequency between us like a wall of water, like a mirror. He's asking me to trust him and his calculations, which he can't prove. I've been there, asking people to trust my numbers. Now I realize how hard it is to put your faith in something you can't see. How far-fetched I must have appeared to Chan.

"All right. You said the Loyalists are a network of criminals. And they're planning a succession of power. So who is their former leader? Whose master-file are we dealing with?" I ask.

A shadow passes across his eyes. "Who else is cunning enough to steal and sell a Blacklist tech made by prodigies?" His expression fades to sympathy.

I sink back against the wall, breathless. Her icy voice swirling like a storm in my head. *I've watched PSS for a very long time.* She told me that years ago. I should have known, should have understood.

He won't say her name, so I do. For the first time in months, it slips over my lips tasting like bitter betrayal—to myself, my father, to the team. In this light, *the lion's den* has a whole new meaning. "Madame."

CHAPTER 23

Warmth is ripped from my chest. It's followed by an onslaught of numbers coming from different directions. Mixed with the height of the roof and the pulsating measurements of a boy's voice, vertigo threatens to claim me.

I slide down, back against the wall to stop the spinning. "Don't tell me she's out of prison."

He sits too. His hand rests inches from mine on the cement. I flinch at his proximity. "No." He shakes his head adamantly. "She's locked up. No chance of escape. I would have never asked you to come if she was anywhere near this place."

The protective tone in his voice sends shivers over my skin. Why is this boy so concerned about me?

"How is this possible?" I ask, but I can't claim ignorance. Madame was in my sims. Clues were all around me. The numbers locked away in my subconscious are still trying to create connections and come to conclusions—to much more than my gift.

Noble pushes his back against the wall. "Madame collected and used PSS secrets long before she met you—some of those are on the master-file. When you opened the door for me to break into PSS during your sims, it also allowed Montego, her former lackey, access. He must have been watching and waiting for an opportunity. I tried to stop him, but I was distracted and then it was too late."

This is all my fault. I sneak a glance at him before he looks away. The helicopter. I distracted him with my foolishness during the sims. When I convinced Harrison and Pens to open the firewall at PSS, I let them both in.

But his eyes don't condemn me. They're dark, round, and candid, but also deep and unsearchable. Everyone thinks he stole the file and anyone who has done research on me knows about Madame. If he's a genius, he'd calculate a cunning way to make me believe him. Which is why I'm here to outsmart him—even though something about it feels wrong.

"If anyone gets control of PSS tech," I say, reaching to my ear, slipping an earring out, "the power they'll have will be even more destructive than Madame's." I rub a bit of smartdust between my fingers. Just enough. Now all I need is to get it on his tech somehow, and the Bluetooth nano-tech can hack in. "How is this deal going down without her?"

"When Madame let you go at the Expo it was because she had already set up a new Successor. With the master-file, the Successor could build a new empire with her network."

"But we exposed Madame's network," I say.

"Madame was too smart for that. She knew the authorities would be able to dismantle her empire, so she deliberately exposed only three-quarters of her contacts. That way, a smaller part of her network could remain hidden and eventually rebuild."

It dawns on me with a frightening feeling that I was her first choice as a Successor. That plan didn't work out because she "killed" me. I wince. "Who is her Successor now?"

"No one knows. Not me. Not even the Loyalists," he says, opening a leather satchel. "Only Montego has information on who the Successor is. That's why he's our key to taking down the Successor, stopping the Loyalists and ending the radicals tampering with the election in Tunis."

"How is Montego the key?"

Noble hands me a small, black holographic thumb drive—a holothumb. "We switch his holothumb with this one—it's an identical holothumb to the one that Montego has with the PSS Blacklist, only this one is encrypted with a program I call, SMOKE to trace all of the files." I gasp. Noble better have good explanation for having our tech.

"Tomorrow Montego plans to sell another item from the Blacklist to the radical's leader, Amir Ben Slimane, thirty minutes from here in Sidi Bou Saïd. Then he will head to the desert where the Loyalist transaction will happen on Friday. If we can switch the holothumbs, when the Successor merges the master-file with the Blacklist files, SMOKE will infect them both. Kai is safe, and the last of Madame's network is exposed." He pauses. "I've been watching him. He's terrified of Madame's reputation. He protected her secrets for months. But he's greedy. After he hacked the FBI private watch on Madame and was sure she couldn't escape and come after him, he started selling older Blacklist tech, like Veil to the radicals. Now we have the perfect opportunity to stop this."

"We?" I ask. "You keep saying "we", but I haven't agreed to anything yet. You haven't even given me proof that Kai is ok. I won't be a puppet."

He keeps his back against the wall in the shadow. "Last time I checked, Kai was fine. I dare say, even enjoying himself."

My eyebrows furrow. Kai has always had a quick mind and quick feet. I'm not at all surprised he convinced a group of terrorists that he belongs. But enjoying it? I doubt that. I'm worried for him. I've seen him after a mission before. "So you have eyes on him?"

"I do."

"Prove it."

"Believe me, you don't want to see." Noble's voice is so absolute; I can't imagine what Kai's been through. But I need to make him show me. It's true I'm desperate to see Kai, and somehow, I know the hacker will buy it. But that is not the only reason I demand it.

"Yes. I. Do," I say, strongly, my adrenaline rising. "Show me Kai right now, or I walk." My gift starts flashing like a strobe light and I have to close my eyes to make it stop. *Why are my numbers so out of control?*

"All right." He sighs, and brings up his phone, taps in a code and pulls up a screen. He swallows hard. "This is live and he's undercover. You might see things you don't like."

"I don't care." I snatch his phone into my hand. The Bluetooth smartdust from my earrings is now on his phone. He doesn't know it, but we're one up on him.

I watch the live video stream of Kai and all thoughts of smartdust fade.

My heart surges once he is in full view. Yes, that is Kai. He is alive...and...my head swirls and bounces to every inch of the screen, taking in every bit of the scenario. I'd been envisioning him with black eyes, starved and sickly, tied to a chair like in the movies, but he's not.

He's sitting at an expensive table in a luxurious house eating and laughing with well-dressed men and women. And lots of girls. Kai is acting completely normal, relaxed. I'm shocked because he really does look like he's having fun.

My face blanches white as Noble, who is beside me, watches along too. Noble's words about him being attracted to danger surface. All his time with the Sang brothers apparently paid off—not to mention following me, his first "case". But he's undercover, I remind myself. He's good at what he does.

I take another look and pay attention to what I see. The rowdier men are drinking, the more refined businessmen are discussing something I can't hear. The girls, all dressed a bit scantily, are parading around the room.

A girl with long black hair, definitely a former X girl judging by the way she moves, sits at the table a bit too close to Kai. She's far too pretty for my liking. Her mouth is moving, like she's telling him something funny, and—she's touching his arm. He's not stopping her. My stomach tightens. Equations flicker around her movements. She's twirling a lock of her hair, slowly pulling it forward, over her bare collarbone. Noble was right. I don't like what I see. But I need a few more minutes to make sure the smartdust connects so I glue my eyes to the screen and pretend not to care.

"Do we have audio?" I ask, irritated at the jealously in my voice.

He raises his eyebrows as if to ask *are you sure you want to do that?* My stern face gives him his answer. "Right there."

I un-mute the video to hear a smooth, feminine voice. "Can I get you another drink?" the girl with long black hair asks Kai. I cringe. I've watched this scene before. The elite X girls were trained to please, to charm, but always with an ulterior motive, usually getting answers for Madame. She uncrosses her legs. "I'll get it for you. You don't have to move a muscle."

"Thank you, but I should be serving *you*," Kai says with a wink. "You're the lady."

To her surprise, he stands and fills her glass. Kai—always the gentleman. He hated how Madame could turn a girl into a pawn, hated the way they were treated. It doesn't shock me that he's trying to instill some dignity in this girl, but I don't like it. He shouldn't be giving her so much attention.

She lowers her eyes, fluttering her eyelashes at him. "Speaking of ladies, do you have a girl somewhere waiting for you?" She sips her drink in an absurdly sexy way and it makes my insides boil. My hand grips the phone a bit tighter, waiting for Kai's response. In fact, Noble even leans in to hear too.

Kai throws his head back with a laugh. The crooked grin I adore curls up on his face, and he sets his glass down. "Whenever I think of girls, all I think of is *trouble*."

My body goes stiff, and my cheeks catch fire as Noble, to my right, clears his throat. It's just like Kai to do something like that. If anything, he's cocky but he's always ready with the right answer. Kai is thinking of me, even if Noble's accusations still linger. I know they're not true. Embarrassed but satisfied that Kai's alive, I quickly hand back the phone, sure the smartdust has had time to establish a connection.

"Thanks," I say, sighing with relief. "All right. Tell me the rest of your plan."

CHAPTER 24

His plan is outrageous. I'd be stupid to agree. My dad would hate it and I will probably be banned from PSS forever. But I think it'll work.

Now I just have to find a way to get PSS to help. Or, like Kai, I will have to go rogue with this hacker.

"Why are you doing this?" I ask.

He looks away. "I have my reasons."

"Tell me one."

He draws in a large breath. "When I needed it most, this country, these people took care of me. They're good people. They've worked hard to build their nation, lay a new foundation. They don't deserve the chaos these radicals are planning. And the Successor will destroy this whole region–and possibly the rest of the world – with those lists. Someone's got to stop all of them."

I stare at him, holding back a hundred more questions we don't have time for and clear my throat. "That was four reasons."

He smirks. "Maybe I'm not as good with numbers as I think."

My lips tug up. Math nerds are always the same. "All right. Count me in."

Noble fidgets and looks everywhere but my face. "With

your gift you should be able to do this."

My gift. "You act like I still have it. But we can't count on my gift unless you tell me how to get it working again, right now," I say.

"Time's up," he says, pointing to my watch.

A second later my alarm goes off. Dang it. His internal clock is like mine. Jealousy rises in me. I used to be able to do that. I want to ask more but he's right, I'm already out of time.

"You have to call your dad." His eyes soften like he's apologetic for knowing my business. "Better not miss that." Before we head downstairs, he picks up a fallen leaf resting on the roof and runs his fingers over the veins then puts it into my hands.

Each step down I'm consumed and frustrated by how he knows so much about me. Even the phone call with my dad. "How long have you been watching me?" I ask when we reach the bottom stair.

He sighs, running his hand through his shiny hair. "Believe me. If your boyfriend hadn't stumbled into a situation where PSS and Madame were involved, I wouldn't have contacted you at all. And helping you get your numbers back is the least I can do." He moves away from me, back into the shadows like he's hiding something more.

"Next time try calling like a normal person instead of hacking into my sims," I say, a bit judgmentally.

"When has normal ever been easy for kids like us?" The frequency of our voices tingles under my skin every time he speaks. He looks away. It's affecting him too, like it stings to be around me. Honestly, it does for me too and I need to figure out why. He looks embarrassed about how much he knows.

I'm about to leave when I turn, finding his dark brown eyes. "Thank you for helping Kai."

He flinches before backing away. "You're welcome, although I don't think you'll thank me later. I warned you once.

He's not who you think he is." Noble bolts back up the stairs and out of sight.

I push the door open, my head swimming with what Noble just said about Kai. It's dark now but a slight breeze blows off the salty ocean clearing my head long enough to see a shadowy figure come at me from out of nowhere. Before I know it, large hands clutch my arm.

"Finally," the man growls.

CHAPTER 25

I'm commanding K2 to shock my assailant when the large hands let me go and the man snaps, "It's me. The one you so kindly tased back in the van."

I stop struggling. "How are you awake? That taser should have knocked you out for over an hour."

"I'm a big guy. Next time use a higher setting. In fact, next time just poison me," he says smugly, dropping my arm. "I told you my goal would be your goal. I'm on your side."

"I had to go alone. I'm sorry."

"Oh, you're not the one I'm mad at right now. My employer warned me that this might be a tough job. But I didn't expect to be tased. It stings like a..." He glances at me and bites his tongue. "Ah, forget it. At least you're not dead. Did you find what you were looking for?" Goliath asks, his large feet tread surprisingly light on the ground as we head to the van.

"Yes, sort of. Are you going to tell Ms. T?"

"Not if you don't. I'd prefer to finish this job without rumors spreading of me getting tased by a teenage girl." He waits for a scooter to pass us, then leads us across the street.

"Deal."

He walks me to the car like a sentinel. His usual stiff posture is calm, completely in the dark about what just happened. It makes me proud for a moment. He's a trained bodyguard, yet I bested him like Phoenix would have. He has no clue that I just met a dangerous hacker inside the museum. Hmm. The best security in the Middle East indeed.

"Let's get back," I say, a bit skeptical of him as we reach the van. He grunts in reply and opens the van door for me.

After we drive off, I pull out my phone, which is working again. "Excuse me, I have to call my father."

My dad picks up on the first ring. "Hey, Dad."

"Jo," he says, like he's been holding the phone a bit too tight. "Right on time. How's Tunis, honey?"

I look out the window hoping the new sights will make my gift spark like inside the Bardo but it's quiet. "It's great. Just finished my first museum tour…" Goliath rolls his eyes at me through the rearview mirror. I tell Dad about the National Bardo Museum, and he's pleased to know I'm spending time with 3000-year-old mosaics instead of criminals. If he only knew.

"What about the job?" he asks, a slight change in his voice.

"We already found the problem," I explain. "If everything goes smoothly, it should be fixed in three days and we're back within the week…"

"That's great news," he sighs with relief. We talk about the landscape of Tunis and the Medina, where we are staying. He seems satisfied I'm safe, for now.

After I hang up, the ride back is silent and confusing. I wrestle with all the new information I've just received from Coral Hacker…*Noble*… and rub my hand over my arms where a tingle lingers from that strange frequency between the two of us.

I don't understand how or why we share this odd connection, and I don't like that I can't control it. I don't know where it's coming from or what's causing it. It's puzzling but

I don't have time to think about it right now. Once we switch the holothumbs, we can stop the radicals and help Kai stop the Loyalists. After that, Noble promised to tell me how to get my gift back and he will be out of my life forever.

The leaf he gave me is still in my hand. The edges are shaped like tiny triangles. I try to count them, but my mind is too full of thoughts swirling around the Loyalists. Agent Bai and Hansen were slowly shutting down the webs of Madame's organization all over the world. I didn't think I'd ever be entangled in her web again. I should have known it wouldn't be over so easily. This deal was already in the works. Regardless of what I want, Noble's right—I'm the only one who knows Madame well enough to pull off this plan.

I take out my phone and scroll through videos of Kai training at the Sang Brother's *daochang*. I touch his face on the screen. That crazy boy convinced a mafia-led loyalist group that he was part of them. I'd laugh to myself if I didn't understand how much danger he is in. But Kai has always held his own. I refuse to doubt him—even if the thoughts running rampant in my head make me sick to my stomach. He was almost killed. Thanks to Noble, who's obviously not a fan of Kai, he's alive.

I groan, rubbing my temples. Kai's new job is my fault. If he had never met me, he'd be safe and working for his dad right now...but he'd be unhappy, dissatisfied, and lost. So, yeah. I wouldn't want that for him either.

But is this the life he really wants? When this is over, I need to find out what Kai wants. More importantly, what *we* want.

Entering Medina, Goliath pulls around to the back of Dar Alzaytun and escorts me inside.

The team scurries over, relief in their expressions. "You said one hour," Pens exclaimed. "We were worried sick. Thankfully, Mr. Qadar called us to say you were fine."

My eyes sneak a side-glance at Goliath, his straight face

revealing nothing. He called the team for me after I tased him? How could he have possibly known I was safe? Had Goliath seen us on the roof? If he saw me talking to Coral Hacker, he didn't say anything.

My gift may not be guiding every decision, but I know enough to pay more attention to Goliath–who he is and what his motives might be.

"I'm fine," I say to my friends. "But everything else is not."

CHAPTER 26

DAR ALZAYTUN
MEDINA, TUNIS, TUNISIA

One of the first times I sat in on a PSS thinktank meeting, there was a problem they couldn't solve. My thoughts had been wandering the whole day, back to the Pratt. Out of nowhere a solution came to me, something I'd do for King. Without thinking, I rattled it off to the team in its entirety, sure it would work, until their eyes gawked wide, and Harrison started laughing.

"You're joking, right? That would be breaking like ten laws."

I snapped back to reality. "Of course I'm joking." I laughed alongside them, but my heart raced like a traitor...a faint pulse of numbers behind that risky idea. I was not Phoenix anymore in an underground prison full of thugs where one makes their own rules. I'm Jo now, but even as Jo, I struggle. How does someone go from giving to following orders?

The gang, squished in my room, has that same horrified look on their faces as I tell them Noble's plan. But this time, no one is laughing. And one thing has changed since then. They're not in familiar territory anymore—I am.

Pens paces the room, one hand taking notes on her phone, and the other hand running through her red hair angrily. "Let me get this straight—not only is an extreme radical group planning a coup in Tunisia with tech from our Blacklist, which is being sold again tomorrow, but our Blacklist will be distributed to a Loyalist group, whose former leader kidnapped you?"

"More or less." My teeth grind together in an awkward smile, weighing how much more I should say. I haven't even told them about Kai yet. Not sure I should.

Pens goes on. "You believe they will wreak havoc on the whole region using our tech, and the only way we can stop them is a plan cooked up by a rogue hacker that we're supposed to be bringing to justice?"

Harrison is sunk into a cushy chair in the corner of the room, chewing on his thumbnail. "Hate to be the one to say this, but isn't this a bit out of our job description?" He pulls up his hoodie, covering half his face.

Eddie groans, his elbow grinding on the desktop as he slaps his face into his hands. "Much worse than we thought."

"We're already facing a threat of PSS being disbanded, but not sharing crucial information with the police about a crime syndicate and partnering with a hacker could potentially land us in prison." Felicia purses her lips, and her eyes lock on mine as if to make sure I've understood. "I knew I should have hacked that phone call back in Seattle. You have a lot to fill us in on. Like why you actually came on this trip."

"I will," I say, "but right now we don't have time. The sale is happening tomorrow. I won't let PSS be disbanded. I'm going to Sidi Bou Saïd alone. So if anything goes wrong, PSS will have nothing to do with it. Do you want to hear the plan or not?"

The room shifts, and I bite my tongue. They're obviously upset I didn't mention my past in Seattle, and I don't want to risk losing this new team by asking too much—they're the first friends I've made that I feel like I can trust. But Harrison is right. It's out of the job description. I hold my breath as the four of them exchange glances.

Pens looks at Felicia, who taps her chin. Eddie cocks his head at Harrison, who toggles his smart-watch, K1, then he holds up a finger commanding us to wait. Harrison juts his chin out at us when he's done. "Room's clean. No bugs."

Pens sits down, cross-legged on the floor. "All right, tell us Coral Hacker's plan."

Even though the room is clean of anti-surveillance, I keep my voice down to a whisper because Qadar is still in the next room.

"It's actually rather simple." I hold up the tiny holothumb that Noble gave me at the museum. It feels like the weight of the world in my fingertips. "The Hacker made a holothumb identical to Montego's except it has an encrypted virus in it called *SMOKE*. Once it's uploaded, it leaves an electronic residue on everything it touches. It will also identify and alter any file unique to PSS metadata. Making PSS files unusable to the bad guys, but traceable for us. Coral Hacker designed it so that it takes 24 hours for the bad guys to notice, which gives us 24 hours to get our files safely into Cyber Island."

"How do we switch the holothumbs?"

First, I explain Coral Hacker's intel regarding Professor Montego, the radicals, and the Loyalists. "Montego planned a sale of PSS tech tomorrow in Sidi Bou Saïd to Amir Ben Slimane, the leader of the radicals. But Coral Hacker messed with the arrangements, sending Slimane off course, so that we can take his place. All we have to do is swap the holothumb, then Montego will deliver it to the Successor."

"Why can't we turn Montego over to the police? And tell them about the Successor?" Pens asks.

"We can't do that. Montego is the key to tracing our Blacklist and stopping the Loyalists," I say, not mentioning that he's also the key to saving Kai. "He's the only one who has access to the Successor. Once SMOKE is infected into the master-file, all the loose ends of PSS tech, the Successor, and an entire network of malicious plans can be stopped."

"If Montego is taken into custody by the police, we'll have enough to stop the radicals, but we'll lose our connection to the Successor. We have to be able to get the rigged holothumb to the Successor and get SMOKE into Madame's Master-file so we can stop the Loyalists and the Successor," I say. "This is the only way the loose ends of PSS tech, the Successor, and an entire network of malicious plans can be stopped."

"Who's going to switch this holothumb with the one Montego has and how?" Harrison asks.

My face turns instantly sober. I squirm, knowing that the stares will come when I open my mouth. Just like the uncomfortable glances that my family gave me when I'd reveal illegal, violent, or criminal actions I'd witnessed or been a part of during my time in China.

I swallow but sit up straighter. "That's the catch. Montego won't listen to just anyone," I say. "Montego has to be convinced that the person speaking to him has authority and is connected to the one person he fears most: Madame. There's only one person on the planet who fits the bill. Who knows her mannerisms, her speech, her past, her networks and her business—and who could pull it off convincingly?"

Their eyes nearly pop out of their head. "You? You can't be serious."

Harrison looks at me. "Jo, these people are the scum of the earth! What makes you think that you can walk in there without something going wrong? Who do you think you are?"

I briefly look at Eddie, whose face is paling. "I have more in common with them than you know." I fold my hands in my lap, trying to shutter out flashbacks of all the Kings and Alexis and Gaos I studied over the years.

I sigh. "There's only so much of your past that you can tell others without having to relive it. That's why I don't talk about it, but I've looked into the darkest souls, calculating their every motivation. I know how they think. How they move. What they want. I know what scares them." A lump rises in my throat. "But it's a bit more complicated than that…" I could tell them about Kai, but that might get me into more trouble.

Pens jumps to her feet. "Before you go on, we need to tell Ms. T what happened at the Bardo."

"Tell me what?" The door swings open, and smooth black eyes survey the room before landing on me. "I'm all ears."

CHAPTER 27

Harrison jumps to his feet to offer Ms. T his chair, which she accepts. Her impeccable posture makes her look like a queen. Something about it reminds me of Chan. If I played hardball with him, I should be able to play it with her, and come to a bargain in the middle. But the motherly look on her face wins out, and I remember the way she fiercely protects the prods she's chosen. The hard tension in me drains away. I don't want to lie to her any more than I would want to lie to Red or my own mother.

Goliath stands at attention near my door, eyeing me and my watch. The temperature in the room jumps a few degrees as everyone turns my way. A trickle of sweat slides down my back.

As a child, I learned that if I acted like that big thing I'd done was no big deal, my parents would change the subject quicker. I lay on thick that old technique now hoping it will work. "I got the answers we were looking for," I tell Ms. T, "and yeah, it was through a face-to-face meeting with Coral Hacker. Hence the extra tech."

"That was precautionary. But you must have known he might be there, and you didn't tell me," Ms. T sits calmly, like a parent talking to a teenager about sneaking out. She's definitely been in this position before—so have I. A sense of honor rises in me. When I was with Red, he challenged me to always walk with as much honesty as possible. I want to do that. But right now, the stakes are too high. PSS. Kai. The Successor. I'll only tell her what I have to now and share the rest at the right time. I just wonder how many chances she'll give me.

"If I had sensed danger, I would have left immediately," I say. "There was always the possibility of meeting him. He invited us here."

"Invited?" Ms. T clears her throat. "Nice choice of words."

I keep my chin up. I can't back down now. "Mr. Qadar was close by. We hired security for that purpose, right?"

"Hmm." Ms. T looks at Goliath. "What's your professional evaluation?"

Goliath eyes me, a funny look hidden there as he purposely fiddles with his watch. I hold my breath. "Everything at the Bardo appeared harmless," he says finally. I release my breath until he adds. "Josephine's ability to handle herself was *shocking*. I won't underestimate her again." Goliath turns back to Ms. T, a smug look on his face. He's not happy, but I'm grateful he's covering for me.

Ms. T sighs. I appreciate that she hasn't called me dicey yet. But her demeanor makes it clear that she's not convinced of anything. She's still weighing every possibility.

"So now what?" she asks.

"It's an in-and-out maneuver with little risk and high reward," I say, explaining the plan and why I'm the one who can pull off the swap with Montego. "Coral Hacker has already made arrangements at a public place, *Ennejma Ezzahra*, the Sparkling Star Palace—a cultural and historical landmark." I ask K2 to pull up an address. Harrison instantly downloads a map. "After we make the swap, we're done, and we get to kill three birds with one stone."

Ms. T studies the other prods and I wish I knew what she was thinking. The team is looking to her for direction and assurance, but she's hunting for something else. She's a good leader with a reputation to uphold. Connections all over the world. Trusted by governments. She even convinced Jason Rivers to let me do the simulations, which was nothing short of miraculous.

"What's Montego's backstory?" The question catches me off guard, as if I'm talking to Agent Bai, and not Ms. T.

"According to Coral Hacker, Montego stole tech for Madame. But to everyone else, he's just a typical low-level money-grubbing criminal, harmless and gutless," I say, gauging her. "With the date set for the exchange, he's been watching over his shoulder for Madame or her closest associates to appear. Coral Hacker thinks Montego will believe anything I tell him if I'm convincing enough. He may even believe I'm Madame. If we *Veil* news on her, he'll believe it."

"What about the radical leader, Mr. Ben Slimane? He'll suspect something's wrong after the Ministry is shut down and he turns up at a deal where Montego is a no-show," Ms. T asks. Her voice gives away nothing, not one ounce of intonation. It's steady, ticking away like a clock.

Ms. T knows all too well how this works. She's asking all the right questions. I tense up. A current of numbers connects a series of events I've recognized in her before.

"I don't know about him." But I remember Noble's eyebrows knit together when he mentioned him, like he was calculating new possibilities. I didn't ask. I'm glad now I don't know.

Ms. T inhales deeply. "Our names and much more are embedded in those PSS files."

Pens starts fuming. "We create these things to help the world, and they twist them to destroy it." With one hand she's tinkering, while her other hand punctuates her words in angry gestures.

"Now you know how I feel!" Eddie says, kicking back in the desk chair.

Ms. T stands, her body rigid, like even her stature is set against me. I feel her words before she says them. "I can't sign on to this. Nothing about it feels right. We don't know enough about Montego, the hacker or the Successor."

"Without Coral Hacker, it would've taken weeks to discover the Blacklist file was here in Tunis or to create a way to stop it," I say to Ms. T. "Who knows when we would have learned about the Loyalists. If we don't act now, it'll be too late."

"Coral Hacker still could be the thief. I guarantee he's scoured our system." She beckons Felicia who jumps up at her command. "Here at PSS, we don't blindly trust someone who hacked our systems as our main source of information."

"Yeah, I mean, he's unhinged, right?" Eddie says.

I keep quiet. My gut says differently, but I'm not above being corrected. Red taught me that the ability to admit when you're wrong is a mark of honor. "It's a possibility. I've been fooled before," I say. "Regardless I believe he's an ally. He led us to this job knowing we're the only ones who can track down our own toys. Just like I know I'm the only one who can meet Montego tomorrow." I take out the holothumb and hand it to Ms. T. "Test it."

Ms. T nods at me like a judge who's finished hearing me make my case. She straightens her suit and takes out a phone. "Felicia, your blacklisted skills are needed right now. Let's see if this "Smoke" does what Coral Hacker says it will."

"Yes, Ma'am." Felicia takes the *holothumb* from her hands and leaves the room.

"Jo," Ms. T says to me, "meet me in my room in one hour."

I swallow hard. "Yes, Ma'am." She charges out like there's a house on fire.

CHAPTER 28

As soon as the door clicks shut, Eddie turns to me. "You can't meet this pyscho professor all alone."

The word *alone* produces numbers bursting like firecrackers and graphs exploding into webs of numbers. It fizzles out quickly but the power that comes from my gift fills me with energy. I steady myself against the desk. Coral Hacker said the adrenaline rush I experience in my phase 3 sims won't get my gift back, but I disagree. That death wish of mine really wants to do this.

"I won't be alone," I say to Eddie. "Goliath will come too. He's a trained professional."

"He's a security bodyguard. And we're nerds, not double agents on a mission." Eddie shakes his head, mumbling something in Korean.

Pens nods as she works on a double set of notes again.

"I trust SMOKE will work, and if so, Ms. T might let me do this," I say.

"I don't know, Jo." Eddie shakes his head. "The bad guys don't mess around." He rubs the scars on his hands, the kind that look too painful to ask questions about. They say when Ms. T found him, he was a mess of broken pieces, but Ms. T took the time to put him back together.

I put my hand on his shoulder. "Eddie, I've got scars too." I pull back my collar and show him my neck. He gasps, and soon Pens and Harrison are gaping at it too. They only know the broad strokes of my time in China. But I owe them something. "This isn't my first go around with people like this either. I'm not afraid."

Pens eyes the scar once more, then locks eyes with me like we're sharing a secret. She nods, a hard smile on her face. "All right, team," she says. "It's not our typical job, but Jo's right. It's our Blacklist out there and only we can get it back. If SMOKE checks out, I say we do this."

Eddie pulls up M2, his own smartwatch, a new expression on his face. "And I want to stop the radicals too. If they're anything like my old bosses, they're planning something else, and I'm going to find out what." Eddie dives into the computer. My chest swells with hope.

Harrison moves over to sit next to me on my bed. "What did you learn about the hacker, Jo?"

The hair on my skin stands up when he asks and my mind races to Noble's eyes and the frequency skating between us. I touch my earring. My throat tightens as I consider giving them the smartdust, but I can't do it. I can't turn him over to them. To even tell them his name seems like a betrayal, though I don't know why. I owe Noble nothing.

"Not much," I say, letting go of my earring, my hand falling to my lap.

"So he wasn't a creepy old smoker with brown teeth like we thought?" he asks.

"Not too creepy." I laugh as Noble's dark eyelashes and the freckles on the bridge of his nose come to mind. I turn my face away, toward the window. Any girl would swoon over a face like his, but I don't say that.

"He's young," I say. "Average height. Extremely alert.

Slightly awkward. Knows far too much about me. Though he wouldn't say how or why. He's going about it in the wrong way, but he wants to help."

"Dude's got issues." He laughs, then stops abruptly as everyone stares. "Sorry, he showed up and surprised you like that."

"Yeah." Except I don't know how sorry I really am. The memory of us examining each other with our gifts, the numbers sizing up the exact symmetry of his face, and how many times he blinked, and mapping out which direction he quirked his lips. Then there's the frequency humming between us. All living things have a frequency, vibrations, sound waves. Maybe I should ask Eddie. He knows all about them. I wonder if he's ever heard of a prodigy who could measure the decibels and sound waves of another human.

Once or twice, Noble had furrowed his brow like calculating the pitch of my voice stung him. Or maybe it repulsed him. But I shake it off. It's a mystery and I don't need it slowing me down.

"So no clues from meeting him?" Felicia asks. "Details?"

"He said something. I didn't know what to make of it," I say. "*It's all written in the stars.*"

Harrison stops, suddenly curious. "Written in the stars? The only other person I know who writes anything in the stars is the NASA Tipper," he says. "Do you think...?"

I scoff at the very idea. The NASA Tipper is a mystery often discussed by the prods at PSS. He or she keeps sending NASA genius ideas that have solved technical glitches in their equipment and helped their scientists achieve new insights into the unsolved mysteries of space.

"Why would the NASA Tipper be interested in a prodigy girl who lost her gift? Hack my sims and fight criminals in Tunisia? It doesn't add up." I want to dismiss his connection, but I'm a mathematician. We don't dismiss anything without considering all possibilities. Regardless, it seems too far-fetched to connect Noble with the NASA Tipper.

"Since he was able to create a holothumb replica from scratch," Harrison persists, "I believe we're dealing with a pure genius here. And the NASA dude is the real deal too."

Eddie looks up from his laptop, rubbing his chin. "Harrison's right. The NASA Tipper created a whole language called Star Coding. It's literally writing messages in the stars. Of course, no one is smart enough to read it yet," Eddie says.

"Oh snap," Harrison says, his face turning to pure mush, like hearing about his celebrity crush. "If Coral Hacker dude is the NASA dude, I'm gonna flip my lid. Totally changes everything. From creepy stalker guy to my idol overnight. You have to find out Jo. If he is, get his autograph for me."

"It's not him. It can't be. This boy is..." I stumble for the right words. "An enigma. And he hacked us! It's crazy to think that the NASA Tipper splits his time breaking into PSS while charting the stars."

"You'd be surprised. Meeting your idol isn't always what it seems." Harrison smirks.

"It's not him. And we're not becoming his fan club, ok?" I say, the room once again feeling overly warm. I need to think about Kai. Not Noble. The exchange of holothumbs is happening tomorrow. "Now, can we focus?"

Felicia bursts back into my room holding the holothumb Noble gave me, panting.

"SMOKE," she says through her breaths. "It's working. Everything checks out."

My chest fills with satisfaction. It won't take much to convince Ms. T now. "Then I've got to prepare for tomorrow."

"Now you're talking." Eddie rubs his hands together. "What kind of tech do we need?"

I raise my eyebrows. I swore I'd never do this again. But here I am. "Tech comes later," I say. "Right now, I need something else."

"Like what?"

They have no idea what I'm about to say. "A cut and color. And a new shade of lipstick."

CHAPTER 29

DAR ALZAYTUN
MEDINA, TUNIS

Impersonating the woman who kidnapped me is not why I came to Tunis, but here I am.

When I walk into Ms. T's room, her eyes are sharp and focused. She's studying me from head to foot, her presence almost as powerful as the person I'm about to imitate.

My new razor-straight fringe hangs just below my eyebrows. Dark brown like the locals, but tinted red, and perfectly smooth. To do this meeting right, I need to look the part and blend in. Every X girl who did a job for Madame was taught to move and act like her. They'd play with people's emotions. Few people actually knew what Madame looked like, so the X girls would tease them like a cat would a mouse.

My new clothes are straight and stiff and expensive. My pantsuit is white and perfectly tailored, my sunglasses are large, covering my face. My lipstick is blood red, and a strong citrus scent, just like Madame's, hangs on my clothes. The scent hides things, like the mist Madame used to knock victims unconscious. X girls always smelled the same. Montego, if he ever came in contact with an associate, especially an X girl, will recognize this scent. Harrison graciously mixed it up. It took over an hour to get the scent just right. My dreams were less than pleasant because of it lingering in my nose.

"You've done a good job. I've only seen photos, but you look just like her." She stands behind me.

"I've had practice." I grimace at myself in the mirror, slightly gagging, and remove my sunglasses.

"Harrison has *veiled* news about her too, I see." She stops in her tracks and takes in a deep breath. "Let's just hope police scanners don't pick up on you. Are you determined to go through with this?"

"You told me to do whatever it takes to get the Blacklist back. I think this qualifies." I stare her down. We both know she could stop me if she wanted to. "You're the experts on this tech. I'm an expert on Madame. We can't fail. If we do, Madame's Loyalists all over the world will end up with illegal tech and gain positions of power. Even the PSS geniuses won't be able to stop them."

She folds her hands. "You're sure this professor is non-violent?"

I soften at her motherly tone. "That's his record. Goliath can interfere if there's any trouble. In theory, this meeting should be simple."

Again, there's a look in her eyes like I noticed back in Seattle—deep understanding. Whatever she's experienced, it's why she mentors prodigies who need a safe place. It's why she understands Eddie and me. She doesn't just choose anyone to be part of PSS. Which is why I trusted her to begin with.

Ms. T knows no plan is a sure thing. I flash through the number of times I've almost died. Like Red, death can't frighten me away anymore from what needs to be done. But what does scare me is not doing what I know I should and losing people I care about.

I picture Kai and a rare memory of Chan comes to mind. I was watching Kai tend to orchids in the pool house when Chan walked in. Chan and I watched him together for a moment, then he turned and said, "When Kai was small, he was just like his mother, writing poems and interested in flowers. He was always strong and smart, so when she died, I made him trade stocks and do all kinds of things he hated. He was angry for so long I didn't get to see his mom and his uncle in him until now. *Thank you.*" My jaw tightens. Chan was right when he told Kai I was trouble. It's because of me that his son puts his life in danger daily. But I won't lose him.

Holding tight to my secret, I look at Ms. T. "I can do this. I have to."

Her body goes rigid like she sees my struggle. "Jo, I chose you for PSS because I believe in you." Her eyes linger on mine like she, too, has a secret but today is not the day to reveal it. "You're strong."

"And Sidi Bou Saïd?" I ask.

Ms. T studies me and sighs. "Don't get me wrong. There's nothing safe about this plan. But we play the cards we get. Right now, we have no other choice. And I get the feeling you'd go, even if I said no. So, we either expose the slime who's selling our tech, or we hand the information over to authorities who can't trace it and won't succeed at stopping the criminals and risk disbandment of PSS. Let's just hope we don't get caught in the crossfire." She leans in. "What I'm saying is, we've got your back."

I was right. She's just as crazy as I am.

CHAPTER 30

DAR ENNEJMA EZZAHRA, SPARKLING STAR PALACE
SIDI BOU SAÏD, TUNISIA

Sidi Bou Saïd is a mosaic of white buildings and blue doors and windows. The sea in the backdrop folds out in various shades of blue, adding to the mystery of this Mediterranean town that they say was born of mystics, sages and saints.

The chalk-white buildings have smooth, straight exteriors but nothing else is as simple. Arches, pillars, window lattices and door frames have geometric patterns carved within them. The entire town is a piece of art. As in the Bardo, everywhere I turn makes my brain buzz with joy. Noble was right. I needed to come here.

The *souk* is bustling with people hopping in and out ofcshops making purchases. Moneychangers and vendors selling fried donuts stalk tourists. Cats lounge on the hot pavement. The cafes are full of travelers chatting in French or Arabic and sipping on strong shots of espresso or mint tea with pine nuts.

Up ahead, museums and traditional *dar* are advertised as historical sites, reminding me that Eddie discovered a list of heritage sites with maps embedded in the Ministry of Education. The radicals may have plans to attack these sites, he said. But we won't let them.

The dust in the air mixes with the faint smell of orange trees and jasmine blossoms coming from the vines spilling over walls and gates. It makes me wish I were here for a vacation—not a clandestine date with a crooked professor.

We park on the street by the historical palace. The sign at the entrance matches many I've seen since arriving here: *Tunis, history at your fingertips.* I'm eager to get inside. Get this meeting done.

The *Sparkling Star Palace* has stunning white arches and ornate stucco walls with more beautiful carvings. From what K2 said, the *Palais* has cool terraces overlooking the sea. An escape from the relentless North African sun. It's cool and shady, and magenta, lilac, and golden bougainvillea overflow down the walls and archways. We don't go in yet but stand a little way down the street from the entrance.

I look at Goliath now. "You understand how this is going to work?"

"My job is to protect you whether you get attacked by a poodle at the mall or meet a terrorist for coffee," he answers.

"Good."

"Besides, the *Palais* is safe. I called around this morning." That's twice he's been too helpful. Who did he call, I wonder? I want to ask when K2 informs me of an unknown caller.

"Answer," I say, and brace myself for Coral Hacker's frequency.

After a second of static, I hear Noble's robotic voice. "Jo. We need to pull out." His voice is sharp, not calm as usual.

"What's wrong?" I say, a slight disappointment at the absence of the frequency bouncing between us.

"Just got new intel. Montego knows something is wrong. Maybe it's because the Ministry of Education was shut down. Whatever it is, he's far more unstable than I calculated."

"What did you find out?" I ask.

He breathes in deep. "I can't prove it, but all my numbers point to him dabbling in the PSS tech. I think he's coming *equipped*."

"Equipped with what?"

He groans. "Fingertips."

"What?" I cup the phone and whisper into it, so Goliath doesn't hear me. "You mean the fingertip bombs Eddie designed for special ops? Only a Navy seal could handle that stuff. It could take out a whole block. And there's no way to dismantle it."

"Exactly. Which is why you have to pull out. The plan wasn't to endanger you."

Goliath is examining the passersby on the road. I snap my eyes shut and focus. "Tell me what you're seeing. The calculations. Is there a better way?" I wait, because in this bizarre way, I trust him—or I trust the numbers we both share. But he's silent. "Noble?"

"We'll find a different way." He doesn't have to write it out or dumb it down. There is no other way. He's calculated it. This is what we have to do.

My head spins with thoughts of Kai. This is our only chance to help him stop the Successor. I can't back out of this exchange.

"No," I say. "We've got this. Our plan is set. I'm moving forward."

"*Kunt 'aerif*," he groans. "I knew you were going to say that. Fine, but Montego's anxious and suspicious. When you're with him, remain calm. Let him know that everything's under control. Whatever you do, don't scare him."

I exhale hard. "Madame lived and breathed threats and so did all of her associates. If I'm going to be believable, I can't show mercy." Goliath narrows his eyes at me when I say that. *Gah.* He's thinking of the taser again. I return an apologetic smile and lower my voice.

"Do you speak French?" Noble asks.

"*Un petite peu.* Not like Madame." I picked up languages really fast because of my gift. But my time with Madame was traumatic. Lev made it even worse. It wasn't until Red that I could focus enough to take it all in. But then I remember something. "Madame never used one language with any-one—" I stop abruptly. Feet are pounding in the background. Noble's breath becomes shorter. "Are you running? Where are you going?"

"Back to my hotel," he huffs. "If Montego finds out you're not one of Madame's Loyalists, he'll flip."

"So you're just leaving me?" I say, horrified.

"No," he hisses, huffing. "I'm going back to get *Dissolve* just in case."

My breath catches. I'm confused. "You mean PSS *Dissolve?*"

Dissolve was Eddie's design to dismantle Fingertips, but he never got it to work without some kind of explosion.

"Yes. I've been working on a solution for a few days now." Noble knows he doesn't have time to explain anymore.

"A few days! Have you even tested it?"

"It's not exactly easy to test a bomb made of mixed chemicals hiding in your fingertips." He's panting, running harder now. "But my calculations estimate an 85% chance it'll work."

Great. I bite my tongue. This is how I sounded to people. Reckless. Unhinged.

I glance up at Goliath. His muscles are taut, he's vigilant. But he has no idea we're about to meet a suicide bomber. "It'll be fine. You know what? We won't need Dissolve," I say. "I have a giant to protect me."

He doesn't stop running. "Short and sweet. Whatever you do, don't use your Taser." His words are choppy now, in between breaths.

"Got it. Switch the holothumb, make sure he takes it to the

Successor on Friday, and get out."

Goliath gives me a head nod. "You'll be fine," he says to me, his eyes scanning the area.

Qadar's body has stiffened even more. He's gone into another mode completely. He's highly alert, on guard and ready to pounce. He knows more than he's letting on. One half of my mind is warning me. *This could be a trap.* But Qadar's voice fills the other half. *Your goal will be my goal.* Something in his eyes makes me believe him.

My gift flickers awake at the beautiful architecture but inside, anxiety rises. "We're here. Tell me this is going to work."

The robotic voice cuts out and Noble's real voice is in my ear. "I'll come back. I won't let anything happen to you."

My arms flush with goosebumps at the sound of his voice and the frequency quenches my anxiety like fresh water. It's all I need to give me courage to step out of the car.

Qadar notices. "All ok?"

I nod. Qadar closes my door. He doesn't need to know everything.

K2 is now routing through a tiny PSS speaker in my tranq-earring. "Harrison's K1, requesting an X line."

"Granted."

Another static vibrates in my earring. "Jo. Ms. T set up a meeting with three police officers down the road just in case. Fuller Montego is on the street, almost to the Palais terraces now. We found his car and bugged it. Eddie doing some forensics, you know, fingerprints and hair samples. Any update on your end?"

I refuse to tell them about Fingertips. "Everything is fine."

"All right then. I'm signing off. If there's any trouble activate K2's SOS, and we'll send those officers in," he says. "And Jo? Ms. T says no risks."

My gift is tingling, right on the verge of appearing. "You mean apart from meeting a dangerous scientist while pretending you're a psycho recently sprung from prison ready to do the greatest deal of her life? Wouldn't dream of it."

Harrison fakes a laugh, for my sake. "You claimed he wasn't dangerous. You better be right." He skips a beat. "There he is—or should I say *target in sight?*" He signs off.

A man with a blank stare crosses the street, entering the Palais. He's looking around, concentrating too much. He walks quickly, not a confident stride, but like he wants to get it over with. He rubs his forehead, then wipes his pants. He's sweating, nervous. His fingers tap against his leg. My stomach knots. I step forward, my heart racing, gift flickering with numbers. I can't let my team get anywhere near this guy.

Goliath leans down. "Jo, this guy's got every warning light going off in my body."

"Listen," I say to Goliath, adrenaline simmering in my chest. "Don't interfere unless I ask, please."

We move to the veranda in the back of the *Sparkling Star Palais.* Montego is heading outside where a few tables are set up under a vine-covered arbor.

"It's money time," I say. Goliath gives me an odd look.

"Sorry. Inside joke. Let's go." With his large hand on my back, he escorts me inside.

Numbers are cast like a net into the sea as I enter the building. For 34 seconds I catch the dimensions of rooms and the distance to the terrace. I take note of the starkly juxtaposed modern appliances amidst old paintings and illustrations and a collection of musical instruments. Then my gift starts to blink, like it wants to come on, but something's pushing it away. The on-and-off is distracting me. It's too hard to piece all of the clues together.

Goliath positions himself at a corner table, awaiting my instructions. Montego settles into his white chair, a small briefcase with him. Anyone could tell he's not a fighting man. He's tall and gangly, extra thin arms and legs. A sunken face. A sad man who looks like he has lost all hope. Most likely easily overpowered. It makes me pause. He probably was once a brilliant professor with a future, full of scientific breakthroughs the world needed.

What made him so desperate or disillusioned at life that he gave up his reputation for money and power at the cost of his own soul to work for Madame, and now the Loyalists? I think back to the Pratt and how gradually lies seep in and take root. Unless someone's there to pull them out and plant truth, monsters grow. A part of me wants to bind the monster and set this man free, like Red would have. But I also know he has to make it to the transaction on Friday or the bigger monsters go free.

And if he believes I'm Madame, he'll most likely be scared of me and do what I ask.

Despite the nausea of those days, I allow my dinners with Madame in Shanghai to sink their teeth into me. Her power. Her cunning words. *Her threats.* It makes me sick, but I take on her persona now. *I am the one who wields the sword.* I strut up to Montego's table as graceful as a doe, as silent as a ghost, as deadly as a kiss.

"Montego, darling," I say, in that icy whisper of a voice. "Nice to see you."

He turns startled, already pushing his chair back. "W-h-ho are you?" he asks, his hands immediately splayed out on his legs. Drips of sweat pour down his forehead. He really is nervous.

"As if you don't know." I pause for dramatic effect. "Ah, now. You're wondering if I am her or an associate. One never knows. That is how she likes it. But she told you she'd show up. And *I* always show up. Your buyer couldn't make it, you see." I sit at his table like I own the whole palace.

"Impossible." He's trembling, his chest is already heaving. I feel sick but my gift is starting to buzz. Just a bit more fear and intimidation, then I will calm him down, set him at ease. Perhaps persuade him to a better life, to get out of the game. But instead, I do what Noble says not to—I threaten him.

"What's impossible is you selling Madame's property without permission. Tsk tsk tsk. Cherie, you had a deal. And even before the big day." I stare, hard and without blinking.

"She's…You're…in prison. Even this morning. I checked. How did you…?" His fists curl in and out.

"Am I the only one who knows the news is a farce? Even after all the tools I've provided for you. You didn't even think to check the FBI's private network?"

Harrison veiled the feed this morning. AI bots went to town creating fake videos of Madame's getaway.

I deliberately cross my legs as she used to, drawing attention to my boots. "They'd never announce an escape this important on National news or an FBI network. No one wants to admit they have a criminal of my caliber on the loose." I hold out the phone to him, a Veil news leak created by my personal team.

He pales to a shade of ash as he reads it. I stare, without blinking, my flickering gift revealing more about him than I like. Nervous energy is jolting off him. His fear is taking over. It's hard to ignore. I shake it off and act hard and cold. Like she would. I'm pleased he believes my performance.

"So who am I? Does it matter? I do her bidding." My gift flinches as the lies and confusion fly out of me, a glimmer of the truth trying to surface. I suddenly understand something. Madame's gift flickered too. Those moments when she saw me for who I was. It was her gift. But it never fully returned. I clench my teeth. I won't let that happen to me.

His face drops as he reads the headline in a Veiled news source. "Notorious criminal Maxima Moreau escaped her high security prison last night. Authorities have closed borders in three countries in attempts to identify her location and prevent her from eluding capture."

Noble is in my ear, running, voice firm. "I'm one kilometer from you. No threats. Switch the file and leave."

I give him a smile that does not reach my eyes. "Now hand me your holothumb. I already know you have it on you. Yours is corrupted now. I have a new one for Friday."

He swallows hard, nothing moving except his hands, which are still rubbing his legs. "What are you going to do to me?"

My gift buzzes with life.

Focus on the file. I know I should but that is not what Madame would do. It's scary how I know exactly what she would say. And I say it.

"Nothing, Cherie," I say as smug as possible. "We have a job to do. And I still need you. You'll still make the deal for me, as agreed, and when this *holothumb* is in the Successor's hand, your disloyalty can be his problem." I take out the little black holothumb. "Here, an updated list without a trace of corruption."

He shifts in his chair. A horrified expression now on his face.

Noble is in my ear again. "Jo, numbers don't lie. Whatever you said, your cover is blown. Call your bodyguard."

"You can't be her," Montego says. "You're not who you say you are."

"Montego, darling, don't be stupid." But Noble's right. My cover is blown. His hands are trembling, he's sweating. Is it because I'm not speaking French? What did I say that triggered him? Whatever it was, I have to fix it. "You don't want to mess up our last job, do you?"

Noble's in my ear. "He's not buying it. I'm almost there. Stall. Calm him!"

But I don't listen because my numbers are spinning out of control now, and I want to fix this. I want the plan to move forward for Kai. Then I do the one thing Noble told me not to do.

"Now, let's get on with it. I'm growing impatient with you.

Don't make me summon the men surrounding this building."
The threat. It just came out. So naturally.

His eyes, crazed, stare into mine like a rabid dog's.

I should tap my watch for Goliath. He's about to make his
move, but I don't because my numbers are surfacing. One more
second and I should know what's to come. But it's too late.

He grips my arm so hard it's like a jaw-locked dog. It hurts,
but I don't register it fully. "I don't know who you are but call
your men off, right now." His voice is laced with desperation.
"We're going to walk out of here, and you're going to let me
go free or this whole building explodes, and we go with it."

With his free hand he waves. All I see are his fingertips.

CHAPTER 31

Think.

My gift is spinning, but nothing is clear especially when K2 barks in my ear. "System override. D2, M2, K1 all have lost visual." Noble's cutting their video. He knows they can't see this. It can still be salvaged.

Qadar moves toward me like a raging bull to intervene. "Stand down," I confirm, but before the words are off my lips he's already pulled back. I half-expect him not to obey orders. He doesn't move, though still strung taut like a lion about to pounce.

With my arms squeezed by fingers with little bombs likely to go off any second, I get up and walk to the door.

"We're going for a little walk." Montego's death grip on my arm tightens, squeezing it so hard his fingernails dig into me. It's going to leave a mark, but I'm only concerned about the bombs. How did Pens say they detonate again?

I follow his instructions and walk to the door. To any bystander we'd seem like a couple leaving for the afternoon.

"If you make any wrong moves at all," he says nervously, "your arm will be the first to go. Then your head."

His threat hits me like a shock wave. Instead of fear, my gift wakes up, rocketing around the room for solutions. I knew it wouldn't fail me. It spouts off equations; within seconds my face falls. The equations line up K2's Taser and an equation for a chemical reaction of *Fingertips*. Bad news hits me right away. Noble was right. It will set off a far worse explosion if I use it.

I grit my teeth so hard my jaw hurts. *Stupid!* If I signal for help or try to use any of the tech on my body, he'll know. My numbers confirm that he won't hesitate to ignite the bombs in his fingers. Then where will we be? He's desperate and not thinking clearly. If I go with him, my chances of survival are higher. But I can't let Montego get into the street and risk PSS seeing what's happening.

Goliath is in the corner, watching intently. I'm obviously in trouble. I expect him to step in somehow even if I told him not to interfere. But the minute I look at him Montego notices, and whips him a hard stare.

"Not one move, or you'll go too," Montego growls.

Goliath cocks his head the other direction, and steps back before I give an order. What happened to taking a bullet for me? Maybe bombs are different. He flicks his eye to the door and cocks his head again to the right. Is he obeying someone else's orders? The numbers around him tell me he is listening. But to who? Is Ms. T in his ear and if so, what is she telling him?

Twenty-four steps now—my numbers spout off an equation. Noble is around the corner –I just have to stall. But what can he do? If Montego is touching me at all, these bombs will rip us to shreds.

Another wave hits me, stronger this time—calculating my odds and how not to die. What will happen if we get into the car and go together? My numbers explode with adrenaline, then completely zap out. My head spins. But in the midst of it, an equation reveals Montego is as scared as I am. There's a speck of something in my favor, a glimpse, one in a million. I need to stall him. But how?

Montego squeezes the back of my neck. We're almost at the Palais exit. "You almost had me convinced, but I knew Madame couldn't escape. Tell me who you are!"

A whisper in my ear, Noble's words answer my question. "Almost there."

We stumble through the exit, and Qadar is left behind.

Alone and out of the building, Montego yanks me forward toward the street.

"You're making a huge mistake." I growl through my teeth, hoping to get him to second guess his choice. "Madame is smarter than you think. I know her better than anyone. I was trained by her side."

He drags me one step forward when suddenly I know what to say. "You're right," I hiss. "I'm not Madame. I'm her Successor."

Montego stumbles back, gasping, horrified. He lets go of my arm. Right then Noble, breathless and sweaty, runs onto the scene like a shadow, slamming something that looks like a needle into his arm.

Montego swings his hands wildly trying to mix the chemicals to ignite the bombs but they're powerless. Goliath flies out the door and to my side and knocks Montego to the ground.

Noble, panting, red in the face, stares at me, his eyes assessing me with numbers and something else much deeper. He takes one fleeting look at the bodyguard then bolts away.

Qadar cocks his head at the boy.

Montego's eyes roll back into his head and he slumps to the floor. The shout of a woman in the crowd startles passersby. Heads spin in our direction.

Ms. T is in my ear. "What happened? All visual cut out."

I don't answer, but snap down, frantically searching for the *holothumb*. We've got to flee the scene before any police get here. I need the Blacklist. Finally, in his pocket I feel the small cold metal device.

After it's in my palm Qadar snags my arm. "We have to leave, now!"

I shake off his arm. I can't leave yet. I need his thumbprint. The sirens are getting louder. *Think!* Then I remember. Fumbling in my pocket I grab the lipstick serum, Sway. I spread it on the top of my hand, then quickly press his thumbprint into it, praying it won't smudge. Then, Qadar whisks me to my feet and ushers me to the van.

Sirens and the Tunisian police are on the scene seconds later shouting in Arabic and French. "Back away! Move back!"

Ms. T signals me again. "Jo. What's going on?"

I catch my breath before I answer. "He didn't cooperate."

In the van, the small holothumb bounces in my hand. We got the PSS Blacklist. We can stop the radicals. But the master-file is still out there. The Successor is still on the move. And Kai is in more danger than ever.

CHAPTER 32

SAINTE CROIX CHURCH OF TUNIS
MEDINA, TUNIS, TUNISIA

SMOKE is already underway.

A light blue sky unfolds with the dawn over the pale city of Tunis as the early morning call to prayer echoes in the distance. From the rooftop of Saint Croix, I observe the sand-colored buildings, minarets, and large signs in Arabic script, trying to take it all in, even study the language, but all I can think about is Kai.

The Arabic signs reminds me of a night I came home from my sims and found Kai teaching my sisters how to do Chinese calligraphy. The brush in his hands looked so natural as he traced graceful strokes, crafting a Chinese poem. After my sisters left, I marveled at the boy-fighter who tended orchids and painted calligraphy.

"You're so much like Red. He loved poetry," I said.

"I wish I knew him like you did," he said, inviting me to sit.

"I'll tell you everything I know about him," I said, peering over his art. "Might take years though."

"I'm not going anywhere." He leans over to kiss my cheek.

"And speaking of poetry...this is for you."

I looked down at the Chinese characters, each stroke artfully brushed in black ink, and read it.

sea and sky invited me for a trip, but i heard your voice, and said no thank you.

gold and silver offered me luster, but i saw your face, and turned them down.

time and mystery promised me secrets, but I held your heart, what more could I want.

Speechless, I threw my arms around his neck and nuzzled my face into his skin, soaking in his scent. "You should write poems more often."

"It's not the first time I've written a poem about you. Just the first time I've shown you."

"When will you show me the rest?" I ask peering into his big dark eyes.

He laughed. "We've got years remember?"

Except, we might not have years, after what happened yesterday.

I shrink down next to the intricate bell tower on the roof, watching the light reflect on the three glass domes. Poor Qadar is sitting in the stairwell, watching me from a distance. He didn't complain when I woke him. He even offered to make me authentic *qahwa arbi*, a Turkish style coffee made with a *zizwa* he carries with him. It's sweet and grainy, but also stiff and strong, biting back with each sip. I need that right now, especially as I wait for a call from my dad.

He rings a minute later and after a brief chat where I recount nothing but a lovely adventure in the blue and white paradise of Sidi Bou Saïd, my dad admits he's doing better than expected, even started making some new business plans. I'm glad he has something to focus on other than me.

After we hang up, I turn my gaze to watch the clouds shift and billow. My conversation with Montego runs over and over in my head. I keep searching for where I slipped up.

No one was hurt, no historical palace was destroyed, but still, I botched the plan. Montego will be locked up and interrogated. There is zero chance he will make it to Friday's deal with the Successor. No chance to vouch for Kai. I can't figure out what went wrong. What triggered his disbelief?

Thankfully, half of our job is in motion. With Noble's SMOKE now uploaded to Montego's *holothumb*, the team can trace the previous PSS tech sold to the radicals, like Veil. The prods already uncovered four attacks planned on historic or government sites in Tunis and identified three names and faces they believe are connected to them. The Tunisian government is now on the case and arrests will begin. The momentum for their coup has slowed, and the radicals are not happy. They're attempting to set up Veil in another government host site. But it's the Successor and the Loyalists who are my concern.

Apart from the coup, Eddie detected Veil in cities in North Africa. Thankfully, PSS can use SMOKE to wrangle PSS software into Cyber Island. The team considers this a victory. But I can't celebrate.

Kai and the Successor are still out there, possibly in the same room. We might stop the coup, but not the Successor's plans if *SMOKE* isn't joined to Madame's master-file. Especially, since no one knows who the Successor is. Madame operated with no one knowing her identity. Every meeting she set up could take place without anyone even knowing she was in the room. She was a ghost. If the Successor is anything like Madame, they'll do the same thing and get away with it. They may even figure out who is interfering with the radicals and call Friday's deal off.

The Tunisian sun is above the horizon now, a fiery orange. It blinds me slightly as I face it. But I welcome its warmth.

I pull out my phone and flip through photos, landing on one of Kai, my dad and I at the beach. That day I'd noticed a group of young men harassing a young girl by the sidewalk. I looked up at Kai, who knew what I was thinking. He gave me a sharp nod, and I strutted up to the group, Kai remaining with my father. Even as I walked toward them, that protective fire started to roar. With one command, the boys wilted and fled, tails between their legs. I spoke with the girl, slowly becoming myself, then watched her climb into her car, safe.

On the drive back, my father looked at Kai. "How did you know she'd do that?"

Kai smiled. "Your daughter has taught me to never underestimate anyone, especially her."

I think of him now, and how he believes what he told my dad even when he sees me at my weakest. I don't let my guard down easily, but Kai's seen it all. He's my haven. When a memory triggered a fear, or a nightmare hit me, I tried to hide it. But he always knew. "It's ok," he'd say, wrapping his arms around me. "You don't have to be strong when you're with me. I know who you are." Not as much as I know who he is. He's every bit Chan's son, smart and commanding, but he's also Red's nephew—a tinkering boy who loves orchids, calligraphy, and wants to save the world.

Which is why he's somewhere in this country and why I need to find him. How will the new Successor punish people who don't deliver on their promises? My thoughts trail off to dark places. I lift my cup and gulp down the last sip of espresso leaving the dregs of coffee grounds at the bottom.

Then I message Noble. *Is Kai okay?* But two minutes later, he hasn't texted back.

My sim glasses are in my bag, taunting me. My mental calculator is what I need to solve this equation, but the sims aren't digging up my numbers fast enough. Still, Noble's words linger in my head. *Your subconscious is gathering clues.*

He's right. I had hints that Kai and Madame were involved with the stolen Blacklist tech before I had proof. So then, what am I missing?

With Qadar watching, and probably wondering what the heck I'm doing, I throw a sweatshirt on the ground, recline onto my back, and slip on my sim glasses.

"K2, load phase two from Monday." A black screen comes on and Tunisia fades away.

Running.

I open my eyes to a thousand people all around me. My feet are already pounding on the cement below. As expected, it's night and I'm in downtown Shanghai, but on the other side of town. My back is covered in sweat. My chest hurts as I pant. Sharp wind slices through my shirt as I run. But I don't stop.

This time I'm not dizzy and I know what I'm looking for. I sprint to the square where the fighting is happening.

Pay attention Jo. What triggered Montego? *Wake up,* I command my gift. *Every detail is important.*

I run until I'm out of breath, I skid to a stop in front of a crowd. Jabs and kicks are already in motion. This time I squint, focusing harder—forcing my gift to wake up—but nothing stands out.

I resort to child's play and count. A new detail pops out at me. Nine people are in the ring. Nine people watching.

There are actually two fights within the fight. What does it mean?

I edge closer, pulling my hoodie down to shield my face. Between swinging fists and foaming spittle and crimson blood, three men all wear sharp suits. Kai is locked in what looks like a deadly battle. His face is so different from the Kai who held me when the world was crumbling back in China. His eye is a black sunken moon, and blood kisses the corner of his mouth, a thin focused line. I can't tell if his face is a mask of focus...or hate.

My numbers go wild, but nothing makes sense, like my mind is trying to calculate a dream that won't compute. Maybe it's because Kai is a bloody mess. He turns and starts fighting a man twice his size. I almost worry until Kai crouches down, rounding up for a kick. I've seen him fight so many times, I assume he'll go for the knee or groin, maybe even the neck, but his foot slams into the man's chest and he goes flying. Kai starts circling around a new opponent in the second fight.

Circle two steals my attention. They're fighting dirty, using weapons, while the clean suits back off. Is one group the radicals and the other the Loyalists?

Then just like last time, the fight ends and Madame yanks on the X girl's arm who trails behind her in perfect sync. Kai leaves with them.

My head vibrates like turbulence in an airplane and I still don't have a clue what triggered Montego. I'm about to follow Kai and the X girl when I notice the man Kai kicked. He's still on the ground. Not moving. *Not breathing.*

My stomach drops. My heart is galloping, like I've had too much coffee. Kai wouldn't kill anyone in real life, would he? He's not that type of guy. He's like Red...right? But the question won't fade. Is this the life Kai really wants? Is this the life I want with him?

A black screen comes on before I know it. My eyes open to the glass domes on the Saint Croix rooftop. The sun is warm on my body now.

The blue sky overhead does nothing to take away the images of Kai killing that man. And for what—an undercover job? It's not possible. Even if the man was like King, Kai wouldn't kill him. I shake my head and try to roll over the details of the scene but there is nothing significant highlighting the Successor.

I need a distraction. Need my gift to wake up. I consider entering phase three of my sims but rule it out for now. I don't need any more action. I need calm. Phase one is my only option. It will distract me. I'm curious, *too curious maybe*, about what I'll find.

"K2, load phase one from last week too, would you?"

"Loading now."

Phase one opens to a distant winter sun. Soft shades of yellow like a field of frosted daises fill my room. I'm at my desk. Rays of light from my bedroom window hit my bed, highlighting the one person who turns my world upside down each time I'm here. My mother, beautiful and alive, sits on my bed. "Hello, Little Seagull."

"Mom!" I don't care I'm in a simulation. I fly from the chair and dive into her arms, burying my face into her shoulder, her scent like roses. Her hair is black and sleek. The petals of her lips blossom into a smile, and she strokes my head, tucking loose strands of hair behind my ears. My heart is ripped from my chest as I hold her tight and don't want to let go. My eyes sting as tears fill to the brim. Foolishly I think I won't feel this way each time I see her, but the grief of missing someone you love never goes away. It just changes form. One minute you're okay, the next, waves of longing to see their face and hold them hit like a tsunami.

I don't talk for fear the sim will end. I don't always get to choose what comes up. Sims are based on memories, recreations of the past, and my thoughts at the moment. It's connected to my synapses. But my mom seems unaware of my grief. And as the sim sinks deeper, I remember why I'm in the room.

"Talking to Mandel again?" she asks.

I blush. It's embarrassing. "How did you know?"

"Well, you talk about him quite a bit, and you're always really happy afterwards."

"Mandel gets me in a way that others don't. We get lost in conversation."

She laughs. "I know. You didn't even hear me when I called you for dinner. That only happens with him."

I turn away. "Can you not tell Dad or Mara? Mara will make fun of me, and I'll be embarrassed if Dad knows."

"You shouldn't be embarrassed to talk to your dad about boys, you know. He gives great relationship advice. Ah, but maybe in a few years, huh?" She sighs and looks out the window. I love how she never rushed. Always in the moment. "How is your friend?"

I look up at her. It's so real, the concern on her face. I want to stare at her forever, talk to her all night. Each time she's in my sims, the real me wants to tell her about China, so she knows, so she can comfort me, but it never comes out. The sims are like dejá vu, like replaying a dream, and the memories are too deep. All I know is that I love her and miss her, and my mouth picks up on a story I already know.

"Mandel's parents treat him really bad, Mom," I say, jogging the past, my heart filling with empathy. "If he fails at anything, he's punished. They show him off like some prize, but they never give him time to himself. They call it family duty. He's not even allowed to do sports. Just school. They say it's for his good but once they locked him in his room until he solved a problem for the National Security Agency. After he came out, they didn't even tell him he'd done a good job."

Mom sighed and squeezed me. "That's terrible. Where does he live?"

"I don't know. Not in our time zone. Maybe London? I wish he didn't have to live with them anymore."

She squeezes me. "I'm sad to hear that. More than anything, kids need to know they're loved and safe. That's what helps them learn and grow. That's what helps you even when you get frustrated with your gift." She rubs my back, as I take his postcard into my hands.

"Mom, how do you know if you love someone?" My face burns red hot. But if you can't ask your mother, who can you ask?

"Ah, sweetheart, there are many types of love and many ways to love. And seasons to learn about love. You'll know more when you're older. For now, just be a good friend."

"Ok. I will. But what do you do *when* you love someone?" My heart feels jumbled. "I want him to be ok..."

Mom smiles at me. "You're doing it now. Love starts by making choices. Love is patient, it protects, it pursues. It gives and lets go. People who love each other also make sacrifices for each other." She hums softly, her hand still circling on my back. "The way you care for people is your greatest strength. You'll figure out what to tell him at the right time." She stands to leave. "Now say goodbye and come down for dinner."

I nod. There's a foggy feeling that I won't see her at dinner, but the mixed reality is too strong. "Thanks, Mom. Be down soon." She's about to leave when that hole in my heart starts aching. "Mom?"

"Yes, Little Seagull?" She turns at the door.

"I love you."

"I love you too, Jo." Mom smiles and leaves the room.

I dive back to my chat with Mandel, scanning our previous messages.

<From sonofaMandelbrot: *I wish I were deaf. I can't take it anymore. The yelling, arguing...the threats—I'm not good enough. I'm disappointing—I need a new sound in my ears...*>

My heart stings almost as much as knowing my mom won't be at dinner later. But the protective side of me rumbles, remembering what my mom said.

<From yougetmydigits: Hey. I'm back, but only for a sec-

ond...What are you doing now?>

<Breathing. Also looking at the tail of a seahorse.>

<What can you see?>

<Swirls of wind in a storm. Steam curling from a teacup. Whirlpools in the ocean currents. Formations in the galaxy...>

A smile spreads on my face.

<My parents don't see it.>

<See what?>

<"That clouds are not spheres, mountains are not cones, coastlines are not circles, and bark is not smooth, nor does lightning travel in a straight line..." >

My face falls. I know that quote well. Mandel repeats it often. It's the opening sentence from Mandelbrot's Fractal Geometry book. In his Chaos Theory he says the natural things of our earth are rarely smooth or straight but hidden inside is a beautiful order. I understand what Mandel is saying. No matter how hard he tries, he'll never be the perfect boy his parents want, and they can't see who he truly is.

<Listen. You're not what your parents say you are. You're going do something great one day, in your own way and time, ok? You're like the lightning. You were never designed to strike in a straight line, but to fractal in beautiful pieces of light across the sky. The lightning still hits the earth, Mandel. > A protective surge burned inside. <So don't let them bully you, ok?>

<I won't, Digits. At the right time, I'm going to run away.>

<Good. When you run away, promise to find me.>

<I'll always find you.>

The Mandelbrot Set Avatar stares at me, daring me to see if that account still exists. Like I *need* to find out if he is still out there. If he's ok. But static clicks in my ear, shaking me from my dreamlike state, and Noble's robotic voice jogs me out of the daze.

"Interrupting something?"

The simulation changes into a computerized blueprint of my room. Ugh. I jump, flying back, suddenly looking around. "What are you doing?"

"Looked serious. Simulations aren't for nerd-dating you know." He jokes. "Something you should tell Kai?"

"Are you in my sims right now?" I ask, slightly horrified.

"Kind of? Sorry. I didn't know you were *working*. I wanted to make sure I could get into the helmet at a moment's notice. Because as you may have guessed, we need to talk. ASAP."

"I thought I told you to call like a normal person?" I stand up, leaning against the Bell Tower.

"I thought I told you normal wasn't my style. Besides, we need to meet. It's urgent."

"Can you see in here?" I ask, my glasses' audio still on.

"Not in the way you think, but yes, in another way. Sorry. I'll leave. I just needed access to give you what I promised."

"About yesterday..." I reach for my arm.

"I know. Go into your room to talk?" he asks me. "It's more secure."

"Sure. Give me five minutes."

"It'll take you six and a half..."

I roll my eyes and start for the stairs.

CHAPTER 33

Qadar's at the door to the stairs. I try to race past him to beat Noble's time but, he's asking me questions, and I also bump into Eddie. By the time I make it inside my room, and put my sim glasses back on, Noble's prediction of six and a half minutes is perfectly accurate. I groan.

Once I sit on my bed, a static buzz clicks in my ear.

"Hey." He's still using the robotic voice.

"No more computerized voice, ok?" I say. "I know the frequency is...I don't know what it is, but I can't talk to a robot anymore."

"That's why I never used my real voice before."

Huh. So Noble knew the frequency would happen between us, even before we met.

The distinct static clicks off. He clears his throat. "But if that's what you want, Jo, I won't use it." His low voice sends shock waves of energy and oscillations down my spine, waking me up like a strong cup of coffee. Maybe I was wrong. Maybe he should turn it back on.

"How's your arm?" he asks.

I rub where Montego squeezed me and nearly implanted a bomb. A purplish bruise has formed. "Sore." I look away.

All it does is remind me that I failed. If it weren't for Noble, it would have been worse. "Thanks for yesterday. We can safely say Dissolve works..."

"Give Dissolve's formula to your team for me." An equation shows up in K2. He's silent for a beat. "I hope you can trust me now."

"Look, I don't know what your plan B was, but I've thought about this all night..." I bite my lip before I speak. "I'm going to bring the holothumb with SMOKE to Kai. But I need your help. You have to tell me where he is so we can arrange a drop-off point..."

"You? No. You're not going to bring it to him. I am. Yesterday was a disaster. You almost got killed. I never calculated the odds of Montego inserting Fingertips. I'm sorry." His voice softens and his frequency does too, a current of warmth over my arms. I rub it away, confused.

"How is Kai?"

"Last time I checked your boyfriend was fine. But he won't be when Montego doesn't show up on Friday. That's in less than 48 hours."

"I want to see him again."

"Then let's meet," he says. "You give me the holothumb, I'll show you Kai. I'll take it to the exchange on Friday. If you really want to help your boyfriend, figure out which of these three men is the Successor."

On the screen, pictures of three men show up with information like a police report.

"I swiped this from Interpol a while back. They think the Successor is one of these. You've already seen the Sheikh in the live stream. But do the others look familiar? Did Madame ever mention their names?"

I study the files: Albert Müller, a successful Swiss banker. Genji Mualim, an ambitious Indonesian Ambassador. And Shiekh Ibrahim bin Aziz, a wealthy landowner of extensive properties in North Africa.

I take a long look. My former math mind memorized faces but nothing stands out. "No. If you brought me to Tunis for information, I'm pretty useless."

"Well, not to be dramatic, but if Kai doesn't give the holo-thumb to the right person, SMOKE won't be merged with the master-file and most likely they won't believe he's a contact of Montego's. I believe there are clues about the Successor in your sims. Working on them is the best thing you can do to help." He pauses. "And I need to know how you communicate with Kai on *the street*. That's the only thing he checks and that's how I can arrange the drop-off of the holothumb."

"Look," I say, "thanks for volunteering to take the holo-thumb, but you know as well as I do that isn't an option."

"What do you mean?"

"You already said I have to go too," I say, finally recognizing the logic. "How many possibilities did you calculate? Of all the solutions, the one that worked had me in it, am I right? That means you knew there was a possibility Montego wouldn't work." He's silent. He knows I'm right. I've calculated the odds on many events, like in China. I knew my plan that included Chan had the highest odds of success, even if it took him a while to come around. "Noble, if the gift you have is like mine, we can trust it, even without seeing proof. It's crazy but I believe it. I'm supposed to come, aren't I?"

He groans. "The plan with Montego was supposed to work. The odds were good." A door closes in the background. I hear traffic and horns and the shuffling of people. He's walking around outside. It makes me wonder what we would have found on him if I'd given them the earring. "The loyalist deal has significantly worse odds now..." He trails off.

"But you predicted whatever chance we have at succeeding includes me. Besides, Kai would do the same for me," I say.

"Regardless of your boyfriend being an idiot, if he were in

my place, would he let you go?" he asks.

Kai is all for adventure. But when it comes to putting me in danger, he is not ok. But I don't say that. It's none of Noble's business. Besides, all I can see is that the next three days are crucial. I can feel it. Helping Kai. Stopping the Loyalists and taking down the Successor. And if I go with Noble, it will give me a chance to understand how to get my gift back. It's now or never. After this trip, I'll be back in Seattle and Noble and I will never see each other again.

"Nothing you say will make me change my mind," I say firmly. "My gift is returning each time I try to use it for something real. Yesterday it almost came back. So you can either help me or I'll go alone."

"You won't get your gift back that way."

"Oh yeah?" I ask. "How do you know?"

He is silent. "Common sense, Jo. Trauma, danger, stress, all those shut a mind down. Only healing and peace open it back up. Danger can make a spark, but it won't light a fire. Go for Kai, for PSS, but don't do this because you want to get your gift back."

I close my eyes. He sounds like Red. Twice now. I think of all the other prodigies down the hall and sink down on my bed, defeated. "Losing my gift is like walking blind..."

He sighs, sympathetically. "Our gift is powerful. I don't envy your loss of it. I promised to help you and I will." The frequency spikes so magnetically between us that the room feels like it's on fire. We don't speak. Surely, he knows how long we're silent, but all I know is the hair on my arms is standing on end and I'm hot and cold and flustered. Until remembering Kai's face in a room full of Loyalists and thugs makes me snap.

"Look, we're running out of time. I need to prepare my team if I'm going to do this."

"Fine. The exchange is happening in Douz, a city called the

Gateway to the Sahara. It's a six-hour drive from here. Albert Müller, one of the possible Successors, is already on his way there. If you're coming, we have to leave soon. Kai needs the holothumb before Albert confronts him. You'd better bring your bodyguard. We may need him."

"What am I going to tell him this time?" I ask.

"Don't worry, I'll take care of him," he says confidently. "You convince Ms. Taylor. I'll call you later. Knock, knock, Jo."

"Huh?" I'm confused by his words until two raps on the door send my heart skipping.

Jealous as an old cat, I hang up the phone. "Come in."

CHAPTER 34

DAR ALZAYTUN
MEDINA, TUNIS

As far as the PSS team knows this is what went down: Montego refused to cooperate so Qadar tased him, and we grabbed the holothumb. End of story.

Noble jammed the video feed after he learned about the Fingertips. Only Goliath, Noble, and I know the truth about what happened at *The Sparkling Star*. Thankfully, PSS was able to Veil news sources afterward too, so anyone watching Montego will think he's still "game on" for the deal.

When Ms. T asked Goliath about the situation, he gave very few details—"Montego refused to cooperate. We needed the holothumb. We took it."

When I thanked him later, all he said was, "My goals are your goals. I was hired to protect you." I can't figure him out.

Ms. T walks in, the team trailing behind her. My long sleeves hide the bruises on my arm.

"How are you feeling?" Ms. T asks.

"I won't lie—it didn't go as planned, but we got what we needed to trace the Blacklist he sold to the radicals." I rub my arms in silence. No one mentions the elephant in the room, so I do. "But now that Montego is in jail, someone has to bring this holothumb to the Loyalist deal in Douz or there could be worse consequences."

"And you think you're the person to do it? Why am I not surprised?" Ms. T asks with a weary look.

In the past, I would have been judging her movements, the direction her eyes flick, the subtleties of her mannerisms. But now I just take her words at face value. She wants the truth no matter what and we'll go from there.

"We have a plan. This time, it should work. He's calculated all the possibilities."

"He? Coral Hacker?" she asks, her hands on her hips. "We're supposed to be exposing his identity, and now you're partnering with him?"

I look out the window at the light brown buildings on the horizon. Several trees dot the landscape. I focus on the leaves and how Noble saved my life yesterday. "I believe he's safe."

"How can you say that?" she asks. "If what you've told us about his surveillance capabilities is true, that means he's illegally hacked into government and other organizations to access those cameras. With what he can do, we can't trust him."

"Eddie, can you open this?" I airdrop the encrypted file for the Dissolve formula to his smart watch. He opens the file and passes it around for everyone to see. Mouths drop. Ms. T, however, doesn't show any expression at all.

"Coral Hacker finished the formula for us. He's a genius," I say, "You specialize in them, remember? Why not give him a shot?"

"For starters, Dissolve is a Blacklist program condemned by the government. Dissolve isn't supposed to exist, and he just completed it." She tightens her lips, but her eyes aren't angry.

"I thought it was blacklisted because no one could get Dissolve to work," I exhale forcibly. There is no point in arguing or trying to convince her of anything. "Look, we only have until Friday when the Loyalist deal is supposed to happen. It's up to us to destroy the master-file. All we have to do is arrange a drop off with the SMOKE holothumb to our guy inside. Trust me."

"Guy inside? So now you have a contact in the Loyalist group too?" She purses her lips. "Jo, I believe in you. I do. But leaving the city again? Your father won't like it. And frankly, even if PSS is in trouble, we are not trained to deal with dangerous criminals. We're polymaths, a thinktank creating solutions. We've got our hands full dealing with the radicals staging a coup here in Tunis. We need to get the authorities involved."

My gift flickers on her movements. It's clear as a polygraph that Ms. T thinks she has to say no to our involvement, not because she believes we can't handle the situation. In fact, I think she believes we *can*. But something is stopping her.

"I'll contact Private Global Forces today." I exhale. To convince her to let me go to Douz is going to require more trust. Red always told me there was a way to do things right. I don't have to go rogue, no matter how much I instinctually feel I should. "We didn't ask for this, but we're not here by accident." I chew on my lip. "Coral Hacker's calculations say there's no other way. I believe him. If there is a way for me to help, I have to do it."

"I won't endanger this team."

"That's why you're staying here. There's a job to finish in Tunis and PSS has to trace the tech. You said they might have stolen four years of files. Douz is our only chance to get SMOKE into the master-file. And I have to do it..." I pause. They have to know why I'm pressing this... "There's more at risk than just shutting down the Loyalists."

"What could possibly be more important?" she asks. Time to come clean. Ms. T's speech about telling the truth and being on my side waves in her eyes like a flag, inviting me in, like my mother's arms. It's enough to make me talk.

"Saving Kai."

CHAPTER 35

My mind floods with a memory of Kai the day before he flew back to Shanghai. He'd spent the whole day in coveralls, covered in oil, fixing my dad's car. I loved watching every minute of it. It's a side of Kai very few people get to see. The boy his father is just now getting acquainted with again.

A smudge of grease was on his face, a satisfied grin on his lips. "Jason, your carburetor is fixed. Feels good to get my hands dirty. What next?"

Dad walked over to him, slapping him on the shoulder. "Don't worry, Kai. I'll have a list of things for you next time. We're remodeling the kitchen. I'll make good use of you." My dad chuckled.

"That's what I like to hear," Kai said. We laughed and talked the rest of the evening.

That night, I'd already fallen asleep, but woke up to the door of my room opening. I almost leaped up, frightened by the unknown intruder, until Kai's familiar scent hit me: A city boy who smells as fresh and woodsy as a mountaintop.

He crept over to me and I reveled in his smile, the one reserved only for me. This is the Kai only I saw.

My stomach flipped as I squinted and sat up. "Kai? What

are you doing? You know my dad's rules." My father would flip if he knew Kai was in my bedroom.

"Eh, his rules are in place for something else. I don't plan on breaking those. I just love watching you sleep." Kai sat down on my bed, his hand moving over my cheek.

I lay back down, my eyes closed, my head resting on his thigh. "You mean because I finally sleep through the night?"

His fingers moved over my lips, then through my hair. "Yeah. That's my job now. Making a world where you can sleep every night like this...Safe....and preferably close to me."

"Do you have to leave in the morning?" I asked, slightly delirious. I snag his hand and pull it close to me.

"If you tell me to stay, I will. I love you, Jo..." The shields of his eyes went down, revealing a pure vulnerability and the deepest part of his heart, where he loves with abandon and holds nothing back.

But I didn't tell him to stay.

Now images from Noble's phone contrast with my memory—Kai sitting with an Arabian Sheikh bluffing his way into danger, to keep his promise to make the world a safer place. I ache thinking about it. Which is why I'm taking this risk to tell PSS.

Ms. T and team silently study me. My gut says I can trust them, but it doesn't stop my heart from hammering.

"Before we left Seattle, I received a phone call regarding Kai, who was also here in Tunisia. I'm restricted from going into too much detail, but Kai doesn't work for his father's company," I explain. Then for the next few minutes I tell my team the bare bones of what Kai does, believing their silence on all things high security will spill over to protect Kai too.

When I finish, Ms. T exhales, her brows softening with concern. Her strength coupled with her empathy only makes me respect her more. "So, he's undercover with the Loyalists right now?"

"Yes, because of me and my past. They believed his cover because he knows everything about Madame, all the details of her take down, things only I would know. Kai claimed he was working with Montego, and he'll be exposed if we don't get the holothumb to him."

Harrison shakes his head. "Kai is a Kung Fu master. He'll be ok."

I glance sideways at him. "Kai's smart and good at what he does but Kung Fu does not protect you from people like this. And Kai's only communication is with me, which is why I'm the only one who can set up a safe drop off."

I expect Ms. T to be upset, instead to her credit, she considers everything seriously. Her posture even relaxes. "Is Kai ok?"

"For now. Coral Hacker saved his life by turning off his biotag's signal. But if I don't bring the holothumb he won't be."

Everything I'm telling her is true and yet more reasons spin through my head. The sim of Kai and the dead man on the ground wars inside me. It bothers me that my numbers couldn't connect the scene when I tried to piece everything together. Kai has always ever been entirely himself with me. But what happens if he goes too far? Noble's words about him being attracted to danger may have some truth and I have to find out what it is.

Kai is the reason we succeeded in China. I couldn't have done it on my own. He shouldn't have to do this by himself either. Kai's strong, but he needs me. My face warms as I remember his last touch, a rough hand brushing the hair away from my cheek, the smile in his eye as we sat in stillness. That was over a month ago—too long, and it may never happen again if I don't help him.

Ms. T narrows her eyes, breathing in and out slowly as she determines her next words. Her self-control is inspiring. "You knew this information before we came to Tunisia...Jo. If you're going to be part of this team, I require full disclosure. We can't accomplish anything if we hide what we know."

"Which is why I'm telling you now about Kai. You said if I tell you the truth, you'd always help me."

"You didn't tell me Coral Hacker would be at the Bardo."

"I had to know what I was dealing with first. I wasn't willing to compromise PSS. The odds of success of Sidi Bou Saïd were high. I thought we could do it." I know I haven't been completely honest, but I'm telling her now. If she isn't satisfied then I'm out of options, no more cards to pull, and my time at PSS is done. She knows I'll go without her permission, but neither of us want that.

Ms. T stands next to me, her hand resting on my arm. "Whether I believe you can do this or not, I made your father a promise to keep you safe. I'm due for a call with him today."

"Don't tell him." I shake my head, a resolve hardening within me. "I can do this. But I also need to work with people who know me and where I've come from. We both know what makes a person is inside, not on paper." Flashbacks of me sprinting into an alley, breaking a bottle over a gangster's head fly by in my mind. Phoenix. That girl wants to come out and play.

Ms. T looks away, like reliving an old memory.

"I see you," I say. "Even without my gift. You've overcome more than just rescuing prodigies and creating PSS. That's why I'm here. That's also why we're in Tunisia. It's why I believe you'll help me..."

"Nice speech." She folds her arms across her chest and sits on the arm of her chair next to me. "There's still one issue. You heading into the desert with the hacker. I don't know enough about him."

Three days in the desert with Noble and the frequency bouncing between us... Even the thought of it has my mind thrumming. There's got to be a logical mathematical explanation for it. He won't look at me when we both feel it, and he obviously prefers to use his robotic voice, which doesn't trigger the sound waves between us. I sense there's more to it—*more to him*. I need to know. But Ms. T needs to know more too if she's going to let me go with him.

My earring.

My gift simmers like a volcano preparing to erupt. "If Coral Hacker helps me, I could learn who the Successor is before the deal. If we can stop the Loyalists, we have to try."

To my surprise, Eddie pipes in. "Our Blacklist tech has already caused damage, Ma'am. PSS started this. We have to finish it. If it's just to drop the holothumb, I think Jo should go. I also think we should help her. And I've got connections in Indonesia. I'll ask around about the Indonesian Ambassador."

Pens jumps in too. "At Harvard I knew some of the top bankers in the world. I'll dig into Albert Müller."

"If Jo keeps K2's com-line open we can track her movements and we can assist her from Tunis." Harrison waves his phone, already pulling up a map. "Should be easy enough. It's a small oasis town with little activity in the Sahara Desert. We can get full surveillance of the location."

Felicia's nodding. "Her bodyguard can go too. He knows his way around the country, and he can partner with the local authorities if necessary." Felicia bites her lip. "Ms. T, you know we're prepared for this, and honestly, we're the only ones who can stop our tech from spreading."

Ms. T nods solemnly. "There's no denying we have to do our part to stop this. But true success comes from teamwork. Calling Kai's agency is a must. I'll also contact a few people. But I will only agree to this plan on two conditions." She looks me in the eye.

"Which are?"

"You get more information on Coral Hacker. His fingerprints, his identity, his real name. Once I know enough to be satisfied that he is not a threat, I'll let you go."

"He'll never agree to that."

"Then I'm sorry," she says.

A pain hits me hard in the gut as I pull out my earring. The smartdust is my last card but it feels so wrong. Even worse than telling Ms. T about Kai. As I roll it between my fingers, the sense of duplicity in my soul thickens.

I place the tiny earring filled with nano-tech in her outstretched hand. "I have a way to do that. The smart dust is on his phone. With its Bluetooth-tech, you should be able to hack into his device and find out all you need." Turning in Noble feels like I'm betraying Phoenix. It makes me feel sick. I know what it's like to want to be hidden until the right time, and I'm taking that away from Noble. But I need to do this for Kai.

Ms. T nods solemnly. She's not enjoying this either. She's keeping her team safe. "All right," she says. "If you promise that all you will do is drop off the holothumb to Kai and go nowhere near the Successor, you may go."

"That's the plan," I say. Low odds of success float around me like specks of dust in the air with nowhere to land. Noble said the plan was riskier than the one with Montego, which I failed. I also have no idea who the Successor is. But I ignore all my doubts, and stand.

"So let's call Qadar and brief him?" I say.

"Not just yet. We have to get you ready." She motions to Eddie and Pens, who run off to grab something.

"I thought I was ready?"

"We're a bit more equipped than you think," Ms. T says. Pens returns with tech I've only seen in PSS files. Ms. T hands Pens the Dissolve envelope, then turns to me. "We won't let you go into this situation unprotected. We created these tools for a reason. And now we're going to use them."

Eddie struts in, a proud grin on his face. "My day has come. Finally, my tech will be used by the good guys."

CHAPTER 36

I'm not a fan of needles but pain has grown easy for me to ignore. My hands are on the table palms up. "Technically, this is illegal, right?"

"Operation Blacklist here we come." Harrison winks, singing an old nineties tune. "It's the end of the world as we know it...and Jo feels fine."

Felicia shoves Harrison. He's enjoying this. He has watched far too many spy movies.

Pens takes a small needle. "This will just hurt a bit. Don't flinch." She holds out a needle and pricks each fingertip.

"I thought Ms. T was kidding when she said I'd get *Fingertips.*"

Pens shakes her head. "Well, we still have the prototype. At your request, we weakened the formula, so the bombs won't be fatal or blast you a hundred feet away. It'll still be effective, so be careful." She takes a cotton swap to sterilize the small pricks in my fingertips and wipes away the blood. "The Fingertip bombs are a mixture of chemicals in miniature liquid gel caps easily inserted into your fingertips. The chemicals in your right hand must mix with the chemicals in the left. After the combination hits oxygen, it will render an explosion. Like this. I've made a low dose to demonstrate."

Pens takes a Q-tip and dips one into an airtight vial. She dips a second one into a different vial. After she takes them out, she makes an X crossing the two chemicals at the bottom of a garbage can. "Now it has ten seconds to react to the oxygen."

After counting down to one, a mini cloud of dust and sparks pop with a loud bang. The garbage can is smoking and there is a tiny hole burned through at the bottom of it the size of my fist.

"They can remain inactive in your body for up to a year. When you want to detonate them, all you need is a small abrasion or cut for the liquid to transfer from your fingertips onto the target, mix them, then run like you mean it."

"Great, so now I have five bombs in my fingertips." My stomach knots. "Is wiggling my fingers ok?"

"Yes." She pats my shoulder. "Think of them like insurance. You don't have to use them."

That's probably what Montego was thinking and look where it got him. Of course, I don't say that out loud.

Pens checks my earrings and my smartwatch, and then sprays something into my mouth. "There you go. That should do it. A 72-hour dose of Sway's resistance, just in case." She hands me a lipstick container.

I shake my head. "I told you. I won't kiss anyone for information."

"Precautionary only. You never know. Remember, SWAY is used to calm someone, to open them up to suggestion without them remembering anything. Take the tech."

"Well, you might as well put *Veil* into my watch."

"I already did. K2 can Veil any narrative you wish."

Ms. T walks over. "Don't forget these," she says, handing me my sim-glasses. "Even now, your mind is working out who the Successor is. The simulations were designed to tap into all of the memories you have stored in your brain, but they're also meant to solve problems you didn't know you had. Subconsciously, your mind is connecting information you're not fully aware of yet. Any free moment you have, do your sims."

Qadar walks in. "The car is ready."

"Be right there." I walk over to Harrison, who is running diagnostics on my earring's smartdust.

Leaning over, I whisper. "Whatever you find on Coral Hacker, I need you to tell me first."

He gives me a strange look. "Why?"

"Please, Harrison. This is personal."

His jaw tightens, but he nods. "Deal."

CHAPTER 37

RUE DE LA KASBAH
SOUK OF MEDINA, TUNIS

Calling Agent Bai was a bad idea.

"You're in Tunisia? *Guaibude.* I should have known." He clears his throat. "Then Montego's arrest was your fault." He rips into me about PSS botching their lead on Montego and the radicals, and how they were forced to reevaluate their operation.

"You don't understand. The Successor is equipping the Loyalists for much bigger plans than Montego and the elections." I give him all I can—information on the master-file, where Kai is, and even the names of the three possible Successors. "Can't you do something?"

"Kai left his mission, missed his check in. There's nothing we can do until his biotag pops up." Bai sighs, muttering in Chinese. "And these individuals have no criminal background. Without direct confessions, we can't bring them in for questioning on a hacker's word." His voice gets a bit louder. "Which is another thing—partnering with a hacker who broke into PSS and dismantled a government-issued biotag? I thought you were smarter than that! The guy's hacking government satellites! You're dealing with someone much more dangerous than you think, *Xiao Feng Huang*."

Satellites. Noble's words race though my mind. *"It's all written in the stars, Jo."* Stars are not satellites, but they're close.

"Just dig into those names a bit more and get back to me. Kai may need our help. I'll be in touch."

"If you talk to Kai before us, tell him *there are sandstorms in the north.* And I advise you to sit this one out. Let us take care of it."

I'm in a bad mood when I get in the car with Qadar. Bai didn't like our plan. Didn't even thank me for the intel. But since he's hands-off until we have confessions, there's nothing he can do to stop us.

On the drive to pick up Noble, I ask K2 to pull up what he can find about the NASA Tipper. One piece of information is interesting. Over the last year, accurate, anonymous tips have been given to countless researchers, not just at NASA, but Space X, Tesla, the Pentagon. But NASA has definitely received more information than any other group.

The NASA Tipper has provided new star charts and innovative ideas for Star Coding, along with breakthroughs in spacecraft and satellite technology, harnessing planetary energy, and measuring vibrations, sound waves, and frequencies in the stars.

In terms of astrophysics, it's cutting-edge research and technology. The tipper provides formulas without asking for any credit. I briefly look into the math required to do something as ostentatious as Star Coding and even I can hardly understand it. Either the NASA Tipper is a genius, who is ahead of his time, or he's as mad as a hatter.

The souk is a collage of color and motion. Qadar opens his window and a warm breeze rushes in carrying smells of oil frying, lamb roasting, and chickpeas boiling. All of this equates to one thing, lunch is almost ready.

My stomach jumbles up in knots when I see Noble waiting exactly where he said he would be.

"That's him," I say to Qadar. Noble is so good at hiding in the shadows he seems almost invisible as he leans against a spice stand in the corner of the market.

He's dressed in dark jeans and a white V-neck and sunglasses. My fingers start tapping at my side and that familiar buzz shoots down my spine. I'm very aware of the risk I'm taking, and my gift flickers.

He's removing his sunglasses, about to look at me in 3...2...1 Our eyes meet, and my numbers pulse, three times more projecting a numerical definition to the market streets.

The number of beautifully crafted mirrors for sale on the corner—29. Artisan rugs—6 unrolled. My mind counts everything—traditional hats hanging on racks, bronze plates in stacks, long dresses on mannequins. The distance between Noble and me. The exact symmetry of his smile. Then nothing...my view of the souk returns to normal. Like a gust of wind, come and gone.

Apart from a small plastic bag of street food, Noble carries nothing with him. Not even a jacket. It makes me wonder where his tech is.

"*Aslema. Labas,*" Qadar greets Noble.

"*Labas,*" Noble replies. For someone who is so serious and secretive, it seems bizarre he's ok with Qadar driving us. Is it because he is a local? I should be asking more questions about them both. Instead, I keep quiet and watch.

Qadar opens the side door of the van and then leans over to me.

"Same boy at the museum, I see." He's not tense at all like he was at the Sparkling Star Palace.

Huh. Maybe that explains his passivity. I hadn't known he'd caught sight of Noble. He's better than I thought at this job. Or my dad paid him a lot extra to keep quiet.

Noble slides into the van and hands me a food container and a paper to-go cup of mint tea that wafts a fresh and tasty scent all over the van.

"I brought you lunch."

I open the container to a baguette stuffed with vegetables, a small fried pastry reminiscent of an egg roll and a salad of grilled peppers garnished with tuna and olive oil. It smells spicy and delicious, but I have no idea what I'm looking at.

He notices. "Tunisian street food. That's *Brik a l'oeuf*— careful the yolk is runny." He points to the sandwich. "That is *keftaji*," he says, sipping his tea. "And this is *salata Mechouia*. Watch out, it's spicy."

"Thanks. I can handle a little spice." I fold back the box. Can't be hotter than what Kai and I eat at our favorite Sichuan restaurant, which reminds me. "All right. You promised to show me Kai."

He hands me the phone and bites into his *brik a l'oeuf.*

The live stream is already playing. My heart stops for a beat. Kai is in a fight. He bobs and weaves as a heavy-set man lays into him raining down punches. But the details sink in and I realize it's just Kai sparring. I relax and watch what I've watched many times before. Kai's sparring partner is North African, from what I can tell. He's well-built and a good fighter. Kai's focused, but he's enjoying the match. His shirt is off and sweat glistens his upper body, defining every muscle tightened to brawl. The same group of girls sit around watching the two men. The fight ends and Kai moves to grab a drink of water. The same girl from the last video waits until the Sheikh is talking to three other men, then wanders over to Kai.

She holds up a towel. "You're not like the other men here. I can tell," she says. "You're stronger than them." She lowers her voice closing the space between them. "Even the

Sheikh." The girl slightly bites her lower lip. "And I'm not just talking about muscles."

Ugh. My skin crawls watching her come on to Kai. The way X girls were taught to move just like Madame makes me furious. I grind my teeth. That's why the Loyalists need to be completely destroyed.

Kai gauges her and wipes his brow. "If you're not strong in this world, you get destroyed." He acts so calm, so natural, like he's two different people. "For what I want to do, I must be strong. Some call it reckless. I call it ambitious."

She laughs, in a raspy cute way. "If you're so ambitious then you won't have any trouble with Albert Müller."

"What do you mean?" he asks.

"He arrives tomorrow night and you weren't on the party list. You'll have to prove your *ambitions* and your loyalty if you want to be part of us."

"*Tai hao le.*" Kai laughs in his arrogantly, charming way. "Finally, a challenge."

"You sound like Madame."

"You met her?" Kai asks.

"Only once. I was too scared to look at her. Her voice was cold, but she told me something I won't forget. That I had nine lives like a cat. Then she gave me this." She shows Kai a small burn on her wrist in the shape of the number nine. She shrugs. "After she was caught, I got out. But I've always hoped the part about the nine lives was true." She looks at him hopefully.

Kai breathes in, listening to her words carefully. The girl might not see it, but he's biting back anger, like I am now, reaching for my own scar, hating that Madame hurt so many people.

Kai rests a hand on her shoulder. "There's still a chance to live all nine lives with someone who cares for you."

Kai slips on a t-shirt and walks away to join the Sheikh,

leaving the girl breathless, a flushed and hopeless look on her face. It's not her fault, I tell myself. Kai is hard to resist, especially the way he fights for people. Still, the way she moves her body bothers me, and the way she obviously wants Kai makes me wonder about this new occupation of his and who else he'll meet along the way.

Noble leans in. "Don't worry. The girl is with the Sheikh," Noble says. "He owns an entire town farther out in the desert—hotels, parties and gambling. He's got everything he could ever want in that little town." The girl joins the Sheikh, slipping her arms around his elbow when he announces. "Come now, everyone," he says, "The night awaits us in this paradise. We have much to plan for."

"What's he planning?" I ask Noble, a bad feeling causes my chest to constrict, but no numbers flicker.

"Don't know. But my numbers say he's eager to test Eddie's *Radar*—the tech that can hack into any Internet Service Provider to track and terminate whichever connection he chooses. Even whole towns. If he wants to take out his competition, this is the perfect way to do it."

"So they're all iron-fisted and bonkers, huh?" I say. Noble nods, his eyebrows wrinkled in thought as he takes another bite of brik. "Do you think he's the Successor?"

"Not sure yet." He chews slowly, finishing it before starting on his salata. "Any clarity from your sims? Any clues?"

"Not yet. Just things we already know. I can't see how Montego and what I've experienced in the sim are connected yet."

"Small details matter the most." His brown eyes study mine. "I think you should do it again. You're missing something."

"Fine, but after lunch." I dig into my first *brik a l'oeuf,* inhaling the pastry as I mumble thanks.

After I finish eating, I decide to make use of the long driving time by reclining in the far back seat of the van to do my sims. I put on my sim glasses. "K2, load *Monday's* sims, all three phases in order—no process time." If I'm going to get it right, I need to recreate it.

Smells hit me first. Salt air. Fresh cut grass. Fresh laundry.

The van's rhythm speeding down the highway mixes with the dream-like quality of my sim glasses, pulling me instantly inside my imagined reality.

A bright summer day warms my face. Rays of sun highlight my desk, a glare reflecting on my computer screen. I pull the computer over to my bed, not surprised that my old blog is up, and Mandel's messages are streaming through. The Mandelbrot postcard sits on my desk. I'm aware—in part—that I've been here before. And my mind is piecing the puzzle together. It's pointing to Mandel. Which is confusing to me. Because each time I'm here, the part of me that knew him, wants to find him. Wants to know him. But it's not fair to Kai. And it's certainly not good timing. I move forward, knowing that I'm doing this to jumpstart my gift. And phase one is as important as any of them.

Dipping into our messages once more, I read a confession. This time, my own.

<I'm considering a PhD when this Master's is over. What do you think, will you get one?>

<Probably not. There's more than one-way to solve a mystery and it's not always in books and schools.>

<Well I have too many mysteries inside me and I don't know what to do with them...I've never told anyone this, but sometimes I see infinity around me, looping, like it's trying to tell me something. I just don't know what it is...>

<Fractals are just another way of seeing infinity, and they're all around us too, speaking all the time. When life is spinning out of control, we're meant to look up and see a thumbprint in the stars or a pattern in the trees and order in the ocean's waves. It's a reminder of who we are and what we're part of.>

<Mandel?>

<Yeah, Digits?>

<You're a mystery.>

<One day I won't be.>

Sim one fades to black, and I'm thrown into phase two.

Before I open my eyes, I know something is wrong. There is no wind tonight. My back is not against a cold brick wall. My eyes snap open. I'm on the other side of town, an area of Shanghai I know well. But it dawns on me. Why is this different? It should be the same as Monday's simulation. But I'm miles from where I should be.

Shoving my hand into my pocket, I find a crumpled assignment. I pull it out and unfold it, smoothing the paper. *Assignment: You're meeting someone. Find them.*

My whole body shivers. I hesitate. I should exit. Reload the sim from Monday. I need to study the fight. Find out who the Successor is. Small details matter. But I don't. Because a small snack shop across the street catches my eye and makes my heart skip.

I've spent hours in that café with Kai drinking tea and eating *xiao chi.*

And he's sitting there now, alone at our favorite table.

Find them.

It's Monday. Kai should be in the square, but he's not. He's waiting for me at the café. He must be. He never meets anyone there but me. I jolt forward to meet him, when I realize it's too easy. The sim never makes my assignment so simple.

Kai must not be who I'm supposed to meet. But I don't care. I run toward him. I want to talk with him. See him. Touch him. Ask him everything, even if it's in a sim. Just like seeing my mom in the sims, it's something.

The sim takes over as I jog across the street. Now I know for sure it's not Kai I'm supposed to find because the sim is pushing against my decision, and making everything difficult, which means answers lie in a different direction. Ms. T says this when I'm fighting against my own mind. I have to follow the assignment. But I can't. Kai is sitting there, waiting for me. He's checking his watch. Playing with chopsticks. I can even smell the garlic and soy sauce in the air.

At the door, I push but it doesn't budge, like it's glued shut. I push harder though I know the sim is fighting me. The doors open, and my feet are stuck to the floor. I'm determined to get to the table. As soon as I come close, Kai looks at his watch once more, and then leaves through the back door to the alley.

"Kai! I'm here!" I shout out to him. But it's too late. He's running. I chase after him. He's heading in the direction of the square where the fight happens.

"Kai!" I scream again. He doesn't hear me. My feet pound harder, faster into the pavement. But no matter how fast I go, I can't catch up.

Numbers flash out at me, telling me my speed, but I don't care because I can't match Kai's speed. The numbers vanish. In previous sims, I'd know I was off course. I'd reevaluate my assignment. But here I don't.

I arrive at the square and remnants of a fight are everywhere. Surely, everyone was here. But it's over now. Kai's gone. I'm too late. Madame and the Successors are nowhere in sight.

I don't know how much time I have left. Minutes. Seconds. My gift isn't coming back. So I keep running, not paying much attention to anything. I failed my assignment. But the blood racing through my body feels good. That's all I want to feel, the pumping of my heart to make me forget. I head to the river, and follow it as far as I can, knowing my sim will fade out at any moment.

At the end of the line, I see a man stooped over the handrail, gazing at the night sky. His hands, old and familiar, wrap around the rails. My breath catches in my throat.

I walk, my face leaning in to see the man. My hand covers my mouth as I gasp.

"Red?"

Loud rotor blades pump overhead. *Whoosh. Whoosh. Whoosh.* My hands vibrate against a set of control levers, sweat already beading against my palms. I'd forgotten phase three would be the helicopter. This time, I'll study the coastlines. This time, I'll fly.

A gush of warm air and a rush of freedom resound through me as my eyes open to a black sky. I'm in the middle of nowhere. Usually, if you fly at night you need at least 30 minutes for the rods in your eyes to adjust to the dark. If not, it could be disastrous, like flying blind. Not to mention bad weather conditions.

Thick clouds swirl around me. There's a light drizzle on the windshield. No horizon in sight. Far from ideal. And my plan to study the coastline is defeated.

The program is too smart. It's designed to challenge me. Night challenges have always been the worst. I think back to the time they made me surf at night. I couldn't concentrate. All I focused on were my legs dangling off my board in the inky water and what was under me. The waves were methodical enough, but it was too much. I panicked. It took one wave to knock me down and steal my breath. I was too far out, lost my board and couldn't swim back.

Likewise, now, I'm too high up, with a storm brewing and nothing to stabilize me.

Do I pull out? But I can't. I don't want to give up.

The gauges display all the information I need. I fly, knowing something will go wrong.

My mind settles into a rhythm and tries to locate any pattern at all. But the night gets worse. A cold front is hitting the summer air, and lightning starts to crack in the sky. Why did they ever put me into these simulations? The smart thing to do is land. Get out of the storm. But as the storm worsens, so does my visual.

Lightning bolts stretch across the sky and my mind shifts to panic. All of a sudden I'm convinced I'm upside down.

Spatial disorientation. A leading fatality in helicopter accidents. It's the only explanation for my confusion. I check all the gauges. They're on track. But my mind whips right and left and all I see is fog, clouds and darkness. Thunder shakes through me and steals the last faculty I have. My eyes race around, searching for any focal point.

Wake up! I need my gift to calculate the space around me. I don't want to trust the gauges—I want to trust my gift. Lightning strikes downward in front of me. I fly away from it, but the more I move in any direction, the more up is down and down is up.

Spatial disorientation, my mind warns me again. But my body is turning inside me. The gauges are wrong. They must be. It says I'm flying downward. But I'm not. I'm too high.

The lightning cracks again and I can't figure it out. The rotor blades are too loud, and the lightning is too bright, I'm about to rip off my helmet when Noble's voice is in my sims. And a surreal feeling that his hand is on my leg. I look down but nothing is there.

"Trust your gauges and pull up."

"They're wrong."

"They can't both be broken. Pull up."

His voice stabilizes me. The frequency. It's even in the sim now. How is this happening? Then I remember. We're in the same van.

"Focus on the lightning—don't look away from it." His voice instructs. "The patterns of it striking. What do you see?"

Even though my whole body says it's wrong, I pull up, because he's better than the gauge.

When the jagged light shoots downward. I know I'm right side up. Another brilliant flash and the crooked lines write themselves in my mind. The strangest thing happens. In the next flash, I don't see lightning, but a river breaking into tributaries on a topical map; then tree branches stretched out in all directions. Peace floods my body, the numbers a gentle pulse, and even the rhythm of the rotor blade above me is a simple calculation. I hear nothing now but a still night.

"It's beautiful..."

Noble is gone. No more voice or frequency. I fly into the lightning. I don't even care if it strikes me. My gift is on. Slowly, the storm fades and the clouds part over the dark shimmering water with a revelation.

I beat the simulation.

Everything goes black.

Noble leans over the middle seat, his eyes on me. My chest tightens and our eyes lock in a raw, beautiful way because he's sharing in this small victory.

"How'd you know about the lightning?" I ask.

"Clouds are not spheres, mountains are not cones, coastlines are not circles, bark is not smooth, nor does lightning travel

in a straight line." The quote slides off his tongue so easily, I
know it all too well and it hits my ears like thunder.

I jolt forward. "What?" I ask, my stomach flipping. "Why
did you say that?"

"Did I say something wrong?" He looks confused, trying
to make out what upset me. "Like I said before, designs make
patterns, and patterns makes equations. I thought you'd get the
reference since you carry a Mandelbrot postcard with you and
almost every prodigy from here to India knows that quote."

I huff an awkward laugh and tuck my hair behind my ears.
"Right. Yeah, I got the reference." My cheeks heat so I peer
out the window to hide them. "Thanks for the help."

A car horn honks outside, clearing the air and bringing
back reality. I shake off his comment and the fact that for a
split second I thought Noble might be connected to Mandel
somehow, but there is no way that could be true. Mandel
was my friend and would never hide his identity from me. He
wasn't a hacker, either. Besides, Noble had brushed off my sim
with Mandel as *nerd-dating*. Wow. No process time between
sims really messes me up. But he's still staring at me like he's
waiting for something.

"What?" I ask.

"Did you learn anything?" he asks, and I remember—phase
two. Friday. The Successor.

"No. This sim was different," I say, trying to piece it together.
"It wasn't the same as Monday. My sims are malfunctioning."

He considers that for a moment. "I don't think it's malfunc-
tioning. I think your reality is overpowering your memories.
I've looked into how PSS designed it, and your sims are created
for this purpose. To give you what you need at the right time.
Eventually, you won't need them at all. It's part of the process.
So nothing new?"

"I ran to the fight and everyone was gone." I don't tell him
about Kai in the restaurant or that Red was there.

Noble is calculating me. "Hate to do this. But you need to do it again. My numbers are going crazy. Everything we need is locked up in there..." He softly taps my temple and I squirm at the way my skin tingles at his touch.

"What I need is my gift back." I mutter, not meaning to snap. I must be tired. "I'll do them tonight when we're out of the car."

"OK. I made an update of sorts. When you do phase three again, don't choose Monday. Let it be automatic. Hopefully, it'll help your gift." He breathes in and his hands fold nervously in his lap. "And...I can also come in with you in person, if you want."

I pause. "What? Do you mean into the sims, not just with audio?"

"Right. I'd be there with you. You'd be able to see me."

"How is that possible?" I look at him, marveling at his ability, but also incredibly taken aback on his offer. Why is he doing this? A thousand questions fly through me. Phoenix would be so suspicious of him. But I'm not. It's the coral. It's the lightning.

He holds up a tiny piece of micro-tech. "With this. It's a neural simulator that can connect to your sims. You attach it behind your ear. It's how I popped into your sims that day on the roof. It's a bit disorientating, but if you think it'd help with your gift, I'll come in." His eyes melt into mine and for a second, I look at him in a new way. Not as a hacker, but a boy who I know nothing about. Whose life is a complete mystery to me. An enigma. An equation I'd like to solve.

A small part of me is curious about what it would be like to have him join me in my sims. He could help me with my gift. He could help me find the answers I'm seeking. But if I'm honest, I'm curious about more than finding my gift. I want to know who he is and why this frequency bouncing between us.

Then all too soon, I'm smiling at the freckles on his nose and our eyes meet, and like an invisible line is about to be crossed, he's moving closer, not physically, but emotionally and...it scares me.

I break our gaze and look out the window.

"I'll be fine alone," I say. "Thanks, anyway."

Noble feels the rejection and takes it as his cue to turn back around. In Arabic, he converses with Qadar until they're laughing like old friends. Qadar's body language is relaxed, comfortable. My years of studying people come into play quickly. Is it because they're both from a common culture or...no, it's much more familiar...My gift flickers at their use of language and their mannerisms. It couldn't be. But everything in me says I'm right. I don't speak Arabic, but these are old jokes between two very close people.

They know each other well. How could I have missed it in Sidi Bou Saïd? Qadar didn't come inside the National Bardo Museum to look for me because he knew who I was meeting...the Arabic phrase book on the bed in Dar Alzaytun—Qadar must have placed it there for Noble when he first inspected my room.

I shake my head. This trip is giving me far more answers than I thought. Thankfully, these are not the first men with secrets I've had to deal with.

Their conversation in Arabic entrances me. I imagine their words like a story opening from the wrong side of the book, moving from right to left on the page—opposite of how I learned to read. The phrase book Noble gave me is in my backpack. He said it'd help me see life in a new way, and I understand that. Learning Chinese, or Arabic, is like breaking out of a box you never knew you were in. It takes focus, curiosity, and courage to think and speak differently, but eventually, new pathways form in your mind, and you start to see and hear a world you never knew was there.

The melody of their discussion lulls me to sleep but not before syllables, tones, and sounds are imprinted in my mind, bringing color to areas I never knew were dull.

When I wake, it's dusk. The busy streets and tramlines of Tunis are long gone. We're on a highway in the middle of nowhere and the land has grown dry, brown, and sandy. We pass a 'camel crossing' sign, and random cars are set up on the side of road selling stuff.

"We're in the Sahara now. Past the Jebil National Park." Noble's frequency rolls over me like small waves in a gently rocking boat. He gives me a shy grin. "Almost there."

We drive through a small town where olive and palm trees cluster around the shops with brightly colored signs and crates full of dates stacked outside them. Large awnings extend from stone houses and trucks rumble past us until we are back in the desert outskirts.

The sky darkens and we keep getting further from town. A billion stars twinkle in the sky, and the moon seems ten times brighter here.

"Where are we going?" I ask, my stomach growling. "I thought we were staying at some touristy place?"

"We are. We're setting up our surveillance in a tent." Noble smiles mischievously.

"Tent? Like camping?" I ask, very confused.

He hands me a brochure with two camels on it, and grins. "Not exactly."

CHAPTER 38

DOUZ, THE GATEWAY OF THE SAHARA
SAHARA DESERT, TUNISIA

Welcome to the Tunisian Sahara, Saddle up and enjoy the Dunes Bedouin-style! The brochure states. Inside there are pictures of several large and luxurious nomadic tents.

"So we're glamping in the Sahara?" My head snaps over to Qadar. "What's going on?"

He keeps his eyes on the road. "You'll see."

We park the van and waves of dunes surrounded by hundreds of palms trees create a beautiful oasis in the desert. I grab my bag and follow Qadar and Noble. We walk on a dusty path through the desert and reach a sign that says, *Oasis Bedouin Dream, Maghreb Style Glamping in the Tunisian Sahara.*

But once I walk through the wall of trees, paradise hits me. These are not like any simple camping tents I've seen. Sophisticated and lush white canvas like small castles spread out in a very specific formation, creating a circular camp around beautiful stone patios with a sparkling blue pool.

Café chairs and patio recliners line the courtyard. Thick

palm trees covered in lights dazzle me.

A group of kids run out and circle Noble jumping all over him.

"Aslema!" they yell, chattering on in Arabic. One kicks a ball to Noble and he kicks it back, tickling them.

"Tourist lodging, huh?" My lips curl to one side.

He smiles and hands me his phone. "I'll explain after your call. Your phone's dead, I rerouted the call to mine. Sorry. It comes with the gift..."

"What call?" His phone rings, and I look down, recognizing the number immediately. *Right.* "Hi, Dad," I say, picking up.

Noble navigates confidently into the maze of tents, heading toward a large elaborate tent in the middle of them all. The canvas is pinned open displaying beautiful diamond patterned carpets, hanging lamps and colorfully decorated tables.

"Hi, honey," my dad says eagerly, an edge to his voice. "How are you?"

"I'm fine. You wouldn't believe this but we're actually *glamping* in the Sahara right now." I set my bag down and wander over to the tree line where an animal is making a strange sound, like a child crying.

He sighs with relief. "Wow, from museums with 3000-year-old relics to desert glamping. No scorpions, I hope?" A nervous chuckle.

"Not yet." I discover the noise is from a herd of camels, tied up to a stall. A pungent scent of dung nearly makes me gag. "Lots of camels though." I plug my nose and wander back to the courtyard. I step onto a beautiful brick lanai lining the crystal-clear pool. Potted jasmine with small blooming white flowers and a sweet fragrance decorates the pool area, which is surrounded by Arabian date palm trees. It's paradise in the middle of miles of dunes. I could stay here all year.

"Sounds fun. I've always been curious about those *cara-*

vans in the desert, I mean, what else is there to look at besides the dunes?"

I'm about to tell him about the pool and the palms when Noble walks out, a glimmer of the setting sun on his bare chest. Wait, bare chest? Why is he only wearing shorts? Is he going—a splash of water sprinkles the patio after he jumps into the pool. The kids from earlier run and scream after him. A full-on splash attack of water and laughter ensues.

"Um," I say, distracted, watching him swim, his lean arms gliding through the water, a huge smile on his face and laugher spilling from his mouth. He looks so happy, so at home.

"Jo?" my dad says.

"Yeah, lots to look at—um—it's really good looking out here." I smack my face with my hand. "I mean, it's exotic and it's a desert. And there are palm trees. And rocks." My fingers pinch my forehead. Get a grip. "Like you said. Sand and sky." I look up. Hmm. Not a lot of light pollution. A good place to study the stars...

"Well, I'm not going to lie, Jo," he says, "Sounds fun. I'm happy to hear that you're safe. Are you guys getting any work done?"

"We have some down time," I say, my lips bunching together. "Can't do much until tomorrow and Friday. Today is prep time." That sobers me a bit.

"What are you up to these days?" I ask.

"You remember those Kung Fu exercises Kai set me up with months ago? Well, I finally started practicing a few. Things are changing, Jo. I feel stronger, like this trip was meant to happen for both of us."

"That's great, Dad."

"I'm glad you're getting your wish to travel and see the world. We still need to do our call tomorrow and Friday, ok?" he says. "Take some pics! Send them my way."

"Sure, Dad," I say. Noble catches my eyes from the pool and

smiles. Embarrassed I'm still staring, I wave and turn away. "Hey, can you put Mara on for a minute?"

"Sure. Talk tomorrow, honey."

A second later Mara's voice comes on. "Sis?" she says. "How's everything?"

"Friday will tell us more. I just needed to hear your voice. My head is too full."

"With the job?"

"And other things. Or boys if I'm honest." I glance at Noble swimming. "Do you remember that boy from my blog?"

"How could I forget? I teased you endlessly about him. You know it was because I was jealous, right? I wished I had a connection like that with someone. Sorry."

"Thanks...I understand," I say. "But the problem is he keeps coming up in my sims now. To make things worse, there's another boy here who I shouldn't be thinking about. And Kai is gone, and I'm really confused."

"Wow. You should really talk to Dad. He's way better with relationship advice."

I stop walking. "That's what Mom said," I mutter.

Qadar makes his way over to me.

"Hey. My bodyguard is here. I gotta go."

"All right, but remember, Jo, you learned to trust your heart in China. You can figure this out too."

We hang up and Qadar reaches down to pick up my bag. "Let me take you to your room."

I pull back the white canvas doors, and my eyes widen. I breathe in jasmine everywhere. Lamp light glows around the tent revealing beautiful woven rugs and tapestries. Lush square and cylinder silk pillows. Ornate wooden tables with mosaic designs carved into them, laden with dates and fruit and teapots.

Colorful drapes separate a large bed from the rest of the room. Vibrant striped pillows are arranged on the floor. Beside it is a bathroom with a fancy copper glass basin for a sink and a beautiful standing bath with copper claw feet. I locate the fragrance—a small vase of jasmine flowers sweetening the air like honey. My first stay in a desert, and I'm not sure anything could ever top it.

"This tent is yours for the next two nights." He points to an adjoining door. "Once again, I'm in the next room. Noble is in the other. You're surrounded by trustworthy people here. You're safe. Your goals—"

"Are my goals. I know." I set my stuff and Noble's phone on the bed.

"Come with me." He leads me into another tent full of people, and we take a low table in the back of the tent, lounging on the pillows scattered on the rug.

"Please." A woman with a gentle face, dressed in beautifully embroidered clothes, sets down three hot cups of tea in front of us. A strong mint aroma swirls in the room joining with an apple-flavored smoke. "*Bishfa.*"

I sip the hot liquid and savor its sweetness. Wafts of spices and meat being cooked make my stomach rumble.

Noble, hair wet, but fully dressed now comes in and sits at the far end of table. It's not surprising he takes the seat farthest from me. The moments where he avoids my eyes make it clear something about me unsettles him, but still there are other moments, like in the car, that feel like we've known each other for years.

"*Aslema.*" Men come in shaking hands, then place their right hand over their hearts, while women come in greeting with kisses. They all stand to meet Noble and Qadar greeting them in Arabic. An older woman caresses Noble's cheek, staring into his eyes endearingly.

"All right," I say. "Time to spill it. Everyone here knows you."

Noble looks at me, then slaps a hand on Qadar's shoulder.

"Meet my uncle." He gives me an awkward shrug. "I may have rigged the bodyguard system so he would be the one to watch you."

I'm shaking my head about to pour out a billion questions when an older woman comes to interrupt him, beckoning him to follow. "Saved." He winks at me and walks away.

"Wow." I stare at Qadar with an eye full of *shame on you.* "Your employer told you this job might be tough, huh? Now I'm the one who's shocked." I purse my lips.

Qadar laughs. "That's why he was late meeting you at the Bardo. He came to 'wake me up'."

It's all clear now. I thought his *employer* was my dad. But it's Noble. Just like that Qadar's words rush over me.

The one who hired me cares about you. You're important.

My body floods with energy and frequencies that rival nothing else. I need to find out who Noble is. And more than that. I need to find out what he won't tell me about Kai.

I sip my tea and let the new flavors and hot liquid roam over my tongue and sooth me. Last year, I was the one who had to be pried open to talk. Things really do come back around.

Qadar grabs a handful of sunflower seeds and starts splitting them with his teeth. "On one hand, I was completely honest with you. Your goals were to meet the hacker and help Kai. I've stuck to that."

I can't deny it. Noble is back in view, carrying plates of food into another room, delivering them to each table, happily chatting away in Arabic. He comes back and the hum of those sound waves mingles with the music in the background. It's like a melody that makes me want to dance. But dancing is not why I came. Noble moves the hair from his eyes, and hands me a map of Douz.

"The deal will happen a few miles down the road. My mother's relatives own this tourist business. If we stayed anywhere else, they'd be suspicious. We're safe here."

"Safe, huh." I laugh, and they do too. Because all things on the table, it's slightly ironic. Safe with a boy who hacked me and rigged my bodyguard. Safe in the middle of the desert where Kai is undercover, and Madame's Successor will establish a new empire.

I'm anything but safe. I should be scared. Instead, my gift flickers.

CHAPTER 39

Only someone with a death wish can brush off being set up by strangers and believe it's the best bet you have to stay alive. But two can play at this game.

"You know I'm a walking weapon at the moment, don't you?" I wave my *Fingertips,* half-jokingly. I don't need to mention *Sway* in my pocket, the taser at my wrist, or the tranquillizer-earrings.

Qadar scoots away, hands up in the air. "Hey now. We both have the same goal here."

Noble's eyes lock onto mine for a moment but a buzz and spike in our frequency makes him look away. He focuses on his tea, both hands cupping it. "You insisted on coming. So, you either trust me, or we're all in danger."

"Nice options." I raise a brow and wrap my fingers around my teacup. Transitioning my gaze to the map on the table, my gift hums trying to decipher the Arabic names written across what looks like nothing but sand dunes. "Look, I'm here to give the holothumb to Kai, but I'm also seeing this through. I won't let the Successor inherit Madame's empire. So, let's get to work. I have a lot of questions...like how can we monitor this deal while glamping in a remote oasis?"

Noble and Qadar exchange glances like I'm the oddball. They obviously know something I don't.

"We'll explain everything soon. But we can't work yet. Something more important is about to happen." Qadar hops to his feet and hurries through the door flaps.

"*Nabil!*" A woman calls from the other room.

I spin my head around the tent anxiously. "Oh no. What is it?"

Noble rubs his belly and laughs. "Dinner." He stands and offers me a hand.

He pulls me to my feet then drops my hand like it burned him.

His arm is extended toward the next tent over. "In Tunisia, you don't keep family waiting, and you always compliment the chef. Extra points if you tell her it's the best couscous you've ever eaten."

I follow him because I'm starving and oddly excited to be in such an amazing place, trying new things. I almost feel guilty when Kai is God knows where and the team is dealing with dangerous radicals in the capital. There's also another part of me that's jittery with excitement. I can't pinpoint why.

We enter the other tent where several large tables, some with cozy pillows as seats and others with benches, fill the room. Heads turn to look at us. They're examining me with bright curious eyes, giving me a head-to-toe once-over. I swallow. It's like walking into one of those family gatherings where you don't know anyone. I wish I had worn nicer clothes than these grubby old blue jeans with a plain t-shirt under a gray sweatshirt.

The kids from the pool run up to Noble. "*Ammi*," they call him. I assume, like in China, it's a familiar greeting like Uncle. Noble leans down to hug them or ruffle their hair. As he sits down next to them, I realize I haven't given him a chance to be a real person. Right now, he looks like someone I would like. He's showing the kids a stack of cards, teaching them something about numbers. My skin warms watching the kids stare at him in wonder.

A woman stands by me, leaning over. "Welcome to my home, Jo. I'm Farah, Noble's mother's cousin." Her accent is heavy, but beautifully soft like music. Her face glows with kindness and sun-kissed wrinkles.

"*Aslema*," I say, surprised she knows my name. "Are these your kids?" I glance at Noble again.

"Not all ten of them." She laughs. "But yes, I have a few in the bunch. Every child here loves Noble. Without him, many would have nothing."

"What do you mean?" I ask.

"He teaches them when he's in town. Some of them don't have many opportunities." Her smile softens, her voice rich with life. "But Noble has made them ten times smarter than any school. And he's more patient than most parents. He teaches in ways that kids like, fewer books." She smiles, a scent of flowers and spice float from her.

I study Noble. Hacker. Crime fighter. Possibly the NASA Tipper. And now, a teacher of children. In many ways, he reminds me of Kai. Smart, charming, generous and brave. Mandel also comes to mind. If he ever taught kids, it would be the same way I bet. It's strange how these three boys crisscross my thoughts at the same time.

The woman sets down a large piece of lamb on a plate. "Eat." She points her hand to a table laden with steaming plates of roasted lamb kebabs, couscous, and *briks*.

"*Shokran*," I say, thanking her. "For hosting us."

"Of course, anything for Noble and his friends." She smiles.

My stomach takes over and I forget about the plans. The lamb is roasted to perfection, and so are the potatoes. I'm introduced to *khobz* bread and different dips, and we feast. I take it all in—the choice of silverware and fancy lace tablecloth.

The family-style platters where everyone reaches for more. An unhurried, enjoyable gathering. There is an aspect I like about not having my gift. Time slows down.

Farah pours more tea into my cup, "We've heard a lot about you. Noble thinks very highly of you."

"Really?" I give her a funny grin. I wonder if he told them he was hacking me. To be kind, I respond. "We actually just met." Which isn't exactly accurate. He's technically been spying on my sims for the last couple of months. My gift flickers and that frequency skips as I catch the sound of his voice from across the room. At the same moment, Noble and I shoot a glance at each other. We blush as our eyes meet, then he looks away, eyebrows knit together in thought.

I want to shake the frequency, but it's hard. It's like walking into this feast. All the new aromas and sounds stimulate my senses, but I can't register them all. It's both wonderful and overwhelming. I suspect he also knows when my gift flickers. As a mathematician, I want to study our frequency. As a person, I want to run from it.

A young girl comes up to me and hands me a beautiful shawl, "*Marhabaan bikum fi Tunis*," she says, smiling.

Farah leans over. "She's welcoming you to Tunisia."

"You have a beautiful country," I say...and we're going to make sure it stays that way.

Soon the kids scramble over to ask me questions and I have to guess what they're saying. Noble and Qadar are no help. They are busy speaking with everyone. Both Arabic with French words are thrown into the mix. I might catch a word or two, but I have no clue what they're saying.

"*Ana asifah.*" I apologize that I don't understand then look at Noble to see if my pronunciation is correct. He nods, impressed. "I'm working on it." I dig out the book Noble gave me my first day in Tunis.

Noble's face brightens. "In all your spare time?"

"My brain needs an update, remember?" I say. "So I'm wiping the hard drive and loading new software, hoping to see the world in a new way." The kids are still around me, chatting and pointing. "What are they saying?"

"You'll have to hit the books to know." He scoots further away and starts a conversation with another boy near his age.

Qadar answers instead. "They're saying you're very pretty."

Noble doesn't turn but fights a smile cracking on his face.

Farah lifts another heap of couscous onto my plate. "Noble looks different with you here." She gives me a smile. "A couple years ago, we thought he might never recover. All he wanted was to be left alone, away from everyone apart from the kids." She sighs as she looks over at him. "But now, he brings you here and his eyes are bright."

"Oh." I blush at her implication. Farah looks at me like there's an angel in the room—and it's me. Definitely not the right time to inform her that her nephew is a wanted criminal, at least according to PSS. "Um. We're not together. He's like a...colleague."

"Really?" she says, "Because from the outside, it looks like you have a connection. Regardless, I'm glad he's happy."

Happy? I wouldn't exactly use that word. He acts like I pinch him when we get close to each other. I turn the conversation away from me and focus it on Noble instead, hoping some questions are answered. "What happened a couple years ago?"

She frowns, a distant memory lodged into her expression. "He lost someone he cared about."

I frown. I know how that goes. A breeze comes in the tent reminding me of Kai and why I'm here. Master Sang once said a similar thing to me. Kai and I were play sparing at their *daochang*, and I kept looking for a way to outsmart him. When Kai showed me a break-free move, I had an idea. "You're holding me too tight," I lied.

"I'm sorry," he said, immediately relaxing his guard, then

I knocked him off his feet.

"Taking advantage of me, huh?" He lay on his back laughing. "You think you're smart, don't you? Or you just wanted me on the ground." He tackled me, and we laughed until we both couldn't breathe.

After Kai went to change, Master Sang found me. "I've never seen Kai laugh so much, neither have I seen such acute focus in him before. You have fine tuned him in a way no one could. It makes me wonder..." he trailed off.

"Wonder what?" I asked him.

"What would happen if he lost you."

I down my last sip of tea and head over to Noble's side of the table. I won't lose anyone again.

"Time to get to work," I say, eager to see Kai and set up the drop off. Noble stands and motions to Qadar. "If our devices can even get a signal in the desert."

He stands, a quirky grin on his face. "Don't worry. That won't be a problem."

CHAPTER 40

Noble and Qadar thank everyone a hundred times and I tell Farah her couscous is the best I've ever had, which is actually true. Then we excuse ourselves.

Noble motions for me to follow him, and we snake through the tents on beautiful walkways made of sand. "This way."

Soon we arrive at another tent, where the canvas is definitely much thicker and bolted to the ground with a heavy lock. Inside the tent, my breath catches. It's filled with the tech of a hacker's dreams. From the outside it looks inconspicuous. But inside it's like PSS and PGF and Interpol all together.

Wireless devices are connected to holographic screens and computers and all the latest systems...even telescopes. Satellite equipment catches my eye, a fantasy world for a nerd. Not to mention, it's in the Sahara, in a gorgeous oasis, under a jet-black sky filled with stars.

"OK, let's dive in."

"First, show me Kai. I need to know he's ok."

He takes me over to a screen showing live footage, but a separate screen with facial recognition on it catches my eye. It's super high-tech and Kai's image is displayed on it.

"Who designed this?"

Noble looks up. "I did."

I look closer at it and there's a sidebar with countless video files on Kai. "What's all this?"

"A database of footage. Originally, I'd just been watching Montego. When your boyfriend came on the scene, everything got more complicated. I have a special camera on him too."

"How far does the footage go back?" I ask.

"Six weeks, more or less." Prods like him and I don't say *more or less*. Noble knows the exact date, just as I would have known it, but for some reason, he won't tell me.

Which makes me think whatever disturbing thing he knows about Kai is in these videos. I'm sure of it. But it's not like I have time to watch weeks of footage to find out. Right now, we've got bigger things to think about.

I slide back over to the screen that is live steaming from Kai's location right now. Noble swipes a holographic button and audio fills the room as I zoom in on the video.

The Sheikh looks across the room at the girl with long black hair sitting on the couch, then at Kai. "Ennéa tells me you knew Madame," he says. I'm surprised the Sheikh knows the girl's name for how little he looks at her. "Is that true, you knew the great Maxima?"

I don't miss the way the girl cringes in the corner the same way I do when I hear Madame's name. My heart goes out to her.

"I did." Kai looks at him with a smooth grin. "In Shanghai. Through her hotels."

The Sheikh's chest puffs up, and he scoffs. "The hotels were small minded. We're going a different direction all together."

"I want in."

"Ah, when Montego arrives to vouch for you. There's

no rush."

"I may be new, but I'm not stupid. You've been planning things this whole week."

"How long did you work for her?" the Sheikh asks, studying Kai.

Kai drinks whatever is in his cup. "Less than a year. My ambitions are far wider than hers ever were. That's what led me to Montego. But let's get one thing straight. You're not choosing me. I'm choosing you." His expression hardens as he plays his role. "Madame was a genius. Until her protégé outsmarted her. Unlike Madame, I don't underestimate anyone. Present company included." Kai's eyes flick around the room.

"Then to Friday and a new reign." The Sheikh offers him a toast. He swirls the last dregs with a pleased smile and then excuses himself. The minute the door closes behind him, the girl rushes over to Kai, sits too close beside him crossing her legs the way Madame would.

"The Sheikh doesn't tell me much," she says, "but I know he won't tolerate traitors."

"Well, I don't tolerate men who don't appreciate good women." He winks at her and fills her glass.

I swipe the audio off. Seeing him undercover is really gut punching. No doubt he's gifted. Believable. Even though I can tell he's strategizing and weighing what each person says. But it makes me feel ill, too. I know what it is to live a lie.

Noble can tell I'm bothered.

"Sorry. Must be hard to watch." He offers me a steaming cup of mint tea. I appreciate his thoughtfulness.

"No," I lie. "He's just doing his job."

It is just a job—until it isn't. Staying undercover, living with another identity and lies can work for a day or two. A short period of time doesn't break you, but weeks, months, years later, it takes a toll on your mind. Eventually you can't tell what is true anymore. And unless you have someone who wades through the lies, snagging you out of the black pit, you could sink in forever. Kai should know that from my experience. Thankfully, this is only for another day or two.

"Did you find anything in the other videos?" I ask moving to the facial recognition screen again. I scroll through the data until I land on one date I won't forget. The day Coral Hacker first messaged me. My gift flickers and numbers pop on, briefly functioning like a calculator.

Noble quickly moves over, punching in numbers and the screen goes black. "Nothing you need to see right now."

"We're in a little too deep to keep intel from each other. You can tell me why you hate Kai," I say, brushing his fingers off the keyboard. "A lot of people have misjudged Kai. They don't know the real him."

"I don't hate him," he says. "I just think he's stupid. Besides, that's your business. If our plans go well, they'll be busted on Friday. You guys can talk, and then he'll be on to his next job."

His next job. The words hurt.

Regardless of what Noble knows, that part is true, and it stings. Another job means more time away from him. I don't want that. I'm getting anxious to talk with Kai. Not to mention anxious about the drop off and Friday. I could ask Noble what his predictions are but my numbers around him are like trees in a dense forest, too thick and hard to see through, yet something subtle beats across my subconscious growing with each second. The numbers, like burning stars, start connecting the dots. It's a maze of constellations, spinning side by side with our frequency and soon it all becomes a frenzy of numbers, all chaos. My head throbs and a dull pain grows behind my eyes until I squeeze my eyes shut to make it go away.

Noble notices. "You ok?"

"Yep. Let's just get Kai the location. Open a secure line for *the street.*"

He opens the undetectable line into *the street* portal where I leave Kai the details. Thankfully, Noble's special messages are delivered only to the person, untraceable then disappear. "Done. All set for tomorrow," I say. "We drop the holothumb. Kai switches it with the Successor's. We set up surveillance. The girl said Albert Müller will arrive tomorrow and make Kai prove himself. So we have to be ready for—" I stop talking because it's useless.

Noble is not listening. His eyes are calculating me again. Whatever problem he's trying to solve is not fun. The way his face wrinkles with each complication. I used to do the same thing. "What is it?"

He clears his throat, eyes on me again. His voice sends energy waves over me. "Kai's an idiot."

"What are you talking about?" I say, indignant.

"He's going to mess up everything for a thrill." His eyes pierce me like I've been shot with a silver bullet.

"You're wrong. He knows what he's doing," I say, defending him. "He's too smart for that."

"Not smart enough." He mutters under his breath.

I'm angry now. "Kai will find the *holothumb* and it will be uploaded to the master-file. He won't miss a beat. I promise. He won't mess up the deal." Noble's numbers fly my direction, mixing with my calculations of his sound waves.

He leans in too close. "I'm not talking about the deal."

Our frequency is spiking, and whatever he's talking about, he won't tell me. Whatever it is he thinks he knows about Kai is wrong. But then the image from my sim flashes to my mind, the man lying dead in the dust haunts me. And Kai just walked away. What don't I know? My mind is too full to think. The chair screeches as I push it back.

"Excuse me," I say, heading for the door. "I need some air."

CHAPTER 41

Whatever I do, and wherever I go, trouble really does find me.

The raven black sky above me, glittering with stars, is so vast and magnificent I'm overcome with emotion. I walk over to the patio area and slide into a reclining chair, watching the moonlight reflect off the pool. Kai is still in my head, along with the pressure building to make sure things go right tomorrow. But I try to focus on the good. Kai could have been dead. But this job won't be the end of it. For all I know, this could be the norm for all of his jobs.

A desert breeze rustles into the camp and tents flap and palms sway under its passage. The sweeping dunes in the distance steal my attention, and I let my mind wander. My hand drops to touch the stones, sand grains everywhere. It's not my ocean's sand, but it brings me comfort. It's new and exciting. What I told my dad about seeing the world wasn't a lie. I always want to be learning. Exploring. Solving problems.

An office job in Seattle crunching numbers was never for me. Although, I hadn't imagined myself in the desert stopping dangerous political factions either.

I recline the chair to a flat position, put my hand under my head, and stare at the stars. After I lost my gift there were no more equations drawing maps in the sky. At first, I was grateful, because for the first time in my life stargazing was relaxing. But it didn't take long to realize I'd lost something special, a way of seeing that others didn't have.

Now in the Sahara away from town, the constellations and even galaxies far away seem closer. A spark of hope alights. The note Noble left in the Arabic phrase book stirs in the air. *Reverse. Learn to read the world differently.*

The dark sky covers the night like a blanket, and I let my mind ease into my surroundings. It's been so long since I could just…be…without worries. But somehow, right now, looking up it feels like everything is going to be ok, like the sky is whispering that anything is possible.

It also makes me read *him* differently. This is the perfect place for an astronomer. If anyone wanted to chart the stars, like the NASA Tipper, this would be the place to do it. With that telescope coupled with his gift. It's possible. Harrison wasn't far off.

The desert has cooled down, and the breeze brings a chill. But I don't want to go into the tent yet. The stars are too majestic, and small traces of my gift murmur deep inside me. Whatever is happening isn't the same as when I'm in danger. It's quiet and still and safe, like sitting here surrounded by these tents, and palm trees, and the endless sand is what I needed, like the spark that lights the flame. Maybe Noble is right about that too—danger won't wake it up, only peace will.

As if he can hear my thoughts, Noble's footsteps echo toward the patio.

"Pretty isn't it?" His voice makes me shiver even more than the night's chill. He covers me with a large shawl. "It gets cold at night though."

He reclines on the patio chair next to mine, a sweatshirt and down vest on, head propped up on his elbow. His brown hair is tucked behind his ears and his eyes fix on mine. "I'm sorry

I upset you. You and Kai are none of my business."

"It's fine. I'm ok. Kai and I have been through a lot. You don't know him like I do."

"All right." He holds out his hand as if to shake on a truce. "Friends?"

I look over, surprised. We certainly didn't start out as *friends*. But what are we now? I think back to the first day he rescued me in the coral. His voice steadied me. Like it did in the helicopter, both times. But then there's the mystery of this frequency...I don't know what we are. But we're not enemies. "Is that what we are?"

"I'd like to be." His mouth curls up on one side.

I take his hand, my chest slightly hammering, and we shake on it. "Friends tell each other the truth."

"Friends are also patient, right?"

I nod. I won't force any information out of him that he isn't ready to share. Again, I've been there.

He looks up, and sighs with contentment. "I could stay out here all night."

"Do you live here year-round?" I ask, wondering how personal I can get now that we're *friends*.

He pauses linking eyes with me, calculating, then throws caution to the wind. "No." He rolls onto his back, and his cell phone drops out of his pocket. I'd forgotten about the smartdust and what Harrison is finding now. "I wish I did."

I stare at him. My gift is silent, but I can see his is at work. The smile playing on his lips as the numbers and equations reveal secrets around us. "I have to admit. You make me a bit jealous. What do you see when you look up there?"

"Everything." He laughs. "It's speaking all the time."

"What's it saying?"

"It's more like an invitation, a path to escape the chaos," Noble says. "What is it like for you to look at the stars without your gift?"

"I can finally enjoy it," I say, feeling a bit childish. "Before the stars would give me a headache because my mind used to…"

"Try to count them? Map them out?" he asks.

"Yeah."

"I've been there. It was an intense battle. But I won."

"How did you do it?" I ask, curious.

"Wonder. It's the best teacher." He looks over at me. "Take my family here in the Sahara for example. They've looked at the sky their whole life, but no matter how many times they've seen the moon or the stars, they still stop to marvel at it. *Look, it's the moon,* they say. *It's so beautiful tonight.* Like it's the first time they've seen it." He smiles wide. "Wonder means we still have something to learn. And if that's true, then we need to see it in a new way. My headache left when I stopped trying to solve everything and learned to play instead. Consequently, I discovered some things."

"Noble?" He looks over at me, glints of moonlight in his eyes. "I know who you are." A feeling stirs in my gut.

He looks up, eyes full of hope, a smile on his face. "Really?"

"Yeah." I look at him. "You're the NASA Tipper, aren't you? It's obvious, the way you talk about the stars coupled with your gift."

His face falls, and he turns away. "Wow. You…um. I didn't think…"

"That I'd figure it out?"

"Something like that." He shakes his head and takes a deep breath.

"Well, am I right?" I say, simply wanting him to confirm it.

Instead of looking away, he sits up and gazes at my face, from my eyes to my chin, mapping out every bit of me. Self-consciousness threatens to take over because I know what he sees. But instead of letting it get to me, I look back at him and dig deeper, hoping to find my gift's hiding place.

His dark eyes flicker under the moon, and the light is just enough to see the small freckles sprinkled over his brown skin. This close to him, I catch the scent of his clothes, fire-smoke and cardamom.

We are not speaking but the frequency sparks between us like a symphony. The wonder of it is almost as strong as the stars. According to Noble, that means I still have something to learn about him. I'm so lost in his face I forget I asked him a question and am startled when he responds.

"Does it matter to you who I am?" he asks.

"Yes."

He looks away and pulls his vest tighter as the desert air grows colder. "Then I'm the NASA Tipper." His voice is so still, so serious. "But the truth can't get out. No one can find me. I don't want credit. It's not why I do it."

A slight guilt in me rises because of the smartdust. One way or another, we will find out his real identity. Ms. T is working on it as we speak. But as I sit with him now, his desire to remain anonymous is all too familiar. Noble may have broken into PSS, but he did no harm. All he did was help me. *But why?*

I have to call Harrison. Stop the process. *Ugh.* Am I thinking like Jo or Phoenix now? I can't tell. My allegiance isn't clear anymore. I roll over and look back up at the stars.

"I won't tell anyone, Noble," I promise. "I know all about being taken advantage of." Then something else dawns on me and I start to laugh.

"What?"

"If the PSS team—especially Harrison—knew I was with the NASA Tipper right now—they'd freak. You're kind of like their hero. Although they're not fans of the Coral Hacker."

"Wow. Couldn't you have given me a better nickname?" he says, laughing too.

"They originally called you the Sim Stalker," I say, my lips pursed to one side.

"Ouch." He shakes his head. "I told you, I wouldn't have contacted you if it wasn't for PSS and Kai."

"Only half true." I point out. "You didn't have to help me with my gift. You also know a lot about me."

"Yeah, sorry about that." He shivers and without thinking I offer some of the enormous shawl to him. Our hands touch as I reach out and this time he doesn't flinch away. My heart skips as electricity pulses through me.

I slide my hand away embarrassed and alarmed by the adrenaline racing inside me. "Sorry. You can take it. I forgot I have to go in and do my sims. Thanks, Noble."

My feet weave along sandy paths as I stumble back to my tent. Once inside, I close the flap-door and grab my bag, snatching out my sim glasses. They sit untouched in my lap. I can't start until my heart slows down.

CHAPTER 42

I'm not on vacation. But the scent of oranges and jasmine, the platter of dates and olives on the table, and the warm glow of the lamp on my tent tries to convince me otherwise.

Lying on my bed, the sim glasses are still beside me. I'm exhausted but I promised Noble I'd do all three sims tonight. I can't seem to begin. Phase one has invaded my mind in a way I didn't expect. Mandel is such a strong memory, and I can't shake him. Then there's Noble and phase three. He said he programmed a new sim that would help me, but honestly, I'm afraid of what I might feel inside the simulation.

So, that leaves me with only one option. Phase two. If I can't find any clues, then Kai is truly on his own. Noble and I can't storm a whole group of Loyalists even with my PSS weapons.

With that in mind, I slide on the glasses. "K2, load phase two please."

It's silent. No wind. No cold. I open my eyes. I'm sitting in the middle of the square in downtown Shanghai, but it's a ghost town. No one is on the street. Not one living thing in sight. No cars or buses, no bikes, or taxis. Nothing but me and the cold cement. City lights from skyscrapers blink on and mix with the moonlight under a thin veil of smog, the night glowing red above me. Shanghai never sleeps. It's eerie, like no sim I've experienced before. Maybe my mind is overpowering it again. And I don't have much time. The fight is what I came to see, to find the identity of the Successor. I stand up, ready to exit the sim when the faintest sound of the river gurgles. A figure, slow and old, walks my way.

I gasp. I thought I'd lost my chance.

I run over to the frail old man. My eyes fill with tears while laughter also spills out. His body may be brittle, but his mind is as sharp as a sword and his countenance that of a young warrior. I snag his wrinkled hand, pulling it close to me. "Grandfather?"

His eyes are focused on me. "What are you doing out here looking so lost, granddaughter? Did you forget what I taught you?"

"No." I shake my head, gripping his hand tighter. "I think of your words every day. It's just—there's something you don't know. I lost my gift."

We walk along the river. "Nonsense. How can you lose something that is a part of you?" he asks, strolling at a snail pace, hands now folded behind him.

"I don't know." My chest squeezes. "The numbers want to return but they're buried too deep. I don't know how to find them." I'm desperate for his advice, and he takes in a deep breath like he knows it.

"Did you know animals walk over gems and precious stones every day with no understanding they're even there? Unlike humans, they have no desire to dig or mine the earth for them. Likewise, the fish of the ocean swim ignorantly past expensive coral or sunken ships with treasure while people search them out."

I stare at him, blank eyed, knowing from all my hours

spent with him that there's a lesson here. "Why are you telling me this?"

He slows to a stop. "Treasure is all around us. We humans are designed to find it. You must look deeper."

I know him well enough to know he is not talking about silver or gold, but I'm not quite sure how this will get my gift back.

"It's not that simple," I say. "So much changed after you left. I was finally getting comfortable in Phoenix's skin, then my family showed up, and my life changed again. Now I'm Josephine and I don't know how to reconcile that girl with who I became in China."

"Every year, we shed a layer and grow. Only for a moment is the new skin tender."

"I don't want to change anymore. I just want to be me and have my gift back."

"Your thinking is backwards. Your gift didn't go through the fire. You did." He faces me, his voice stern but comforting. "Your math is not the gift. *You're the gift.*"

When he says that, a small burst of mathematical diagrams start popping up around me. I look at his face. "There's something else I need to tell you."

"Go on then," he says.

"Your nephew Kai and I are...well, he's wonderful, and I..." I'm stumbling over my words, because this is a sim. If this were real and Red was alive, what would he say about our relationship?

His eyes widen, even glisten. His smile is the widest I've seen. "You have my blessing. Now wake up before you're too late."

I jolt up in a tent full of shadows. The clock reads 3:30 in the morning. It's Thursday. Drop off day.

I must have fallen asleep during my sim. Was Red a dream

or part of a sim? I might never know. My eyes are heavy. I close them again, but my mind is restless now, bouncing between my simulation with Red to wondering where Kai is sleeping. More thoughts clamor for my attention: who is the Successor...how to get my gift back...Noble quoting Mandelbrot...then back to Red telling me to wake up before I'm *too late*...for what? It's all one big chaotic mess in my head, which makes going back to sleep useless.

Inside the tent, the black oscillates to a subtle gray with the coming dawn. The bed is warm and cozy, but the desert is calling my name. My eyes adjust to the dark and a whistle of wind on the dunes calls to me. I want to watch the sunrise over the hills, the waves of sand sweeping across the horizon. I need time to think. To clear my head.

My phone vibrates, alerting me. K2 announces a private voice message. It's early, probably my Dad.

"Play message."

"Jo," it's Harrison's voice. "You never checked in last night. Ms. T isn't happy. But that's the least of our problems."

CHAPTER 43

I pull on the same jeans and hoodie, tie my boots and slip on my backpack. Unzipping the tent, I slip outside and a dry breeze rustles in the palms. I need a private place to chat with Harrison.

I sneak past the pool, dipping in a finger. It's cold but refreshing and I want to dive in and swim to the bottom right now, but I can't.

Unfortunately, just miles away there are Loyalists setting horrific plans in motion that could take all this beauty away.

I slip past the camels to climb up a small ridge and plunk myself down in a pile of sand, pulling my knees to my chest. "K2, get Harrison D. George on a com-line."

Harrison answers. "I wondered when you'd wake up."

"Jetlag, and bad sleep." I pause. Lots of noises blare in the background. "What's going on over there?"

"Putting you on speaker."

"Jo?" Pens voice breaks in like a train wreck over the noise. "Do you even know what we're dealing with over here in Tunis?"

"No."

"We're basically at war with the radicals for control over

SIMULATED   243

this city." An alarm goes off. "Once we uploaded SMOKE, we were able to locate our tech, and initiate the kill-switch. Now, as they lose the ability to use Veil and other designs, they're scrambling. Trying to shut down other ministries. Schools."

"Eddie—get on that!" Felicia shouts in the background.

"What's happening?"

"Well, they do have old PSS tech, which we don't have a thumbprint for. And they're using Eddie's RADAR to shut down the city so no one can vote. But we're after them, re-routing servers to warehouses and alerting authorities. We're currently acting as the eyes for the police."

Felicia cuts in over another alarm going off. "They even cut the power to a hospital. Harrison was able to get everything back up for them. But they're mad, and we are literally the only ones who can stop these attacks because they're using our tech."

"Where is Ms. T?" I ask.

"Briefing the Tunisian National Guard." Harrison shouts into the phone. "We don't know if we're fast enough to find everything and shut it down. This is a lot more pressure than our usual jobs."

"Isn't SMOKE working?" I ask.

"It's working fine, but Coral Hacker designed it to take 24 hours so that the thief won't know you've infiltrated them, and we still have to trace the PSS tech and move it into Cyber Island before they find out. It takes time, and meanwhile the radicals are burning tires in the streets and trying to shut down the city. We've got plenty to worry about."

"Oh no...my dad! What if he watches the news?" I groan.

"Don't worry. We've *Veiled* everything your dad sees on his phone or in his home, but you never know when someone might mention it to him. The reason we're calling is that a group of the leaders has disappeared. Mr. Ben Slimane, the head of the radicals, made it clear he wasn't happy we took away their new toys. Most likely, he paid good money for them."

"All right, send me the details on the leaders who are missing. Coral Hacker has facial recognition tech. Maybe we can locate them."

Harrison laughs nervously. "Search *for really angry men in old fashioned army fatigues*—I'm sure you'll find them. More than half of them aren't even local. Anyway, whatever deal you have to stop, please make sure it doesn't fail. We can't risk this chaos spreading."

I'm silent, my mind moving in a hundred directions. "Did you find anything about the Successors?"

"Not much. Albert Müller just landed in Tunisia. Apparently, he vacations here often. The Indonesian Ambassador is in meetings the rest of the week at a summit in Europe. It doesn't look like he's headed here. We could be wrong. The Sheikh's a businessman, and he looks clean."

My jaw clenches. "Ok. Keep digging."

"Ms. T wants to know how things are going on your end?" Harrison asks.

"We drop the holothumb to Kai tonight. If things go smoothly, Kai switches it, SMOKE is uploaded, and we get the rest of the Blacklist and the master-file."

"Who's making the drop-off?"

"Qadar. I'll be totally out of the picture," I tell him. He doesn't need to know that I plan on watching from a distance. I need to see Kai. In the flesh. "I'm in a safe location. Qadar is here. The hacker is helpful." The earring smart dust comes to mind. "Harrison? Can I talk to you off speaker for a moment?"

"Yeah, Jo." The noise dies down a bit, but I'm still cringing at everything the team has to do. "OK. Just us. How's life with Coral Hacker?"

"Enlightening. You won't believe this, but he even found a way to enter my sims in person." I sigh. "Have you found anything with the smartdust?"

"Jo. You're right. The guy's a genius. Even his data is immune to the Bluetooth nano-tech. It's like he has a guard dog protecting his stuff. Without a password, I can't break into anything. But," he whispers, "there are sure a lot of hints that match the NASA Tipper. I know you said it wasn't him, but I ran tests. I'm 97% sure the charts that the NASA provided to NASA are coming from exactly where you're standing."

Oh snap. He knows.

I'm silent. "Harrison. You can't tell anyone. Please, nothing you find out about him goes to anyone but me until this is over. Trust me, it may ruin everything if we do."

"That's a lot to ask, Jo." Harrison sighs. "Ms. T is my boss. But...we are busy, so I can wait until the drop-off. Afterwards I can't promise anything."

I wince. Making him promise not to tell his boss is what Phoenix would do.

"You're right. I'm sorry for asking you to compromise, Harrison." I shake my head. "I'll tell Ms. T everything myself soon." My insides bunch up in knots as Noble's face runs through my mind. "Believe me, he's not the criminal we're looking for. And if there's anyone who needs to know his identity, it's me."

CHAPTER 44

The sun wavers over the horizon now, glowing in the distance. The tents are still silent, so I let the desert steal my breath away before the chaos of the day comes.

My mind travels down the golden waves of sand. The arid land makes me feel small and full of wonder. It reminds me of what Noble said, that I have a lot left to learn. There is so much to know and explore. What would it be like to sleep outside all night in this desert, under the stars?

The dunes are magnified in the morning sun and the splashes of green palms in the oasis point to paths and lost wonders. Unfortunately, for me it's not a path to paradise but to Loyalists and Blacklists and a world hurting like an open wound. My fingers run over the soft grains of sand. I understand too. I've spun out of control before. Lost myself so deep I couldn't think straight. There were moments where I was blind, and no one was there to lead me back.

Just look up. It's always speaking. The words feel so true they hurt. Like they're as big as the universe and as small as a seahorse. Out of my backpack I grab the sim glasses, thinking of doing phase three. Wondering what it is Noble put into my sims ...Noble tells me my gift won't come back with danger.

But how can he be so sure?

Even if he has the same gift, he's not me. He might have been able to get my numbers to come back for longer periods, but they still haven't returned fully. Now in the light of day, connecting him to Mandel because of one quote was foolish. Last night I overreacted.

Lots of prods, mathematicians and math students—heck, anyone who studies science—knows of Mandelbrot. Even pop culture knows about him. He's been written into books and songs and movies. Major scientific discoveries have roots in his work. And Noble told me he saw the postcard. It makes sense for him to quote something I know.

I wander over to a palm, my mind like a sandstorm of thoughts. I need clarity, but I feel blind.

People are up now, and the kids are playing under a group of trees. It's a type of math-based game only Noble could have taught them.

Curious, I stop and watch. At first it looks like they are making stew with rocks and leaves and everything they can find. Even I did that as a kid. But watching closer I see they're playing a complex game of equations with very specific items.

A tap on the shoulder startles me. Farah is holding what I think is breakfast. A steaming bowl full of chunks of bread topped with chickpeas, with scents of garlic, cumin, lemon and peppers. "This is *Lablebi*. Tried it before?"

I shake my head, and absently take the bowl into my hands. "Thank you." She's about to walk away when I stop her. "Farah? What are they doing?"

"A game. It's called The Thumbprint of God," she says.

Chills shoot down my spine. "Noble taught them, didn't he?"

"Yes." Farah smiles wide. After I thank her again, she walks away leaving me speechless.

They're studying fractal geometry. Like flashes of lightning, memories of Coral Hacker and my sims come to mind.

Everything he told me to concentrate on during my sims were fractals. The order in the chaos. If my heart could tremble, it's doing it now.

A hand on my shoulder shatters me apart. It's him.

"Good morning," Noble says. The oscillations of his voice tremor through my skin even with my eyes closed. This connection...it's impossible. "Qadar and I are going to set up surveillance at Ksar Douz and the old ruins where the drop off is. The International Festival of the Sahara will be starting tonight. It's the perfect cover. Tourists and journalists from all over the world will be there. We'll be using my family's tourism business and camel treks to set up nearby."

I don't answer because his face looks like a collision of stars, and trees, and dreams. A thousand conversations fly through me, making me reach into his eyes for answers.

"Jo, are you ok?" Noble asks, a crooked grin. He recognizes I'm scrambling for numbers.

My eyes shoot to the ground. "Yeah," I say, pinching myself—whatever I'm making up in my head is fantasy. I get a grip and look up. "Without my gift, I can't find any new details in the sims, that's all. It's making me a bit worried."

"Did you do your next phase three yet? I think it'll help a bit with the confusion." He gives me a shy grin that reaches his eyes. He feels it too. Whatever is between us is deeper than we can comprehend.

"Thanks," I say, a battle raging inside my chest. "I don't think I can handle any more challenges right now."

"No, it's nothing like that. Trust me," he says. His big brown eyes stare back at me. Will I ever get used to this frequency between us?

"Trust the infamous Coral Hacker? The NASA Tipper? Noble, the enigma who lives in the desert?" I tease.

"We're friends, right? I agreed to tell you the truth."

My whole body shivers when he looks at me. His eyes

plead for me to agree with him, like if I say no it's the same as plunging a knife into his heart. My sims are mixing with reality and messing with my head. I'm delusional. It's wish fulfillment. He said it himself. What I'm thinking can't be true. "All right, I promise I'll do it later, when things are a bit less chaotic."

"There will always be chaos. It's the calculation we find inside the chaos that reminds us of who we are and where to go." He slips a piece of dry coral into my hand. "For you. Be back soon."

I'm breathless as he walks away.

I unfold my fingers and examine the coral. It's not just any coral, but something called Stony Coral, with a very specific pattern. A fractal pattern.

I close my eyes. "K2, get Harrison on the line."

CHAPTER 45

I pace in front of the camel stalls ignoring the smell as I wait for Harrison to pick up. Finally, after the one-billionth ring, he answers. "What? You ok?"

My fingers can barely hold the phone, they're trembling so much. "I think I figured it out." Camels cry and screech behind me.

"What are you talking about?" he says. "And what is that in the background? It sounds like Chewbacca!"

I cup the phone, guilt digging into me, like I'm a thief picking a lock. But I need to know. "I want you to try something. A password to crack Coral Hacker's codes."

"Give me one sec." I picture him sitting down in front of his screen. "Got it. Which one?"

I stare off in the distance at the kids. "The Thumbprint of God."

Harrison laughs. "Jo? Are you having some spiritual moment? Too much desert heat?"

"No," I say. "$fc(z) = z2 + c$. The equation for the Mandelbrot set."

"Interesting. Any reason why you've come up with this?" he asks.

"I've just seen the world in reverse."

"Fine, give me some time. I'll get back to you." Harrison pauses. "Jo. Do you know who he is?"

My hands are shaking. The sound waves. The oscillations. The coral. The way I trusted him in my gut. The way he looks at me and says my name, like he's known me for years. What if he *has* known me for years? What are the odds?

My eyes squeeze shut. I'm silent because everything else on the inside is screaming.

"Not yet," I answer Harrison, "but I'm going to find out."

I hang up as Farah waves me over. Questions I need to ask her fly to my mind. I'm running out of time. I stroll over to her, forcing my outward appearance to hide the chaos swirling inside.

Farah hands me a tray of more snacks—olives, dates, a baguette and a pot of tea. "Noble said you would be working while he was gone, so I wanted to bring you more food."

I take the tray. "Thanks." Before she walks away, I stop her. "You said Noble lost someone he cared about. Do you know who it was?"

She cocks her head to the side. "A girl. That's all I know."

"When was that?"

"A couple years ago now." She smiles. "Don't worry. I think he's over her." She winks at me and runs after one of the little kids who is heading for the pool.

My eyes reach again to where the older kids draw spirals in the sand.

I fly back to my tent, zipping the door closed. I take out my bag to find Mandel's postcard of the Mandelbrot Set.

The image of the fractal comes alive. My mind flashes to the trees. The oceans. The desert. The hills. The maps. The coral. What do they all have in common? Fractals. Are. Everywhere.

Back in Tunis, Noble's first instructions were to find the tree. "Everything has a design. Designs make patterns...patterns produce equations…" He was training my eye to see fractals.

The calculations that started in my head are now pounding in my heart. These equations are never simple. Never cut and dry. Never with a clear answer. The heart is rough and messy, like the waves in the sea and clouds in the sky, like water you can never hold. As a girl, I want to rule it out, but as a mathematician, I can't. The questions have to be asked.

What if Noble is not just the NASA tipper? What if he's not just a prodigy who's obsessed with the stars? What if he's a boy who stayed up for hours talking with me online…a boy who made plans to run away and find me? A boy designed to light up the sky?

What if Noble is Mandel?

The first boy I ever loved.

CHAPTER 46

My head is dangerously close to overcapacity and the drop-off is happening in less than an hour at dusk.

Albert Müller is already nearly at the Sheikh's Dar. Kai knows the drop-off time. Now he just has to make it there alone. I speed over to the tech-tent where Noble is sitting at one of the three desks. The facial recognition software and the small tab of footage on Kai haunts me. That is the last thing I need.

Noble is monitoring the live stream. I keep waiting for Harrison to call back. But he hasn't yet.

Noble notices as I walk in. "Hi," he says softly. "Did you do phase three yet?"

I shake my head, staring at him. He looks away disappointed.

But my eyes stay on him. Every inch of his face is different to me now. Every strand of his brown hair. Every freckle. If this is what Mandel looks like, he's more beautiful than I imagined him to be.

I'm delusional. Noble can't be Mandel. Mandel and I never had a *frequency*. Even as a kid, I wouldn't have forgotten it. And if Mandel had experienced it, he would have told me. But Noble somehow knew it would happen, that's why he used his robotic voice whenever he contacted me. So maybe he can't be Mandel. It's too much to think about.

"Any news?" I ask, conflicting emotions rolling around in my stomach.

"Not much. Just watching Kai on the job. They're all preparing for something. Probably Müller's arrival. Kai's getting ready to go out to meet us. I think he's planning to use the girl as his cover."

"The girl? That's a bad idea. X girls, former or not, aren't loyal." I move to the screen, but immediately wish I hadn't. The girl's long hair is down her back, and everything about her is sexy. Her dress flutters open to expose her upper thigh just like Madame would have wanted. Inwardly, I cringe.

She greets him by rubbing his arm, then goes to sit next to the Sheikh. Kai smiles, a nonchalant confidence about it. When did he get to be such a good actor?

Then again, Kai was always good at keeping secrets. He kept mine from Chan. He helped me do a hundred little things Chan never knew about. The rebel side of him that skipped work was always there. I believed it was because he hadn't found what he was passionate about. Has he found it now?

I watch him because I miss him and this whole thing with Noble is tearing me apart. If I'd never gone to China, would I be chatting with Mandel now? And where would I be without Kai? He's been a rock in my life, grounding me. He never gave up on me. Kai didn't get the chance to know Red, but that same power and passion of Red lives in him. Kai saw the good in me when I was hard, cold, distant, and angry. He pursued that girl, knowing all I needed was to be loved.

Even though Qadar will make the drop off, I refuse to stay at the camp. I will see Kai tonight. We won't be able to actually touch or talk, but even being near him will comfort me.

On the screen, Kai sits there almost like Madame, so hard to read. The Sheikh is assessing the room. He knows something, like a captain on the sea before a storm. He's more nervous than I expected. Is it because Müller arrives tonight?

"Are you here to accomplish your plans or the Successor's?" the Sheikh asks Kai, grilling him again.

"We're all here for our own plans, am I right? But I came here because I seek a leader with vision." To an outsider, Kai might look relaxed, but under the surface his whole body is on guard and ready. He reminds me so much of the brothers back in Song Valley. They taught him well, not just the art of Kung Fu, but how to truly use power.

"Ah, yes, then you won't be disappointed. Grand plans and plenty of resources will come with the Successor," he says, leaning in with a refined laugh. "Where do you plan to base your operation?"

"My territory is Shanghai," he says, smoothly. "I came for the master-file and to be part of the Loyalists."

The Sheikh grunts. "Good. Because my territory is here," he says. "And soon it will all be mine."

Kai gives him a coy glance. "Then we should stay in touch."

"Isn't there anything that would persuade you to stay in this region?" the girl pipes in from across the room.

"I'm always open to persuasion," Kai laughs softly, staring at her. "Excuse me." Kai stands, winking at the girl as he exits the room. She picks up on his hint that she's meant to follow. I squirm in my seat. He's really going to tell her? Kai should know better.

"She can't be trusted," I mutter to Noble.

"Are you sure it's not jealousy?" he asks.

Kai leans in, his large hand covering her petite shoulder. "Ennéa, I'm going to check out the location before the others arrive to make sure it's clear. No one else seems concerned. But I know better. I'll be back in an hour. If anyone asks, please tell them I'm in my room." He slides his fingers over her hair, and I burn up inside.

How can he do that so easily?

"I'll do it." She flashes him a nervous smile.

"Ennéa!" The Sheikh beckons her.

"I have to go." Kai glances back in the direction of the Sheikh. "You deserve better than him or any of the men here."

"Deserve or not, one can only hope for someone loyal." Her face falters, beautifully broken and shattered, and yet a faint smile spreads across her lips.

Kai reaches for his jacket.

The Sheikh calls again, and the girl turns to go back inside.

Moments later my phone beeps, alerting me to a message on *the street*. I look down. "Kai sent another message—in the emergency stock."

Noble opens a portal into his cloaked tech world, and I log in through a backdoor.

"What's he saying?" Noble asks.

I look at Kai's message. A photo pops up of Kai and I when we went to the Seattle Piers one night. We're leaning against the dock. The picture was taken right before a group of seagulls attacked us, trying to steal our fish and chips. That night was a disaster. Everything went wrong. We missed the show we'd come for, and after the birds swarmed us, my wallet fell into the harbor. We'd ended up laughing about it all night, but still, why would he send this photo?

My cheeks flush with embarrassment. "Sorry." I shake my head. "It's personal." He occasionally sends pictures or notes but never to the emergency portal. Maybe it's because he knows he's in hot water. Or maybe he misses me or needs to remind himself of the truth.

I look at the message once more then watch it disappear. Tonight can't come soon enough. This deal needs to be done.

I shouldn't even be here, and neither should Kai. Suddenly, I'm angry at everyone. At Kai for taking this job. At Noble for not telling me who he really is or what he knows about Kai or what I need to do to get my gift back. I'm mad at myself for failing Mandel long ago and letting my feelings for him take over my mind. I'm mad that when I look at Noble, I want to figure him out, but he came at the worst time possible. I'm even mad that Madame didn't tell me who the next Successor would be.

A week ago, things were simple. Kai was mine and I was his. But then my conversation with Mara returns and I know it was never that simple. Now I'm mad at myself again for never saying "I love you" to Kai. The words were so often on the tip of my tongue but never able to come out, and he can say it so easily, even while he's undercover.

I stiffen and shake it off. This isn't me. Phoenix would never let these emotions gain control over her. Kai and I can talk when the mission is over. I just need to focus. People's lives depend on it.

As if on cue, Qadar walks in. "We have to get to the military ruins after dark. Do you think Kai is ready?"

I snatch my jacket, jumping to my feet. At least I'm sure about one thing. "Ready as he'll ever be."

CHAPTER 47

INTERNATIONAL FESTIVAL OF THE SAHARA
DOUZ, TUNISIA

It's almost sunset. We hop into a Jeep and set off for our destination—the middle of the desert where an old Roman palace lays in ruins—the drop off point. Noble's cousins run a camel trekking tour out there. This week is particularly busy because tourists are visiting for the festival.

We park behind the *H'naiech* Stadium where crowds of international visitors bustle around, talking excitedly about camel and horse races. Signs point to traditional Bedouin wedding parties and snake charming displays. Musicians play horns, drums, and bagpipe-type instruments around us. Traditional dancing is going on in different corners of the desert festival grounds. The pandemonium is a welcomed cover. All five of my senses light up and I'm drawn in every direction.

My fingers start tapping on my thigh, searching for my gift like an addiction I crave. I want to count every motorcycle, food stall, tourist, and animal in this place. I need my numbers to come back in full force, but without being grounded, the result will be nothing but trouble.

We weave through the crowds and arrive at a stall where Noble's family is busy setting up a caravan of camels.

"This way," Noble says. He points beyond the stadium to a stretch of desert where special Sunset Races will take place. "Bedouin traditions will be displayed as part of the festival. The most popular camel ride through the desert is at sunset. If we're near any of the caravans at that time, we shouldn't be noticed. That's why we chose this spot. It's close enough to the ruins but far enough away if we need to escape into the crowd."

"What about your family?" I ask, avoiding his eyes. He knows I'm struggling with something. His eyes are calculating my every move. He's being very careful with me. He probably thinks I'm still jealous. He has no clue that I know who he really is—if what I believe about him is true.

"They know how to hold their own, and this is their territory," he says, zipping up his vest. His desert boots and jeans make him look American, but then there's the other half—the dark hair, the loose white button-down that makes him look local. Whatever ethnicity he is, he blends in. "Qadar will make the drop off. We watch from a distance. If there is any sign of them using PSS Radar, we won't be able to use anything more than a cell phone." Noble doesn't spell it out, but PSS Radar tech is what enabled him to pick up on a government-protected biotag.

Noble hands Qadar the small device, a circular black holothumb the size of lipstick. It's so small, and yet it carries the most dangerous secrets in the world.

Qadar will trek ahead to the meeting point on foot, while we join a camel caravan. Beside us, tourists fill the area, giddy for their own romantic moonlit camel rides into the desert. They're joking and seem to ignore the loud bellows and groans the large beasts make. Not to mention the smell and the spitting. Guides from other caravans begin describing all the Roman and Phoenician ruins scattered throughout the desert in Tunisia.

Noble and I are going to a ruin that's not on the list, a place the locals call Ksar Douz.

Noble brings a camel over to me. He makes it kneel so I can climb on.

My legs grip around the beast, and I take hold of the saddle. Its back legs go up first throwing me slightly forward. Then its front knees push up. My legs strain in a new position, gripping onto the animal, using muscles I never knew I had.

We wander down a sandy path, riding side by side, at the back of the train of camels. Noble is sizing up everything around us, almost showing off.

I'm starting to feel frustrated. My gift has not returned yet but Noble acts like he knows exactly how it's going to come back. PSS said the sims would work. Noble said to give him three days. Apparently, no one knows how I function. Not even me.

"Tomorrow is my last day, you know," I say darting a glance his way. If he's Mandel, I want to give him a chance to tell me himself. He should. He still owes me answers. But he's silent. Somewhere in the back of my mind, I know I shouldn't push this right now, but I can't help it. My sims are highlighting Mandel for a reason—unless Noble manipulated them, in which case I'd be even more upset. "So if you want to tell me anything. Now's your chance."

"Like what?" he asks blankly, pointing ahead to a large, ruined stone structure that used to be an ancient palace. Inside, there is a circular courtyard made of stone. Ksar Douz.

My gift blinks on for a second, showing me the layout of the land, calculating every small detail before me. I'm hopeful that it's going to stay until it abruptly fizzles out, making the fire in my bones even hotter. "For starters, like what will help my numbers return. You said three days would be enough."

"Relax," he says, finding my eyes. "Your gift is there. You don't know it, but it is. You'll get it back and we'll find out who the Successor is." He steers us away from the group. "We're here. This part is tricky."

He hops off his camel then offers his hand to help me down too. His hand holds tight to mine, completely covering it. The feeling is distracting, warm and soft, and I almost trip. What is wrong with me? We tie up the camels and walk north to a different set of stone walls, a few hundred feet from the larger ruins. We can see directly inside Ksar Douz from where we are, but we're hidden pretty well from anyone at the ruin in front of us. He checks the cameras he set up earlier inside the Ksar and returns to me.

"May I?" he asks, touching K2.

I stretch out my wrist, and after he punches in a few numbers, we've got visual of the Ksar courtyard and all audio is routed to my earrings. When he's finished, I snap my wrist back.

"Easy." His calm is annoying me right now. The numbers inside him give him all of the advantage. As he confirms the nano-tech audio-earbud with Qadar is working, a debate goes on in my head.

On one hand, I want to ask Noble if he is Son of a Mandelbrot, on the other hand, I don't. Because if he is...then I won't know what to do. Every emotion tied to Mandel is too strong and with Noble in front of me, and our frequency mingling like it's meant to be entwined...I can't interpret what it means right now. It's all too much. My hand starts tapping furiously against my leg again.

Soon Noble is standing beside me, handing me a device that deceivingly looks like a cell phone. It's actually a mini satellite with more bandwidth than I've ever had. Noble is utterly amazing. Why didn't I use my gift to chart the stars or something like that after my mom died? Why finances and investments? Then I remember Mandel is the one who told me about the stock markets, and in my grumpy state I'm happy I now have someone to blame.

"We haven't detected any radar tech in use yet. Looks like we're in the clear."

"And you're sure the Successor won't be able to detect SMOKE on the holothumb?"

"Not unless the Successor is like you. And we both know the odds of that." He smiles.

"Don't you mean like *you*?" I ask, rolling my eyes.

"Jo, on a prodigy aptitude scale of one to ten, I might be higher than you. But in terms of the gift inside each of us—you're ahead of me. On that note, how did your sims go?" he asks.

"Terrible." I answer shortly. Confusion and anger are bubbling up. He says there's no pressure, but what he really means is we need to find out who the Successor is before tomorrow. We have one chance and I'm letting everyone down. Kai. Ms. T. My dad. Noble.

His face is straight, hiding any real emotions. He's probably feeling sorry for me, which makes things worse. He hacked *me*. Brought *me* to Tunisia. Lied about Qadar being his uncle.

"Don't worry, after the drop off you can do it again." He tucks his hair behind his ears in a charming way that bothers me.

"I don't think it's going to help," I say. "Each time I go in, I see nothing new. My gift has gone blind."

"No. It hasn't. There's something you're missing." He's so confident talking about *my* gift that my irritation grows.

"It's always the same. Two fights. Madame walks away unscathed." My hand is tapping up a storm. I'm all worked up. "Your bet's on the Sheikh, right? You're the genius here. I'll take your word for it."

"No. You can do this. I believe in you. We'll figure it out." Noble's voice softens. He can tell I'm upset. "What about phase three?"

Why does he keep mentioning phase three? "I told you. Phase three is too much for me right now." It's true. I don't know what I'll find there.

"Ok. What about phase one?" he asks.

I shake my head. I can't tell him about phase one either—especially not until I'm sure about his identity.

"All right," he says. "I know how you feel. You're not seeing what's around you yet, but your gift is there, and it will come back. Everything will be fine."

He's trying to be nice, but it snaps my patience because we're arguing about my gift when all I want is the truth.

"How can you be so sure everything is going to be ok, Noble?" My voice is raised. "You haven't really told me anything—who you really are, why you know all about me. You didn't tell me Qadar was your uncle. You could tell me what you know about Kai, but you haven't."

I'm fuming. My back is pressed up against a cold rock and it's digging into my shoulder blades. Here I am in the desert waiting on my boyfriend who lies to terrorists for fun, while in front of me may be the boy I haven't talked to in years who thinks he truly knows me.

"How can you stand there and tell me you know what it feels like?" I ask, my whole body tense. "You don't know what it's like to lose your gift. You've only ever flaunted yours in front of me. It feels like my eyes were ripped out. Like my whole world is crashing just like that stupid helicopter. Like my fingers are trying to learn braille but I've suddenly gone numb! I used to see infinity. And now I see nothing."

I turn away, frustrated, leaning my forehead against the crevice, waiting for Kai to show. I don't want to talk any more but then his warm hand is touching mine.

He gently pulls me away from the gap in the rock, slipping his other hand directly behind me where the rock wall has been digging into my back. His arm blocks the bumpy surface, like he knows the cushion will make it feel better. And it does.

"You're wrong, Jo." His whisper, sharp and strong, is so close I can feel it in my chest. The frequency is like a crescendo of music—or waves raging in a storm. "I do know how it feels."

"How can you say that?" I ask, shaking my head.

His eyes burn into mine with intensity. "Because I lost my gift once too."

My breath catches in my throat as numbers so vast and intense explode around us like fireworks. The only thing keeping me from spinning into chaos is the frequency that creates a tie to his stable numbers, and a thousand heat waves between.

"Oh yeah?" My voice is rough, snappy. I'm in his face now, a breath away. I lose myself in his eyes but I'm still an angry child demanding to know. "When?"

Our eyes lock in a showdown, of who will look away first. His hand moves from my arm to my face. His other hand joins it. My chin is now cupped in his hands—they're warm and strong. I don't move because everything about him pierces my insides even before he speaks.

"Two years and 156 days ago."

My heart shatters like a bomb was dropped on it. Every piece of that date is engraved on my mind forever. It sealed my fate for good. And now this—*him*, another equation, is added into it...the day they announced my death.

A hundred questions—no, a thousand—race up my throat, are on the tip of my tongue, about to spill out over my lips, but a voice shatters the moment.

"Kai is here," Qadar says. "But he's not alone and whoever followed him doesn't look happy."

CHAPTER 48

KSAR DOUZ
DOUZ, TUNISIA

A cloud of dust follows us as we crouch into position behind the ancient remnants of the Roman structure. Noble's jaw is tight, that same tortured expression on his face. Like learning to read Arabic, my mind is skipping backward, erasing all I know about him. Reading him in a new language altogether.

Qadar sounds again. "There's an entourage behind him. I can still make the drop off. But they're dangerously close behind. Someone might see me. Is Kai good for it?"

"Yes." I'm sure of it.

Noble's device is scanning for any sign of PSS Radar. "That's Albert Müller. The flashy one. No trackers. Go for it, then get out of there."

Qadar dashes into the ruins and places the holothumb in a secure hole under a stone ledge next to an old pillar. But all too soon Müller's men surround the ruins and the Sheikh's helicopter lands about a football field away. The Sheikh and the X-girl join the entourage.

Qadar is stuck, looking for a way to make it out unseen.

He slinks slowly into an alcove in the crumbling walls, waiting for the right moment to make a run for it, but even without my gift I can tell it doesn't look good. He's stuck. Thankfully, there are layers of walls he can hide behind.

Noble looks at me. "I don't like this," he says. Then to Qadar, "Hunker down until they're gone. We don't know why they followed Kai."

"They obviously don't trust him," I whisper.

I scan the ruins for Kai, and finally, I spot him.

Kai's walking forward like the desert belongs to him and he doesn't have a care in the world. He was supposed to come alone, but he doesn't look the least bit concerned the Loyalists are surrounding the area. That boy. What is he thinking?

Kai won't have time to reach the drop off point without it being obvious that he came to pick something up.

As soon as the Sheikh and the girl reach Müller and the fortress, Müller's lackey, a large man grabs Kai, but he yanks himself free.

"What is this?" Kai asks.

The Sheikh walks over to him, a sour expression on his face. "The meeting is tomorrow, isn't that right?"

They shove the girl forward and she whimpers. "I'm sorry... they forced me to tell them where you went."

"It's ok," Kai says to the girl. He turns to the men. "I came out to do recon of Douz and the stadium before tomorrow's meeting. No one else bothered to check it out to make sure it was clear of surveillance."

"No one else had to," Albert Müller says. Three more very large thugs walk up behind him.

This was unexpected. To make matters worse, Noble looks at me and mouths. "*Radar.*" Which means he has to turn off the PSS tech on K2.

Kai laughs confidently, and cocks his head, gauging what he's up against.

"You claim to be a Loyalist," Müller says. "You claim to have Montego's Blacklist. But we know nothing about you. And we just got word Montego's been taken out."

"Well, if you knew anything about the former empire," Kai practically spits, "you'd know Madame hid all her favorite associates until the last moment."

The girl on his right steps up. "I can vouch for him. He knew Madame. He's an ally." She's a liar, obviously, but at least she's protecting Kai.

"Someone shut that girl up," the Sheikh barks just like King. "How is it that Montego told you about this deal with the Loyalists and then he gets caught?"

Kai backs up in the direction of the holothumb. "That's unfortunate for him. That's why I was the backup." He stares down the Sheikh with an intimidating smile.

"Ah, so you have the device?" Müller asks.

"That was always the game."

"Then if you don't want to remain out here in the desert forever, I suggest you show me the holothumb."

Kai shakes his head. "The handoff will still happen on Friday." They circle toward Kai, but he moves his feet toward the drop-off location. He's almost there. The holothumb is not very well hidden. Just under a ledge two feet off the ground.

The Sheikh laughs. "I still don't believe you. None of us know you. We were all summoned here by the Successor. But you weren't."

"There's no way he'll be able to pick it up tonight," Qadar whispers.

"Don't say another word. Radar signals are popping up everywhere."

I lean over to Noble. "They're going to hurt him if he doesn't show them proof," I say. "We need a distraction so he can grab it. What if I let off one of these Fingertips? Kai will pick up on it."

"No." Noble shakes his head. "It won't work. My equations say it will fail."

"I've beaten the odds—"

"Look at Kai. You're the one who claimed he wouldn't fail in this operation."

I press my face against a hole in the rock wall, to get a better view. "He won't. I guarantee it. That doesn't mean he won't need a little help."

"We can't do it." Noble calculates our surroundings. "There are too many unknowns. Too many tourists. It could blow his cover. Expose us. And there could be more lackeys nearby. With such limited tech and visual, I can't be sure."

Müller and the Sheikh, along with several of their men surround Kai. "We can only assume you had a part in Montego's arrest."

"You assume wrong. Montego messed up. He sold information to the wrong people. I stuck to the plan."

"Nice story," he growls. "Maybe you need a bit of persuasion to tell us the truth." He nods to a very large man cracking his knuckles.

"I'm always open to persuasion." Kai takes off his jacket.

"You might not be after this."

Kai laughs confidently. "I wasn't talking about me."

CHAPTER 49

A giant of a man swaggers forward from the group of thugs. His tight black t-shirt makes his torso look like a solid trunk of oak. Tattoos cover his arms. His hands are so big they look like they could crush Kai's head like a small dog. Kai might be shorter and leaner, but they have no idea what he can do.

The man barks at him. "Which weapon?" He pulls out a knife, thumbing the blade in a show of how sharp it must be.

"I don't need one," Kai says, cracking his neck and tightening his fists.

The man scratches his mouth and smiles. "You sure pretty boy?" He points the knife at Kai like he's sketching his face with the blade.

No. I grip my forehead and moan. I do not want to see this.

Kai starts moving around the sandy arena, jumpy, on his toes likes he's getting ready. "Yeah, I'm sure." He flicks his wrist. It's an odd movement. What is he thinking? "You don't look sure though. That knife looks new. Betting it's never been used." Kai circles. I bite my lip and prepare to watch.

"You won't think your jokes are so funny in a minute, pretty boy." The big guy sneers.

"I don't tell jokes," Kai says rolling his neck, "But you're right. This fight will be over in a minute."

The big man grunts. Kai fakes a jab. And the fight begins.

We watch from the gaps in the stones as the big man lunges. Steel glints in the moonlight. Fists and feet fly just as I remember from watching Kai in China, like angels across the sand kicking up clouds of dust. Kai's so quick and methodical, so elegant that I find it hard to picture him as a real fighter—until he's actually in a real fight. He's trained hard to know just how to interpret his opponent's moves and beat them. But Kai isn't really fighting. Not yet anyways. He's dancing, circling. He's like me with my numbers, but in the arena.

The man swings and Kai steps in close and blocks the man's arm and then drops down and sweeps him off his feet. The man recovers and jumps up, then attacks. Fists, jabs, hooks, and kicks. It's all happening so fast, but Kai isn't giving it his all. His form looks sloppy, almost on purpose. His hands are down, but he's still circling. Then I realize—his farce is intentional. He's playing the fight, using it for his own purposes. Kai has a different plan all together. He's looking for the *holothumb*. This is his way of finding it.

There are no numbers in my head to help me understand the fight, but Noble's eyes trace it all and give me a numerical play-by-play. After a minute, he leans over to me. "Kai is close enough to the holothumb now." Then he cringes. "I'm pretty sure he's going to—"

Slam. The tattooed man hits Kai square in the face. Kai drops to his knees and throws himself over the stone ledge. *The ledge.* Exactly where the holothumb is.

The big man doesn't slow down. Sensing an advantage, he charges, swinging the blade wildly.

Kai tucks his shoulder into a roll as his fingers stretch and grab a handful of sand. It looks so natural I don't immediately understand what he just did. Then, like the snap of a snake he slides the holothumb into his boot as he rolls to his feet, and the rest of the sand flies out of his hand at the man's eyes.

"Nice punch." Kai wipes the blood from his lip. A sly grin spreads across his face. Ooh. I don't envy what is coming for this man. That grin means only one thing. Kai was going easy on him. Now there's nothing left for him to do but finish this fight. *Finishing* moves are no joke when you want to end a brawl. They can break a neck, a knee, an elbow—some of them are fatal. Kai knows how to do them all, but I don't think he ever has. Phase two of my sim returns with a feeling of dread.

The man charges, but Kai is ready. He redirects the blade with his forearm, then twists his torso as it slices through air. Now side by side and a few feet apart Kai snaps a kick and the chunky sole of his boot lands hard and square on the big man's left knee. There's an audible pop.

The big man is down, obviously in pain, but he's tough. Kai shoots forward as the big guy is pushing himself up. Kai's knee connects with a crunch to the man's jaw. I cringe. The knife falls from his hand before he even hits the sand. The beaten man groans in the dust.

"48 seconds," Noble mumbles.

"What?" I can't take my eyes off the scene.

"Kai said it would be over in a minute…he's not punctual…"

"Enough." I roll my eyes, not wanting a millisecond play by play.

Kai stands over his opponent, bends down and picks up the knife. In a flash he whips around and the knife thuds into the sand. Directly between the feet of the two remaining thugs.

"Which one of you is next?" Kai taunts. He seems so feral, like his swagger and confidence have a lethal tangibility right now. But he has seen what these people do to others. He's seen what King and Madame have done to me, and he never wants it to happen again.

Müller urges his other two thugs forward. He's still not convinced of Kai's loyalty. The two charge Kai at a full-on sprint. But even from where I'm sitting it looks easy. They're both leading too much, showing Kai what they're going to do. As the first guy swings, Kai slides under the punch and comes up twisting with his elbows in tight. Like a hammer, he connects with the thug's face and the guy folds in half. Carrying his momentum, Kai continues his spin, kicking the second thug in the groin. He drops to his knees, then with the same elbow Kai clocks the other man in the back of the head. Both of them are down.

"5.8 seconds." It's the first time I hear awe in Noble's voice.

Both thugs lie in the sand, dizzy and down for the count. Kai is reaching for his boot, pulling something out as he stares down the Sheikh and Müller.

Everything happens so fast that everyone is still processing what Kai just did. No one has even reacted to him yet.

With gritted teeth Kai leans in close to Müller. "I didn't come here to fight. I came here for the master-file."

Finally, some of the other lackeys snap to action and draw their weapons on Kai. The desert buzzes in silent tension.

Kai slowly raises his hands above his head. It's been mere seconds counting by my pounding heart. It feels like I've run a marathon. I can't blink. Noble grins.

Kai's hands are still in the air, and I finally see why Noble is grinning. It's so small I didn't see it at first. Kai presses the only button on the side of the holothumb and a hologram appears, with the sign of the Loyalists.

"Well done." The Sheikh nods. "You proved you can fight, and you have what you promised. You are still welcome in my Dar. Madame always chose her people well."

"Not well enough," Kai spits out with a playful wicked laugh as he looks at Müller. It's meant to be a threat. He's playing their game and he is doing it well. He doesn't even sound like Kai.

Müller meanders over. "So you can fight. That proves nothing to me. I want loyalty. Bring him out." When he says that, a sound rustles behind us. Noble pushes me to the ground.

Noble's hand covers his mouth and he's motioning for me to stay low. "No," he gasps.

The next thing I know, men are rounding the corner, dragging another man into the arena.

Qadar. They found him.

"This man says he was on a caravan nearby. Are you sure he wasn't here to meet you?" Müller asks, eyes pointed and cold.

"Never seen him before in my life." Kai is telling the truth.

"Good. Then you won't miss him when he's gone. The Successor demands loyalty, and for you, the test is to make him disappear. Consider it a gift for the Successor."

My stomach sinks because I've seen that look on Kai's face before. He's ready.

CHAPTER 50

Noble's fist pounds the ground. We're crouched down behind a stone wall in the corner of the ruins, but Noble's legs are flexing like he's about to stand. "There are three possibilities to save my uncle's life right now—"

My sims fly through my head. The man in the dust. Not breathing. He was big, like Qadar. No, it couldn't be. I refuse to believe it. Kai would never take a man's life just to prove to the Successor that he is one of them.

I grab Noble's vest, stopping him from moving. "Wait. We can't do anything. He won't do it," I say, mostly convincing myself. I draw on everything I know about Kai. I've watched him train a hundred times. I can read his movements without numbers, like I have the last few months. I watch him now. Kai is warming up for something. He has a plan; I just don't know what.

"Jo, the numbers aren't good. He's jumpy. He doesn't know what he's going to do. And if he doesn't go through with it, they will." Noble's fidgeting hardcore.

"No, just wait. Kai will know what to do." But Noble's right. Kai is nervous. Or extremely focused. It could be either. And if I'm wrong then the Loyalists will end Qadar before we can save him.

"I'm not going to watch my uncle die because you trust your boyfriend!" Noble hisses under his breath. His eyes dart across the Sahara taking in every possibility, a sheen of sweat on his otherwise smooth brow. I don't need numbers to know Noble's about to do something foolish. "He's all I have." The words are a slap of desperation, matching the wild look in his eyes. His foot angles to the right. He's got a plan of his own. But I grab his hand and squeeze.

"Trust me. I know you see things I don't, but I know Kai." It's there, in my gut. I can feel it. At the same time, I can't prove to Noble or myself how Kung fu could win in this scenario. My hands grip his vest tighter, even though I feel him pulling away. I refuse to let go.

Noble's fists tighten and his eyes drill into mine. To him, I'm choosing Kai over his uncle. I'm trusting Kai's ability over Noble's numbers. It makes no sense to him. But I know without a doubt if he interferes, no one will make it out of here and all our plans will be ruined.

"I can't, Jo." He shakes his head and moves to stand. "I'm going down there. Please don't stop me."

As he lifts his legs, I know the movement will mess up everything. A move Kai taught me springs to mind, and without thinking, I kick his feet from under him. I push him to the ground once more. I'm straddling his chest, facing him. Holding him down. He's going to resist me. I see it in his face. I don't know how to reach him, to get him to trust me. Then the word just slips out.

"Mandel." The use of his old nickname is like an electric shock. He snaps forward, looking at me in a whole new way. "Mandel. I've trusted you until now. Tunisia. The Bardo. Montego. Now trust me." The frequency surges inside us as dense and turbulent as a sandstorm. I feel everything chaotic in him. Which means he must feel something stable in me.

We lock eyes, and the frequency connects dots in my mind to an outburst of numbers that stirs memories of Harrison back in Seattle.

Kai may even teach me the death kick.

That's it. Harrison was talking about a move Kai had been studying. It's not a death kick, but that's what it might sound like to an amateur like Harrison. The Masters called it *Tou-Qi.*

"Noble, I know what he's going to do. If you go in there, you're going to ruin everything."

I remember the day Kai begged his masters to teach him this technique. They said if he wanted to learn it, he had to have it done to himself, so he knew what it felt like. Kai, in all his eagerness, agreed. Tou Qi means to "steal breath". It temporarily suspends respiration and circulation, reducing a person to a state of almost comatose, so that they appear dead. This state can last up to 20 minutes. If any doctor were to check the victim in those moments, it'd look like a heart attack took their life.

I remember when the brothers did it to Kai. I'll never forget his moans. He couldn't eat or talk for a few hours, alternating between feverish groans and bouts of vomiting. He barely even recognized me. But he recovered. It took Kai a good 24 hours of pain and headaches for him to bounce back to normal, and the technique doesn't leave any internal damage—if done correctly. That's what he's about to attempt.

I also understand why Kai is nervous. He has never done it successfully. And if he fails this time, he has something to lose. A real person at his mercy. Qadar, a man who promised my goals would be his. Noble's uncle. Kai can't fail.

I squeeze my eyes shut, tapping into anything my gift might offer me, but all I hear is a silent prayer. "Don't worry. Qadar will be fine." My eyes narrow. "Hurt, but fine." I'm saying it out loud to believe it myself.

"Jo..." Noble's eyes are like a wild animal's, calculating

everything at a hundred miles an hour. His whole body is tense, restraining himself. "I can't lose him."

My hands hold his face forcing him to look into my eyes, see my certainty. "You won't. Don't trust your numbers this time. Trust me."

Noble squeezes his eyes shut, forcing the muscles in his neck and shoulders to relax. I know how hard it is to do that. To block out your numbers. Especially as a sign of trust. More so when someone you love is on the line. I slowly back off him, and lean against the ruin's stones, eyes on Kai. Noble moves next to me, his fists still in a knot.

Kai rubs his wrists, warming up. An average fighter might not pick up on why this move isn't deadly. A fatal blow is usually to the head or neck. But this is to the chest, in a very specific place—to steal your breath.

The girl, Ennéa, who followed him out to the desert, is watching from the perimeter of the Ksar Douz as the desert cools down. The Sheikh backs up beside her. He leans against the crumbling stone walls, peering through the cracks to see if any danger lurks. But Müller's men sufficiently surround it.

Kai looks at the girl who's watching every move. "Please turn away," he says to her. "I don't want you to see this." But she doesn't.

"Please," Qadar says to Kai. "I have to get back to my family. There are sandstorms in the north."

I grit my teeth. The message for Kai from Private Global Forces. Qadar is a genius. Only Kai would understand it. The slightest twitch of his lip. "How unfortunate to be on their own."

Now I get it. Bai's message is that he can't help, that his hands are tied. That Kai—and us—are on our own. Suddenly, the weight of this whole operation is crashing down on me.

Kai cracks his knuckles, walks over to Qadar. All eyes focus on him. To Qadar's credit, he doesn't look scared.

Noble is staring in disbelief. I pull him closer to me. "Don't watch. Please." His ragged breath is in my ear. He's squeezing his eyes shut, trying to turn off the calculations. Because he knows the odds are slim. He's choosing to trust me but it's taking every ounce of self-control he has. His body is shaking as he holds it back.

All I can do is have faith. Kai can get this right. I trust in his goodness. In his ability. That boy thrives on pressure, it gives him focus. I believe he can do this. He has to.

Müller removes the blade Kai threw at the ground, and hands it to Kai. "Go ahead."

"I already told you. I'm dangerous without weapons." Kai's knees bend and eyes close. He focuses himself, drawing in a deep breath. As he exhales, Kai walks up to Qadar, doesn't pause, doesn't say a word and in a blink, his hips flex and twist. Like a loaded spring releasing a storm of fury, all his energy and might are executed into one jump. Time stands still, specks of sand fly off his boot. And with one kick, his heel smacks and plants itself into the center of Qadar's chest. There's a gasp, choking, a forced exhale. Like the main sail of a ship snapping as the wind drives it. Qadar wavers, his eyes roll back into his head. He falls to his knees and slumps sideways onto the sand.

My throat tightens and my stomach locks up as I see a replay of my sims.

The Sheikh ushers a man over as the other lackeys stare in awe and fear. The servant rushes over to Qadar. They check his pulse and breathing. My flesh chills and my heart pounds in my ears. I believe in Kai, but sometimes seeing makes believing so hard.

The servant looks up at Müller. "He's dead."

Müller slithers over like a snake, his band of men behind him. He stretches out his hand to Kai. "Welcome to the Loyalists."

CHAPTER 51

It takes all the strength I have to hold Noble back, his heart slamming its pain against my chest.

Müller's lackeys drag Qadar's body behind another archway of stones leading into the interior of Ksar Douz. Müller and the Sheikh don't let their eyes off of Kai. Their entourage of thugs stare at him in awe like he's a newborn legend or a fearsome madman.

Kai smiles, that same winsome grin I've seen when he accomplishes a new challenge. Does that mean the body behind him in the dark will still be alive in twenty minutes? He should be—he has to be.

Sweat drips down my forehead, tickling me in this small, cramped space. Noble must be asking the same thing. He's completely still but his muscles are taut as a bowstring, surely counting down the seconds to when he can get to Qadar.

The Sheikh joins Müller next to Kai. "I see now we have much to discuss. Let's go."

Müller motions for everyone to head back, except for a few of his men. "Search the perimeter. There may be others." He nods towards Qadar's body. "Keep watch on the area until the festival dies down." A passing caravan with a string of camels meander past, tourists' laughter and conversation tickling the air, not a hint of what is near them in the darkening ruins.

"What about them?" one of Müller's men shout.

"They're tourists," Kai replies. "Don't draw attention to us." Then men scatter in all directions.

The girl Ennéa walks up beside Kai as he's stuffing the holothumb back into his boot. He stands up. She touches his face where it's red and swollen.

"Sorry you had to see that," Kai says. "You'd better stay with the Sheikh. He's upset that you followed me."

"He doesn't care about me." She looks his direction, then back to Kai. "Why are you so intent on this meeting?"

Kai stands under the moon, peering out over the desert in my direction, like he's searching for me. Then he draws the girl close to him, her back to me. They're body to body. His hand swings low around her waist, caressing her but not in the same way he touches me, this is different. His hand still on her waist, he points west.

He knows I'm watching. He's telling us to go west, but why? His other hand slides up her body in a way I hate watching, then circles back over her bare arms. He gently pulls the girl's head close to his, the way he's done to me so many times. "I told you," he says close to her ear, "I'm ambitious. And loyal."

He smiles into the dark night before he walks away with her to an uncertain tomorrow.

CHAPTER 52

Noble and I sit in agonizing silence for twenty minutes waiting for the rest of Müller's entourage to leave the area.

Noble's jaw is clenching and unclenching, and his hands are sticky with sweat. "I'm going down there now." His face is contorted with worry.

"Wait. One more minute." My knuckles are white, still holding on to his vest. "There are still men in every direction. Check the tech again." Hopefully, this will distract him.

He winces. "They're scanning everything with PSS radar," Noble says. "We're pretty much blind right now, at least for an hour. We can't use any PSS tech, but we have to get to him. Now. I can't wait any longer." He lunges forward into the desert.

I sprint after him and push him back against the ruins. "You're not thinking clearly. Let me go first." I inch over to the edge of the broken structure that shields us. As the night's festivities continue, Müller's men are heading toward town. There is a small entrance on the north side for us to sneak into Ksar Douz. Qadar's body was near that side of the wall. But if Qadar is alive, he might not be able to stand for more than a few minutes.

"Noble," I say, "send a text message asking your family to drop another camel near ours tied to that palm." Then I point out the small entrance. The minute I do, the calculations on Noble's face are clear. He's not waiting. He dives out of the structure and dashes to the Ksar. I have no choice but to follow. Apparently, Noble's numbers help him avoid detection because no one seems to notice us.

The inside of Ksar Douz is empty now. There's nothing but piles of stone and a vacant ancient courtyard covered in dust and sand, with spots of blood from Kai's fight. But there are a few of Müller's men still left patrolling the area. We stay low, sneaking over to where they dragged Qadar. We find him on his back, arms sprawled out on the rocks. His clothes are dusty, and his arms are scratched from being dragged over the rough stones. His face is deathly pale, and his chest is not moving—or at least that is how it appears. When the masters did this to Kai, he was limp and cold. It wasn't pretty. It was frightening seeing him in that state, even though I knew he was alive. Now, with Qadar, it's the same. But he should have woken up by now.

Noble frantically checks his pulse, then sighs with relief. "Faint, but there. But he's not breathing well enough."

"Adjust his hips, it'll open his lungs."

Noble nods, knowing exactly what I'm referring to. He lifts his hips upward, the way you would to a person who has had their breath knocked out of them. Qadar draws in a large breath. Noble's relief is palpable. Tension drains from his mouth and shoulders.

Then Qadar moans loudly, like he's drunk out of his mind. My head shoots up to see if anyone notices. No one cares or turns a head.

We sit him up and the moaning gets louder. Noble tells him to quiet down, but he's delirious. He sounds just like one of the old camels back at Farah's camp. Someone is going to notice us if we don't get him out of here.

"I don't think I can carry him to the camels," Noble whispers between clenched teeth, struggling to hold Qadar upright. "But bringing them to him will draw too much attention."

"Kai said west was our best bet." My eyes chase the moonlight across the desert and forsaken ruins to a distant haze of lights and voices.

"The festival," Noble says. "There's a night race coming soon, it'll be the perfect cover. Let's head that way." He shakes his uncle. "Qadar, you have to stand." Noble manages to get him to his feet. Qadar's staggering, but like Kai, he's strong. We check the area and wait for Müller's men to face the other direction. Just as we do, a group of tourists bumble down the path, making their way to Ksar Douz, drawing their attention to the south side. We head like mad for the camels tied up near the northwest dunes.

We stagger out. Qadar slouches over both Noble's and my shoulders.

"Let's hope no one notices a dead man walking," Noble mutters. "Thankfully, it's festival time. Staggering men are common right now."

We make it to the camels and lower one of them down for Qadar to get on its back. Noble has to tie Qadar on to the beast. He's completely slumped over and still moaning. Then he throws up all over the saddle blanket.

"That was Farah's favorite blanket." Noble's face bunches up. "Let's get him to my family."

As soon as we start moving toward the noise and crowds, some of Müller's lackeys pass us on the north side of Ksar Douz. They go in the same place we came out. Which means, if they investigate further, they'll discover the body is gone.

Noble notices the same thing. He grabs Qadar's reins. "Let's move. Get behind that caravan now."

A caravan is moving slowly making its way back toward the

Festival and the commotion of crowds and stalls and tourists. Thank God it's tourist season. The camels start jostling up and down. I didn't realize camels could move so fast.

As soon as we're near the caravan, Müller's men exit the Ksar yelling to each other. I'm not sure what they're saying but I can guess. My heart seizes like a bird caught in a cage. But Noble's doesn't miss a beat.

"Come on. I know this desert like the back of my hand. Follow me!" He leads us across the vast plain nudging the camel faster.

The men notice that we're speeding forward. A few start running, picking up the chase close behind us, while others scramble to where a few motorcycles are parked, but we're headed where the camel riders are preparing to race. Crowds are gathering to watch. We've got about a hundred feet to go when my phone starts ringing.

"It's my dad." I yell.

"Don't answer it! We have to get out of here!" Noble rushes us through another group of palm trees. "Sorry!" he says to tourists and caravans stooped over a water station.

"I have to answer this. Or he is going to kill me!"

"What do you think *they're* trying to do?" Noble shakes his head, knowing my next move.

I answer the phone, catching my breath. "Dad, hi." I laugh awkwardly. The camels bump up and down. My voice goes up and down with each thump. Qadar is groaning like a beast in the background. Noble zips around the hills, leading the way.

"Hi Jo," he says. "How are you?"

I look over my shoulder at three men chasing us. "Interesting day engaging the locals."

"You sound out of breath..." he asks. "Everything ok?" The sound of hooves pounding, and now music and horns, and camels groaning in the background only intensify my panting.

"You'll never guess. I'm riding a camel, actually. And, um,

it's sort of a race. And I'm in the lead, Dad. I really gotta go if I'm going to win this thing. Can I call you tomorrow?" I arch my neck back. Three men are still trailing us from the south while three more arrive on the north, trying to box us in. But they can't be sure we aren't tourists because we're now mixed into the pandemonium of the oasis where horses and snake charmers and tents and foods stalls fill the area.

A few of Müller's men are up ahead ditching the motorcycles and jumping into jeeps.

"Don't you guys do any work?" Dad chuckles. "Well, Jo. You were right. Seems like I was worried for nothing. Just glad to hear your voice. One more thing—"

Noble yanks on my camel to pull it alongside his, and the animal bellows.

"I've been learning from your example—not letting fear hold you back. And I just want to tell you that I believe in you and I'm proud of you. You're right to choose a job that can change the world," my dad says, "Now go win that race!"

My face blanches. "Thanks, Dad. Talk tomorrow?" No time to savor my dad's words, I hang up just as my camel charges forward with Noble's. "See? That wasn't so bad."

Crowds line up to see a Berber wedding and all the beautiful people dressed in traditional clothing, performing songs and stories. Other men parade brilliantly decorated horses through the area. Noble leads us to a line of tent stalls and a hitching post for camels.

"We have to ditch the camels at my family's stall and get to the Jeep." Noble jumps off and ties its lead rope to a stake in the ground. He helps Qadar off the camel, but he nearly falls to the ground.

"Dehydration from the races." Noble explains to some curious onlookers.

But Qadar looks so drunk, everyone laughs. "Sure he is." They laugh. "Too much huka!" Someone shouts. "Look at that drunk!"

I have no idea how to make the camel bend down, so I pull my legs over the side and slide off the beast. Noble's cousin recognizes me and takes the reins. We get Qadar into the tent where he collapses on the floor just before Müller's men come around the corner.

In Arabic, Noble explains something to his family and their faces frown. Farah is worried. Qadar's eyes roll back into his head. He looks bad, but he's actually tolerating the pain far better than even Kai had. Noble bends down, a hand on his forehead and whispers something in Arabic to him. Qadar's head sways a bit.

Then Noble stands, taking an off-white colored shawl from a chair, and veils me in it. He takes a traditional Berber robe that looks like Obi Wan Kenobi for himself. "We have to get out of here. Lead them away from my family," Noble says.

Noble's cousins come back inside, whispering to him. "There are men patrolling the major roads." I peek outside of the tent. The three lackeys are still searching for us in the crowd.

"Ok." Noble looks at me, his numbers clearly at work. "When the races start, we make a dash for the Jeep."

I nod. When a loud bang in the night air signals the race, Noble grabs my hand. We sneak to a lot where many cars are parked, find the Jeep and hop in.

"Fold in the mirrors."

"Why?" I ask.

"It's gonna be a tight squeeze." He looks at his watch, calculating the right moment. He starts the engine not a second sooner than the moment when the night's largest festivities explode with fireworks and music. He hits the gas and plows a narrow path through the oasis palms.

"What is this?" I shout over the roar of the car.

"A camel trail. Don't worry. No one uses it at night." We

speed through, palms and sand flying past us. Engines roar to life behind us in the background. I'm not sure if they're following us or blocking the roads.

Noble zigzags back and forth, then pulls over and cuts the lights. It's so dark I can barely see his face. I'm almost glad I can't because now that we're alone our conversation from earlier is returning. Except it's muddled with Qadar and Kai and—Mandel. I gulp the thought away.

"What are you doing right now?" I whisper.

"Calculating." His tone is low, the frequency rolling much more like a quiet brook. "Sorry. No tech, not even a light right now. Anything could draw them this way. At least the moon's out."

"How long?" I ask.

"We have roughly an hour to wait until the radar won't work on our tech. My family is pretty upset at what happened to Qadar. I told them to take him home in an hour. You'd better be right."

Grimly, I agree. I better be. Inwardly, I'm also fiercely proud. Kai did it. But how long until his moves run out? The deal is tomorrow and there are so many unsolved equations. If we can't figure out who the Successor is, Kai won't know who to give it to, and the master-file will be spread around the globe to an A-list of world's worst criminals.

"So now what?" I ask. "We just sit in this Jeep for an hour?"

"No, we head back to the camp. We've lots to do." He starts the engine and pushes the gas pedal, slow but steady. "Buckle up."

I grip the car door handle. "Are you crazy? It's pitch black out."

Noble scoffs. "The map is in my head."

I snap my buckle closed. "Of course it is."

CHAPTER 53

At the edge of the oasis Noble parks the car. "Let's walk the rest of the way, just in case."

It's still black as ink, minus the star-dotted sky. My gift buzzes in the dark like I'm in the helicopter again. With each step, I feel disoriented and find myself dodging phantom branches while Noble walks as if it's daylight.

Without me having to ask, he moves closer and grabs my hand. "I'll help you. This part is tricky." He draws me around a labyrinth of rocks and hardened sand. "This way."

He weaves us through what seems like a maze. His hand squeezes lightly, leading me this way and that. I stay close to him, the same smell of fire-smoke and cardamom filling my senses. At one point, I even close my eyes and follow his movements—it intensifies the frequency between us, which is still alive and undulating.

A normal person would get lost. But not Noble, not with *our* gift. The numbers map out areas, constructing blueprints forever stamped in the mind. Evidently, it also keeps him oriented like it used to do for me. A flutter shoots through me. It's the strangest sensation in the world to trust someone who knows what you know and what you've experienced.

But apparently neither of us are ready to talk about the *elephant* in the desert. Kai's face is still clouding my mind. Watching him fight and risk everything. Noble is right. He thrives on danger. If his father saw him now…

The lights around the pool come into view. The windless night makes the camp feel especially still. No one is in sight. Everyone is at the festival. I welcome the much-needed calm and breathe in deeply.

"All right," Noble says, slowly dropping my hand. "No one is behind us. I think we're safe." We follow the sandy path. I notice all the shrubs poking through the terrain and I miss counting them.

The lights over the blue pool sparkle. When we pass it, I stop. I fiddle with my earring, wondering if the Successor has enough PSS nano-tech to trace the smartdust to this location.

"Don't worry. They didn't steal that tech yet. They don't have *Sway* either," he says looking at my lips. I blush again. The lipstick is still on—72 hours. I could use this on Noble and he would tell me everything. He wouldn't even remember I asked. But I couldn't do that to him. Noble has a right to tell me his secrets in his own time.

Suddenly I'm embarrassed to be in his presence. Very aware of my messy hair, and the dirty clothes I haven't changed since I arrived in the desert. I try to act normal, but it's much harder than expected. Especially now that I know…

"Do you need anything?" Waves of Noble's frequency wash over me. I can't get over the intensity of his eyes at Ksar Douz. Right now, they send a sweet and dreadful invitation like the night itself is asking to talk, but you know you only have until sunrise.

The water looks so calm in the pool that I wander over and sit cross-legged on the patio where we talked the first night about the stars.

"You said we had an hour until we could do anything,

right?" My eyes say it all. We need to talk.

His face lights up like maybe he thought I'd never ask. He nods, a grin on his face that silences me. He walks over and plants himself next to me. My stomach flips. Attraction is another science altogether. The longer you are near a person, the more you help one another, bonds form, opinions change. We're both aware that everything will change tomorrow. We don't have time to waste.

We face each other, both of us trailing our fingers in the water, most likely wishing we could dive in and swim instead of facing all the chaos around us. But for this moment, everything is still.

We stare at each other for several hushed beats, capturing a space and time where unspoken sensations do all the talking. In an untouchable place where feelings collide and thunder, where fires burn in the undefined reaches of the soul. All the words in the world can't explain what a heart is saying in that place and if they do, they'll mess it all up. But I know, eventually, words need to be spoken.

So I take a deep breath and touch his cheek, my eyes seeing something out of a dream. "Mandel." The frequency between us vibrates like a plucked harp string. "You're real. A person. With a name. And a face." It's almost too good to be true. As a girl of thirteen, I dreamed of this very moment. "I need to know, Noble. Everything. I don't want you to be a mystery anymore."

"I always promised one day I wouldn't be," he says, touching my hand on his cheek. "Digits."

CHAPTER 54

Noble looks up at the stars as if they've already heard his story a hundred times. He draws in a deep breath, and his eyes shift to mine.

"The day I learned you died was one of the worst days of my life. The world stopped and I started spinning. I had nightmares for weeks." He shakes his head, and exhales. "I'd already been looking and watching for you since the news announced your disappearance, then abduction." His brow tightens.

"I'd come so close to creating a facial recognition software that would scour the earth for you. Every text of audio that I had on record. Every photo that was on the Internet."

I interrupt him. "Is that the same software in the tech-tent?"

"Yeah," he says. "I was going to find you. It could see anywhere, find anyone. It was almost ready. I had two more adjustments to go, then the news of your 'death' came."

Noble's face falls, as if he's reliving it. Back then, I only thought of how my death affected my family. They mourned for months, years. I didn't think about how it would affect my teachers, my friends, or Mandel…and looking at his face now, it hammers me to the ground. One of Red's old mantras skitters to mind. "We live knowing our lives affect others."

Noble's face straightens. "Grief hit me in a way I never knew was possible. The next day I woke up and everything was a blank slate. My numbers were gone. Silent. Everything you've experienced with the loss of your gift. The madness, the blindness, feeling the world stripped bare. Felt like my strength was taken from me. Like I had no protection. To make matters worse, my parents didn't believe me." He shudders. My throat tightens thinking about it, and a surge of protectiveness bubbles hot.

He folds his hands into fists. "You don't need to know what happened after that. But that's when I ran. My mother's brother, Qadar, was the only person who seemed safe to me. I found him, told him everything. He believed me. Promised to protect me."

Noble runs his hand through his hair, surely recalling that kick to Qadar's chest. His reactions at the Ksar Douz make much more sense. I want to apologize for what I put him through, but he moves on.

"Qadar took me to the last place my parents would look. The desert in Tunisia, out among the stars, where all I could do was heal and dream. Qadar became a father to me. I don't know if my parents are looking for me or if they even care I'm alive."

"I always wanted you to run away," I say, watching him, pondering the similarities he lived through with his parents and me with Madame. "I'm glad you found Qadar. He's a good man."

"Yeah. I'm glad Kai didn't take him out." He huffs a shaky laugh, more to himself than anyone.

"Me too." We're silent for a moment. Kai is an obvious wall between us. But my heart is flying at a hundred miles an hour. At one point in time, Mandel meant everything to me. "Go on. Please."

He gives me that shy grin. "After that, I tried to adjust to life without equations. I'll admit, it was chaos. I was so used to performing that I felt worthless. Qadar insisted I learn Arabic, which at first made me feel even worse. It was like I was five years old again, learning to read and write backwards. It didn't help that the little kids were finishing their homework before me." He tucks his hair behind his ears then leans back. "But being out here, looking up at the stars, hearing nothing but the sand moving on the dunes and wind in the palms, I forgot about tests and formulas and expectations. Slowly, all that weight was lifted off me and I just explored. That's when I started to remember."

"Remember what?" I ask.

"Mandelbrot said *'for a thinking person the greatest mental illness is not knowing who you are'*. I remembered that I loved fractals. Finding order in the chaos. To fix my eyes on what was unseen and find its secret." He picks up a shriveled palm leaf on the patio. "Like the coral. Like the lightning."

My skin chills. "Then your gift came back?"

"It flickered for a while, like yours. I took note of what triggered it—long nights peering up at the stars, water rippling, bark on trees. The numbers started to define things in a new way, like Arabic did for me, like a child. I started to trust my gift was there, even if I couldn't see it. When it came back, I didn't even notice. One day, I just started to operate in it again, like it'd never left." He looks at me and puts his hand on my arm. Goosebumps shoot down my back. "That's why I know it will come back for you, Jo. I can't explain it, but I see your gift thriving inside you. It's very much alive."

"So that's how you became the NASA Tipper? Out here?"

"Smart girl. I started fiddling with my tech again and as you can see, this place has almost zero light pollution. I researched the energy the planets emit, started tapping into satellites, then I got an idea for star coding. One day, NASA needed help. My gift clicked. I had a solution for them, and I didn't think twice.

I sent an anonymous tip, they tried it, and it worked. So, I kept helping when I could. I liked doing what I loved without the pressure of performance and expectation."

"Don't we all?" I smile at Mandel, still marveling that he is the same boy from my blog. "So who knows your real identity? You said you don't live here year-round. Do you live alone?"

"Not totally alone. I talk to people when I go out. Which I do—go outside. I'm not a hermit. And despite what you might believe, I interact with people a lot. I just don't like them knowing who I am or what I do. And I'm in Tunisia a lot because of Qadar."

"So no one here knows you're the NASA tipper, not even him?" I ask.

"Qadar knows everything. He's never told a soul. Everyone else thinks I'm smart, but that's it. They treat me like a normal guy, which is an indulgence for people like us." He smirks, his lip curled up on the right side. His magnetic eyes make it hard to look away. A shiver shoots through me. My face flushes with heat. Maybe it is better if he doesn't look at me.

Dang. Now I'm blushing even more. The numbers give me away. He sees it. For the first time, he admits it.

"Jo. I feel the connection we have too. Which makes things really difficult for me. But I would never compromise you and Kai. Honor is something I learned here. Without honor, things are spoiled. The only reason I'm hard on Kai is because I know he's not right for you...and I don't want you to get hurt."

My fists curl in my lap. "Tell me what you know."

"It's between you two. He'll tell you. That much I know." He looks out over the dunes. I wish I had my numbers right now, predicting what he'll do next.

"Then tell me how you know all about me," I say. "When? How?"

He turns back, a painful look of restraint on his face. "Much later, after my gift resurfaced, I snuck back to my parent's house and retrieved all my tech for the facial recognition software. One day, I plugged in the tech I created for you—yours was the only face that was programmed into it. When I booted it up, it immediately started to alert me that it'd found you."

"I was shocked, then ecstatic." He bites his lower lip. "Until I saw you were at some EXPO and it looked like some crazy woman was threatening you. I was about to call the police, but seconds later, you were with a swat team explaining everything. To my horror, I heard everything you reported to them about Madame and King. I also saw you with Kai."

"I turned it off. Glad you were alive. Not knowing what to do. But as news came out about Madame and King's arrest, then the economy and Kai's father's company...it wasn't hard to put all the pieces together. No one else could have done that. I knew who it was."

"Why didn't you reach out?" I ask.

"You had Kai and I wasn't ready to reveal myself." He looks up again at the sky. "I was wary of people. I'd had an anonymous life for almost a year. You'd never responded to my other emails...and I'll admit, Kai's some tough competition. Honestly, a year ago I didn't even know how to look at myself. I certainly didn't know how a girl like you would look at me." He turns away, fingers trailing in the water.

I stare at him now, so beautiful and brilliant. Sometimes, it's a shame we can't see ourselves through other's eyes. He turns, feeling my stare. Our gazes mingle, the frequency filling the space between us. I'm certainly looking at him now.

"The more I read about China, the more you inspired me. I started using my tech for good. That's about when the radicals started wreaking havoc in Tunisia. Montego soon entered the scene. Then, one day, Kai stumbled into the picture. And here we are..."

"How did you know about the frequency?" I ask.

He grabs his head and groans. "Don't be mad, ok?" he

says. "When the news announced you were back in Seattle, you had a small press conference, remember?"

"Of course." I hadn't wanted to go, but it was big news.

"I was there, in the room. When you came in and started speaking, the frequency connected me with you. I didn't know what it was or why it was happening. It was powerful." He pauses, squeezing his eyes shut. "Like electricity. Like magic. And then it was..."

"Scary?"

"Yeah." He looks up at me. "But you couldn't feel it. You flinched for a moment, I thought. But I could tell you couldn't see or feel what I was feeling. Because you..."

"Didn't have my gift."

"Right. I figured it out pretty quickly. I kept thinking of ways to help you. Because I'd been there. I knew you needed someone. But I couldn't talk to you because Kai was there. The last thing you needed was some weird boy from your past dropping more heavy news on you. Hence the sim invasion..."

I sigh, thinking back to my first interactions with the Coral Hacker. "What about in my sims? How did you make it so I found your emails in phase one?"

Noble shifts his weight on his other side, a red glow on his cheeks. "Even that surprised me." He finds my eyes. "I can't control your memories. It's why I only ever entered phase three." He smiles. "Phase one was all you. I guess you were thinking about me too..."

I play with my hair to hide my face. It's true. I was thinking about him a lot. Because of Coral Hacker. The connection I felt to him having my gift. I must have subconsciously connected it to what I felt before with Mandel. I marvel at how our minds know things before we do. The brain logs every small connection we've ever had.

"How could I not think about you?" I say, his eyes staring into mine. "You were so important to me. I cared about you.

I never got to explain what happened, why I never talked to you again..." I finger my lips, dry from the desert's air. I look up at him, very aware of his body next to mine. Aware of his hand, close to my fingers. Aware of everything he has done for me. Aware of our connection. And knowing time is short, I become bolder. "Why do you think my death..." I swallow hard, "...affected you so much?"

His dark brown eyes peer up at me under those thick eyelashes, examining my face with an intensity of numerical layers clashing inside of him. I wonder what his equations are telling him about me, what they're predicting or revealing—perhaps something I am not even aware of. But right now, I don't care. I wait for him to speak because I have to know. I've waited for answers, and answers bring you peace, right? We're connected in some way. Knowing why will help me see clearly and I'll know what to do.

He leans in closer, his hand resting on my knee.

"Because in this broken world, you're my fractal," he finally says, his eyes dark like the night, but bright like the stars. "I've loved you since I was thirteen...and I still love you now."

A thousand shocks ripple through my chest. Images of Mandel and Kai and oceans and cities and thousands of moments and memories slice through me laying bare every crater of emotion my heart has ever opened. I've been near death and I've felt new life, but the power of love surpasses them all.

I thought getting answers would bring order to this mystery. Instead, it brings more chaos.

CHAPTER 55

A Jeep tears into the camp, jolting us back to reality.

Farah screeches to a halt with Qadar slouched in the back seat. "Noble! He's been vomiting since he woke up." Her face bunches with worry.

Noble jumps up, looking at his watch. "I'm going to help her but then we've got to get back online. Meet me in the tech-tent?"

I nod, and hurry over to Farah and squeeze her hand. "He'll be ok. Just give him another few hours. I'm sorry."

Noble sprints to the Jeep, opening the door to Qadar who chokes back an agonizing moan. "Noble?" he rasps. "Are you and Jo ok?"

"Yes, Uncle," Noble reassures him, slinging his arm over his shoulder. "Thanks to you." I remember Kai was like this too, but worse. He spent the whole day in a fetal position. At least Qadar can walk, albeit with help.

Noble darts a look at me. "This will take moment or two. Be there soon." He smiles shyly, but I swear there's a hint of caution—*or reality*—breaking in.

The moment he's gone, I rush from the pool patio, my mind full of thoughts I didn't know were so heavy. Noble's voice, the way he looks at me and makes my whole body turn to fire. And then there's Kai who is loyal and brave and understands me in a completely different way. Kai's face in the desert. Kai risking his life. And here I am, surrounded by luxury tents and a hacker who was my first love and a whole mixed-up stew of feelings I don't know what to do with.

I am with Kai. Kai loves me. Do I love him? I need to talk to him. To see him face to face. To discuss our future. To remember why I chose him. Remember that we were going to beat the odds.

I race over to the tech-tent, where I know I can at least see the live stream. I don't even care if he's with the girl. I just want to see if he's ok. I try to calm myself as I go. Kai should be safe at least until tomorrow. They believed him. Kai's on top of this.

But what about the Successor? How can Kai give the ho-lothumb to the Successor if he doesn't know who it is? And if it gets into anyone else's hands, it won't be merged with the master-file.

I'm failing Kai on so many levels—my feelings for Noble, no help with the case. After I check the live stream, I'll do my sims again. This time I'll figure it out. I know it. I need to cage these feelings. I don't need these emotions warring in me. Not here. Not now.

Inside the tent, I pull up the live stream. But a black screen comes up. All visual is gone. Noble said the surveillance would be on alert for an hour. He also said they weren't tracing any signals. Hasn't one hour passed?

As I try to get it to work, the facial recognition footage catches my eye. Those videos aren't live, but recorded and stored data. Kai is in them. But they're locked with a password. Out of curiosity, I punch in $fc(z) = z2 + c$ the equation for the Mandelbrot set, and all the files open.

I scroll through weeks of data. Noble's intel on Montego.

I'm not looking for a way to find the hidden secret about Kai. I want to see his face, hear his voice.

I'm about to click on a random video when my mind flickers on a certain date, and like a light everything turns on around me. That's the date Noble first contacted me. The day he first warned me about Kai.

My gut squeezes tight like I'm wringing water out of a wash-cloth, and my mouth goes dry. A voice warns me to choose a different video. To wait for Kai, like Noble advised. Even Noble believed Kai would tell me everything. But numbers bombard me, and whatever fuels that death wish is lurking, tempting me to press play.

Noble's voice is in my head. *I don't want you to get hurt...*

I've denied that Kai could hurt me. I've avoided this since I didn't want to believe anything was wrong. I dread what I'll find, but time is short, like I told myself on the patio about Noble.

I probably shouldn't do this, but I hit play anyway and the video starts.

CHAPTER 56

Kai sweeps onto the scene with buoyancy in his gait and victory in his grin that suggests he just conquered the world. He's got a small bandage on his upper right cheek, and his lip is cut, but he's ramped up, and eager to please. It's the same energy that says, *Don't worry, Trouble, I loved every minute of it.*

My numbers are not operating, but my mind jumps into action sizing up the room. The map on the wall. The red and white striped flag with a yellow moon and sun against blue. The different languages on various signs. He's not in China. Not in Tunisia. This in Malaysia where Private Global Force's headquarters are.

"Good morning, Director Kane. You wanted to see me?" Kai asks.

"Kai, welcome to HQ." The director, Agent Bai's superior, stands welcoming him and shaking his hand. "Please take a seat." He motions to a chair by his desk.

Kai sits, back straight but with a pose that always manages to communicate he's both relaxed and confident.

"First, I'd like to thank you for your work," he says. "The world is a lot safer with you out there."

Kai beams. "That's why I'm here."

"I've been watching you with great interest since you joined this team," he says. "Bai tells me you were the only one who could handle the mess in Thailand, and you got out without a hint of fire on you. Well done."

"Thank you, sir." Kai clears his throat, not used to such direct praise.

"Because of it, you caught someone we've been tracking a long time." Kane has the same expression on his face as Bai, evaluating, contemplating, preparing.

"I'm ready for the next round."

Kane huffs an odd laugh. "We can tell. Has Bai briefed you on the job in Tunisia?"

Kai leans forward, nodding. "Yes, sir, I'm all in. It'll be no problem. Whatever you have that others don't want, give it to me."

"I'm glad you said that, Kai." He leans back in chair. "You're unlike any recruit we have ever had. Your aptitude for combat and fast solutions, characterizations, is higher than anyone I've met. It's off the charts. We haven't seen anything like you in years. You're faster, smarter, and braver than more than half of our present agents. My fellow directors and I believe you're the guy we have been looking for."

"For what, sir?"

"A promotion of sorts." Kane studies Kai. "You'd go undercover with a bunch of highly trained criminals to expose countless webs of activity. We've been following them for a long time, with little progress. I want to be clear; this is a very dangerous covert mission."

The word dangerous doesn't deter Kai. He comes alive. "This is why I'm here. To stop all that." His smile is wider than ever and the excitement radiating from him is contagious. This is something he truly loves. "Count me in."

I love the way Kai never backs down from a challenge. But it reminds me of what Noble said—he's attracted to trouble. And apparently this will be his next job. I think of everything I've seen here in Tunisia—the girl, the fights, the terrorists. Is this the life Kai wants? Is this what I want him doing every night?

Regardless, this can't be the video Noble is referring to because Kai told me he got a promotion. He said there were difficult circumstances to him accepting it. Was he talking about the danger level? Did he think I would be worried? Because seeing his face shows me, he is clearly not concerned. He is hungry for this job in a way I've never seen him before.

Director Kane rolls back his shoulders. "Great. It requires one to three years. During that time, you'll have to create a new life, a new name, new history, new friends, everything. For your safety and that of your team and mission, as well as the ones you love, you'll have to cut off all personal relationships."

I gasp in shock. One to three years? It's like ice water has been thrown into my face. My stomach plummets to my feet.

Kai's face falls. Not enough for the director to notice, but I do. "All relationships, sir? Even family?" Kai's composed, but the intensity on his brow clearly shows there is a conflict going on inside him. He's thinking, weighing it, *actually* considering it.

My fingers feel cold. I can understand a month or two. Kai loves this job. But would he cut off our relationship—me—for one to three years? Or is he plotting some way to keep in touch, with disposable phones and *the street*? Even so, whatever he's thinking won't work. I've been driven insane waiting four weeks. After losing my family for two years, waiting to see people I care about isn't something I want to do again. I want them near me. I thought he understood...but watching him now, it's clear as day he doesn't understand, or worse, might not care.

My heart is in my throat and I tense, on the edge of my seat, as Director Kane answers. His words are precise, sharp as razors, leaving no room to misconstrue his meaning.

"It means exactly what you think. Your life will end as you know it, and another one will begin. Until the job is done." Director Kane says, setting the pen down. "It's a high-risk operation and a long commitment. You may be the only one who can complete this assignment."

Turn down the job, Kai.

Kai's back straightens, his chest thrusts forward. "I know I can get it done. I want to be an agent who makes a difference. But..." Kai's eyes flicker across the room.

As my eyes bounce from Director Kane to Kai, my gut is wrenching.

"This isn't like what you've faced before," Director Kane says, his voice low and serious. He leans forward, stiff. "This type of operation will require every ounce of your ability and dedication. Going under for this long is as dangerous as it gets. In this type of op, your pocket litter can be the end of you. There's zero room for error."

"There's not an ounce of fear stopping me, sir. But I'll need some time to consider it," he says.

I breathe again, but Kai's jaw clenches on and off. This is hard for him. Noble was right. He said Kai was young and impulsive, that he loved danger and he loved me because I fulfilled that part in him. Is he considering it because I'm some math nerd doing nothing?

"Of course," Director Kane says, his expression putting Kai through training. "After Tunisia, you can give me your answer."

"Just to be clear, *all people* are cut off?" Kai asks.

"That's correct. Everyone. Family. Friends...*Girlfriend.*" He leans back in his chair. "It's not like it hasn't been done before. Thankfully, you're young. Family waits and girls come and go." He studies Kai, then folds his hands across the desk. "That's what's holding you back, am I right? Some girl waiting around for you?"

Kai considers the question. A shot of hope rises in me because—hands down— he's thinking of me. But Kai breathes deep and pulls his eyes up, looks him square in the face. "No, sir, she's not waiting around for me."

The tent feels like it's closing in on me. *What does he mean I'm not waiting around?* I thought losing my gift was bad. This hurts worse. I stop the video. I can't watch anymore.

Is Noble right about him? Am I not dangerous enough without my gift? But then a fire flares up in me. Then what am I doing here in Tunisia, trying to save him?

Kai loves me. I know he does. I don't understand. We were supposed to talk about our next steps but now I see those next steps might lead to a closing door...

My eyes are wet and a part of me goes numb. Beat down with emotions, like a waterfall is pouring down on me, pushing me under. I can't reach the surface. Chaos is winning because I see no perfect answer.

A chair moves behind me, and I jump around to see Noble's straight face, his jaw locked tight.

My eyes red and cheeks wet, unable to hide my pain.

Noble calculates everything. He bends down to look at me. "You saw the video."

I nod, my lips tight. Little by little, my heart hardens, like the Phoenix I once was. A set of equations zigzags across the room, alerting me to a job we still have to do.

"I'm sorry, Jo."

I shake my head, feeling like an idiot. "Don't be. You warned me."

CHAPTER 57

Tell me we can beat the odds, and I'll never leave your side.

When Kai said these words to me in China, I believed him. When did things change?

He didn't say it outright. But it was in his eyes. He wants the job. The way his face fell when Director Kane mentioned the time frame. The way his eyes narrowed when they talked about being young and having a girl... *She's not waiting around for me.*

Kai's words reverberate in my mind until they're taken over by K2 announcing Harrison's call. My body jolts forward.

"Answer call," I say, my mind a gyroscope of thoughts.

Harrison's voice hits me like a fire alarm. "Jo. Where have you been? We've been trying to reach you for over an hour!"

Ksar Douz. Qadar. The festival. The patio...the scenes flash through my mind like they happened over the span of a week and not just the last few hours. I take in a deep breath. "I'm sorry, we couldn't get online. They're using PSS radar over Douz."

"Oh no," he gasps. "You don't know."

"Know what?" I ask, aware of Noble behind me, flying to the desk trying to make the live stream turn on. "What's wrong?"

"I've got a string of horrible news," he says, "What do you want to know first?"

"Just hit me, Harrison," I say, already in a bad mood. "We don't have time for this."

"First, more radicals left the city hours ago and we don't have the manpower to track where they went," he says. "Next, PSS tech is lighting up all over North Africa, especially in your location. Eddie's on bank watch, and lots of money is being transferred from Douz to an unknown location as we speak. And the Swiss Banker guy, who also might be the Successor? He's meeting several big wigs from the European Union and the Indonesian Ambassador early tomorrow morning in Algeria, and the Sheikh is heading to Abu Dhabi to meet with some powerful men. Are you hearing me? All of them are leaving on private flights tonight."

"No." I shake my head. "That can't be right. We just saw them. The transaction was supposed to be tomorrow night..." I look over at Noble, who's at his desk, tapping into every signal he can, without luck. He's fidgeting, definitely concerned. He shoots me a look that fills me with dread. "We don't know who the Successor is yet."

"Jo. Then we missed it. Because something big is happening right now. And I don't need to remind you that if Coral Hacker's SMOKE isn't uploaded to the master-file, our tech will be unstoppable." He pauses. "Ms. T is still in meetings. She'll be back in one hour."

Streams of information intersect in my mind. Two of the possible Successors followed Kai to Ksar Douz. When Kai said he came to *check out the place because no one else had,* Müller's response was, *"No one else had to..."*

But then they allowed Kai to join the Loyalists...

Red told me to wake up before I was too late. I ran to Kai in the square, but he was already gone.

My equations flicker to the photo Kai sent on *the street.*

We'd missed the show that night because we'd gotten the date wrong. It had been the night before. How did I not pick up on this?

"Don't worry, Harrison. Kai has the holothumb with SMOKE," I say, wanting eyes on Kai as soon as possible. "It'll be fine. They believed Kai. He'll get the job done. We'll check it out."

"Two more things..." Harrison breathes in, killing me with his slow pauses. "Ms. T knows who the hacker is. Noble J. Adams, Tunisian-British mother, American father. Went missing two years ago. Jo. He has been in our system, far deeper than your sims. Ms. T is convinced he's hacked more than PSS, maybe even government secrets. She thinks he's dangerous. She hasn't said it, but we think she's sending someone out there, to retrieve him. I'm sorry. I know you think of him as a friend."

My eyes shoot over to Noble—*to Mandel*—with a pang of dread. *What have I done?* A sledgehammer to the gut would feel better than this.

"Tell me the last piece of news is better?" I ask, not knowing if I can handle any more.

"It's worse. We just detected a government biotag in the area. It came on in the last hour. And it doesn't look good."

My fingers go numb. My throat is tight. "What's going on?"

"Not entirely sure. The readings coming from the biotag are connected to the host's body vitals and they've reached the top of something like a 'red zone'..." Harrison's voice turns grave. Then he confirms the news I already know. "We think... they're torturing him."

CHAPTER 58

My body feels cold as the concrete floor in the Pratt in winter, numb and stiff. A strength I haven't felt since then also returns. Nothing in me cares about what I saw in that video. All I can think about is saving Kai.

"I have to leave. Now." I stand up, grabbing my backpack. Noble jumps up at the sound of my voice. "Give me the keys to the Jeep."

"Jo. What did he tell you about the deal?" Noble is asking, his hands on my shoulders now.

"We're too late. Whatever the Loyalists are doing it's happening now. We're missing it." Everything is caving in on me. The deal... Kai's biotag... He's on his own. Noble's now a target. My breathing is shallow. But my head is clear.

"There's more you need to tell me," Noble demands. "I can see it. I want to help you."

"No." I shake my head. "You've got to get out of here right now. Ms. T knows who you are. Because of me." I touch his face, so many mixed emotions, before heading to the door. I won't ask him to risk himself for Kai—again.

"What else, Jo? Trust me." Noble blocks the exit, almost not caring what I said. His frequency surges erratically like waves in a storm.

"Did you hear me?" I shout. "She knows who you are. You have to leave."

Noble spins me around, tenderly taking me by the arm. He pulls me close to him, his face full of concern. "Forget about me right now and tell me what is happening. I want to help you."

I relent. "They must have used Radar to turn Kai's biotag on...they know who he is..." My face explains the rest. "I'm going there. I won't let them hurt him anymore." A rushed plan forms in my mind. Noble's face tells me his mind is working on one too.

"All right, let's do this," he says. "We'll help Kai and stop this deal." Noble flies around the room snatching up a backpack and packing it with tech like a mad man.

My head spins. He's only ever told me *my boyfriend* was stupid. "Why do you care about helping Kai?" I ask.

Noble stops to look at me. "I care about you. And he's important to you." The frequency skips, locking me to him. But he doesn't waste time. "I only need three minutes..." He jumps into action, punching in codes and passwords, and grabbing things from drawers. He's mostly taking software chips and small devices. It's obvious he has a protocol for this type of scenario. He's closing down shop as fast as he can, but it feels like molasses. We've got to get to Kai before they...I push away images of what I've seen in the Pratt.

"What happens if they go through this tent?" I ask, worried now for what they'll actually find on Noble. "PSS will be able to track you. Imprison you. They're the best."

"Maybe, but not better than me." He pulls out another locked box. "I've got some tricks up my sleeve. By the time I'm done, it'll all look like star gazing equipment and software. No one, excluding present company, could possibly decipher it, at least for a few years. Qadar knows what to do with the rest."

Every minute we waste, Kai could be inching near death. A rage is burning in me against the Successor. Whoever it is will not make it out of the building. I won't let them get away with this.

Noble is finally done. He shoots across the room. "Come on."

We hop into the Jeep and tear down the dark back roads at a ridiculous speed. Thank God it's nearly midnight and not many people are on the road.

I try to get Bai on the phone but it's useless. Even my numbers don't respond to the small kick I give them. But Noble's equations are going into hyper-speed. I can feel it. It's all I can do to trust his mind right now, the way he trusted me at Ksar Douz.

"Do we even know where we're going?" I ask, watching the palms whip past us.

"No. We're running blind right now. If Radar is being used at all, they'll detect us coming. We won't have any tech to give us visual." His hands tighten around the wheel. "Qadar is useless at the moment. Private Global Forces won't help. Jo, we don't have any back up."

"What are your numbers saying?" I ask, scared to hear.

"We're outnumbered and we're not Kung Fu masters." He's driving as fast as he can.

"Then why are you still driving?" I ask.

"Because if we put our minds together, we have a chance." Noble shakes his head and exhales loudly. "Kai might be right. Life with you *is* trouble."

The last thing I want to do is bring PSS deeper into this mess. And I certainly don't want them to know what we're about to do. But they can still help.

"We're not totally alone," I say. "PSS is out of the Radar's zone." I get my phone back out. "K2, get Harrison and the team back online."

Harrison answers immediately. "We're here, what do you need?"

"Eyes. We need to know where that signal is coming from."

The Jeep is speeding through town. I brace myself as it races over cobblestone and flies through the narrow alleys.

Pens hops online. "We're ahead of you—5 miles west from where you are. But we'll need a minute to get the imagery."

Felicia cuts in. "I'm on it. It will take some work, but I can probably get something in 15 minutes."

I grimace. Kai had pointed west in the desert. This whole time he was trying to tell us things were changing. "We might not have 15 minutes," I say.

"I'm searching for blueprints of the area now," Harrison says. "I'll download them to K2 once I find them. I'll also send body heat scans of the area once Felicia gets a satellite lined up."

"Sounds good. What are his vitals now?" I ask.

Pens is silent for a beat. "You don't want to know."

A lump bulges up in my throat at her answer. Kai's last message on the street, telling me he loves me. My inability to say the words doesn't mean I don't feel it. After having been kidnapped and in the Pratt, love became weighty, like gold. Like if love were real, but you treated it even an ounce less than its true value, it would become worthless. But I know that's not true. Love is costly and more brave and beautiful than anything I've ever known.

"Ok, we're going to check it out." I look over at Noble processing everything as he redirects the Jeep.

"You weren't supposed to go near the deal," Pens says, a serious tone.

Eddie is in the background. "Not a good idea, Jo."

I grit my teeth. "Trust me. I won't do anything I haven't done before." At least that wasn't a lie.

CHAPTER 59

Harrison's directions lead us to an even smaller town near the lake of *Chott el Djerid*. There are several large, gated compounds in the area. All of them are luxurious, isolated, and very secure. We don't know which place it is until we see the outline of the Sheikh's helicopter in the shadows and moonlight.

Noble pulls the car to the side of the road. "My calculations say this is as close as we can get. Let's ditch the car and go on foot."

Everything is quiet, a ghost town out here. We approach the compound from a distance. There's a large wall made of sandstone surrounding the entire property.

"Harrison, give me the details," I say.

"Alright. It's called *Dar du Sable Doré.* The House of Golden Sand. There are four outbuildings and in the center of the compound, is an old Dar surrounded by gardens and courtyards. You're looking at 20-30 people inside, and a parking area."

"Where's the biotag signal?" I ask.

"It's doesn't give us an exact location. It's in range, somewhere on the compound."

Noble's mind is gauging everything around us. "Ten-foot-high wall, two feet thick. We're looking at a 20,000 square foot compound—half an acre. Fancy. Vehicle tracks are the same as Müller and the Sheikh's men at the festival." Noble squints his eyes. "The meeting will be in the center room of the old Dar. But from what we saw at Ksar Douz, most of the men will be guarding from the outside. There's no telling where Kai will be."

If they're torturing Kai, it means someone used the Blacklist tech, or they wouldn't have been able to turn on Kai's biotag. But who did Kai give it to? Because if they didn't believe him and the deal went down, it means the SMOKE didn't merge with the master-file and now it's going out to all of their contacts and there will be no way to track those files down. We can't let anyone leave this compound.

"The Successor is in there. If they think Kai's a traitor, he's not walking out alive." My hands are tapping like crazy, but my gift is silent. "We're going to stop this. All of it. I don't care how we do it, we're going to stop this deal and save Kai."

We sneak behind a group of date-palms, knees in the sand, twenty feet from the Dar's outer wall. Noble puts a hand on my shoulder. "Jo, leave getting inside to me. Once we're in, we need to know *who* the Successor is. You said it yourself. They know how to get out and start over. And we're only two people. We're only getting out alive if we use everything we know to our advantage."

Resolve hardens in me, solidifying like water to ice. "So how do we get inside?"

"We draw a few guards outside. Then I'll calculate the rest. But we need them to believe we're not alone."

My tapping stops, and my mind becomes sharp. "That's it." I say into my watch. "K2, tell Harrison to veil these co-ordinates. Make whoever is in the building believe there's an army outside. We also need a blueprint of the compound." Even without my numbers, a plan forms.

The building schematics arrive instantly on K2 but with a strict warning from the team. "We're notifying Ms. T right now about the deal and your location. Do not enter the building."

"We're going dark now." I cut off K2 and turn to Noble. "Now for your part. You're the brains."

Noble gives the numerical stats. "Ok, from the blueprints and heat scans, they've got about ten men doing rotations around half an acre of enclosed property. The most secure room is in the center of the Dar. Ten for ten, the meeting is in there. Numerous possibilities, but according to my equations, our best bet is to sneak around the south entrance and draw them out. Rotations at five minutes a pass, we'll only have two guards to handle. Then we can disable the vehicles."

"Once we're inside, if we don't get confessions, Bai said his agency can't do anything. The Successor has to confess. Müller, the Sheik. All of them." My gift is tingling inside, like its buried under the sand. So deep.

Noble looks at me. "You brought your backpack, right?" I nod. "Good. I have an idea on how we can get confessions."

As he explains it to me, I nod my head. "Mandel, I always knew you were a genius." I take off my watch and put it around Noble's wrist. Then I grope around for small stones on the ground. I pick up five rocks and put them in my pocket. "Now for weapons. K2 has two Tasers left. I have two tranquilizer-earrings. And you still have your pocketknife, right? Can I see it?"

Noble takes out his small pocketknife and hands it to me. "This might slash the tires, but it won't help with anything else. Jo, they have real weapons."

I draw in a deep breath. "So do we."

I cut my fingertips.

CHAPTER 60

A drop of blood mixes with the oily chemicals, forming bubbles on the tops of my fingers.

"A walking weapon, remember?" I smile. "Your brains. My brawn. Never thought I'd ever get to say that." I give a shallow chuckle. But then I see his face. Reality is hitting him.

"I can't do this." He's staring at me, that same wild look he had when Qadar stood in Ksar Douz in front of Kai. He grabs hold of me, pulling me close to him. His breath is heavy now. "Odds are one thing, a real person is another. Especially you. You already died once. I didn't bring you to Tunisia for this. Now that we're here, I can't put you in danger."

"Noble, you said my gift is alive. You said it's there. That means there's a chance we can stop this. I need you. I need your eyes, your mind. Our plan is to deceive them." I lift my fingers. "This is only a contingency plan. We can do this." I lean into him with my shoulder, careful to cup my oily fingertips.

"I'll never forgive myself if anything happens to you." Noble's jaw is locked.

"I'll never forgive myself if anything happens to Kai."

That snaps him back to reality. He shoots me a look, a sobering glint in his eyes. "You're right. He may be stupid, but we can't let him die," he says, a twinge of hurt in his voice. "And we came here to stop this deal. Alone or not, we can do this." He runs his hand through his hair and focuses on my fingers. "You cannot mix the left with the right until you know your targets. And I never thought I'd ever say this to you, but...don't touch me."

Noble and I sneak to the south entrance. There is a door in the stonewall with a lock. Noble pulls a tool from his bag and opens it easily.

"Breaking and entering skills?" I whisper. Ms. T was right. There's a lot I don't know about this boy. He shrugs, and we both hold our breath to listen. Hearing nothing, we sneak through the entrance.

Several SUVs are parked in the corner. We stay low and get behind them. Noble takes the knife, which barely punctures a hole in the back tires of each vehicle.

Further in, we enter a beautiful courtyard with a manicured garden, and large potted palms, and a tranquil pool. From behind an arch, we watch as several guards talk to each other, while others patrol the grounds. Noble calculates the guard's rotations, looking for the perfect moment to make our move. His eyes dart back and forth taking in all the possibilities until he finds one with the highest odds of success. When the guards switch rotation, we dart into the center courtyard to one of the outbuildings. Noble hacks into the compound cameras, and freezes them, also giving Harrison access.

Noble presses his fingers to his lips. When a guard turns to patrol the south, we dodge into a pathway, and press ourselves against a wall. When he comes around the corner, Noble taps K2 and the smartwatch zaps the guard. He falls to the ground in a heap of shaking. Noble pulls him to the side, behind a large pot full of jasmine.

We move further inside where several stone pathways lead to the center of the Dar. Three men patrol the outer path near the wall and two more circle the path in the center. Again, Noble is calculating. He motions for us to move forward, and another military-looking guard comes around the corner and spots us. Before he can alert anyone, Noble uses the last taser on him and he, too, drops like a fly to the ground. A moan too quiet for others to hear.

"We're in." Noble's voice is in a whisper. He points to my earring. "I may need one."

I show him my fisted hands. "You have to take it out." He pulls out one of my tranquillizer-earrings, the same one he picked up on the roof of the Bardo. My gut wrenches. "Ready?"

"Yes." All the while my mind is replaying my sims and my meeting with Montego. I need to find Kai. I need to find the Successor.

The last time I ran to the square in the sims, I was too late. Kai was gone. Just like now. My sims. They were telling me something. My gift was working, like Noble said, putting clues together. So what else did I miss?

Noble fiddles with his tech again. "The Sheikh's phone is located in the center of the Dar. We don't know who has the master-file."

"I'll figure it out. Give me a few minutes," I say, but Noble's slipping up to another guard I didn't even notice, and before I know it, he takes one of my earrings and jabs him in the neck, catching him and slowing the guard's fall so it's soundless.

Because of Noble's stealth, we're inside now. Staying down, we creep through beautifully tiled rooms and ornate archways, and dodge behind a pillar. We hear girls' voices coming from another room. But up ahead the billowy laugh of the Sheikh confirms we're close.

The room is securely locked and fortified. "I can open this. Give me a few minutes." Noble bends down, about to break it when his hands pause "Jo, I don't think…"

"What? We're running out of time."

"That's just it. My numbers...if Kai isn't in there, there might not be enough time to save him after dealing with the Sheikh."

"Then I guess this door is my first target," I say. "Back up."

I swipe right and left on the locks, and we dart behind the pillar.

Ten seconds later the door blows open. Shards of splintered wood litter the hallway. The door now has a huge crater in it. Not a huge explosion, like Pens, says, but effective.

We climb through the hole into the room. The Sheikh and Müller and a dozen Loyalists are crouched under a large table, surprised at our entrance.

I scan the room for Kai, but he's not here. My throat feels as bare as the desert after a strong wind. The men's faces gleam up at me, assessing and examining us like guards at the Pratt. I force that storm away and narrow my gaze. I know who I am.

"We're here for the list," I say. "And don't make another move. Or this whole room is going to look like that door."

CHAPTER 61

I'm in the lion's den.

A dozen hostile Loyalists all vying for Madame's master-file and the Blacklist tech suddenly jump up, ready for action.

Noble shouts. "The table!"

Knowing exactly what he means, I wipe my fingers and throw another stone as fast as I can into the center of the room. The table erupts into fragments of debris, knocking the men back to the ground again. Smoke and splinters fill the air.

Regardless, weapons are pulled out and aimed at us within seconds. The few girls, including the one who clung to Kai, shriek and flock to the corner. But Kai is nowhere in sight.

Noble sizes up the room. "I wouldn't do that if I were you." Noble nods in my direction. "She's got enough firepower to take out this whole room."

He's bluffing, but I hold up a small stone. The X girls start shrieking.

Müller cocks his head. "Ah, but you're out numbered."

"Are we?" Noble motions to the security cameras up on the wall. "We have a whole swat team outside. If we get hurt, this whole building goes down. Go ahead, have a look." The Sheikh motions for his men to check the visual.

I look around the room, fifteen men are there, three girls. Something isn't right. My gift is simmering, spinning. The Successor is in this room. I can feel it. But Kai is dominating my thoughts. He's hurt. I need to find out where they're holding him. The Sheikh's girl is staring at me. An image of Kai's hands sliding against her back in the desert curls in my stomach.

I try to push it away, but I can't. This is going to be his life now, fighting bad guys, near death injuries, and rescuing helpless girls...it's what he lives for. Beating the odds and slaying dragons. And yet all I see in this moment is every single video I had to watch of him flirting with her.

Suddenly, I stop. Mind reeling. My phase two simulations are cut up and pasted alongside my meeting with Montego and the surveillance with that girl. She was in every single live stream, listening and watching.

An X girl, whose face I never saw, was in my sims next to Madame. As plain as day. Every movement in sync with Madame's. Just like every X girl in real life. Just like *Ennéa*. Our eyes lock onto each other's again. My sims replay on fast-forward. Kai walked away with her each time. Unscathed. The other men were always beaten...*beaten*. But *she* walked away. Just how Madame would have done it.

The Sheikh's men confirm Noble's intel. "We're surrounded."

Thank God for Veil technology and the PSS team.

"Now, if you give us the holothumb, we'll cut you a deal." Noble moves forward, strategically.

"What kind of deal?" Müller says to Noble.

"First give us the holothumb."

Müller shifts his feet, eyes on me. I know the eyes of a hard man, like King, or his cronies and those in the Pratt. Muller isn't one of them. He's a banker, a businessman. He's looking for a way to win.

But I drown out their conversation. I'm still looking at the girl. The meeting with Montego runs through my mind in slow motion now. He stopped believing me the moment I talked about the Successor. It wasn't *when* I talked about the successor but *how*. I told Montego that he would be *his* problem. *His*. Not *hers*. He stared at me in disbelief until I told him *I was the successor*. I'm a girl—and that's when he believed me. Montego didn't know who it was, but he knew the successor wasn't a man.

I shake my head, hating myself for not seeing it earlier. Madame would have never handed her empire over to a man.

The story the girl told Kai. 9 lives. A scar. I fracture into pieces. *Nine*—I was the *eighth*. Octavia. Elegant and simple. Just like Madame's codes. She always laid out her plan in the light of day to flaunt her genius.

Ennéa. It's Greek. Even her name means nine. There's always something in the name. The girl arranged this meeting right under their noses. She's setting up the men, getting their money and the plans will be hers. I figured it out—just not early enough.

"You're too late," the Sheikh says. "The transaction is done."

No. My body stiffens. The master-file and Blacklist have been sent out.

"Then it's worthless. Toss it to me," Noble shouts, snapping me back.

Müller huffs. "Tell us who you are!"

Müller acts like the leader, but he has no idea he's a pawn. I answer his question, but I stare at the girl. "A Successor who wants what is hers." I tilt my head and pitch a rock up in the air and catch it. They understand the threat, and seconds later, the holothumb lands in Noble's hands.

They believe us. Relief courses through me. We can fix this. Noble pulls off his bag, about to check the holothumb. I step closer to him, keeping my voice low. "The Successor. It's the X girl." With my eyes hard and locked onto the girl, I call out.

"Where's the loyalist with Montego's Blacklist?"

But Müller can't answer because a loud crack has us all snapping backward. What's left of the door crashes to the ground. A group of very angry men in old army fatigues flood the room. The radicals from Tunis. The team said they left the city. They knew about this meeting and they're not happy they weren't invited.

"Don't believe a word they say," growls the radicals' leader. All the goons' weapons are pointed at Noble. The leader gestures at the holothumb. My mind spins frantically. This wasn't a part of the calculation. "There's no one outside but us. We were promised Blacklist tech and we've come to get it." He lunges toward Noble.

The room erupts into mayhem, and the girl goes running.

CHAPTER 62

Why does everything I do almost get me killed?

Harrison warned us the radicals were furious that they didn't get the last tech promised to them by Montego. He warned us they were headed our way. I was so distracted by the news of Kai I forgot to tell Noble. He would have factored it into the equation.

From the look on Noble's face, numbers are tearing through his mind like the running of the bulls in Spain. "Time to use those weapons!"

Something in our frequency makes it clear where I should aim. My grip on the stones tightens. I swipe left and right on two stones, throwing one at the radical leader and the second stone at five more men coming at us. Then I run for cover.

Noble dives forward as a loud bang pops the air, and a bright light flashes. Mr. Ben Slimane is knocked off his feet, his head against the wall.

An explosion of smoke and light slams against them like a bully shoving them to the ground. I grit my teeth—the bombs aren't strong enough. Why did I ever tell Pens to make them less potent?

Three of the five men rise to their feet, a bit hazy but not taken out. All I want to do is follow the girl, Ennéa, who slipped from the room and into the courtyard in all the confusion.

"She's getting away!" I shout to Noble. He dashes in her direction, but three radicals tackle him to ground with a thunk, connecting his face to the hard tile floor. Noble shouts at me, but before I hear his warning that someone is behind me, the back of my knees are kicked in and I'm shoved to the ground, cheek against the floor. My eyes lock onto Noble's, our breath and frequency a wildfire between us. One last stone is in my hand, but Noble shakes his head at me, warning me not to use it yet. He's right. It would be worthless against so many.

We failed. The Successor is getting away. Kai is going to die. Even if we call Harrison it won't work in time.

I'm yanked to my feet with my arms pinned behind my back. They're just as rough with Noble.

"No more games, or you won't be getting up off the floor next time." The leader, his face now bloody, spits at us. "Give us our tech or no one gets out of here."

They pin Noble's body to the wall and wrangle the holo-thumb from him.

The Sheikh and Müller stand behind their own thugs, but the radicals have them backed into a corner.

Müller steps out. "We've got more where that came from," he offers, "and we've got more funds than you can dream of."

Noble is calculating something. His frequency stabilizes to an even calm, making even my numbers peek out. Thoughts of coral and lightning flow through my mind, and a quiet comes over me. Numbers erupt out of me, igniting possibilities and equations in every part of the room...I see it. Even in this whole mess of chaos, there is hope—until a radical starts screaming in my ear to hand over the backpack. The voice shatters my numbers, and I clutch my bag. I won't give it to him. If there's any hope at all, I need the sim glasses. I bite down and prepare for a beating when his voice is overtaken by shattering glass.

I'm shoved to the floor again and Noble shouts for me to close my eyes. I don't understand why, but I do. Somewhere, another window is kicked in. A loud explosion assaults my ears, even behind closed eyes, I know the room has turned blinding white. My ears are ringing. The vibrating is also in my stomach, making me feel nauseous. Mayhem is happening all over again. Boots are storming in with heavy thuds and crunches.

Rolling over, I open my eyes. Men in bulletproof Kevlar vests, helmets, and goggles gain the tactical advantage with an overwhelming force. They're not scrappy fighters like the radicals. These men are trained, marching in with the discipline and strength of Navy SEALs. Tables are breaking, boots are stomping, orders are being shouted, men collapse with thunks to the floor.

The man holding me won't let go. He's dragging me out of the room. In the chaos, Noble sees it, and thrusts forward, but a radical grabs him from behind, a weapon trained on his head. My heart skyrockets and adrenaline stabs into me, waking up my numbers for five seconds. Two things course through me: Noble has three seconds to live and one chance of survival. Like clockwork and destiny, the trained man behind Noble spins around, his arm extended, ripping the weapon from the radical and with one hit, knocks him to the ground. A man's voice I recognize is shouting an order and the man who helped Noble charges after the man holding me, who has let go to flee the scene.

I watch as the trained men subdue the radicals and the Loyalists with precision and strategy, in what seems likes seconds.

The pandemonium slows as more men storm the room, flooding it with weapons and manpower. The leader in the invading team removes his helmet and goggles, his shrewd eyes sweeping over the room and stop on mine. Bai. That familiar smug grin now filled with concern. I exhale. He came. Just when our odds ran out. Relief floods me.

Bai rushes over to me and helps me stand. "You ok?"

I'm shaking with adrenaline. "Kai's biotag..." My eyes are wild.

"That's why we're here. Find him. We'll take care of this." Bai's men are handcuffing Loyalists, waiting orders. "Which one is the Successor?"

"It's the X girl."

"I broke a lot of rules coming here. If we're going to keep this clean, we need confessions."

Noble walks up to Bai. "Leave that to me." He passes me the small neural simulator he showed me in the van on the way to the desert, and places it behind my ear. The numbers zipping across his face are full of warning. "Find Kai. I'll check the holothumb."

I race out of the room taking the same path as the Successor. My mind snaps, once then twice. But my pulse is staccato, and nothing about my gift is stable. Whole sections of the room are blinking in and out with graphs like broken mosaics. Sound waves or energy waves fluctuate in the air and just like Noble's voice, I'm calculating them in fractured pieces. I gasp. *What is happening?*

I need to breathe, focus. I need to find the peace in the storm.

For a brief twenty-two seconds the layout of the compound is clear in my mind. I don't lose a minute. I jet toward the farthest outbuilding near the gate exit. As I get closer, a sound more horrible than I can imagine fills my ears. Kai's muffled, guttural scream.

I picture Kai gritting his teeth so he doesn't show his pain—it's the sound of an animal walking into a slaughterhouse, a ship about to sink, of sirens in the distance. All the things this world shouldn't have but are there.

I run forward, searching every room, listening for and block-ing out his cries. We weren't designed for chaos. We weren't designed for heartache and pain, but they exist and just like

Noble said, if we didn't have something to look up at to find the order in it all, we'd all be swept away.

Kai's moans are hoarse, but I'm closer now. Then he is silent. *Hold on, Kai.*

I sneak into the last room on the right. It's nothing like the Pratt except a lingering feeling that the walls have witnessed unspeakable things. The air holds a brokenness I had hoped never to meet again.

The girl is here. I sense it. She's with him. I already know her game plan, under the surface my gift is piecing it all together.

I calm my breathing. Two fingertips left, one bomb to go. I grip a small stone in my hand. I won't let the Successor leave here. I won't waste it. I need her to be unconscious at least for a moment for what we have planned.

I tiptoe around the poorly lit garage. It smells of motor oil and smoke. My fingertips tingle and I start tapping. The steady rhythm hones my focus. There are no numbers, but a boldness takes over, sweeping away all the chaos. All my thoughts are bent on saving Kai—and putting myself in harm's way is only a passing thought…maybe this is what Kai feels when he's out there. How the sacrifice can't compare with the lives he saves.

Finally, I spot him. He's tied up, sprawled out on the ground, blood pooled around him. Delirious, but awake. Kai's breathing is labored. It's far worse than the last time. He's holding something to his stomach, blood is everywhere, like they cut him and he's trying to stop the bleeding himself.

I bend down, placing a hand over his beating heart, like I used to in China, that steady calming rhythm. "I'm here, Kai. Hold on. We're going to get you help."

At the sound of my voice, his bloody and bruised face turns to horror. "Jo, get out of here. The Successor, she's in here…"

I gasp. He said *she*. He knows it's her. But I can't ask more because he fades out again.

A shadow darts across the room toward the exit.

"Don't move. I know who you are." I grab my last stone as I turn around and face her. "Show me your hands."

She cowers, body shaking. "Please help me," she begs. "Let me go. I need out of here. They're going to hurt me."

"I don't believe you."

She moves to the door, shielding her body and crying.

"Don't move," I say. "I don't want to hurt you."

But she's still backing up. "I'm trying to listen but I'm too scared." She looks up at me, wild eyed. Eyes I've seen before. Did I make a mistake? All I see are the girls that Madame ruined. The ones she stole away and twisted into what she wanted. My head is spinning, and Kai is moaning, trying to speak.

She points at Kai. "I tried to help him," she claims. "They hurt him, badly. He needs help. Quick. Please help him."

The chaos in her eyes threatens to sweep me into it. A thousand broken girls. Müller. The Sheikh. King. The Successor. The master-file. They all need to be stopped. Am I wrong about her?

The girl studies me, a glimmer in her eyes, like I believe her. She's sunk her hook into me, and I'm a goner. "The Sheikh has plans for the whole region," she whispers. "You have to stop him. I can tell you everything..." Her voice trails as she steps through the open door into the courtyard.

My mind is spinning. I follow after her. I don't want to hurt her, but I catch a glimpse of her wrist. The burn. The number 9 etched into her skin and the sound in her voice—it's all wrong. Underneath her begging, it's icy. My mind clears as everything in me screams her words are false.

"I don't believe you," I say. "I'll give you one last chance to cooperate." If she is the Successor, she's planned this moment for months. She'll never confess, and she wouldn't have to. Her record is spotless, as white as snow. No one knows who she is. Custody will be a few days then she'll get out and wreak havoc for twenty years.

I look at Kai on the floor and back to her.

"Your time's up." My hands pull out the stone, now oily and bubbling, as I mix the chemicals. Her eyes widen. She leaps into the courtyard, dashing toward an open vehicle. But it's too late. The stone is in the air. I'm praying it doesn't miss as I jump back. It explodes at her back. The blast catapults her forward. She crashes to the ground; her eyes are rolling back into her head. Good, I think. I have two minutes.

Bai's medic storms the garage a second later. He sees me with the girl and hesitates.

"Help Kai!" I scream, rushing over to him. I bend down and hold his hand as the medic moves quickly, assessing Kai, tying tourniquets, and bandaging him up. I touch Kai's face. I don't want to leave him. I want to be near him, but the girl...

The medic looks up at me, as if he knows what I'm thinking. "I can stabilize him."

Nodding, I step away, toward the girl. I won't let Kai's work here go to waste.

She's babbling now, her skin slightly burned. She's not conscious enough to register anything around her. I walk over and bend down to roll the girl over. Then I open my backpack.

Noble's plan had better work.

CHAPTER 63

There is no wind. The warmth of the sun beats on my face. I'm on a penthouse rooftop with a view of an old city. There are green hills spotted with richly colored villas, and beyond it lies a deep blue sea and what looks like a volcano.

I don't know where I am. There's no way of knowing unless I want to give myself away.

Under a beautiful wooden arbor covered with grape vines, Ennéa is lying on a chaise, her eyes barely fluttering open. Finally.

Drawing a deep breath, I move to her side and cross my legs like Madame. "You're not hurt," I say, in a sickly, sweet voice. "Everything is going to be ok. I got you out. Your identity is safe."

"How did we get here?" She grips her head, her long dark hair cascading past her shoulders. She's looking at her clothes now, which are different. They match our environment, wherever we are. She's confused.

"I brought you here. I know all about you."

She shakes her head, eyes disoriented. "There's no way you know about this place. And I'm not who you think I am. You're wrong." Ennéa rubs her dark, round eyes.

"Oh, I know exactly who you are. Like you know who I am."

"I've only heard rumors of the girl Madame loved. The protégé who betrayed her." She gives me a once over, as if I'm not what she expected.

I lock my jaw, and stare at the vines, trailing and clinging on to anything they can.

"I had to betray her. It was necessary to take up her mantle. She trained me to be ruthless. To hide who I really was. Like she trained you. Do whatever it takes. Mask your identity. Be unknown to all." I smile, that power in me rising, threatening to steal my soul. "She told me about you though. I had to see if you knew what you were doing. I have the master-file and Blacklist tech too. I certainly don't need yours. But you did well. Organized, planned...quite the set-up, all without a soul knowing who you were. Except the boy. But he's dead now. Quite brilliant."

Her eyes turn innocent again. She's shaking her head. "They lied to me. Whoever you think I am, I'm not her." Then she looks around the roof, piecing together a puzzle. "How did we get here so quickly? We're not even in Tunisia."

I ignore her. "You have much to learn." I sigh, shaking my head and walk to the wall surrounding the rooftop. My back is toward her, but I continue speaking. "This empire is mine, but I want to make you a deal. First, we rid ourselves of the radicals. They are beneath me. I never work with such volatile trash. I was surprised you did. The Sheikh was a nice choice, but he's gone now. But if you did what I think you did, you got the money." I turn back and face her as I add my stipulations. "If you prove that to me, we can be partners. Unless you want out, in which case, I'll let you go if you surrender the plans you've already set in motion. Madame wouldn't be so kind. But I respect you."

"I don't know what you're talking about." She stands, checking everything like it's fake. Being in this setting is the only thing working in my favor. She rummages through a drawer, and an envelope is there. My numbers flicker on an address in Sicily but I need to hurry, because I'm getting dizzy.

"Ennéa? I know that's not your real name. I know Madame chose you. Because she chose me too. We can trust each other." The words are bitter on my tongue. I pull the hair from my neck to reveal my scar. I'm disoriented. It's hard to focus. Just like Noble said it would be.

Her eyes grow cold at seeing my scar. She's connecting with me. Almost there.

"In the bedroom, there's a small device." She runs to retrieve it. She comes out with another holothumb, different from the master-file and Blacklist. She hands it to me. I press the bottom button, and a hologram fills the space between us. It's another master-file. Every plan she'd put into place across North Africa and the Middle East. Accounts. Names. Dates. Governments. Targets.

She looks up at me, her eyes proud and sad at the same time. "I did everything she taught me. I set them all up. Every one of them will take the fall except for the ones I put in place, which have not yet been exposed. We have more than enough money for years to come."

I stare at her brown eyes, a sour taste in my mouth and an ache in my heart. She's nothing but a broken soul looking for a home. I'm not satisfied at all by my task though I know it had to be done. And I can't take another minute.

"Thank you for your cooperation, Ennéa." I push the red button and the screen goes black.

I peel off Noble's neural simulator from behind my ear and look to my right. Noble is there, waiting anxiously. "It was recording. Did it work?"

"It worked." I look over at the girl, surrounded by Bai's

men, removing my sim glasses from her. Her disorientation is now fading as she's escorted from the room. My stomach lurches like a ship at sea.

Noble comes over to me, taking my arm to lead from the room. "The radicals are subdued in Tunis."

"Good." My head is in a cloud, but Bai rushes into the room.

"It's Kai," he says, "Come quick."

We race behind Bai to the courtyard where a medic SUV is parked outside. Kai is in the back of the car, moaning and talking deliriously. His vitals are dropping fast.

The medic looks up. "We've got to get him somewhere with more equipment fast or he's not going to make it."

"You told me you could stabilize him!" I shout, gripping Kai's hand. "I wouldn't have done the sim if he wasn't stable!"

"He was stable," Bai barks, motioning to the medic to get in the car with Kai. "Now, he's not. Now get in the car." Bai is trying to stay calm, but his eyes are darting from Kai to the big mess in the *Dar*. He can't leave because he's in charge and has to clean up this operation quickly.

"We have a safe house in Tozeur with a medic and the equipment to save his life." The medic climbs in the SUV to drive.

Noble checks Kai's heart rate. "I'm sorry. My calculations say...you won't get there fast enough. From Douz to Tozeur in a car is over an hour."

Bai hits the hood of the car, frustrated. "Then what do you suggest?"

My eyes shoot across the darkened sand to a trial I've never faced in real life but have dreamed about since I was a child. I know what I have to do to save him.

"I can get him there in time," I say, pointing. "In that."

Bai cocks his head. "The helicopter?"

CHAPTER 64

Bai looks at me like I've lost my mind. "I won't lose two people tonight!"

"I can fly it, Bai," I shout. "Now get him in there and give me the coordinates. We don't have time!"

Bai curses under his breath, then shouts to the medic. "Hurry! Help him carry Kai to the helicopter."

I race over to the machine. It's much smaller than it looks from a distance. It turns on easily enough, just like in the sims. Noble's close behind, standing outside the cockpit.

They bring Kai around on the other side and secure him. The medic digs through the bag bouncing on his hip, putting pressure on wounds and checking vitals. "I need to travel with you."

Kai is feverish and pale, but he's fighting. His eyes are spinning but he sees me. "Jo?"

I touch his face. "I'm here, Kai." I say. "Hold on. I'm going to get you to help."

The medic's instruments are already spilling out over Kai. The helicopter fits two, and Kai is sprawled all over the cockpit, and the medic beside him.

"I can come too," Noble offers. No one knows my history in

a helicopter more than Noble. But it's a two-person helicopter and it's already cramped with the medic who has to ride with Kai. Besides, Noble told Bai he'd help get the confessions.

"I can do this, Noble." I give him my backpack with my sim glasses inside. "After you help Bai, take the Jeep and get out of here."

He takes off my watch and puts it on my wrist. "You'll need K2."

Rotor wash from the blades swooshes down against Bai who's pacing beside the machine, shouting orders and cursing.

Noble reaches up and grasps my hand. "Don't listen to Agent Bai. Look at me. I wouldn't let you do this if I didn't believe you could. Trust your gift. Look for the fractals." He cups his hand to my face. "I'll meet you there, Jo."

I nod. "Thanks."

Noble and Bai duck and run away from the helicopter, then from a short distance away turn around to watch with anticipation.

Before I take off, I close my eyes, and breathe. There's an invitation in the chaos, all I have to do is listen. I picture the helicopter from my sims and open my eyes. The rotor blades thump as the engine whines and revs. I move my hands over the controls lightly. I grasp them, wrapping my fingers around them, and then we're up in the sky.

I glance down at Kai, focusing on his face and not the blood seeping through his bandages. "Hold on, Kai."

His eyes flutter open at the sound of my voice. "*Xiao Fenghuang?*" Kai uses my Chinese name. "When did you learn to fly a helicopter?"

I laugh. "You don't want to know."

The palm groves wave under us now. And it's dark, so dark. The helicopter pitches and rolls like a car being overcorrected on an icy road.

K2 is spouting coordinates, but I don't hear them because

I'm fiddling with gauges, needing to finesse the controls. It's not a smooth take off and I'm still pitching forward. The medic tightens his straps, surely wondering if I even know how to fly this thing. Technically, I don't, but I refuse to tell him that. Because somewhere inside me, I have everything I need.

The dense clouds above me that covered the moon are dispersing now. There's light in the sky, but my numbers still aren't surfacing. The helicopter proximity warnings go off in the cockpit. Terrain indicators squawk, too. I need to gain elevation and get up higher over the trees before I smash into something.

*Sometimes all we need is to look up...*but I can't focus, until I see an auto-hover button on the flight director panel—my sims never allowed me to use one. It was too easy of a way out. But this is real life. I push it, and the helicopter hovers, stable in one place.

"What are you doing?" the medic yells. "We don't have time to hover, we need to move!"

But I ignore him because we won't make it if I can't find peace.

My eyes dart up in the dark sky, and a starry host grabs my attention. I let my mind fill up thoughts of stony coral and bright lightning splitting into tributaries of light. *Don't think of what you see, but what it took to produce what you see.*

Dunes. Oceans. Stars. The sound of the wind. The smell of the rain. The tail of a seahorse. Wonder grows in me like a toddler's first visit to a playground. The boundaries of the sea. Above me, below me. Fractals everywhere. The never-ending patterns in the chaos around us. Treasure hidden in plain sight.

The key to unburying my gift is so close, within my grasp. All I have to do is see with new eyes.

I think about love and what it makes us do. How it grows in the dark like a seed in the ground, unformed, until water and light trickle down. Then it splits into a pattern growing both up and down, in two directions, beautiful replicas of each other but in different ways. It's like roots and branches—one outstretched toward the sun, bearing fruit. The other unseen but securing life and holding the earth together. I turn off the hover and fly.

We're high above the trees now. Safe from crashing, but it's still a rough flight. While my sims helped to this point, I'm struggling to keep the helicopter in control.

I look down at Kai. He looks up at me, one eye swollen shut. "It's pretty up here...you're pretty up here..." His voice is slurred. His eyes roll back into his head. "Jo, I love you..." His bloodstained hand reaches out to touch mine. Then, it drops and he's unconscious.

I think of what it took to produce what I have with Kai. Trust. Risk. Time. Love.

Numbers flash like lightning through the sky. The cockpit lights up, a familiar filter of angles, equations and numbers, and something new—charts measuring *sounds, frequencies.* Miles of patterns and scales unfold before me, until I'm flying with a map of my own. Every button on the dashboard is numbered and ordered.

The chop of the blades is a sweet rhythm in my ear. Noble said everything is speaking and now I'm somehow measuring it. Like unmapped territory, there are numbers and tools in my gift I don't understand. But right now, I don't care. The speed and distance now pulse in sync with numbers in my head. I can count every control switch and I have organized them within seconds. The dynamic systems around me make sense and flying a helicopter is as simple as playing with a new toy. I take the controls with confidence.

My numbers flow from inside me, a peaceful current like the sea, unhurried and deep. Then I see it—calculations in the midst of chaos. The world is spread out like a mosaic. Beautiful broken pieces so intricately put together that it forms the most stunning piece of art I've ever seen.

I fly over the earth, its chaotic perfection curving around every bend, the rough and complex meeting in the middle. The equations become like stories, defining everything I see. The very earth beats around me like a human heart declaring life, proclaiming the layers that make us able to love deeper even when trouble comes.

This time my gift is tangible in a way I've never felt before—like new growth on a plant in spring. I don't fully understand what it means, but it's more alive than ever, like the infinity around and inside us. A hope that nothing and everything lasts forever.

I fly into the sky, my mind zipping with numbers. I'm measuring—*not sure how*—twenty-eight sounds around me, but it feels silent, peaceful.

My gift is back.

It's not going to leave me.

But the boy slouched next to me in the cockpit still might.

CHAPTER 65

TOZEUR SAFE HOUSE
TUNISIA

The safe house in Tozeur is easy to locate with the emergence of my new gift. It's exactly two miles out of the city, tucked behind a grove of palm trees. I bring the helicopter down smoothly on a sixteen-by-ten patch of gravel. It's not a landing pad, but it will do.

Thirty feet away sits an inconspicuous old Dar, smaller than the one in Douz. Three men stand outside waiting for us. It's been twenty-three minutes since we left Douz, and fifteen minutes since Kai passed out. The medic is yelling orders concerning Kai.

Even though an internal clock is ticking, it feels like slow motion as agents rush out of the safe house and over with a gurney, and lift Kai. I follow close behind. As we enter the house another man, clad in a bulletproof Kevlar vest, leads me into a nice room with a brown corduroy couch and a small table.

Within seconds, my gift has already calculated the number of rows the fabric has, the dimensions of the windows, and what percentage of the walls have paint flaking off.

Then I wait, with my eyes closed because the numbers swirling inside me make the future all too real. They've calculated the odds for Kai. It's not helping. I stare out the small window and do the one thing I can, study the stars and look for a thumbprint.

After an hour and seven minutes Noble arrives at the door in a fresh change of clothes. I stand, but don't rush. My numbers outline his physical features, and highlight small movements in his face, each equation telling me the numerical story of a boy.

"Hi." His voice sends waves of frequencies undulating in the room. Coupled with my equations, they're so strong I almost need to sit back down. "You made it."

I nod, shakily.

"You were right about Kai. He didn't fail. The holothumb was merged with the master-file. SMOKE is currently exposing networks all over North Africa and the Middle East."

I sigh with relief and eight questions are ready on my tongue, chiefly, why he's still here and not fleeing Tunisia. But Jace, the medic who rode in the helicopter, comes into the room, and pulls my attention.

"Kai's stable and awake. He wants to see you." He holds the door open. "You have ten minutes before Director Kane arrives. Agent Bai said you both need to leave before he shows up."

Noble juts his chin toward the door. "Go ahead," he says. "I'll wait."

CHAPTER 66

The boy lying on the bed is beautiful, bloody, and bruised but not defeated in the least. The minute he sees me his face lights up, bright and victorious. He pushes himself up, all his energy directed toward me. "Hi, Trouble."

He doesn't even care about his banged-up body. Director Kane's words about his aptitude for pain and recovery being off the charts return to mind. Was Kai born for this? Suddenly I don't know what to think. My numbers are coursing over his beautiful face, and every time he saved me replays over and over in my head...I just want to know what Kai really wants.

I walk over to him, gently nuzzling my face into his.

"You smell different. What is that?" he asks, his eyes squinting playfully.

I sniff my sweatshirt. "Fire smoke and cardamom." I sit on the edge of the bed. "I'm glad you're not dead."

"Me too." He shakes his head and lets out a sigh.

The bruising of his right eye jogs a memory from China. "Well, you're on brand by sacrificing yourself for others."

He smiles. "For you." The blood caked on his face earlier is now washed clean revealing swelling everywhere. Under it, all I see is the boy who saved me over and over again. A boy who risks his life so I can sleep.

For the last year, he's been a spark of light in the midst of darkness, a sign life goes on. But what about now?

He tries to sit up.

"Lie down," I say, gently pushing him back. "It's finished. You solved the case. You're the hero."

"I had a plan to make it out, too, you know." He stares at me as if I'm his medicine, his drug. The only thing keeping me together is the numbers zipping up and down his face like the first time I saw him in the pool house in Shanghai, shirtless, fixing stuff and watering orchids. The boy no one gets to see but me.

"I know you did." His skin is still hot and feverish. Then he gives me a funny grin. "What?"

"The way you're looking at me," he says, piecing something together. "Is your gift back?"

"Yeah," I say, amazed at how well he can read me. "It happened in the helicopter, with you. It's been on for one hour and twenty-seven minutes and well, you get the idea..." I smile. "There's something new about it though. I don't quite understand it yet. Basically, I'm weirder than before."

"Jo. *Tai bang le*! I'm so happy for you." He squeezes my hand. "And who was that guy talking to you by the helicopter?"

My thoughts pause for a millisecond. Noble is outside waiting for me. I breathe in deep. "The hacker. Turns out he's an old prodigy friend. He helped me remember where my gift came from."

Kai grimaces. "He's lucky I could barely move. I didn't like the way he looked at you. Don't tell me you were with *him* all week? I thought you were with some bodyguard?"

"The bodyguard is his uncle." I purse my lips with the thought. "And the guy you did Tou Qi on."

He groans. "Please tell me he's ok."

"He's fine," I say. "But Bai was pretty upset you left

Montego. It was a dangerous move."

"Montego was a pawn," he says. "I had to think quick when he told me about the Loyalists. I knew I had to stop the Successor, and it worked out. The world's safe. You're safe. All the remaining parts of her empire are gone now. If Bai was there, it means the good guys won, right?" He smiles.

"Yeah." I smile back. He stopped the deal, took down an entire syndicate, and prevented the PSS Blacklist from ruining the world. "How did you know it was her?"

"Because of you. You taught me never to underestimate anyone." Kai reaches out for me. He said as much, even to the Sheikh in the live stream. My eyes were on Kai, but Kai's eyes were on the girl. He knew even then. "When did you give her the holothumb?"

"In the desert at Ksar Douz, after the fight. I had to touch her in a creepy way to do it though." His face bunches up. The scene comes unbidden to my mind, the way his hands glided over her body. I laugh thinking of it now.

"Did she confess anything?" he asks.

"Yeah. Everything." I clear my throat, "And Noble, um, the hacker, I think is helping Bai with the Sheikh and Müller's confessions."

"Noble?" Kai's confused, and slightly bothered. "A lot happened this week, I see." Kai's hands find mine. They're scarred and rough, but gentle.

"More than you know." Over the last five days I flew to Tunis to save a boy. PSS infiltrated two networks. Stopped a coup. Stole a holothumb. Kept up with Noble. Met Mandel face-to-face. Flew a real helicopter and my gift came back... and I learned Kai might leave me...

Kai threads his fingers with mine. "I'm sorry you got involved. When I went after them, I didn't know you'd come."

"Never apologize for doing the right thing, Kai," I say, the words trembling on my lips. "I just want to know what you want next. What's important to you?"

"You're important to me." He lays back and peers up at me. "When I heal up, I'll come to you and we'll take long walks on the beach. We'll make our plan."

"Long walks on the beach, huh?" I ask, my insides squirming. "What about your next job? What about the promotion?"

Kai's eyes dart to the wall. "We don't need to talk about that now. Doesn't matter."

My stomach squeezes into a knot. Every number says he is hiding his true thoughts. He doesn't want to hurt me. How will I ever get the truth from him? If he won't tell me what he really wants, I'll never know if I am the one stopping him from his dreams. Unless...I finger my lips.

There is one piece of PSS tech I have left. One I swore I'd never use. Never thought I'd have to. Until now.

I lean down and kiss him.

CHAPTER 67

Sway's serum works instantly. The irises of his eyes sway large and small, and he slurs his words. "Trouble, what'd you do? The room is spinning."

"Of course, it is," I joke. "I kissed you."

He laughs. "That would do it. Your power over me is much stronger than I like to admit." He groans and grabs his ribs.

I move my hand to gently touch his bandaged chest, my insides squirming at his labored breath, the cuts traversing his ribcage, his swollen face.

Sway is fully operational, and yet he gains his bearing and focus on me much quicker than what I heard was normal. Pens says it's like a bad headache, or a thick hangover, a haze over your mind. It's not surprising Kai is fighting it. He's strong.

"Kai, can I ask you a question?" I ask, sitting down next to him.

"Anything."

"Why do you want to be an agent?"

"So you can sleep at night." He takes my messy strands of hair between his fingers. "I made you a promise. I won't let you live in a world where anything bad can happen to you, where anyone like Madame exists. I want you safe, always."

I bring his hand to my lips and kiss his fingers. "There's more to it than that. Please tell me."

"Why? What's wrong?" Kai knows me too well, even with Sway in his system.

"I know you were offered a long-term undercover position," I say, directly.

"I was going to tell you." His eyes try to focus on mine but fail to stay still. "How did you find out about it?" His head is swaying.

"That doesn't matter," I say. "I just need to know what you want, Kai? Not for me, but for yourself."

He's fighting Sway, trying to hold back what is inside. "I love you, Jo."

"I know you do." This boy is hard to crack. "But what else?"

He finds my hand and squeezes hard. His eyes roll, like he doesn't want to say what's next but does anyway.

"Remember when you were in the Pratt, and Red taught you to claim your gift and find the destiny you'd always dreamed of? The purpose you felt? You knew you had to do it. You could never go back to a normal life, even if it hurt?"

I smile sadly. "I remember."

"That changed my life. *You* changed my life. I can't explain it, but that's how I feel when I'm out there, like there are lives that only I can save. That I'm brave and quick for a reason. It's like your gift, but invisible. A compass inside me, guiding me." Kai takes a deep breath, head wavering heavily now. "You gave me the greatest treasure, Jo. You woke me up."

"Five minutes until Director Kane arrives." K2 warns, but I don't need a watch anymore. I knew that before it spoke. It's comforting, knowing I can beat a machine.

Kai ignores K2. "I've always wanted to save the world. And I know I can do this job. But I won't leave you." He shrugs. "Not for 1-3 years..."

"You told Director Kane I'm not waiting for you."

He grips his head. "How did you hear that?" His eyes narrow, full of hurt. It's not fair, our conversation. He has no way to lie right now, but I don't want him making the wrong decision because of me. My numbers are back, and I need to know what he wants, what I want.

"You're not waiting, Jo. I'm the one waiting. For you. You think I can read you so well, but I don't always know how you really feel even if I act like I do. I know you care. But..." The tone in his voice stings because it's true. I've never told him how I really feel. "Jo, maybe you don't see it, but you're the one who needs to make a choice. Even now, I see there's something bothering you, but you won't tell me what it is." He grabs my hands, his big brown eyes looking up at me. "But if you love me and you want me to give up this job. I'll choose you." He coughs, and swallows hard. His eyes struggling to focus.

My heart soars like we're back in the helicopter. He's telling the truth. He'd give it up. He's proven that a hundred times, but how could I let him? Since I met him, he's done nothing but make sacrifices for me.

The sim in my old bedroom with my mom returns. *"People who love each other also make sacrifices for each other."*

Time freezes as I look at him. His dark eyes sink into mine, and my heart crushes inside me. He's one of the most loyal men I know, willing to give it all up for the woman he loves. But Kai was born to be a hero. Born to save lives. He needs to do this for himself. I won't make him give up his destiny for me.

As much as it hurts, it's my turn to make a sacrifice for him.

Three months without my gift altered me drastically. One week with Noble showed me a world I didn't even know existed. What will happen in a year or two without Kai?

Ninety-six seconds left.

"You're silent. Even if you don't love me now," Kai says,

his shields fully down. Then as if to stick the knife deeper into my heart, he says, "I'll wait. You're what keeps me alive out there. You're my center."

I grip his hands tighter. His eyes battle the chemicals that lurk in his conscience. He's so strong. The world needs him. I need him. And yet, for the first time, I grasp the weight of his love in my heart. Like gold. It's so pure, so real, it finally pushes me over the threshold I never thought I could cross.

"Kai," I say, a hot tear trailing down my cheek. "Truth is, I love you. So much…" Once the words are out of my mouth, a freedom I've never known is unlocked in me. "I love you, Kai." I lean over him, our lips brushing.

He grabs my face and kisses me over and over again. "That's all I've ever wanted to hear." Our kiss intensifies like floodgates, once held back, are now broken down. I count his heartbeats between our breaths. The number of months, and days, and hours, we have been together. Memories and dates where he chose me are logged and filed away. All his smiles and touches and habits are numerically defined and written.

Two people who love each other is a beautiful mystery. There may not be a formula to follow, but there is evidence of what makes it grow. Eventually, our kiss turns tender, and he nestles his head into my hair and breathes deep. It's even clearer now, what I have to do.

K2's warning beeps again. My time is up.

"Goodbye, Kai," I say, wiping a tear off my face and already missing our slow walks on the beach. "I love you."

With those three words, I've made him the happiest man alive. Unfortunately, by tomorrow he won't remember I ever said them.

CHAPTER 68

There is no red button in real life. We can't opt out of difficult phases. Instead, we have to face them, head on, with our eyes open, looking for that small trace of infinity and order in the chaos.

I step out of the room where the medic rushes me to the back door. I exit the safe house and step into the chilly desert air. Noble is waiting for me, like a beacon, like a balm...like a perfect storm.

"Hey." His frame, perfectly numbered and his voice a low whisper. Our frequency collides now with my gift fully turned on and alive. He's watching me and I'm watching him.

I wipe my eyes. "Did the sims work for the confessions?"

"All of them. It's done." He says, moving closer to me, leading me toward his Jeep parked down the way. "And Harrison was right. Ms. T sent a squad of detectives out to find me. I have 30 minutes to get out of town."

I shake my head. "I'm sorry."

"How's Kai?"

I can't answer. All the words are caught in my throat. I'm tightening my lips and locking my jaw.

He frowns, seeing my face. He knew this was going to

happen. Only he thought it would be Kai leaving me...

He wraps his arms around me. "It's going to be ok." His words slay me. I shove my face into his chest, and breathe him in. He's lying. Nothing is going to be ok. He's leaving too... but hearing the words makes me feel better.

Noble opens the car door and I hop in. I don't even ask where we're going. I know it's not his family's camp—that place is compromised now since Ms. T knows who he is.

Noble's quiet as he drives, calculating the right moment to speak. And we have a lot to talk about.

I never believed in coincidence—and without a doubt, Mandel, or Noble, prepared me for this exact moment in time. And if he's anything like me, his numbers are spinning with possibilities and sliding puzzle pieces together to make sense of the week. But numbers only go so far. They don't open a person's soul and share its secrets.

But they do tell me this. There's more I need to know about Noble. He's uncharted territory, like my new gift. I need time to map him out and understand him. But time was never in our favor. *You have five days.* And that's over.

He drives, his hands on the wheel, looking straight ahead.

"Where will you go?" I ask.

"Another haven I have out in the wild." He's ambiguous on purpose. It's smart. It's better I don't know. I don't want to know, just in case PSS grills me.

He pulls over where another van is parked by the entrance of a highway. Someone is slumped over the driver's wheel.

"Who's that?" I ask.

"Qadar. Ms. T called. They've handed everything over to the security council. She ordered him to drive you back tonight." He sighs.

"How can he?" I ask, shocked he even made it this far. "He can barely move."

"He's stronger than you think." We hop out. Noble walks

over to the van and opens the door. Qadar gets out, staggering like he's still drunk. Noble says something in Arabic, hugs him, then returns to me.

He swings open the back of the Jeep and grabs a full bag. "Farah packed your stuff. And here are your sim glasses back." He takes out a small chip and puts it in my hand. "Give this to PSS."

"What is it?"

"Ms. T may have been right. I've hacked into everything. I also broke into the PSS main server and other secure files. PSS has fun toys."

"Harrison told me." I look at the chip before putting it in my pocket.

"On the chip are solutions to many of the problems the team has been working on. I just wanted to help." He shrugs. "I'm working on being normal, remember? For what it's worth, tell Ms. Taylor I'm sorry, and tell Harrison I admire his work."

Every number around us is squeezing me to pieces.

"Noble," I say. "I'm the one who's sorry. I'm the reason you have to leave. The smartdust from my earring on the rooftop of the Bardo, you knew what I was doing. Why did you let me do it?"

He skims my ears where both earrings are gone now. "I took a risk on my numbers—and you. I had to believe in this moment right here, where you'd see me for who I am and trust me...and that you'd let me go."

Noble's frequency skips like mad raindrops on puddles. My gift tries to predict his numbers, like building blocks, and yet nothing is more unquantifiable than the emotions rocking between us. It scares me.

We walk to his Jeep. "You know I have to go, if I don't want to get caught." His jaw locks.

"Mandel. I ruined everything..." My mind is clouded over. Everything is jumbled, because I love Kai, but what is it I feel for this boy?

My numbers tell me plainly that confusion makes the worst mistakes, and hasty decisions are usually wrong. But the smell of his skin, fire smoke and cardamom, seem to balm my pain of saying goodbye to Kai. Even with my gift I can't think clearly. This is Mandel. Everything in me bounces from past to present, spiraling with a dangerous question, *what if?* I don't know what I'm doing because every sensation is teetering on the edge of my skin. What if I never see him again?

I step up to him. My hands slide over his waist. I lift my eyes to him. Our eyes are locked in one of our intense battles but now they sing with numbers, clashing with my hurt of losing Kai and the joy of finding Mandel. That bewilderment and hurt becomes reckless, a part of me I don't recognize. All I notice now are his jaw, his lips, soon my fingers curl around his neck all while pictures of Kai war in my head. I don't know what I'm doing.

Noble exhales hard, then removes my hands. "Jo." An equation shows the redirection of his strength to change his motion. He's restraining himself. "You're making it really difficult for me."

"Questions have burned in me all night..." I whisper.

"Me too, but..."

"But what? What is this?" I motion between us, our obvious connection. "Our past. We just found each other and..."

"Jo," he says, gently, brushing my hair behind my ears. "I've wanted to kiss you since I was thirteen. I've loved you since the first time we spoke...but I've wanted it for the right reasons. Right now, your head is too full and I'm not the only one in it. Without honor, things are spoiled. This is one thing I don't want to risk ruining. I've waited too long, but I'm willing to wait some more for the right moment."

I run my hand through my hair, my face on fire. My eyes shoot to the ground, focusing on the sixteen pebbles in the sand by our feet. What was I thinking?

"You need time to understand this new gift," he says. "Things might change now. And whether I want to admit it or not, you need time to understand what you want."

He's talking about Kai...

He digs his feet into the sand. "Jo. I claimed Kai only loved you because of the trouble and danger." His gaze is steel. "It's not true. I watched him write your name in the sand twenty-two times. Whisper your name in his sleep eight times. You were never just trouble to him. Wherever he was, you were on his mind."

My heart crushes inside me. "Why are you telling me this now?"

"I want you to choose me for the right reasons. It's a risk I'm willing to take."

He draws me into his arms and pulls me close. My face buries in his chest. It's new and familiar at the same time. I don't know what to make of it, and time won't give me a penny.

"How can I find you?" I ask.

His lips warm my forehead with a kiss, and his hand slips down my arm, then away from my hand. "It's all written in the stars, Jo."

He climbs in the Jeep and closes the door. I watch him drive away until the frequency fades and the dust settles. After ten minutes, an engine rumbles. Qadar is signaling me. It reminds me when I get back to Tunis I'll have to face Ms. T.

I head over to the van.

Qadar stumbles out. "It's time to go back." His voice is slurred.

I shake my head at his half-closed eyes and crooked stature. "You can't drive. You need to rest for at least a few more hours."

"You're my responsibility. My charge. I'm taking you

back." He attempts to stand straighter, but fails, catching himself on the car door. Noble was right. Qadar is strong and won't admit defeat.

"You can take me back, but I'm driving." I slip past him, into the driver's seat, and buckle up. "Get in."

"You don't know the way."

I look up at the night sky, a laugh on my lips. A highway of coordinates, speeds and distances have already calculated in my mind. "The map is in my head and you can't stop me."

Qadar gives me a funny glance like he's heard that from someone before. Without arguing further, he climbs into the back seat, and collapses with a thunk. I glance into the rearview mirror but can't meet his eyes because they're already closed. A smirk plays on his face. "Your goals are my goals."

CHAPTER 69

The drive back to Tunis is a desert of fractals, questions, and dreams. My view is different, like I'm a year older and an inch taller, and can finally see above the counter.

The equations around me have changed, pointing to things I don't yet understand. Which is why I know I still have a lot to learn. I'm a child on a journey, learning how to read life backwards, so I can see.

Red was right. Each year, we shed a layer and grow, whether we want to or not. The truth is we're better for it. We're made to grow. Sometimes that process means we lose our perspectives like the leaves of last year. So that when they grow back, they're fresh and new in the right season. Maybe that's why treasure is often buried in the ground. You have to dig for it. You have to go low and believe it's there even when you can't see it. And sometimes you get dirty. It's humbling, but Red always used to say true humility would always win you the best seat at the table.

Seven hours and nine minutes later, the inky blue-black gives way to pinks and purples as dawn breaks over the capital up ahead. Qadar, who slept most of the way, is awake and stable now. He climbs into the front passenger seat.

"Any water?" he asks. "My mouth is as dry as Douz." He finds a bottle Noble must have packed. After several long gulps and a pause, he finally speaks again. "I'm not flying back with you. Ms. Taylor doesn't think it's necessary."

I glance over at the giant, a pang in my heart at the thought of saying goodbye to him. Qadar's the only person, apart from Noble, who knows what really happened on this trip. Who knows what Noble feels for me. A part of me longs to be back at Farah's tents with hot mint tea, oranges and olives but I'm going home to Seattle. Alone.

"Where do you think he'll go?" I ask.

Qadar looks out his window. "He never says. He'll let me know he's ok when he gets settled."

"Do you think he'll try to find me?" I keep my hands on the wheel, and eyes focused on the road.

"He's tried to find you for as long as he's lived with me." He smirks. "What do those odds tell you?"

I smile, slowing for a red light.

"Is that what you want?" Qadar asks.

"I'm asking myself the same thing. I don't know."

"That's why he's giving you time. Noble doesn't do anything with half a heart."

I nod because I believe it's true. Qadar must notice how my face falls. He offers a squeeze on my shoulder.

We roll up to the Kasbah, and I pull around to the back and park. "Thanks for everything, Qadar."

"*Min gheer mziyya*," he says. "You can call me anytime." Then he walks with his hand on my back, leading me into Dar Alzaytun.

Ms. T meets us at the entrance. "Welcome back." She turns to Qadar. "Well done. Please meet me in the conference room for debriefing with the other bodyguards." Qadar nods, and slowly makes his way down the hall. Ms. T turns to me. "What happened to him? He looks like a truck hit him."

"He did his job..." I stifle a yawn; the long drive is getting to me now. My eyes are heavy, red, and stinging.

Ms. T notices my exhaustion. A set of differential equations predict she'll place a hand on my shoulder. I don't move. Even my numbers welcome the warmth of a motherly touch. Her hand comes down with a light squeeze. I receive it. At least she hasn't excommunicated me from PSS yet. "We fly out in three hours. Go pack and rest up. We'll debrief in Seattle."

I walk to my double room in silence, the *Dar* a different place now. Every tile in the floor comes alive, assigning numbers to patterns and colors. Every mosaic in the house fills with geometrical equations like a delicious banquet for my mind. And yet, there is new math, measurements around me I don't understand yet. Just like in the helicopter.

Inside my room, I collapse on the bed, too tired to pack. But there's a loud knock on the door and before I can answer, the PSS team rushes in.

Pens sets a baguette and a plate of fried vegetables with harissa on the table. "Hungry?"

"Tired." The rich spices fill the air but all I wish for is to be back in the tent, under the stars. "What about you guys?"

"Not our usual job," Felicia says. "But the government is safe. The election went well. Everything is back online. We updated their security system. But we don't care about that. We want to know all about you and the NASA Tipper."

I glance at Harrison. "Hey," he says. "I kept it a secret for as long as I could. Once Ms. T knew, the news got out."

I sigh, too tired to care. "He wanted me to pass on that he admires all of your work. Especially yours, Harrison."

"Me?" Harrison's face cracks into a wide grin and his glassy eyes tell me he has floated off to some distant place.

"Details. Now." Pens and Felicia plop down on the bed next to me. "What was he really like?"

I yawn, and lie down on the bed, thinking of Noble, the boy who is bright, brilliant, and complex, the way he struck my life and lit up my sky, then was gone just as fast.

"Like lightning."

CHAPTER 70

SEATTLE, WASHINGTON

It's eleven p.m. at the airport and everyone's family picks them up except mine. By the look on Ms. T's face, this is on purpose.

She wraps her arm around my shoulder. "I asked Jason if I could drive you home."

I nod, and we walk to the parking garage where she unlocks a car. We get in, and soon we are on the road amidst the slow night traffic.

At first, we're silent. I count how many times Ms. T checks her mirrors, or switches lanes and the patterns in her speed fluctuations. But eventually, after seven minutes of moving in and out of the slow lane, she speaks. "Are you going to tell me what happened out there?"

I shrug, counting the buildings as they pass. "Kai and the Blacklist are safe. The Successor and her associates are in custody, and the elections went well, no more radicals…" My mind skips to Kai's feverish bandaged chest, then to Noble saying goodbye at the highway entrance. "There's not much else to tell."

Her face puckers. "The records say differently. As do all ten of your fingertips which should have bandages. K2, which is PSS tech, reported no tasers left, and your earrings are missing."

My eyebrows rise. "There may have been *a little* action."

She nods, her patient self-control taking over. "Qadar's face yesterday proved that." She sighs. "What about you? You haven't said a word since we left Tunis. Are you ok?" We take the exit for West Seattle Bridge, and head toward Alki Beach.

Apparently, I'm not an expert on hiding my emotions anymore. Ms. T can see something, *or everything,* has changed. "That depends."

"On what?" she asks, pulling off the freeway.

I turn to look at her. "What you're going do with the information about Noble's identity."

Her features soften and she sighs. For the next twelve minutes we drive in silence, until she pulls down my street and parks in front of our beach house. The front porch light is on. There's also a glow in the kitchen and the garage. They're awake, waiting up for me.

"You don't know where Noble went then, I suppose?" Ms. T asks.

"No, but he wanted me to give you this." I dig the chip out of my backpack. "He's not running because he broke any laws. He's good, a prod worth protecting. All he wants to do is help."

Her motherly eyes don't miss the way I speak about him. "And did he help you?" She's referring to my gift.

I breathe in, the numbers defining every ringlet in her hair, the pattern of her floral shirt, and the fractals in and around us. I pause, taking note of the new scales and measurements being drawn from the car to the house; the vibrations and frequencies speaking, traveling in sets of equations I don't yet understand. I'll tell her everything, but not tonight.

"Yeah. He showed me I have a lot to learn." Under my hands I feel the sim glasses in my backpack. I don't need it anymore, but I'm not ready to give it back. Noble programmed something for me in phase three. I just don't know when I'll be ready to see it.

Ms. T gauges me. "Jo, I've decided to put the information about Coral Hacker, Noble Adams, into Cyber Island."

My eyes light up. "Thank you."

She takes a deep breath. "I want to tell you something. A bit of history," she says, her voice an octave lower. "I believe I can trust you and it's easy to tell you've been wondering about my past." She folds her hands in her lap. "When I first started PSS, we had a special partnership with the government for some very complex cases, like this one in Tunisia. My prods helped solve over 200 cases a year. At that time, there was a girl, like you, brilliant and brave. But not with the same life experience you have…" She swallows hard. "We lost her because she didn't follow protocols. There's no need to go into the story now, but after that, I shut the unit down to focus solely on projects that will bring goodwill and prosperity. Last year, the government asked me to open that special unit back up." She stops talking, like even the reasons she is telling me this are raw and unfiltered.

"What did you tell them?" I ask, my mind piecing everything together.

"I told them that although I trust a few of my prods to do jobs like those again, I hadn't found anyone to lead them." Her eyes fix on me. A stack of live streams, and finger bombs, and desert fights fall on me as I realize it's both an answer and a question. One I'm not ready to explore.

"Thank you for trusting me," I say, my mind sinks down in a sea of numbers, possibilities, and memories. Maybe there's treasure there, but right now I can't hold my breath long enough to reach it. "I'm not ready."

"I understand. Then we'll see you on Monday?" she confirms, and I nod. "Tell Jason I said hello. He's a brilliant man, you know."

I take my small bag out of the trunk and walk to the house. I slide the key in the lock and open the door. I brace myself for frantic hugs and vital checks, but only Mara is there to greet me.

"Welcome back, sis." Her eyes are sleepy, but she rushes over to greet me with a hug. "Everything ok, with what we talked about on the phone?"

I bite my lip, and she frowns as she takes in my face.

She sighs. "I guess we have a lot to catch up on."

"Yeah, but in the morning. It's late," I say. "Where's Lily and Dad?"

"Lily's with Cullen," she says, her eyebrows raised. "She's had more freedom this week than she's had all year. She's indebted to you. Dad's in the garage practicing his new hobby. He's waiting for you."

On the way to my room to drop off my stuff, I pass the den and my mouth drops. It looks like Noble's tech-tent. Where did my dad get this equipment? How did he set this up while I was gone? And why?

I hurry over to the garage, swing open the door, and come to a halt. My dad's punching into a sandbag hanging from the ceiling, and the garage looks like a mini *daochang*, the kind where Kai works out. Numbers map out every new thing, but what I care about is my dad.

His cheeks are rosy and full, his gait straighter, his shoulders are back, his chin up...and his eyes—they have light in them again. The fire my mom fell in love with and the strength that started his multi-million-dollar company before I was born. Waves of goose bumps travel over me. This is the dad I knew before China, before he lost his business.

"Dad?" I'm laughing as he walks over. "What happened to you while I was gone? What did you do to the den? What's with the garage?"

"It was time to change," he says, swinging me into a sweaty

hug. "Remember long ago when you worked in the office with me?" I nod. "I used to tell you success wasn't out there," he points outside, "but it started here." He taps his heart. "I finally remembered that."

After he hugs me again, we walk into the house, toward the kitchen. He turns on an electric tea kettle. "I promised myself I wouldn't ask you to tell me every little thing about your trip. You can just share what you want."

I'm shocked and pleased. "Where's my dad? Are you really Jason Rivers?" I ask, laughing. My numbers go wild. It's rare that a human can surprise me. "Why don't you explain the office first." Two desks are set up, side by side like when I was younger and first started attending business meetings with him. In a time when I had no idea what I was capable of.

A big grin grows on his face as he pulls out two mugs and, to my delight, puts in mint tea bags followed by boiling water.

"I'm going back to work," he says, eyes twinkling.

"You don't ever need to work again," I say, not with the amount of money we have in savings.

"You know as well as I do, life isn't about doing a job. It's about using what we've been given. And it's time I got back into being me. I used to help people too, you remember?"

Pride swells in my chest. Mom would be so happy. "So what, you want me to work for you again?"

"Nah, I want to work for you." The energy in his voice is filling the air. "I want to talk to you about a few ideas I've got up my sleeve. It's a new season, Jo."

I'm excited about what he is saying, but I frown, because he's right. It's a new season...one without Kai. He'll soon be on some mission far away. And Noble fled to a hidden place somewhere in the world. And I'm here with thousands of numbers but zero answers...I drop to the chair, a lump in my throat.

My dad notices right away. "What's wrong?"

I cock my head, not sure how to answer. I want to listen to him and rejoice in his news. I also want to tell him my gift is back and I calculated every car and plane and route on the way home. But everything about Tunisia has me choked up.

He pulls up a chair, his hands on my knees. He's fully tuned into me. "Hmm," he said. "Looks like boy trouble."

"How did you know?" I ask.

"You may not know this, but relationships are kind of my thing." He shrugs, his eyes inviting and safe.

I smile, shaking my head, remembering my mom in my sims, and even Mara's advice. I take a deep breath. "Have you got an hour?"

He's already placing a mug of tea in my hands. "For you, I've got all night."

CHAPTER 71

RIVERS RESIDENCE
WEST SEATTLE, WASHINGTON

Five days later...

Jetlag is a welcome beast right now. It's 3 a.m., and everyone is asleep but me. It's silent, and warm, and after 128 days of living in this house, it's the first time it feels like home.

My phone is turned off and in my bedroom. Not like I'm getting any calls. PSS already changed my number and upgraded the security. But I can't look at it because it's filled with photos, videos, and messages between Kai and me. He already found my goodbye letter on *the street* explaining that we need to take some time apart to understand what we want. I asked him not to come, not to contact me. That it'd be too hard if he did and I'd reconsider everything. Of course he called. And despite every equation screaming in my head, I didn't answer.

Kai is hurting badly. I can feel it. The new part of my gift that I don't understand lets me sense it in a way I've never experienced before. Somehow, I know he feels my pain in a unique way too. Which makes things worse.

I don't know if I'll ever be able to let him go. His face, his scent, and his words are always with me. He understands me like Red did. He found me in the dark and pulled me into the light. Kai believed we could beat the odds. Promised me he'd never leave my side. Letting him go was a risk I had to take. For both of us.

He doesn't understand why I'm leaving him this way. But hopefully he will later, then he won't regret his decision. Maybe by then I'll understand too. All I know is that even my numbers confirm he has to do this job.

Truth is, I need time to understand what I want and to comprehend what is happening to me. My gift is operating on a whole new level. Each day there are new equations that confound me. I don't know what they mean, but I know I need to figure it out before I can move forward. I have so many questions, and there's only one person who can answer them...Noble, a boy who has seen me in a way no one else ever could. He's the other equation I need to solve...

The sim glasses dangle in my hands. The phase three that Noble programmed haunts me. I've been battling internally whether or not to do it.

I wander out to our back porch, which looks out over a sandy beach and the Puget Sound. Settling into a deck chair under a thick blanket, I listen to the waves, calculating their sets coming at me with not only beautiful numbers but new oscillations and frequencies with each splash and break of water on the shore.

I look up. It's a clear night, and a host of stars tease me, holding back their secrets. With each twinkle, they're putting off energy that no doubt Noble is harnessing. Somehow, I know he's there writing something in the sky, his mind calculating at light speed. His star coding comes to mind. Experts said the codes are so complicated no one has learned to read them yet. I wonder what they say. I wonder at our connection and if he had told me sooner how he felt, what would have happened. I also wonder where he went.

With that in mind and a buzz in my stomach, I slip on the sim glasses. "K2, phase three, please."

A rustle of frosty breeze brushes against my ears and cheeks. The tip of my nose is cold, and as I inhale, fresh, chilly air tingles my senses. But it's not salt-air. It reminds me of mountaintops and pines.

My eyes open to miles of white rolling hills. Trees everywhere blanketed and dressed in beautiful white gowns. The sky is a thick wall of gray, and it's snowing.

My hands are gloved and I'm wearing a long, down parka. Even the boots on my feet are so warm I couldn't be more comfortable. Snowflakes are falling around me in droves. I cover my mouth, almost giggling. I haven't seen snow in years. A gift, from Noble.

The flakes are larger than the ones I saw as a child. I stretch out my hand, watching them fall on my glove. Laughing, my mouth opens to catch them on my tongue.

I want to play in it forever. I fall to the ground to make a snow angel, then roll over and over. I pack it together to form the biggest snowball and toss it downhill.

I wade through the snowy land, thankful Noble said there would be no danger here. Up ahead, a path in the snow leads to a small table under a tree. There's a lamp on it, a thermos and two mugs. I look around, wondering if Noble is somehow going to join me. But no one is there.

I pour the liquid into the mug. Hot chocolate, perfectly sweet with a dash of savory. There's a note under the second mug. I pick it up.

Digits. I always wanted to give you a billion snowflakes. I hope you're eating fractals right now and enjoying them. It's the most intricate, infinite art you could ever taste.

Yours, Mandel.

The lump in my throat returns. He planned to tell me who he was in Tunis. I inhale the snowy air and muse as I sip on my hot chocolate.

What do you want? Qadar had asked me. I don't know, but I can't move forward until I understand what is between Noble and me. A whistle in the trees catches my attention. Vibrations and numbers calculate every tree, distance and detail. I perk up. Every element of this sim is perfectly placed. The table under the trees. The path in the snow.

It dawns on me. This is a real place. This is Mandel's memory. *So where am I? Where is he?*

I look up, intentionally scanning the sky, searching for the brightest spot in the thick cloud cover. Thank God for my numbers because the sun's position is enough to calculate that this place is in the northern hemisphere, and very far north. Looking downhill, there's something hidden behind a group of trees. I'm drawn to it, but the minute I jump up and head that way, the screen goes black.

I take off the sim glasses, breathless and once again draw in the salty air. I tighten the blanket around me. *It's all written in the stars...*

Was that Noble's way of telling me I could find him? Does he think I can crack his code?

The clear night dares me to look up and when I do, my numbers reach into the heavens, drawing lines across the sky and digging for treasure.

I set my gaze on the stars. It's high time Noble had a little competition.

EPILOGUE

LÜDERITZ, NAMIBIA

February, Three months later...

The world is upside down.

In reality, I'm in the Southern Hemisphere where the earth is tilted toward the sun, so unlike Seattle right now, where frost covers every leaf and blade of grass, here in the arid city of Lüderitz, it's summer and a blazing heat radiates over a rainbow of brown terrain colliding with a deep blue sky. So it's not exactly upside down, no matter how life feels right now.

I'm sitting outside on a sandy ledge in shorts and a tank top, wiping sweat from my brow, staring out at the South Atlantic, calculating how many hours it would take to sail the 3635 miles to Rio de Janeiro. Behind me, Felicia and Pens are wrapping up the final tests at a solar-powered workstation we set up on the coast, two miles north of the city. Working with the Namibia United Energy Research and Development team, PSS helped develop new tools and techniques to locate and recover renewable energy sources in safer, faster, and more sustainable ways. Harrison and Eddie are installing the last of the PSS updates to their new tech at the NUE headquarters in town.

"One last test and we're done," Pens says, satisfied. "After seventeen days of working on this project, we can finally be beach bums and go sightseeing." She gulps down a bottle of water.

Felicia snags her bathing suit, and dives behind the workstation door to change. "Harrison and Eddie want to explore the shipwrecks off Skeleton Coast," she yells from inside. "I think we should head to Victoria Falls in Zambia. What do you say, Jo?"

"Huh? Sure. Meet you there," I say, distracted as my mind measures the sounds coming off the ocean. The global wind patterns—or the polar easterlies—and the eddies forming in the sea are so different here. No wonder so many ships have run aground and there's often heavy fog.

"Jo, you're not paying attention again," Pens yells over. She sighs, shaking her head. "Fel, where are the X-2 chip readers? I can't find them."

"Harrison has all the micro-tech in his bag. He'll be back in 15 minutes." The oscillations of Felicia's voice collide with a car speeding by in the background. My mind buzzes, listening to it all.

"Fifteen minutes is too long when I'm this sweaty. It's hotter here than our last job in Saudi Arabia," Pens whines, fanning herself. "Jo, do you have that old phone from China?"

"Yeah, why?" My gift tracks the familiar pitch in her voice.

"The tech we've installed is super advanced, but we need to make sure it can read anything, no matter how outdated. Can I use the sim card? That should work for this test."

"No problem." At least my nostalgia is good for something. I take out the old phone from my backpack and rub the edges. I don't know why I carry it with me. It's not like I ever turn it on. It's sort of a reminder I'm free. It was the first piece of tech

I used after escaping the Pratt. Chan gave it to me. It's also loaded with old messages from Kai. I toss the phone to Pens and stare out over the ocean. I wonder where he is right now.

"Thanks," Pens says. "This should be done in one minute. Then, we swim."

"I'll meet you there," I say. "I want to read up on the new PSS jobs before swimming, so we'll be ready to make a decision on where we're going next. There are jobs in Benin and Mozambique, or we could move on to South America?"

I don't really care which job we choose next as long as I keep moving. Seeing the world in a new way has been like getting another PhD. In every location, I'm creating new charts, new graphs, new logs of information. Everything is numerically recorded—sounds, sights, rules, languages, maps. My brain is filling up and filing everything away like it's preparing for something. But I don't know what. The capacity of my gift is increasing, but it's also creating more questions—that no one here has answers to.

"Jo, we've been on the road since Tunisia," Pens says, not looking up from the machine. "Don't get me wrong. We've never accomplished this much. And we love it, but we're not the one who lost a boyfriend."

"And actually, I gained one," Felicia says, coming out ready to swim. "We just want to be sure you're doing ok."

Namibia is the ninth country we've been to since Tunisia. We finish one job, go home for a few days, then fly out again. We're not on any special operations. There are no fingertip bombs, gangsters, political or economic crisis, terrorists or weapons. It's just regular PSS jobs—solving problems and helping people. It's relaxing. Jetlag doesn't even affect me anymore. I calculate flight times and sleep patterns and now I adjust within hours. A small, but welcome perk of my gift.

"Even at night you don't sleep much because of your *hobby*, which is cool but..." Felicia glances to the new PSS telescope and the math book on the table beside me.

I shrug an awkward grin. Bouncing all over the world also helps my research. I track, chart and record the stars from as many positions of earth as possible. Like tonight, I'll take advantage of the low light pollution here, and work on the hardest code I've ever tried to decipher in my life. I've spent months probing galaxies and following asteroid patterns, analyzing sun and star energy and scouring the solar system for formulas and equations until finally a tiny pattern started to emerge. A puzzle in the light, a semi-morse code in the stars. I started to recognize coordinates, an address in the sky...and then the trail went cold. No more messages.

"Fine. I'll come swimming. And you guys can choose the next job."

I grab my bathing suit, about to change when Pens called out. "Jo. It's asking for your pin number. Do you remember it?"

"Yep." When my numbers came back, all the memories associated with my gift returned as well. Once again, I'm a walking directory of everything I have ever learned or observed. I walk over and punch in the old password. The machine starts beeping wildly.

"What's happening?" I ask.

"Well, it can read the card, which means, the equipment works, but strangely, it's picking up a message that was sent to this number over a month ago."

"What does it say?" I ask, walking over.

"It must be a wrong number. It's written to someone named Mila," Pens says.

Goosebumps roll over my arms, despite the heat. "Read it, please."

Pens gives me a quizzical look. "OK," she says. "Mila. I need your help. It's urgent. *Per favore.* Call me."

My hands drop to my lap, a rush of memories taking over my thoughts. *"Non ci credo...*I don't believe it.*"

"Who's Mila?" Pens wrinkles her nose. "Jo? Are you okay? You've got that look on your face…"

"I'm fine," I say. "I just haven't heard that name in a long time."

It's one of my old names from China—after Double-Eight and before Phoenix. There's only one person on the planet who calls me Mila.

Rafael.

DISCUSSION QUESTIONS

1. What are some examples of fractals in nature? (Look them up online for visuals. Why are fractals so appealing to Jo and Noble?

2. How do the three phases in Jo's simulations help her heal and move on from trauma? What does she avoid in the simulations? What elements in the simulations help bring Jo's gift back?

3. There are three women who strongly influence Jo's life: her Mom, Madame and Mrs. T. How do each of these women shape Jo's character and the choices she makes?

4. Several characters in the book face the choice of letting go of something they are holding onto: Jo, Noble, Jo's dad. What do they need to let go of and why? What might have happened if they had made a different choice?

5. The PSS prodigies, including Jo, each have extraordinary gifts. If you could have any of their talents, which gift would you choose and why?

6. What place, experience or food in the book appeals to you most?

ACKNOWLEDGEMENTS

Once again, I need to thank a whole crew of people who made this book possible.

Thank you to my stellar agent, Amy Jameson, who always has my best interest in mind. Without your keen insight, this book wouldn't be half as awesome as it is.

Thank you to my publisher Rachel Del Grosso and the entire Wise Wolf Books crew, for once again giving me a chance to birth a book into the world. Thanks for all the work behind the scenes to make this book a success.

To my Simulated lifesavers: my amazing critique partners, Ellen McGinty, Candace Mieding, Rebecca Woo-Krauss, Chelsea Bobulski, Rebecca Alexandru, Becky Dean, Amaris Glass, Hilary Magnuson, Ernie Chiara, and of course, Ira McBee. My biggest 'thank yous' for this book belongs to you all. This book would not have been written without many tears if I didn't have you. You stayed with me in the game, encouraged me, sent feedback, read pages quickly and at odd hours, talked through plotlines, showered me with great ideas and loved this book from the beginning. You kept me focused and fueled me to get this book done.

Thank you to my early beta readers, Michelle Tsang and

Jenni Claar, for devouring the book within a couple days, then calling excitedly to tell me how much you loved it—that meant so much to me.

Special thanks to Kirsten Mount for your math insight and suggesting I look into fractals.

Thank you to Katylin Wonnell, who read, edited, checked language and other details, and created discussion questions for both Calculated and Simulated. You're awesome!

To my Street Team, especially Megan Walvoord and Heather Kelley—your enthusiasm and love for this series gets me fired up.

To my KidLitNet ladies, especially Elizabeth Van Tassel and Lorie Langdon.

Thanks to all the readers who have reached out, left reviews, pre-ordered and sent messages telling me how eagerly you were waiting for book two! That made me nervous, but also so excited! Thank you!

Special thanks to Justin Gardner, professional hacker extraordinaire, who gave me incredible feedback to make my prodigy team sound legit—your insight was invaluable!

Thank you to Abdulqadar Dawood, Doug Magnuson, Martin Woodruff for answering my questions and sharing your stories, insight, and suggestions on Tunisian culture and Arabic language.

Thank you, Glenn Fleishman, for sharing your experience and insight regarding gifted teens and adults.

Thank you to my parents, Richard and Hellen Schmid, who not only kept me alive by feeding me while I holed up in their downstairs basement every day during my deadline but cheered me on daily and helped with the three wild things, so I could finish. Special thanks to my dad who also read Simulated early, gave great feedback, and loved all the twists and turns. To Isaac, Olivia, and Leanne, (my big brother and two younger sisters)—where would I be without your constant support and love? I love you guys.

Chrystal and Brad Bowen, the most thoughtful award goes to you. You dropped off numerous meals to my family while I was on deadline so I could focus on finishing the book instead of cooking. (You may have saved Ira a few times, too!) You guys are the best!

Thanks to my three wild things. Even though you didn't like that I was on a deadline, you still got excited about Simulated whenever we talked about it. You may not think that writing books is cool now, but you love anything "story" and jump at any chance for me to tell you one. I can't wait for the day you can read the Calculated series. Thanks for your patience, my sweet-sweets.

Thanks to Ira McBee, my husband—you just know the craft of a good story and are always upping my game from good to great. My stories wouldn't be as cool without your feedback. You also took on the full responsibility of the three wild things while I was on deadline and you survived without any gray hair. How do you do that?

Lastly, thanks always to Jesus—in a world of chaos, you're my fractal.

ABOUT THE AUTHOR

Nova McBee is a hopeless nomad and culture nerd who has lived and worked in Europe, the Middle East and Asia. She speaks multiple languages, including Mandarin, and lived in China for more than a decade writing books and teaching English and Creative Writing to teens and adults. She thrives on complex plots, adventure, making cross-cultural connections and coffee. She currently resides in the beautiful Pacific Northwest with her husband and three children.

CPSIA information can be obtained
at www.ICGtesting.com
Printed in the USA
LVHW101811070422
715624LV00018B/550/J

9 781953 944122